The
LAST
TOURIST

ALSO BY OLEN STEINHAUER

The Middleman

All the Old Knives

The Cairo Affair

An American Spy

The Nearest Exit

The Tourist

Victory Square

Liberation Movements

36 Yalta Boulevard

The Confession

The Bridge of Sighs

The
LAST
TOURIST

OLEN STEINHAUER

Minotaur Books
New York

First published in the United States by Minotaur Books, an imprint of St. Martin's Publishing Group

THE LAST TOURIST. Copyright © 2020 by Third State, Inc. All rights reserved. Printed in the United States of America. For information, address St. Martin's Publishing Group, 120 Broadway, New York, NY 10271.

www.minotaurbooks.com

Library of Congress Cataloging-in-Publication Data

Names: Steinhauer, Olen, author.
Title: The last tourist / Olen Steinhauer.
Description: First edition. | New York : Minotaur Books, 2020. |
    Series: Milo Weaver ; 4
Identifiers: LCCN 2019048501 | ISBN 9781250036216 (hardcover) |
    ISBN 9781250036209 (ebook)
Subjects: GSAFD: Spy stories. | Suspense fiction.
Classification: LCC PS3619.T4764 L37 2020 | DDC 813/.6—dc23
LC record available at https://lccn.loc.gov/2019048501

Our books may be purchased in bulk for promotional, educational, or business use. Please contact your local bookseller or the Macmillan Corporate and Premium Sales Department at 1-800-221-7945, extension 5442, or by email at MacmillanSpecialMarkets@macmillan.com.

First Edition: March 2020

10 9 8 7 6 5 4 3 2 1

Again, for Margo,
who asks the right questions
and should never stop asking them

PART ONE

EXPENDABLE TURTLE

7 8 9 0

TUESDAY, JANUARY 15, TO THURSDAY, JANUARY 17, 2019

1

It's easy to forget, now that so many facts have been laid bare, but we once lived in a state of holy ignorance. We didn't believe this to be the case. No, we studied the world and examined facts and argued over their interpretation. We took newspapers with a grain of salt, because to depend on strangers for knowledge was foolishness. Verification was our go-to word. We even debated whether or not the facts themselves could be trusted, and this sort of meta-analysis made us feel like we were truly critical, that we were looking at the world unencumbered by Pollyanna notions. We were wrong. Sometime over the past fifty years the center of the world had moved, and we hadn't noticed.

You would imagine that I'm talking about regular people, citizens going about their days focused on bread and love and children. I could be, but for fourteen years I had worked as an analyst for America's premier foreign intelligence agency, and even in the halls of Langley, armed to the teeth with secret information and specialized enlightenment, we wallowed in the same kind of ignorance. We made policy recommendations and sent employees out into the world, sometimes to die, based on a basic misunderstanding of how the world functioned.

For half a century, we were distracted. We let the wrong people grow stronger, so that by the time we were able to look directly at them and see them for what they were, it was too late to draw up search warrants and set court dates and frog-march them in orange vests to Leavenworth. That would have been a better, cleaner solution.

I joined CIA from graduate school in 2005, seduced by a pale poli-sci professor who had spent a mysterious part of his youth in Prague. Though my stated interest, when asked, was international relations, that was only an excuse to get at the thing that truly excited my younger self: secret knowledge. Fieldwork was naturally attractive, but I'd quickly discounted myself. My social skills have always been lackluster, my physical courage less a known fact than a hypothetical, and confrontations have never gone well for me. In short, I was temperamentally unfit to be a spy, but I knew how to strategize, and I knew how to analyze. Despite my inability to charm them, I understood people because I had always observed them from the outside, as if through a microscope.

It helped that I looked different. In Boston, among the pink-cheeked children of America's aristocracy, or the striving descendants of the African labor that had built the country, I was never quite one with any of them. My skin set me apart from the former, my lack of enslaved pedigree from the latter. When I told them my people were Sahrawi, they blinked ignorantly, and I knew I could fill that void with whatever I liked. That we were Saharan royalty, that we ran caravans loaded with gold, that we kept our own slaves. I didn't, but I easily could have. And when my older brother later died in the African hinterlands, I could have made that part of my mythology, too, but I didn't have it in me to do that.

What my professor understood, which I hadn't, was that this outsider status was precisely what would endear me to the Agency. He said, "You were born here, but your parents weren't. How does that feel, Abdul?"

I told him that it made me feel mildly schizophrenic. My soul was in this country, while my heart was tied to a place I didn't know.

"And you speak Arabic."

"Hassānīya Arabic, yes, and I've studied modern standard."

"Do you dream it?"

I smiled, shrugged, nodded.

"Photographic memory, I'm told."

"No. Just a good one. Like, I don't have to take notes at your lectures."

"I've noticed," he said. Then: "Sunni, yes?"

Four years earlier rogue members of the Sunni faith had declared war on America in an explosive fashion, so it was inevitable that I hesitated. "I was raised that way," I told him.

"How does that make you feel?" he asked pointedly.

I was unsure what he was getting at. "It makes me feel that the world is more complicated than people believe."

He might have pressed further but chose not to. Instead, he moved to the core of his pitch: "And you want to understand how the world really works."

"Doesn't everyone?"

He rocked his head, chewing the inside of his lip. "No, Abdul. Not everyone. Most people don't. But I can connect you with people who *do* understand."

Which is to say that he fooled me, just as he was fooling himself, because fourteen years later neither of us knew how the world really worked. We only looked at it through a more sophisticated lens and believed that our lens was the highest resolution that could be achieved short of divinity. Belief usually isn't enough.

In the outside world, what some would call the real world, I'd fallen in love with another first-generationer, Laura Pozzolli, a beautiful linguist with a biting wit and an instinctive sense for right and wrong that I could never match. By January 2019, we had been married seven years. Our son, Rashid, was six.

There is nothing like a family to help you discover the limits of your abilities. At the office I swam like a shark from one project to the next, my analytical skills put eagerly to the test against country after country, yet at home I was a turtle, graceful in one moment, struggling on muddy banks the next. The tension between home and work did not get better with time, and when the phone periodically rang in the middle of dinner and I had to drive off to examine time-sensitive cables or captured documents from terrorist safe houses, the look on Laura's face told me more than her occasional outbursts ever would: This was not what she'd signed up for. She'd been raised by a Communist father who had always endeavored to take on half of the child-rearing himself, and when her parents met me they warned her that, no matter how good my intentions, I would inevitably fall back on the ways of my culture, leaving her with the babies and housekeeping. We'd laughed about that, though I never told Laura that after meeting her my mother criticized the girth of her hips, then pointedly asked in Hassānīya how many grandchildren she could expect.

I'd like to say that I worked overtime to alleviate my in-laws' worries, but when I look back there's little sign I really tried. When Paul, my section chief, called, I never said no, and when Laura pointed this out I asked her who she thought was going to pay the mortgage. Quite rightly, she accused me of becoming my father.

It was on such a night that the phone rang, and Laura glared at me from across the table as I answered it. Rashid was twirling spaghetti on his fork, unaware of the tension. By the time I hung up, Laura was covering my plate with plastic wrap on the counter. I told her I didn't know what time I'd get back, but that wasn't news. Security prevented me learning anything until I'd arrived at headquarters.

2

On the cold drive to Langley, I listened to NPR. For the past three weeks, the president had refused to fund the government, demanding money for his southern border wall, leading to a shutdown of basic government services. Then the news turned to the Russian-tainted 2016 presidential election; Nexus founder Gilbert Powell had testified before Congress on his company's extensive safeguards against foreign attack. Unlike his contemporaries from Facebook and Google, Powell soothed his audience with a mix of charm and perfectly remembered statistics. I couldn't help but wonder, as I drove, if tonight's cable or fresh intelligence might touch on this or another of our current national obsessions.

The interconnected offices of Africa section are in the original building, looking every one of their seventy years. As I passed through security there was no visible sign of the government shutdown. Agency work went on as usual.

Paul was in his office, the air bone dry from the overworked radiators, with two women who chose not to stand when he brought me inside. Though they were vague about their positions and only shared their given names—Sally and Mel—it was clear that they were creatures of the seventh floor, because Paul always deferred to them, something I'd only seen in the presence of the director himself.

"We have an issue in Western Sahara," Paul told me.

Sally passed over a thick yet heavily redacted file. Inside, I found a graying white man staring back at me. Oddly familiar—where had I seen him? Late forties, though photos on later pages (surveillance shots on mildly familiar European streets, one in Manhattan) suggested he was older. The flesh around his eyes was dark, and his long nose, in one shot, looked as if it had been broken. On the third page I found his birthdate—June 21, 1970. His name was Milo Weaver.

Most of the things I learned in that office didn't come from the blacked-out file but from Sally and Mel. They explained that Weaver had once been one of ours, though no one wanted to tell me which department he'd come from, and in 2008 he had left to work with the United Nations. Again, no one wanted to tell me whether or not the split was amicable, and the page that might have told me this was a mess of thick black lines. The only entirely unredacted page was in the back, a list of twenty questions that began:

1. Please list your locations between October 4, 2018, and today.

October 4 . . . yes, now I remembered—Milo Weaver's face had shown up on an Interpol Red Notice in October. The Red Notice, as far as I knew, was still live.

"These questions are for him?" I asked.

Mel, a tight-lipped Latina in a beige pantsuit, tilted her head and nodded. "Weaver's been on the periphery for years. We catch sight of him in the background at UN functions. Periodically shows up at their New York Headquarters. Supposedly part of UNESCO, but we know better."

"I don't. What does that mean?"

She ignored my question and pushed on. "Then in May of last year, he was in New York meeting with the Bureau."

"With Assistant Director Rachel Proulx, out in the open," Sally picked up, smiling grimly.

"The *Bureau*," Paul said contemptuously.

The women grinned; everyone enjoyed teasing the FBI.

"Rachel Proulx," I said, remembering newspaper headlines and cable news talking heads. "Wasn't she connected to the Massive Brigade case?"

"Yes," Mel said.

"Why was she meeting with UNESCO?" I asked.

"She doesn't talk to us," Mel said bitterly. "But Weaver—you'll see in the file. Long history with the Massive Brigade. In fact, he saved Martin Bishop's life in Europe ten years ago, and continued to help him, all the way to 2017. A lot of people are no longer with us because Weaver aided and abetted that terrorist."

It didn't make any sense. Why would the UN help a radical group that we'd put on the terrorist list? Or was this Milo Weaver acting independently? Either way, it was a damning connection. Martin Bishop's Massive Brigade had terrified the nation for a long time until the FBI took out its leadership. But then, unexpectedly, the remnants of the Brigade rose up, as one. Their second reign of terror last year had spread with bombs, shootings, bank robberies, and demonstrations that crippled whole cities, all led by a stern-looking middle-aged acolyte named Ingrid Parker. Her face had been plastered across every screen and front page for months; she became the representative of chaos. The last big act they committed had been in June, when a truck bomb exploded outside Houston's Toyota Center during a basketball tournament, killing three. And then, for the last half year, silence. Not a single sighting or online screed.

"I thought the Massive Brigade was disbanded," I said, because this was what everyone assumed.

Mel looked over at Sally, who raised her eyebrow. "Well," Sally said, "we've got word from the Germans that Ingrid Parker was seen in Berlin. Coordinating with European radicals."

"Which would explain their silence," Mel pointed out. "We might not know what they're up to, but you can bet it's big."

I tapped the file. "And you think Milo Weaver can tell us what it is."

"Bingo," Mel said.

Sally leaned closer. "He dropped off the grid in October. Then, yesterday—three whole months later—we find out he's in Laayoune, Western Sahara."

"Why there?"

"Why do *you* think, Abdul?"

Laayoune, which the Spanish called El Aaiún, is the capital of the disputed desert expanse just south of Morocco called Western Sahara. It's where my people come from. Yet despite my knowledge of its industries and history and culture, I was no expert on the city itself. The closest I'd ever come to it was a disastrous week in Rabat with my brother, Haroun, in 2000, when I was still a teenager. We'd been looking to connect with our heritage. A mugging and a visit to a questionable brothel was as close as I'd ever gotten, though Haroun returned to explore further and pushed on, making it all the way to Laayoune. He, however, was no longer available, and it looked like I was the most qualified person in the building.

"Milo Weaver is there because it's an excellent place to hide."

This seemed to satisfy them, in the same way that we're all satisfied when experts give us unequivocal opinions. We forget that everyone has an agenda, even if it's as mundane as keeping their jobs.

"And the position on the ground there?" asked Sally. "I'm not familiar."

I gave them a quick history lesson. In 1975, after controlling the area for almost a century, Spain handed it over to Morocco and Mauritania. By the next year, the Polisario Front had proclaimed an independent Sahrawi republic and was at war with both countries, supported with arms from Algeria. Mauritania pulled out in 1979, and in 1991 the UN negotiated a cease-fire with the promise that Morocco would hold a referendum on independence the next year. "Twenty-eight years later," I explained, "that referendum still hasn't been held, and the UN's peacekeepers—MINURSO—are still there. But violence hasn't broken out. Yet."

"Didn't you write something for outside publication about this?" asked Sally.

She knew about my one academic credit, a short piece on Sahrawi identity under French and Spanish domination, published in *Foreign Affairs* a couple of years ago. "Tangentially. The important thing is that Western Sahara remains disputed territory, and people are impatient."

"So there's no one for us to piss off," Paul said.

"Everyone's already pissed off," I said, and that earned smiles from Sally and Mel, whoever they were.

"Your, ah, brother," Mel said, for the first time sounding unsure. "He passed away in that region, yes?"

"South of there. Mauritania. 2009."

"What was his job again?"

Again? It was a peculiar word to slip in, a subtle way of rewriting history. "Consultant. For foreign investors. He worked most of the continent. I'm told he was good at his job."

"Right," Mel said, nodding, and it struck me that even though they were coming to me for answers, they still weren't sure they trusted me. As if Haroun's loyalties might say something about my own. But he'd been gone ten years now, and few people can maintain loyalty for so long.

"Who told you?" Sally asked.

"What?"

"That your brother was good at his job."

"I cleared out his desk at Global Partners. His coworkers were devastated."

Sally seemed to accept that, and Mel chewed the inside of her cheek. Paul cleared his throat and said, "Rest assured, Abdul. We'd feel the same."

By the time I returned home, midnight had come and gone, and Rashid was asleep. Laura was watching television. Over the last few years political news had become a spectator sport, and like any spectator sport it brought us together even when we weren't otherwise talking. I sat with her a moment as a so-called expert in security discussed progressive groups that were using some of the protest techniques invented by the now-defunct Massive Brigade, and there again was the face of Ingrid Parker—hard and unforgiving. They flashed through shots of Massive Brigade graffiti, its initials stylized as M3, as Parker, in her half-year silence, had gained the stature of a folk hero. More than anything, I wanted to tell Laura what I'd heard, that the Massive Brigade might be ready for a revival, but I only told her that I had to leave for a couple of days. "I'll be back by the weekend."

"Where?"

"Africa."

"It's a big continent," she said, but knew I couldn't be more specific. She turned back to the television. "Your shirts are in the dryer."

3

By the next day, I was dragging my carry-on through the busy Terminal 2 of Mohammed V International Airport, outside Casablanca, looking for *pastilla,* a chicken-and-*werqa*-dough pie that, after seventeen hours of travel, was the only thing I craved. Greasy bag and pile of paper napkins in hand, I sat near a large family of six children and two wives, watching how the patriarch, a heavy, grizzled man, sat with his knees open, his gut hanging over his groin, and a phone pressed hard into his cheek, talking quietly while chewing a toothpick. One of his wives sat on a bag "nexting" (as Rashid called it) with N3XU5, or Nexus, the social media app that boasted absolute privacy—no GPS tracking, encrypted text and video, and no message retention in the cloud—and had become ubiquitous outside North America, to the delight of Gilbert Powell's shareholders. One of the children, a boy, hung over his mother's shoulder, half asleep, half reading her messages.

I was thinking about that visit with my brother back in 2000. Haroun had been older and more worldly, having served in the army with C Company when Operation Uphold Democracy got rid of the military regime in Haiti, and after 9/11 he reenlisted for two tours in Afghanistan. But during those in-between years he'd fallen into a funk. He'd had trouble finding work and spent his free time reading political news and growing cynical. The idea of a trip to Western Sahara had been mine, casually tossed out over drinks, but it had given him something to work toward. He took it and ran. "Look, Abdul—before you disappear into some hole at Harvard, you need to see the world." I saw how energized the idea made him, and so I let him take control of the trip. He struck up conversations with strangers using our desert Arabic that, more often than not, earned us replies in English. To the cosmopolitan citizens of Rabat, I imagined, our slurred dialect made us sound like drug addicts. But that never slowed Haroun, and even after getting mugged and deciding to cut the trip short, not even having laid eyes on our ancestral homeland, he was already making plans for future trips.

My phone bleeped—Rashid was nexting me. Though I'd resisted, Laura had pushed for Rashid to have a phone. It was a way for her to always know where he was, which, in an age of school shootings, felt like a necessity. He wrote:

When are you getting home dad?
　　　　　　　Soon, Monster. Late tomorrow or Friday. Everything ok?
Had a test. I was shook.

"Shook" was Rashid's word for describing any little trauma at school.

　　　　　　　　　　Did you do well on it?
Ok.

I suddenly realized what time it was in DC.

　　　　　　　　　　Wait. You're not allowed
　　　　　　　　　　to use your phone in class!
Haha gotta go.

An hour before my connecting flight was scheduled to take off, over the speakers I heard the muezzin's call to prayer. Most travelers, including the grizzled patriarch, stayed where they were, but a few men got up and followed signs to the prayer rooms. After a moment's hesitation, I took my bag and joined them.

While that long-ago trip to Rabat had blunted my desire for adventure in the wider world, Haroun's was only enhanced. He became a student of Africa and after returning from Afghanistan went to work for Global Partners, advising Western corporations on the potential benefits and downsides of investing in the region. He traveled extensively, writing reports and sending me emails full of passion and excitement, littered with photos of camels and locals, tourist shots all. He got to know so much of West Africa that even after I started with CIA I sometimes quizzed him about on-the-ground knowledge our files sometimes got wrong. Guinea-Bissau, Sierra Leone, Liberia—he knew these hot spots like the back of his hand. And he was, in a way, the inverse of me. Where I needed silence and study to comprehend the world, he required noise and stink and human contact. Haroun was having the time of his life before it ended.

In August 2009, he was in Mauritania, working up an analysis of the feasibility of petroleum exploration in Taoudeni Basin, when he returned from the field to meet with his French clients. Nouakchott was one of his favorite capitals, an assessment I'd never understood. With Dakar to the south and Marrakesh to the north, why love a city so crushed by poverty that it couldn't even keep its harbor in working condition? But he found things to love, even choosing to rent rooms from locals rather than hide away in the air-conditioned modernity of the Semiramis or Le Diplomate. So on that day he took a taxi from run-down Sebkha to reach the French embassy.

August 8 was a hot day, though I suppose he was used to it. Outside the embassy, I understand, there was only a little foot traffic. A couple of gendarmes out jogging, a few passersby, and a young man, a jihadi, in a traditional boubou robe that hid his suicide belt.

The gendarmes and one passerby were injured. Only the terrorist and my brother were killed. That was ten years ago, and when I thought of West Africa I still pictured Haroun outside the French embassy, under the hot Mauritanian sun. I suppose I always will.

Beside strangers in the prayer room of Mohammed V International, I bowed and prostrated myself before God and, for the first time in many years, prayed.

4

Unlike Casablanca's international hub, Laayoune's tiny Hassan I, from above, looked ready to be swallowed by the Sahara. Despite the long-ago name change from Spanish to Western Sahara, the Arabic sign over the passenger terminal also read AEROPUERTO DE EL AAIÚN. Beyond, the flat, hard desert and dusty sky were ominous, and I wondered again why I had been picked for this particular mission.

The late-afternoon heat outside the airport was stifling, but I soon found a free driver smoking against a beaten-up Peugeot with functioning air-conditioning. He seemed surprised when I spoke the Hassāniya my parents had always insisted we use at home. He asked a lot of questions, wondering if I was part of the UN peacekeeping force, but I deflected with questions of my own, asking where the best meat pies could be had, the best markets, and the best cafés—subjects taxi drivers the world over can't help but elucidate on.

Outside the car, a desert wind was picking up, but the crowded salmon-pink buildings protected the streets from sand and sun. Locals filled the sidewalks, the colors of their robes touching something in my DNA. I felt a desire to call home and describe everything I saw to Rashid, to Laura. The feeling swelled so quickly that I even took out my phone before stopping myself. Paul had made clear that this wasn't allowed at the destination. And besides, I thought as I pocketed the phone again, the separation was probably good for us. Laura and I weren't trapped together in a small suburban house, walking on eggshells. We could breathe again, and perhaps with a couple of days' reprieve we would remember again why we'd chosen this life together.

That charmed feeling evaporated inside the sand-colored Hotel Parador, where the lobby was full of dozing foreigners who gave me weary looks. The MINURSO peacekeepers had brought with them the regular assortment of diplomats and carpetbaggers, and it looked like most of them had taken up residence in the Parador. Cynics and small-timers all—I'd spent a lot of my career reading reports from people like these, for whom the world was so much smaller than it really was, and I found their petty braggadocio tedious. Most analysts I knew felt this way, which was inevitable, I suppose, given our illusion of grander knowledge.

The hot water only lasted half my shower, and after washing I ate an energy bar while examining a map of the city, charting a route to the address Sally and Mel had given me before Paul sent me off to my cubicle to absorb whatever was still legible in that decimated file.

"A simple interview," they had told me. "Just the questions on the list."

"And if he doesn't want to talk?"

"Find out if it's just us he doesn't want to talk to, or if he's locking out the whole world."

So why not a phone call? Why not send these questions to someone already on location? Why send me, who had spent the last fourteen years behind a desk? Their answers had been equivocal, but the sad truth was the one I had suspected from the moment I first looked into their faces: They simply had no one else who could blend in as well as Abdul Ghali, their deskbound African.

I jumped at a knock at the door. *"Na-rħam?"* I called, folding the map.

"It's Collins," said an American voice.

Collins—yes, our local friend, very loosely attached to the UN mission. Paul had explained that Collins would set me up with anything I needed, which again raised the question: Why not just ask Collins to walk across town and do the interview? No one seemed to have a good answer for that.

I let in a balding man in knee-length shorts, tennis shoes, a Texas Tech baseball cap, and a dusty, sweat-stained jacket. We shook hands, and Collins looked around the room, sniffing. "Should've asked for a back-facing room. Gets noisy as hell here."

"I won't be here long enough for it to matter."

Collins grinned in a way I didn't like, then reached into the cargo pockets of his shorts. "We live in hope, man." He took out a flip phone and held it out to me. "My number's the only one in it." From his other pocket he took out a small semiautomatic pistol, checked the safety, and tossed it on the bed. "Colt 2000. Nine-millimeter, fifteen rounds. It'll get you where you're going."

I stared at it. "What's this for?"

"You're going into the slums, aren't you?"

"Yes, but I don't . . . I mean, I'm not—"

"Look, kid. It's there to make you feel better. You take that out, and whoever's giving you trouble is going to think twice. I hope to hell you don't pull the trigger—I don't need that kind of paperwork. But take it. Okay?"

I nodded even though my brain was saying no. After a day of traveling in solitude, this sudden bluster was disconcerting, and the addition of a pistol made me think again of 2009, and my brother. It shouldn't have—he'd died in another country and had only sung the praises of Laayoune—but it did. Maybe because we'd never been able to bury him ourselves. His body, we were told, lay on the outskirts of Bissau, in a cemetery only our father had had the heart to visit.

Still not touching the gun, I said, "You're the one who found him?"

"No. And it doesn't exactly reflect well on me that after two years in this dump I didn't notice our little newcomer. I mean, *him* of all people. He apparently made a *phone call* to the States. Stupid slip."

I wondered about that.

Collins furrowed his brow, eyeballing me. "Look, all you have to worry about is your twenty questions. Okay?"

"And you?"

"Me? Don't worry about me."

It wasn't him I was worried about. "You're not coming?"

"Sure," he said. "I'm coming. But you're not going to see me. You see me, *they* see me. And we don't want to scare anyone off. HQ's been looking months for this bastard. Let's not lose him."

"But if I need—"

"That," he said, pointing to the flip phone still in my hand. "You call, I come. No more than a minute or two. And unlike you, I don't have a problem carrying." To prove his point, he opened his sweat-stained jacket to reveal a shoulder holster and a worn pistol grip. Then he considered me a moment, judgment all over him, and said, "You don't need to be scared, okay? Things they say about this guy? He probably made them up himself. His dad was KGB; making up shit is in his blood."

"What do they say about him?"

Collins opened his mouth, then shut it. "How much are you read in on?"

"Not a lot. Ties to the Massive Brigade."

"That's it?"

I shrugged.

He cursed under his breath and stepped away, toward the windows, flexing his fists. "They send you here without . . ." He shook his head, unwilling to finish the sentence, then turned back to me. Made a smile that filled me with unease. "Maybe it's better you don't know. Why fuck with your nerves, right? Keep your calm."

At no point during this conversation had I felt calm about anything, but now Collins had pushed it to the emotional equivalent of nails scratching a chalkboard. So I took a baby step closer, looked him square in the eyes, and said, "Collins, I need you to tell me exactly what the hell I'm walking into here."

5

The sun was almost gone when I finally faced the busy evening streets. A few vendors approached, and in hard-edged Arabic I sent them away. My face and speech might have helped me blend in, but no one had given me a new set of clothes, so the best impression I gave was of a local boy who had grown rich in the West. And why else would I have returned but to spread the wealth? I was a magnet.

The western wind, coming off the Atlantic and pushing inland from Foum el-Oued across twenty-five miles of desert, had cleaned some of the dust from the air, and as I passed teahouses and fruit vendors I felt another urge to call home. At the very least, I could take the same kinds of tourist shots my brother had once taken, so that I could show them off to my family later. But no—if Collins, who I assumed was tailing me at a distance, saw me pulling out my phone, there was no telling what would happen.

I chose to walk the entire distance, about an hour's stroll. I wasn't worried about taxi drivers asking questions or collecting records of my time here; I simply wanted to breathe in the culture that I'd always held at arm's length. I might have spoken my parents' language at home, but as soon as I was out the front door I'd tried to become like my friends, a child of McDonald's and MTV, of fads and convenience. To my younger self, American culture was superior simply because my friends knew of no other, and there was no way I was going to draw them into mine by dragging them home to our bi-level shrine to West Africa. My mother's Daraa robes and dishes of goat meifrisa would only scare them.

Even as a child I was painfully aware of my limits.

Now I was in a land that I knew but did not know, and I pressed on, thinking of my destination.

"So you know about the Library," Collins said, and when I shook my head I thought he was going to punch a hole in the hotel's stucco wall. "Okay," he said, calming himself. "Tell me they at least told you he works for the UN."

My nod provoked a happy sigh.

"Small favors, right? Well, remember what I said—Weaver's dad used to work for the Russians. But then the old man moved to the UN, where he created this thing called the Library. His thinking, we gather, was that the intelligence agencies of the first world countries have a monopoly on what is known and not known in the world. And we work together—us and Israel and the UK, Russia and China, all of us together—to filter and alter intelligence to suit our own ends. So he put together his own outfit, the Library, and hid it deep inside the United Nations. Inside UNESCO."

I tried to picture it but couldn't. "The UN can barely fund its central air-conditioning, much less an intelligence agency."

Collins shrugged. "That part's a mystery. But however they did it, it functioned. And when the old man died back in oh-eight, his boy took it over. Been running it ever since. And from all accounts it worked well, completely under the radar, until it was blown back in October. Same time he disappeared."

"Blown?"

"Wide open," Collins said.

"Then why haven't I heard about it?"

Collins wagged a dirty fingernail at me. "Not to the plebes, man. That's seventh-floor knowledge. Don't know who uncovered it first, but soon everyone knew—us, the Europeans, the Chinese . . . hell, even the Iranians got word of it. And do you know why it was blown?"

I didn't.

"The Library stopped collecting intelligence; it started *creating* intelligence. It became an agency of active measures. Liquidating people. Remember Lou Braxton?"

I did. Braxton had been a Silicon Valley darling, founder of Where4, Nexus's only serious competitor in the encrypted communications sector, until a couple of years ago when he died on a Beijing–San Francisco flight. "He died of cardiac arrest," I said.

"With a full gram of sodium fluoroacetate in his system." Off my ignorant look, he said, "Compound 1080—it's used to kill pests. The company kept that quiet, but it didn't help. A year later Where4 was bankrupt."

"The Library murdered him? Why?"

Collins asked. "Who's to say? They're *global*. You hear of Joseph Keller?"

"He's in the questions. Number eight—explain the circumstances of his death."

Collins looked disappointed. "That's all? Well, he was a British accountant. Worked for the Russians—MirGaz. We heard he had a side-gig laundering money for the Massive Brigade, so we put out a Red Notice on him. Then in October, when everything was blowing up, Paris cops found him buried in a park out in the burbs. The Library killing off its weak link. That's the theory."

"Jesus."

"They're even connected to piracy."

Though I felt stupid saying it, I couldn't help but blurt, "*Piracy?* That makes no sense."

"Not to me either," Collins said. "But all that? Someone was bound to notice. Us, the Europeans, the Russians, the Chinese. *Everyone* noticed. And everyone tried to take it *down*."

"Did they succeed?"

"I suppose so—why else would the Library's director be hiding out in this hellhole?"

"And the Massive Brigade?" I asked.

Collins opened his hands. "Weaver protected them in the past—that's documented. Whatever you do, don't underestimate him, okay? He's hard as shit."

There was no discernible change when I entered the slums of what Collins called a hellhole. The old Spanish architecture remained, and the dilapidated windows and shallow terraces and crumbling façades lining the narrow streets were just as they had been a few blocks back. But now there were more children running around columns and through alleys, slipping in and out of shadows, while others sat on steps and stared at me as I passed. It was unnerving, but when the fear crept up I thought of Haroun, who had for years traversed places far more ominous than this without anything more than a scratch. He hadn't been killed by the greed of the world's poor but by a blind religious fury that could have found him in Paris or London or New York.

I've always had a head for geography, and I reached the three-story walkup on Boulevard Al Hizam Al Kabir without a misstep. Like many other buildings I'd passed, it was dead looking, and I gazed up at the shuttered windows, thinking about the children around me, watching from a safe distance. I thought of Collins, watching from among them, and I thought of the uncomfortable gun in my waistband at the base of my back. And I thought that this truly was not part of my job description. I looked at data, and I interpreted it. I did not go searching for the data; that was what people like Collins were paid to do.

In the darkness I found a light switch on a timer, and in its bright glare the stairwell was surprisingly cool, dark, and clean. The banister shook when I touched it, so I left it alone as I ascended to the second floor. Off to the left a family was making noise, and a radio played a Haifa Wehbe hit. Weaver's apartment—identified by a handwritten *4* on the door—was to my right, and when the timer ended darkness fell. I stood blind, listening to the high melody of Arabic pop but hearing nothing from behind number 4. Then I stepped forward and knocked three times.

Silence. I considered walking away. A man exiles himself in Western Sahara—that means he's not interested in talking. And from what little I knew from the file, and from the mysterious nuggets Collins had given me, Milo Weaver wasn't the kind of man who would talk if he wasn't interested in talking.

But I stayed, if only because I didn't want to return to those warm, dusty streets so quickly. I knocked again and said, "Hello?"

To my left, a door opened, spilling light into the stairwell, and a small girl peered out at me. The noise and aroma of a family meal wafted out with the Arabic dance music, then an indecipherable father's shout; the child shut the door. Then number 4 opened quickly, accompanied by dim light, and a sunburned face peered out at me. A scatter of bristle, some of it gray, reached to his cheekbones, and there was gray around his ears. Big, bruised eyes.

Looking nothing like his photos, yet exactly like his photos. Sandals, linen pants, a light-colored shirt he was still buttoning.

"Milo Weaver?" I said.

A pleasant enough smile crossed his face, and with a voice rough from disuse, he said, "Well, you certainly took your time."

6

"You expected me?" I asked.

Milo Weaver blinked a few times, as if he were just waking up, then glanced at his wristwatch, saying, "Of course."

I hesitated, then stuck out a hand. "Abdul Ghali."

He didn't take it, but he did step aside and open his hand to a small room stocked with a mattress, a column of a dozen books, a sink, a hot plate, and a small table with two chairs. There was a door that presumably led to another room, but it was closed.

"Take a seat," he said.

I settled at the table, discovering that one of the chair's legs was shorter than the others, and this instability kept me from relaxing.

"And put the gun and phone on the table."

I got up again and reached behind myself to take the Colt out of my waistband. Laying it on the table, I felt a sense of relief—that, at least, was out of the way. Then I placed my personal phone next to it.

"Unlock it?" Weaver asked, and I used my thumbprint, then handed it back. He looked at the screen, swiped to the next page, and his eyes widened. "Shit—*Nexus*?"

"What?"

He ignored me, then pressed on the application and deleted it.

"Hey!" I shouted involuntarily, but he didn't care about me or my conversations with my son. He just powered off the phone and set it back on the table.

"Is that your only one?" he asked.

I'd forgotten about Collins's phone, and while I might have bluffed my way through it, something told me that it wouldn't be the right move. I handed it over and watched him disassemble the flip phone and remove its battery. I held up both hands. "Want to search me?"

Weaver didn't answer. He went to the stack of books and took a pack of Benson & Hedges off the top. He lit one with a Zippo and, as an afterthought, offered the pack; I shook my head. As he smoked, he stood looking down at me. He made no move to relocate the pistol farther away; nor did he speak. He seemed to be measuring me with his eyes.

"I have some questions," I said finally.

"Did you draft them?"

I shook my head no.

"Who? Foster?"

"I don't know who drafted them," I said, not knowing who Foster was. "I saw your file, but most of it was redacted." He just stared, so I went on. "All I gathered was some of the outlines—your work history, your family. Your connection to the Massive Brigade."

"Massive Brigade?" he asked, seeming surprised. "Really?"

"Are you denying it?"

He shook his head. "But I haven't been in touch with them for a long time."

There—that had to be a lie. I looked closely, trying to find tells in his face and hands, in his posture. Some kind of baseline to use for his other answers. But I found nothing. Hoping for another chance, I thought of question eight: "What about Joseph Keller? Can you tell me what happened to him?"

Weaver stiffened, closing up. He took a drag.

"Look," I went on, "this is not my usual gig. It's the first stamp in my passport for years. I just need to ask these questions, and I'll be out of your hair."

But Weaver only stared at me, sucking on his damned cigarette, blinking from the smoke.

I said, "They've been looking for you since October. You vanished. Then you showed up on their radar. Here, in Laayoune. The edge of the world. And I was called in."

"Why you?"

"Me? Language. Background."

"What background?"

"Sahrawi."

He nodded, then looked toward the window and its closed blinds, as if alerted to a sound, but there'd been nothing. "They've been good to me," he said toward the window. "The Sahrawi."

"A hospitable people," I said, then regretted it. I sounded like a tourist guide.

Weaver didn't seem to notice. He just turned back to me and said, "Office?"

"Africa desk. Langley."

"But why *you*? What are you bringing to the table?"

He was asking the question I hadn't been able to answer myself. Familiarity with Arabic or Sahrawi culture might be a plus for this job, but it certainly wasn't a requirement. Why not send Collins across town? After a day of pondering I had convinced myself, immodestly, that I had been recruited for some intangible virtues Paul had been too reserved to point out in front of Sally and Mel, but whatever those virtues were they were so hidden that not even I could find them. I told Weaver, "I'm bringing myself to the table."

Understandably, he wasn't impressed.

"So will you play ball?" I asked.

Another smile swept across Weaver's face. He wiped at his dry lips. "Sporting metaphors. Haven't heard one in a long time."

I waited, but he didn't follow up. "So?"

"You found me here," he said finally, "so you'll find me anywhere."

"Certainly."

"Maybe," he corrected.

I looked around at the mottled walls that might not have seen a fresh coat of paint since they were built. "You can give it a try," I told him. "Say the word, and I'll walk out of here. I'll tell them you'd already left town. But then, in a month or two, I'll come knock on your door again. Me or someone else. Just do us a favor and choose someplace like Cannes, or Bermuda."

This time, Weaver's smile was open and full. He approached the table and took my gun and placed it on the stack of books along with the cigarettes. The titles of the books, I saw, were in three languages—French, English, and Russian. Weaver came back and sat down opposite me. "Shoot."

"Isn't that a sporting metaphor?" I asked.

Weaver wagged an index finger at me and grinned.

I had memorized the questions while sitting in my cubicle at Langley, and although the first question, asking where he'd been since October, was a fine way to begin, I instead chose number fourteen. I leaned my elbows on the table, which proved as rickety as the chair, and said, "They'd like to know the origins of your investigation."

"What investigation?"

"I don't know. I'm assuming you know."

"That's a big one," Weaver said, indirectly admitting he did know what investigation I was referring to. "Quite a commitment."

"They're not all so big, but once that's answered maybe the other questions will fall into place."

He cocked his head, regarding me. "Bad interrogation style. You're supposed to start with the small, easily disproven questions."

"I didn't realize this was an interrogation," I told him, and watched, slightly put off, as he laughed quietly to himself.

"Every human exchange," Weaver said, "is an interrogation."

I wasn't going to debate the point, so I just said, "Do you mind if I record this?"

"Go ahead." When I started to get up to go for my phone he said, "Not that," went to the kitchenette, and picked up something I hadn't noticed before, a digital voice recorder.

"You prepared for this," I told him.

He handed me the device.

"You knew I was coming."

"Of course I did," he said. "I sent for you. For someone like you."

It was more than a surprise; it was a shock. Everyone I'd spoken with believed they were on top of this situation. We'd believed we were way ahead of this man.

Or maybe we were, and Milo Weaver, like any good spy, was just a talented showman.

"Why would you send for me?" I asked.

"Because we're out of time."

"Out of time for what?"

"For what comes next."

It was an annoying answer, so I turned my attention to the recorder. As I got my bearings with it, he said, "Okay, then. You know about Tourists, right? The Department of Tourism?"

The way he said this, I knew that I should know, and that it had nothing to do with tourist expenditures or the annual count of visitors to the United States. I shook my head and pressed RECORD.

He considered me, blinking slowly. "Really—why *did* they send you?"

My earlier reasoning—language, culture, some unnamed personal virtue—felt less and less plausible. But we weren't going to get anywhere with him mocking my ignorance. "I do know about the Library," I said.

He just looked at me, waiting.

"I know it is, or was—its status isn't clear—an intelligence service hidden inside the United Nations. I know that your father created it, and that you took it over. And at some point you changed the rules. The Library became an active player. This, I'm told, led to its downfall."

That seemed to take the air out of him. "Is that the way they see it?" he finally asked.

"I don't know. This is just from one source."

He settled into a chair. "Maybe that's right. Maybe it is all on me."

"So you're admitting the Library *did* engage in active measures?"

He looked into my face, then nodded. "In 2009 I took an active measure when I decided to save Martin Bishop's life. We know how that turned out, but I guess I didn't learn my lesson, because four months ago I tried to save Joseph Keller's life."

"Then you killed him," I said.

His smile was so sad. He shook his head slowly and said, "Joseph Keller never had a chance, Abdul."

And then everything exploded.

7

The bedroom door—or what I had assumed to be a bedroom door—burst open, and a woman stepped through. She wore the kind of bright-colored robes that my own relatives wore when they felt alienated from their culture, but her skin was much darker. Bright eyes flashed, and when she spoke I was surprised to find no accent. At least, no accent from the African continent.

"It's time," she said to Weaver.

He sat straight, more alert than at any moment since I'd arrived. "That was fast. How many?"

"Two, maybe more. I recognized my old friend from Hong Kong."

"What?" I asked.

As he abruptly rose from his chair, Weaver said, "We have to move. Once I saw you I knew they'd come in to close it down. But I thought we'd have at least twenty-four hours."

"It's Collins," I said as I, too, stood. "He told me he would just keep an eye on me, but . . ." Realizing that Collins had played me, I even said, "I'm sorry."

Weaver wasn't listening. He ran around the room, collecting items he stuffed into his pockets.

"Let's move it," said the woman, impatient, then looked behind herself into the far room before turning back to eyeball me suspiciously. "He coming?"

"Yes," Weaver said as he snatched my pistol—Collins's pistol—off the stack of books.

"Wait," I said, because the prospect of running off with them was, well, crazy. I had come to sit down and have a conversation, not flee from people who were probably my Agency colleagues.

"Do you want the story, or not?" Weaver asked pointedly.

"Yes, of course. But—"

"Then *come*."

There was force in his voice, enough to get me moving, but I didn't yet leave the room. I thought of Laura, and how she was sitting at home thinking that her husband had flown off first class to have some fun with men of power, leaving her to be the milkmaid to our son. What would she say now? What would she advise?

Don't go.

"Look," Weaver said, his patience wearing thin. "You don't know who they are. You think they're your friends, but if they're who I think they are, then they're going to kill you. They're going to kill all of us."

"Milo," said the woman.

Weaver held out my pistol, grip first. "Please."

And that was all it took, the magic word. A request rather than an order, and it was enough to cut through my indecision. I took the pistol and followed them into the next room, which turned out to be another apartment that led to a low door in the cracked wall that took us to a very narrow set of concrete steps leading down into cool darkness.

The woman took the lead, and I followed Weaver. They moved quickly, with an urgency I hadn't thought Weaver had in him. At the bottom of the stairs the woman pushed open a door, letting in moonlight along an empty alleyway. They hurried toward the far end, where a white pickup truck was parked, and as I chased them past old broken furniture and pails and trash cans I noticed something glint to my left. At first glance I didn't register what it was, but after two more steps my brain put it together. I halted abruptly and turned to look. Spread out against the stone wall lay Collins. The left side of his head was a mess, what I would later understand to be an exit wound, but I recognized him by the other half of his face and his blood-soaked clothes. The Texas Tech cap had been blown against the wall.

"Wait!" I called.

Up ahead, Weaver stopped and turned back to me, but the woman kept going.

"It's—" I couldn't get the word out.

Weaver's gaze moved between me and Collins's body. "Now you understand," he said.

"I don't understand anything."

Weaver raised his head, looking past me. "Run, Abdul."

"What?" I looked back, and at the far end of the alley a man appeared. Not a local—he was as pale as Weaver and wore a suit. He started to run toward us, a long-barreled pistol in his hand.

"Run, Abdul."

I ran straight toward Weaver, who took his own pistol out of his jacket and, as I passed him, fired twice, loud explosions just behind me. I didn't look back, just kept running toward the white truck, which was idling now in a cloud of carbon monoxide.

"Inside!" Weaver shouted, and I leapt into the rear of the truck, landing hard against the steel bed. Weaver banged down next to me. "Go!" he called, and the truck began to move.

As I was still catching my breath, Weaver scrambled into a crouch and aimed his pistol out the back. Flat, shadowy buildings passed, and occasional children gazed at our truck. Then, maybe thirty yards away, the man we'd seen before emerged from the alley, pistol raised and firing at us, the shots muffled by a suppressor. Milo fired back, the noise cracking in my ears. But the man didn't stop; he kept running at full speed, firing. No bullets hit, but the shooting continued until Weaver was out of ammunition and we had taken the next corner.

When he turned and settled into the bed of the truck, breathing heavily and watching me with an indecipherable expression, I said, "Are we going to the UN compound?"

He shook his head no.

"But aren't you—"

"I suppose they came from the UN compound," he said between breaths, then turned to look out the rear again. "Only way they got here so fast."

This made no sense to me. "Wait," I said. "Who the hell *were* they?"

"Remember I mentioned Tourists?" he asked. "The Department of Tourism?"

"That was a Tourist?"

He rocked his head, back to looking like the laconic man I'd met a half hour earlier. "Or something like one," he said.

The buildings fell away to reveal desert. We were out of the city, and I was so confused.

"Why was he shooting at us?"

Weaver didn't seem to hear me. He raised his head and looked out the back, where a few rusting cars trailed along far behind us. Then he turned and frowned at me. "Now I know why they sent you."

"What?"

"You're expendable."

8

The shock took a while to fade. The idea that the Agency considered me expendable, yes, but more than that I couldn't shake the image of Collins, tossed against that stone wall, the way his head had lost its form. His broken body stuck with me as we drove north, into the wide black desert that had been a home to my people, but to me looked like the antithesis of home, a terrain that left nowhere to hide. Just above our heads, the moon followed us.

I was cold, and I had to urinate, but Weaver explained over the wind that we didn't have time to stop. We couldn't know how close they were—all we knew for sure was that they were following.

"Who?" I demanded. "What the hell is a Tourist?"

Weaver wiped at his nose, then checked his fingers, presumably for blood, but it was too dark to be able to see anything. He moved to where I was being jostled against the back of the cab and leaned close so I could hear him above the engine. "In my day, years ago, Tourists served as the sharp end of American foreign policy. We were headquartered in Manhattan."

"I never heard of them."

"That was the idea. We had some notable failures, but more often than not we did all right. And we kept our secret until a decade ago, when the department was closed down."

"Why?"

"Because it was wiped out. Dozens of Tourists killed by our rivals in China, all in the space of twenty-four hours."

I rubbed my aching forehead and wondered if I was going to be sick. The noise and constant bumping through potholes, and now a story of mass murder by the Chinese. "You were one?" I asked.

"For a while. Then I moved into administration."

"I see."

"You don't," he said, "but you don't have to."

He was right. All I had to do was listen and remember, so that at some point in the future—a point that was growing increasingly distant—I could sit down with Paul and Sally and Mel and spill the entire story. It was their job to understand.

"Wait," I said. "If it was closed down, who was shooting at us?"

"All I said was that it had been shut down, not what happened later."

I looked out into the night, eyeing the moon. I could make out craters. This was not where I was supposed to be. "Why all this?" I asked him. "Why didn't you just come to DC and tell your story? Dial a phone? Send a fucking email?"

He didn't answer at first, and when I looked over I saw he was also staring at the moon. He said, "Everything would be intercepted. Any call. Any email. Letters." He shook his head. "Me."

"Then send someone else."

He shook his head again. "I can't put them at risk."

"Of what?" I demanded. When he didn't answer, I said, "Who cares if they intercept an email?"

"Because they can't know what I know. And they can't know who I'm telling it to."

"Who are *they*?"

"We'll get to that," he said, and his answer angered me so much I couldn't even speak.

At the Moroccan frontier, we blew through what seemed like a ghost village, a scattering of buildings and a single gas station; then we were back in the desert. Though it felt like forever, only an hour and a half passed before we were pulling into the coastal town of Tarfaya. I could make out wide, dusty streets and single-story buildings in the occasional streetlight. Faraway dogs barked. Though I'd never visited Tarfaya, I had an image of it from Haroun's emails when he'd taken a day trip there. The cafés with their molded plastic chairs, the long, deep beach, and the rowboats tied up along a rocky port. And people: grizzled men chain-smoking over thimbles of coffee, robed women with piercing, beautiful eyes, and children smeared with the grit of childhood kicking soccer balls in the streets. Now the town was asleep and empty.

At the gate to the port, a policeman stopped us, and the woman behind the wheel had a short conversation with him that I couldn't make out. Eventually the cop stepped around to smile at me and Weaver as he slipped some bills into his shirt pocket, then glanced at the empty space around us as if we weren't there. He grinned like someone who'd been well paid for his blindness. He wandered away, and we began to move.

We finally climbed out along the water's edge, where fishing boats bobbed in a cramped line along the port's narrow peninsula. I looked in vain for a bathroom, then peered deep into the blackness of the Atlantic. I remembered what Haroun had called Tarfaya: *The end of the world.*

From one of the fishing boats came a man as white and out of place as Weaver, who nodded in my direction. "What about him?" he asked in what sounded like a German accent.

"He's coming with us," Weaver explained.

"*Christ.* Phones? Signals?"

"He's clean."

"I'll find out."

Weaver shook his head. "We don't have time."

The man, still angry, pointed at me. "This way."

I looked at Weaver, who nodded, so I followed the man up the path to the piers. "I don't have anything," I said, trying to reassure him, but he didn't answer. He just kept walking down the gangplank. Only the one boat was running, its engine grinding and gasping unconvincingly.

"In the water," said the man.

"What?"

"You heard me."

I knew what he wanted, and why, but I decided to stand my ground. "No."

With disconcerting speed, the man grabbed my lapels and swung, using centrifugal force to propel me off the edge and into the cold water. It was deeper than I'd thought, and I was submerged completely. When I came up, chilled to the bone, the man was on his knees, peering down at me.

"Stay there a moment," he said.

"Fuck you."

He smiled, giving away the reason for his perpetual frown—his teeth were small, discolored nubs. He turned to look at the black woman running down the gangplank toward us. At that moment, I felt the warm release of my bladder emptying into the murky Atlantic, bringing on a mix of relief and shame.

"He's clean now," he called to the black woman, then turned back to offer me a hand. "Come on."

I didn't move, only treaded the dirty water. When the woman reached us, she said to him, "Griffon, you're taking the truck to Ben Khlil."

"No, Kanni, I am not."

"You want them to be waiting for us?"

He withdrew his hand and stood up. "Fine. I'll see you in Switzerland."

As he skulked off she squatted and held out a hand to me. "He's a dick," she said as she caught my hand and tugged. "But he's our dick."

9

Shivering down in the filthy hold, wrapped in a blanket, I rocked back and forth with the beat of the waves and the clatter of the engine as we headed out into the Atlantic. A single bulb swung from a wire, stretching and shifting shadows in the pungent space, the constant movement keeping me off balance. The struggling engine moaned. My head was full of questions, but the fear that had gripped me back in Laayoune was starting to recede. Not because I was less afraid, but because I was exhausted from the breakneck speed of our escape and my jet lag finally catching up with me.

What I wanted was to be dry, to lie down in a hotel bed—any hotel, anywhere in the world—and call Laura. I wanted to hear about whatever trouble Rashid had caused that day, and maybe even discuss our marriage. Not come to any great conclusions or make big decisions, but simply speak about it, openly and honestly. Instead, I was chained to a man I didn't trust, a man who was involved with domestic terrorists, as people called Tourists tried to kill us—all to listen to a story that I feared would take days to get told. A story that might only be made up of lies.

Unbelievable.

When he came down the steps, dipping his head to avoid a concussion against the steel frame, Milo Weaver gave me a smile and reached out to switch off the light. He became a silhouette then, lit only by the moon through the open hatch, a form moving around the hold until he finally settled on the long, low bench beside me. He said, "Need more blankets?"

I shook my head before remembering he couldn't see me. "No, I'll survive."

"Let's hope," he said.

Both of us had to raise our voices to be heard above the engine.

"Where are we going?" I asked.

"First? Arrecife."

"Canary Islands?"

"Then a ferry to Spain. Once we make it there, everything's taken care of."

"Everything?" I asked. "What the hell is going on?"

He gave me silence for a moment, and I saw his silhouette turning to peer in the direction of the steps, and the moon outside. "Well, I'm trying to save both of our lives. And the lives of a bunch of other people."

"That's not an answer," I told him.

"You're right. How's that recorder?"

"Shit," I said. It was in my jacket, and when I used the blanket to pat it dry, I was sure it was ruined. But a press of a button brought up the small, bright screen.

"Good," said Weaver.

We both turned when the engine went dead and footsteps sounded on the stairs. The woman who'd driven us out of Laayoune and pulled me out of the water in Tarfaya—Kanni, apparently—stopped halfway down the stairs and squatted. "They'll be here in five."

"No worries?" asked Weaver.

She shook her head. "But I can't get Griffon on the line."

Weaver touched his face, rubbing, then stood up. "Come on, Abdul."

I followed him up to the deck, where a cold, salty-tasting wind knocked us around. In the direction of Africa there was darkness. To the west Spain's Canary Islands glowed, bright even during the off-season. That was when I noticed, cutting through the lights, a black shape approaching. "You see it?" I asked, but Weaver was already looking in that direction.

It turned out to be a fifty-foot sailing yacht that pulled up silently beside us. On the deck were two young men, one Japanese and another who spoke French with a Moroccan accent. Kanni threw over our line, and with a little effort we all climbed onto the yacht. The Japanese man shook Weaver's hand and spoke to him quietly, then climbed into the fishing boat. Within ten minutes, we were on our way toward Arrecife, the Moroccan at the wheel, while the fishing boat headed back to the continent. Weaver and I returned to the hold and pulled the window blinds shut. The light here was fluorescent, and there were cushioned benches to stretch out on.

"They all work for you, then?" I asked.

He scratched at his stubble, noncommittal.

"For the Library?"

He finally focused on me. "The Library is no longer."

"Looks to me like it is. All these people, they work for you."

He shook his head. "As soon as it became known, it stopped existing. If a tree falls in the woods and no one's there to hear it . . . well, the Library is the opposite of that. Yes, some of the old librarians have stuck with me, but they won't forever."

"What about your family? Where are they?"

He grimaced but said nothing.

"A wife and daughter. It's question eleven."

He chewed the inside of his cheek. "I'm not answering that."

"Are you going to tell me more?"

"We don't have time now. Soon."

I accepted that because I had no choice. In truth, now that much of the fear had fallen away, I was able to see Weaver with clearer eyes than before, and he irritated the hell out of me. He acted as if I were another of his Library employees, a stenographer who had been summoned to take down his precious thoughts.

But that wasn't the situation at all—not really, was it? He *had* been hiding from us, and the idea that he had summoned me was delusion. He was a professional liar, and it was quite possible that he'd lied so much that by now he was lying to himself.

I'd met his type in the corridors of Langley, as I occasionally drifted into the periphery of interagency skirmishes. Political motivations, though rare, occasionally did raise their heads, more so since 2016, and it brought out the worst in people. Black was white, and patriotism was treachery. Some had the gift of coloring the truth just enough to make it look like a lie, and to carefully prune a lie until it passed the smell test and became accepted truth, not just to the intended audience, but also eventually to the liar himself.

10

It was still dark when we pulled into Arrecife, and up on the hill the lights from flat-faced houses twinkled down at us. The Moroccan went to speak with the harbormaster while the three of us found an all-night café along the stone harbor. In Spanish, Kanni ordered a round of espressos, and we sat at a plastic table on plastic chairs and looked out at the water. When the Moroccan arrived, he gave Weaver a nod, swallowed his coffee, and headed off again.

"Ferry doesn't leave until morning," Weaver told me. "I need to go talk to someone."

"Okay . . ."

"Kanni will stay with you."

She kept staring out at the sea, as if she hadn't heard a thing. When Weaver finished his coffee, he stood and stretched, suppressing a yawn. "Maybe you'll want to get her story while I'm gone. It's very interesting."

I gave her a look, but she still wasn't looking at me, so I said, "I'd like that."

"Good," Weaver said, then walked off, hands in his pockets, casual, up toward the town.

"Would you like to tell me your story?" I asked.

Kanni ran a tongue over her teeth behind her lips and finally looked in my direction. "No."

I finished my coffee and tried to get as comfortable as possible in the uncooperative chair. What I wanted, more than Kanni's story, was a phone to call home. Home, not headquarters—I was suddenly unsure about them. Did I believe I was expendable, as Weaver had said? That I had been sent on such an unlikely mission to keep Weaver occupied until the wet works team showed up? No. There was no way I was going to take Weaver's word over the Agency's. But he'd planted a seed of doubt, and that was enough to make me hesitant. Which, of course, was precisely what he'd intended.

The jet lag was returning with a vengeance, and when I closed my eyes for a moment's rest I dreamed of a day when Rashid was a baby. During an afternoon nap, he rolled off our bed and hit the floor. He woke, crying, then vomited a little, and fearing a concussion I scooped him up in my arms and with Laura sped the ten blocks to the hospital. Along with fear for my son's health, I'd feared that this new thing, parenthood, was something I was particularly unsuited for. I feared that eventually I was going to kill the poor child.

When I woke, back aching, the sun was high over the African horizon, and in the golden light I could finally get a good look at Arrecife's harbor and the houses in the distance. Kanni was gone, and Weaver was sitting in her place, a phone to his ear, listening somberly to someone. When I sat up, I felt the weight of Collins's pistol in the pocket of my jacket. How had they trusted me with it?

On the table was a plastic bowl filled with some kind of paste. It turned out to be *bienmesabe,* a sweet almond pudding that would have been delicious even if I hadn't been famished.

As he listened to the phone, his bleak expression deepening, I thought of his child, Stephanie, who according to the file had been born, curiously enough, on September 11, 2001. Seventeen years old. Almost a legal adult.

Sometimes your inabilities take time to show themselves, and just when you think you've made it, when you've muddled your way through parenthood and are ready to release your child into the world, you screw up in the homestretch. Now his child was in hiding. His wife, too. His actions had led to their exile from the world, which in itself was a kind of death. I wondered how that made him feel.

"That's our boat," Weaver said as he hung up, nodding in the direction of a large ferry that hadn't been in the harbor when we arrived. Birds circled it and cawed loudly. The bleakness in his face dissipated, but only a little. "Like your breakfast?"

"It's sweet."

"Everything here is sweet," he said, then pushed himself into a standing position. "Let's move."

I followed him down to the harbor, and we found Kanni waiting among tired-looking European tourists and fishermen drinking beer. She, too, had a phone to her ear, and when we approached she hung up and said to Weaver, "You heard about Griffon?"

He nodded, that miserable look returning. "Let's make sure his family's safe."

"On it," she said, and headed toward the ferry, making another call.

When I asked what that was about, he rocked his head, considering whether or not to answer, and finally made his decision: "The guy who threw you in the water. Griffon. He drove on to Ben Khlil, but didn't make it. He was found in the truck outside town."

I remembered how, for a moment there, I'd wanted to kill Griffon. "Dead?"

"I suspect they wanted him alive," Weaver said somberly, "but he made that impossible for them." He eyed me as we walked. "Griffon was one of our best. Smart and loyal and airtight ethics. It's a rare and wonderful combination."

"And you'll take care of his family?"

Weaver squinted because behind me the sun was bright. Ahead of us, people were climbing the gangplank and driving cars onto the ferry. "As soon as they ID'd him, his wife and two children became visible. We have no choice."

Weaver's family wasn't the only one to suffer because of his actions. "How long can you hide them?"

"You'd be surprised," Weaver said, then opened his hand to usher me onto the gangplank first.

Unlike the other travelers, Kanni, Weaver, and I were taken by an old sailor with a limp to a locked room near the bridge. Inside was a modest cabin: two cots, a cabinet of drinks, and a tiny bathroom. I excused myself and peed like a racehorse, then washed up and settled in one of the cots. Kanni stepped outside, and Weaver took the other cot and told me to take out the recorder.

"This ferry takes thirty hours to reach Spain," he said. "That should be enough time."

"For absolutely everything?"

He leaned back in the cot, cupping his hands behind his head. "No one knows absolutely everything, but the things I don't have direct knowledge of I can make educated guesses about."

"And then?" I asked. "Once you finish telling me absolutely everything?"

"You report to headquarters, just like you planned. And get back home."

I sighed involuntarily. It was the best news I'd heard in a while.

"And if everything works out," he added, "I'll finally get back to mine."

PART TWO

THE ELEPHANT

MONDAY, SEPTEMBER 17, TO THURSDAY, OCTOBER 4, 2018

FOUR MONTHS AGO

1

Milo Weaver rode the Narita Airport escalator up from arrivals to where the enormous departures board floated above travelers' heads, displaying seemingly random cities, first in Japanese, then English, and back again. His personal phone was pressed against his ear, and he said, "It's a different world now."

He was replying to his wife, Tina, who was lamenting their daughter's recent dramas in high school, where she had been targeted by a girl whose family had recently arrived in Zürich from Lebanon. "She shouldn't have to deal with bullies," Tina had said. "I never had to."

Which was when Milo reminded her that this world was different than theirs had been.

He might have gone further, telling her that his own schizophrenic high school experience had been riddled with bullies, the kind who would make today's bullies look like mice, and it had taught him the value of confrontation, but he didn't want to dig a hole for himself when he was going to have to hang up any second. He hadn't seen his family in a week, leaving the day after Stephanie's seventeenth birthday party, and once he was done with Tokyo he would be able to once again settle into the comforting obligations of domesticity.

"What does the teacher say?" he asked.

"They don't *believe* in obstructing the natural developmental curve."

"What?"

"Exactly."

"You're the one who wanted a progressive school."

"You sound like your sister. Progressive isn't synonymous with mean."

Milo searched the faces in the crowd as he made his way to the exit. "Why don't we talk to the kid's parents? Even if I'm delayed I'll be back by the end of the week, so let's set up something for Friday."

"I don't *want* to talk to them."

"Then what do you want to do?"

There was silence on the line as he exited to the curb, rolling his carry-on, and the noise of arriving taxis swelled around him. Across the busy access road, he found the face he'd been looking for: a man in his early forties, Kaito Fukaya, whose work name was Poitevin. Poitevin noticed him as well, then turned to look in the other direction, to where a Boeing Dreamliner rose whining into the sky.

"Okay," Tina said as he crossed the road. "We'll talk to them. You better be back by then."

"I promise."

By the time he hung up he was close enough to Poitevin to reach out and touch his shoulder but didn't. Instead, as they both walked the long arc that connected the three terminals of Narita International, he let Poitevin remain a step or two ahead of him, and as they conversed they never looked at each other. To an outside observer, they were strangers heading in the same direction.

"Your plane was late," Poitevin said in his heavy accent.

"We had to refuel in Mozambique," Milo answered, which was just the passphrase. In reality, he'd flown direct from Manila, where he'd gone to confer with the UNESCO field office about an arrest warrant hard-line president Rodrigo Duterte had issued for Senator Antonio Trillanes IV, a prominent critic. It had led to a standoff, with Trillanes holing himself up in the Senate building, the one place in the country he was immune from arrest. The newspapers were going crazy, and the UNESCO officers, who thought of Milo as some vanilla representative of the central office in Paris, told him they feared unrest and a crackdown by Duterte. Milo should have been in and out in a day, but the airport closed as category 5 typhoon Mangkhut made landfall, and he camped out with a UN lifer at his apartment in the upscale Pasay district, drinking imported whisky and listening to his host's complaints about a country he loved turning sour. More interesting was the man's girlfriend, a corporate lawyer negotiating the sale of Asia-Wide, a local shipping company that had recently filed for bankruptcy.

"The pirates did it," she'd told Milo. "Last month was the third attack. A dozen sailors and fifty million worth of cargo sunk to the bottom of the Pacific, between here and Guam." That had been the final nail in the coffin of what had been one of the largest shippers in the Philippine Sea. Given the dangers, only one brave company had stepped forward: Salid Logistics, a conglomerate out of Oman. With a resigned shrug, she'd summed it up in a single word, "Globalism," and reached for her glass.

By the time Milo was able to fly out, fifty-four Filipinos had been confirmed killed by mudslides, another forty-nine missing. Then he'd gotten Poitevin's flash alert, forcing him to change flights and come to Japan.

"She's in Tokyo?" Milo asked him.

Poitevin shook his head. "Not anymore. Yesterday she flew up to Hokkaido. Staying in Wakkanai."

This was a surprise. Why had the woman he was looking for moved to the northernmost tip of Japan, twenty miles off the coast of the Russian island of Sakhalin? "What's she doing there?"

"I think she's hiding."

"From whom?"

A shrug. "You'll have to ask her. I put her address on the server."

"Anyone else watching her?"

"I didn't see anyone."

The flight to Wakkanai left from Haneda Airport, so Milo had to take an hour-long taxi ride across the southeastern end of the city, skirting the edge of Tokyo Bay. He filled his time on the phone, talking to his reference librarians in Zürich. One of them, Noah, reported that Stabyhoun, a librarian in Greece, had uncovered Turkish agents giving financial support to antigovernment protesters. Milo, intrigued, suggested Stabyhoun follow up on his observations with a preliminary report they could share with the patrons.

Kristin, the other reference librarian, told him about a report from Whippet, in Paris, that the French had been monitoring Chinese efforts to mass-produce 3D-printed plastic pistols that could defeat detectors and cross borders. "How far along are they?" he asked.

"Same logjam as everyone else. They shoot one bullet beautifully, but the barrel explodes."

"Not very useful."

"Depends on how many bullets you need," she said, then told him about a message that had come in: Kirill Egorov, the Russian consul in Algeria, wanted to speak with him.

"What's it about?"

"He wouldn't say. Just called the old central number and demanded the message get to you. I sent you his callback number."

Though he knew of Egorov, and had even met him once, the old Russian's connection to the Library was to its previous chief, Milo's father. Once upon a time, Yevgeny Primakov and Kirill Egorov had been colleagues in Russian intelligence, and when Yevgeny took an abrupt turn and landed at the United Nations, most of his old friends had scorned him. Even Egorov had turned his back, but a few years later their paths had crossed over Iraq, and they began to talk again, trading secrets like baseball cards. But since Milo had taken over ten years ago, Egorov, then a consul to Germany, had gone quiet, and Milo had only kept track of his late career from a distance, a series of foreign postings in steadily less important lands, now Algeria.

"I'll call him," Milo told her. "How's my sister doing?"

"Hold on," Kristin said. "She needs to talk to you about something."

Once he realized he'd be delayed returning home, he'd asked his sister, Alexandra, to watch over the Zürich office. Reluctantly she'd agreed, and when she came on the line he immediately said, "I'll be back soon, Alex."

"No you won't," she said gloomily.

"Why not?"

"The patrons are demanding a meeting at Turtle Bay. Soon as possible."

"Shit," Milo said, wondering if he'd been too optimistic promising to be home by Friday.

He waited until he was through security at Haneda before checking his messages, which required face recognition and two lengthy passwords to reach the server, which was encrypted to a degree that only the hackers in the Library's employ knew how to describe. All this just to retrieve two small items: an address in Wakkanai, and a phone number with an Algerian country code. He called the number, and Kirill Egorov picked up on the second ring with a wary *"Allô?"*

"Privet," Milo said, and continued in Russian, "I heard you were looking for me."

"Thank Christ," the old Russian said, sounding relieved. He didn't say Milo's name on what was presumably an open line. "I didn't think the number would even be in service anymore."

"It won't be for much longer. What can I do for you?"

"I have someone who needs your protection."

"We don't protect people. That's not what we do."

"Tell me about Martin Bishop, then," Egorov said, sounding smug.

Milo closed his eyes, irritated. "That was different."

"It wasn't. You helped an innocent whose life was in danger through no fault of his own. You made an effort to ensure that he would remain safe. This is precisely the same situation."

Egorov had been his father's friend, but Milo didn't know what kind of man Egorov had become since then. How, for example, had he survived this last decade in Putin's Russia? What compromises had he made? Men of his father's generation had spent their entire lives compromising, and by a certain point it became second nature, so that eventually you lost track of whatever principles you once had. "Who," Milo asked, "is this innocent?"

"Did you hear of Anna Urusov?"

"The dissident blogger in Moscow? She died last month."

"It's connected. This person is connected. He fled Moscow and landed in Germany. I found him in Paris."

Milo sighed. "Are you the one protecting him now?"

"I have been, but I can't anymore."

"Where is he?"

"I cannot tell you."

"Then why don't you get your people to protect him?"

Now Egorov sighed. "Your father never would have had to ask that question."

It wasn't the first time someone had thrown his esteemed father in his face, and it wouldn't be the last. "And now he's dead. If you want to talk in more detail, we can send someone to debrief—"

"No," Egorov cut in. "I cannot trust this with anyone else. You'll understand when we speak."

Milo didn't want to give in, but . . . "Look, I should be able to lay over in Algiers by Wednesday. We have a secure location there."

"Thank you."

"Don't thank me—I don't know if I can help."

"But you will." The old man was nothing if not persistent.

"I'll tell the office to get in touch once we know my timing."

"Thank you," Egorov said again, and before Milo could temper his expectations the Russian hung up.

2

Wakkanai Airport was a small affair after Haneda, but it was efficiently laid out, and soon he was taking a taxi past a big open field into town. He didn't know what to make of Egorov's call, and he regretted how quickly he'd promised to go to Algiers. The week was becoming packed, particularly with the patrons demanding a New York meeting. Ever since taking over the Library he'd found himself making concessions—not just to the patrons, who had worked from that first day to siphon his power, but to his father's old friends. Yevgeny Primakov had been profusely social, getting what he needed by way of charm and cleverness. He'd been the kind of man who changed the flavor of a room just by entering it, and as it turned out such traits were not hereditary.

Poitevin's address led him to the Wakkanai Sun Hotel, a few blocks from Soya Bay. The hotel was wildly misnamed, at least on this cold afternoon with its slate-gray sky and ominous black clouds pushing in from the east.

Whether or not he found her, he needed a place to sleep before boarding his next flight. There had been a time, long ago, when constant movement had been his friend—but he'd been a different person then, a Tourist, popping amphetamines before skulking down alleys, living on the periphery of real human existence. Anything had been possible before life finally came knocking. Age had undermined him. Parenthood, too.

Through the windows of his fifth-floor room, he tried and failed to find

Sakhalin Island through the gloom, then shut his blinds and thought back to his reason for being here: He had come to make the offer of a job.

The last he'd heard was that she was making her way consulting for Amsterdam-based Maastricht Securities, but then a year ago, after a stint in Nigeria, she had abruptly quit. He'd had a conversation with her chief in their office on the banks of the Maas River, a pale thirtysomething with too-efficient manners who considered her departure a stroke of good fortune. "We are here," he told Milo, "for the good of our clients. This is a dispassionate business—it has to be."

"You're saying she was emotionally involved?"

"I'm saying she was all emotion."

The description had troubled him, because even though he hadn't seen her for ten years his memories were of a fiercely committed professional who, despite a flair for the dramatic, was never undermined by undue emotion. But looking at her old chief, who patted his mustache dry after each sip of Aquaviva, he suddenly trusted his own memories a little more.

It had taken a while to track her down. There had been a security detail for visiting businessmen in Malaysia, an unexplained appearance in Cape Town, and then, two days ago, word from Poitevin that she'd been sighted in a Tokyo nightclub with two members of Naikaku Jōhō Chōsashitsu, the Cabinet Intelligence and Research Office, Japan's largely disrespected foreign intelligence agency. Poitevin, who had his own contacts in Cabinet Intelligence, learned only that she had come to sell some information and move on.

But she hadn't moved on. Instead, she'd flown to the northernmost point in Japan and checked into the Wakkanai Sun Hotel, where from the windows, on clear days, you could see Russia.

Milo showered and changed into some crumpled clothes, then went downstairs. The restaurant was mostly empty, the only other diners elderly Japanese who were too polite to stare at the Westerner struggling to debone his grilled rockfish.

Noah had looked into the hotel's computer system and come up with two rooms attached to Western names and passports. In 215, Mr. and Mrs. Gary Young, British, and in 306 Ms. Deborah Steele, American. It didn't take a genius to figure out which she was, but he didn't want to rush it. If he trusted his memories, then he knew that a forward attack wasn't going to end well for him. Ideally, he would make himself known by doing this—sitting in the open clumsily eating fish—and she would come to him.

So he read brochures in the lobby and took a walk down to the bleak-looking harbor and peered at a large yacht with Chinese markings as the sun fell, then returned to the hotel. On the way, he noted a yellow M3 spray-painted on a wall, and wondered how the Massive Brigade was inspiring Japan's youth.

Back in his room, he sat on the bed and checked messages, sent requests and, remembering Egorov, searched for the website that, until her reported suicide last month—by placing her head in her gas oven and asphyxiating herself—had been maintained by investigative journalist Anna Usurov. Russian journalists died faster than coal miners, and younger: Usurov had only been twenty-eight. Her blog, *RESIST,* was no longer up, and a government notice informed him that his IP address had now been logged.

He called home at eleven-thirty. Stephanie had just returned from school, where there had been another run-in with her bully, Halifa Abi, which had resulted in a trip to the director's office for them both. Halifa had loudly critiqued her singing ability after the audition for a school show, and when Stephanie tried to ignore her, the girl called her a cunt. In reply, Stephanie had called her an anti-Semite.

"What?"

"But she *is.*"

"She might be, Little Miss," he told her, "but it's a rough thing to call someone."

"And cunt isn't?"

"You're right, you're right," he muttered, wishing for the old days when her school fights were simple bursts of jealousy that could be unraveled with an evening chat and a glass of warm milk.

Tina came on and told him that she had confirmed a Friday meeting at four thirty with Halifa's parents, and that he'd better make it. "Wouldn't miss it for the world," he said.

After he hung up, he thought about his daughter's troubles and wondered how, exactly, the fight had gone down. Was it possible that this Lebanese immigrant was so bold as to attack Stephanie outright, unprovoked? After all, Halifa was a newcomer to the school, and it seemed unlikely that she'd go out of her way to make enemies so quickly. Had Stephanie said something, even something innocent, that hadn't made the story's final cut?

But this was his problem, wasn't it? After so long, living in a world where the obvious story was seldom the truth, he couldn't help but question his daughter's version of events. What he knew was that, come Friday, he could let none of his doubt show. Loyalty would have to come before objectivity.

And, he thought as he got up and put on his shoes again, he couldn't sit around waiting for people to come to him. At this rate, he would never make it home. So he trotted down to the third floor and approached 306. Knocked and waited. Nothing. He knocked again and said, "Leticia, it's Milo. Let's have a conversation, shall we?"

When she opened the door, she was wearing a plush red robe that he didn't remember seeing in his own closet, which meant that she'd taken the effort to bring her own. Which was very Leticia Jones. But even though she looked as if she'd settled in for the night, she'd recently reapplied her blood-red lipstick, and now she smiled at him. "Milo, did you *really* think I'd come to you? Please."

3

Her room was larger than his, with a sofa and a couple of chairs at one end, where she'd placed a shoebox-sized package of airline Scotch bottles. "You were expecting me."

"If I'd known it would be *you,* I would've gotten vodka." She leaned close and kissed him on the cheek, then settled herself on the sofa, legs crossed at the ankles, robe opening naturally to her thigh. He'd forgotten how she did this, putting men in their place so quickly. Or, rather, he hadn't forgotten it; he had just forgotten how effective it was. He settled on a chair, opened two of the bottles, and passed one to her.

"I haven't had a drink in three weeks," she said.

"To abstinence."

"Chin chin," she said, raising her bottle, then downing it.

For propriety's sake, he did the same thing, and his throat burned.

"Looks like your shoulder healed nicely," he said.

She grinned and pinwheeled her arm to prove his point. The last time they'd seen each other, in 2008, Leticia had been shot in the shoulder by Chinese State Security. "Malaysian doctors," Leticia said, "are miracle workers."

"Is that why you disappeared? Alex and I searched the whole hotel."

"I left because I knew you weren't done," she said. "If I'd stayed around I would've ended up helping you, bad shoulder or not. And I needed a break."

"I wouldn't have pushed you."

"You never do," she said with a crooked smile. "You just show off those sad brown eyes."

He smiled despite himself.

"Besides, I didn't fancy working for you."

Though Milo held on to his smile, he felt a tinge of disappointment. "I don't think you know what working for me entails."

"No?" She shrugged. "Ten years ago I see you working with Alexandra Primakov, your sister, who's got some weird, undefined position in UNESCO. Soon afterward, I find out that you're also working for UNESCO—as was your father, old Yevgeny, before he was killed. I've got all that right?"

Milo echoed her shrug and waited.

"So I start checking other names. Lo and behold, Alan Drummond, former Tourism director, *he's* also got a position with UNESCO. I mean, when did *that* rowdy crew get interested in education, science, and culture? It's a curiosity, and you know I'm nothing if not curious."

"It's a well-known fact."

"So I reestablished some old contacts, one of whom had also started working for the UN. For the Library."

"Hmm," he said thoughtfully, though what he really wanted to say was *Who the hell spoke to you?*

"Does it make you happy?" she asked.

He was taken aback by the question; it wasn't the kind of thing people in their business asked. "I don't know," he said. "Does anything?"

She leaned forward, not bothering to clutch her robe shut as she grabbed two more bottles and tossed him one; he caught it.

"What about you?" he asked. "Are you happy now that you've thrown off your employers? Now that you're free?"

She smiled at him, blinked slowly, then took a sip of Scotch. Quietly, she said, "April, four years ago. I was in Lagos. Working for those assholes in the Netherlands."

"Maastricht Securities. I met your old boss."

"Doing your homework," she said. "One tight ass, that one."

"Agreed."

"It was pretty straightforward. We had some investors—American, French, Russian, and British—who wanted to scoop up one of the large coltan mines the Nigerian government was selling off."

"Coltan?" Milo asked.

"Columbite-tantalites. Used to extract niobium and tantalum. Tantalum helps make your computers and phones work."

"Okay, I get it."

"Well, the state had never run any of its mines well, and the deaths of a couple miners a few months before made it a hot potato they just wanted to get rid of."

"Why were you there?"

"To fix a problem. There was a local consortium of business leaders that wanted to buy it for themselves. Keep the money in Nigeria. The newspapers were picking up on the story. Not good."

"You do some nastiness?"

Leticia gave him a hard look. "I got the job done, okay? And no one got hurt."

"Glad to hear it."

"Are you going to keep acting like that?"

"No, no. Go on." Milo leaned back, took a sip, and resolved to shut up. But it was hard, because it truly was good to see her again, and part of the pleasure was the sparring.

She said, "We were closing the deal when Boko Haram kidnapped those girls in Chibok. I asked Maastricht for leave to look into it. They wanted me back home, but I could have a week on my own dime. Fine. Whatever. I hauled myself across the country to Borno State and took a look for myself." She hesitated, looking deeply into his eyes. "I've seen a lot, Milo, but I've never seen anything like that. Two hundred and seventy-six girls. Gone. It breaks a village right in half."

Milo wanted to speak, even felt she would have welcomed a word from him, but found that he had nothing to say.

Eventually she continued. "I met with local law enforcement, and I'm not going to call them saints by any means, but this hurt them as much as anyone else. They knew, right then at the beginning, that nothing was going to happen. They knew that in the capital, in Abuja, they didn't even exist. Why? Because they didn't have coltan deposits. They didn't have diamonds or gold or iron ore. All they had was a little glass sand, bentonite, some diatomite. Nothing worth protecting. Which left them at the mercy of Boko Haram, or anyone who wanted to remake them in their own image."

"But they drew attention to their story," Milo pointed out. "It was an international scandal."

"And they still don't have all their kids, do they? And a year later the government tried to deny them voter ID cards, so they couldn't even use the only power they really had."

"I didn't know that."

"Why would you? Why would anyone? When I got back to Maastricht, I put it to them that we had the network and the resources to go in and find these girls. No, there wouldn't be a big payday, but I asked that asshole to imagine the goodwill Maastricht Securities would receive if we brought those kids home. Know what he said?"

"I could guess."

"He said that we're not in the business of goodwill. He told me to join UNESCO." She shook her head, grinning. "If only he knew, right?"

"But you didn't quit until last year."

"I found Maastricht's network useful for my purposes."

"What purposes?"

"Trying to *do* something about it. Amsterdam didn't need to know. By the time I did quit, I'd exhausted their usefulness."

"And?"

"And what?" she said.

"Last year, July 2017. A hundred and twenty more girls were kidnapped by Boko Haram. Did you approach Amsterdam again?"

"I did. He still said no."

"And what did you tell him?"

"I told him to lick my clit."

He knew better than to ask if she'd really said that, so he just reached down for another tiny bottle and handed it over to her, then took another for himself. Together, they unscrewed their caps and drank.

"So," Milo said. "That's what moves you now? Injustice?"

"Don't say it like that."

"Like what?"

She didn't answer but said, "What moves *you*, Milo?"

"The usual."

"Not the usual," Leticia said, shaking her head. "Back when I knew you, there were only two things that moved you. Tina and Stephanie."

"They still do."

"And that's it? You look around this shitty world, the one you're leaving for your daughter, and you don't find anything that you feel you *must* fix before handing it over to her? Is there nothing you see that must be repaired?"

He licked the bitter whisky off his teeth. "Yeah, actually. There is something," he said, then told her about the thing that kept him up nights. The shift, in country after country, to authoritarian leadership and the growing distrust of objective facts. As he rattled off his grievances, she settled back and laid her arms along the back of the sofa, her features relaxing into an expression one rarely saw in Leticia's always alert face. If he didn't know better, he would have thought she had fallen asleep with her eyes open. But he did know better. He knew that she was listening very carefully.

When he finished, she said, "Fascism, huh?"

Milo opened his hands. "Populism. Authoritarianism. Maybe it's just law and or—"

"It's *not* law and order," she cut in. "Call it what it is. It's us against them. It's fear of the Other. It's racism."

He nodded. "Racism, then."

"Don't say it like that."

"I'm agreeing."

She frowned at him, distrustful, and said, "Okay, then. Tell me what, exactly, the Library does about this wickedness? Go on, Milo. Sell it to me."

He knew by the way she asked it that the question was a setup. But he'd flown to Japan for this meeting, and all he could do was play his part. "We observe," Milo told her. "We report. That's why it's called the Library. Spread the facts, unvarnished by politics or spin, and let the governments take care of the problem. That's their job."

Leticia shook her head, looking mildly disgusted. Straightening, she said, "You know who *would* do something?"

"Tell me."

"Back in January, I got another visitor. Like you."

"Just like me?"

"Ain't no one just like you." She winked, but there was something cold in that move that made him anxious. "Calls herself Joan. Recruiter from DC.

She tells me I'm wasted where I am. Tells me it's time to come back into the fold."

"Into the fold?" Milo blinked, his head buzzing. He understood what she was saying, even though he could hardly believe it. "You mean—"

"I told her," she cut in, "that I could never work for the Department of Tourism again. I *told* her that I was there when the Chinese killed thirty-three of us. Then I asked what she knew about that. Joan was a soft-looking woman, but she didn't blink. For all I know she had no idea what I was talking about."

"Then how do you know she was Tourism?"

Leticia rocked her head. "She used my old code. *The commander of the Sixth Division reported . . . that Novograd-Volynsk was taken at dawn today.* If Joan isn't Tourism, then she's got all the files."

The surprise was heavy, pressing him down. He'd heard rumors over the years that CIA had resurrected the department, but it was in the nature of Tourism that every kind of rumor was to be expected. Rumors became legend, and legends provoked fear in America's enemies. You could win a whole fight by scaring your enemies into submission, all for the cost of a little gossip, and this was what Milo had convinced himself was going on. Maybe he'd only convinced himself of what he'd wanted to believe.

Milo finished his Scotch, scratched at his nose, and placed the bottle on the table. "You know what was wrong with Tourism? Other than its security vulnerabilities."

"Tell me, Milo."

"It became an instrument of political violence. Not governmental. Political. Any politician who got their hands on it started playing their own game."

"And the Library is different. Tell me who pays your bills."

"Independence is a long-term goal."

"That sounds a long way away."

He didn't bother to reply.

"And that's why you don't have to even ask me the question."

"What question?"

"Whether or not I'll become one of your librarians. You're living in a dream world, Milo. To change the world your way, the people you give information to have to be honorable. They have to want to do good. Do you really think that a report on a fascist tide rising across the globe is going to get liberal democracies to push it back?" She shook her head. "No, baby. Politicians and businesses in those democracies are just going to calculate how to cash in on the new world."

4

Milo woke late, the suddenly bright Wakkanai light cutting into his cursed hangover, and when he looked out his window and squinted he finally saw it in the distance: the Russian island of Sakhalin. Two islands . . . no, just one, but he was seeing double. He'd drunk with Leticia until three, at which point she had suggested that if he stayed any longer they were going to have to have sex, so he staggered to the door and accepted the kiss she planted on his lips, as well as the advice she left him with as her large, beautiful eyes peered deep into him: "You have to make a choice, Milo. Either you're on this earth to do good, or you're wasting space."

He nearly missed his flight back to Haneda Airport, and once he reached it he planted himself behind a counter and ate fried crustaceans until his nerves settled down. For the rest of the six-hour layover, he alternated between reading field reports forwarded to him by the reference librarians, and thinking about his failed recruitment of Leticia Jones. It was a blow, though not entirely unexpected, for she had always followed her own path. And now she'd discovered a conscience. A need to *do* rather than just witness. Were a few hundred kidnapped girls what it took to soften one of the hardest hearts he'd ever known? Perhaps. Or maybe she was playing a game of her own with him, which he wouldn't understand until weeks or months had passed. That, too, was possible.

Long game or not, her questions still weighed on him. Was he merely an observer? Of course he was, because that's the business he was in. No one faulted journalists for remaining separate from their subjects' lives, and in fact when they did become involved it meant they had broken one of journalism's ethical tenets. This dispassionate approach to the Library's intelligence work had always been attractive, because even when the world was falling apart he could remain at arm's length, describing it for his patrons. The world was never his responsibility, nor his fault.

Certainly there had been times—in Germany, in China—when he'd tossed out that ethical rule book, when his sense of right and wrong had gotten the better of him. But could he really say the world was a better place because of his escapades? How had saving Martin Bishop gone?

He didn't have to look far to find a world in disarray, slouching toward oblivion. Two hundred seventy-six, then a hundred and twenty, girls in Nigeria. Millions of refugees streaming out of Syria. Venezuela ripping itself apart. Pirates on the high seas. Typhoons burying Filipinos in mud, hurricanes and heat waves and melting poles. Electorates in Russia, Poland, Brazil, Egypt, Turkey, and the UK voting for their own dark futures—not to mention the political turmoil in America.

He couldn't save them all, but could he save some?

What if? What if he did choose to do more than just report on travesties to the Library's more upstanding patrons? To step into the currents of history and redirect a few streams?

He knew what would follow: The nations that funded the Library would react immediately, rightly fearing that one day Milo would come knocking on their own doors. No one wants to pay for a policeman they can't control. The cash would dry up, and the sixty-eight librarians spread across the globe, both full- and part-time, would be unemployed. Or worse.

He upgraded to a particularly pleasant business class for the Emirates flight that took nearly eleven hours to reach Dubai, and on the plane he wrote two reports on the concerns he'd listened to in Manila. After he landed he sent one report to Paris for UNESCO to keep in its files, and the second, more detailed one went to Zürich, where the reference librarians could add it to their enormous database that, stuffed with fifteen years of secret knowledge, was probably the Library's greatest asset. He made a few calls before boarding the next flight to Algiers, and once on the ground at

Houari Boumediene, he asked Zürich to tell Kirill Egorov that he would be at the Library's local safe house until early evening, when he would have to fly on to New York to find out what the patrons wanted from him.

The half-hour taxi ride took him along the Bay of Algiers, where the blinding afternoon sunlight bleached shipping freighters and fishing boats. To the north, Palma and Ibiza were so close and yet a world away from North Africa. Eventually his taxi turned inland to reach the Hotel La Famille in Bab El Oued. Milo paid the driver and took his bag inside, standing in the cool lobby until the taxi had left again. He smiled at the proprietor, an old man with a large set of keys hanging from his belt, then walked out of the hotel without saying a word.

It didn't take long, walking west along Avenue Colonel Lofti, to find Rue Rosseti, where he knocked on the inconspicuous door. The old, round woman who answered wore a black jilbab, only her face and hands visible. *"Où sont les autres dilettantes?"* she asked, almost spitting the nonsense passphrase.

"Ils sont derrière la grange," he told her, and as she took a step backward into the gloom she grunted in irritation.

She led him up the dark stairwell to the second floor and worked at a heavy door with bars over the window until it popped open to reveal a small, humid studio apartment, blinds down, a table with a couple of wooden chairs, and a sad-looking sofa against a water-stained wall. From the looks of the place, this janitor wasn't earning her stipend. There was mold along one edge of the carpet and ancient cracks in the walls that made him worry the building's foundation might be damaged. The counters in the kitchenette were filthy.

After the French passphrase, she didn't say another word to him, communicating with her hands and eyes. It was possible that she didn't know any French beyond the code. She showed him that the refrigerator, which was dead, contained six large bottles of water. She demonstrated how the door would lock on its own when he left, then made a big deal about pocketing the keys so he knew he wouldn't be trusted with them.

Then she was gone, and Milo went to turn on the overhead light, but the switch did nothing. He tried the kitchen, and then the floor lamp by the sofa. She hadn't even paid the electric bill. He sighed and went to peek out the blinds down to Rue Rosseti, and saw their useless janitor hurrying down the street and back to her life.

5

Alexandra Primakov had been a lawyer by trade, and for the first half of her adult life she'd settled into a properly structured life in London with regular hours at the law firm of Berg & DeBurgh and a steady stream of lovers she kept at arm's length. It suited her, always knowing where she would be, and when, fifteen years ago, her father convinced her to abandon her life of stability to join his intelligence operation hidden in the bureaucratic labyrinth of the United Nations, her one demand had been that she would stay in London.

For she was of two minds. On the one hand, she was, and would always be, Yevgeny Primakov's daughter, and like him she would always be attracted to the grand aims of the Library; at the same time, though, she was the daughter of the late Ekaterina Primakov, for whom stability and repetition had been the only route to happiness. These two influences cursed her with a mild schizophrenia, and she knew she would never really be satisfied with the choices she made. A man or a dog? As soon as she chose a mutt from the animal shelter, she would begin to wonder about the man who might have taken its place. Oddly, the idea of getting both never occurred to her, and this was one of the many reasons that, by her forties, she had neither.

From a small rented office in the Overseas Development Institute on Blackfriars Road, she took care of the legal intricacies of international intelligence from a structured place. She did travel, of course—the librarians sometimes got into trouble, and when it couldn't be taken care of remotely she would fly to Kuala Lumpur or Kinshasa in order to assess the situation and approach officials with the legal weight of the United Nations behind her. A couple of days in too-warm offices sitting across from small-minded bureaucrats, and then she was back in her Hampstead flat, toying with the perpetual dilemma of either buying a dog or finding a husband.

So when Milo, six years her senior, called from Manila to ask her to take over the Library's Zürich office "just for a few days," she resisted.

"Can't they run it themselves?" she asked.

"Probably," Milo said, "but I don't think it would look good."

"They're not children."

"You're right," he said, "but if something goes wrong, I'd rather have you there, in the apartment, with Tina and Stef."

There it was. He wasn't asking her to come as a necessary part of the Library but as the comforting auntie for his family. She tried not to be insulted but was anyway, and thinking about the kind of husband her brother had become convinced her that she had never really wanted to marry. A dog it was. As soon as she got back from Zürich she would visit the RSPCA.

So she'd flown down on a morning Swissair, and Noah waited in a Library Mercedes to drive her to the Weavers' two-floor apartment in Oberstrass, half of an old Habsburg villa on Hadlaubstrasse. It was good to see Tina. She'd always gotten along with her brother's wife better than she'd ever gotten along with him, and when she'd met their spunky daughter she'd seen a little of herself in young Stephanie. That, perhaps, was when she'd started to consider the idea of a family, but never strongly enough to actually do anything about it. And by now, at forty-two, her chances, rightly or wrongly, felt like they were slipping away.

Though she stayed in the guest bedroom and took breakfast with Tina and Stephanie, most of her time was spent at the office in Escher Wyss, on the other side of the Limmat River. It was a large second-floor apartment with a kitchen and five rooms. One was full of electronics, a second full of documents, while the third acted as Milo's—and now her—office. There was a fully appointed bedroom and another office used by the two reference librarians, Kristin and Noah. Kristin was previously an assistant for the Canadian ambassador to the UN, and Noah, back in 2005, had been a mathematician her father had found working for a French environmental group. Kristin was in her midthirties, Noah in his fifties, Alexandra the buffer between them.

She missed her little office in the ODI, and the silence, and the way that there was no one to push back against her decisions. Here in Zürich, young Kristin seemed suspicious of her very presence, often saying, "Why don't we wait until Milo gets back?" Noah was less contrary but felt the need to show that he was the person in the room with the most knowledge. For example, when a request came in from a librarian in Cairo for permission to cultivate a source in Egypt's General Intelligence Directorate, Noah delivered a lengthy soliloquy on the history and extent of the Mukhabarat's use of dangles to flesh out foreign spies. Kristin listened intently and finally said, "Why don't we wait until Milo gets back?"

And Alexandra thought, *I'm going to get a big dog.*

In her downtime, which she was surprised to find there was a fair amount of, she read reports and watched videos from New York of the First Consultation of the Liechtenstein Initiative, the first in a series of UN meetings aimed at doing precisely what its full title said: the Liechtenstein Initiative for a Financial Sector Commission on Modern Slavery and Human Trafficking. The UN wasn't known for ambiguous titles, not even for the individual presentations: Timea Nagy's "Follow the Money," Kofi Annan's "Fighting Child Slavery—A View from the Frontlines," and the antitrafficking organization Polaris's "How Do Traffickers Use the US Financial Services Industry?"

That evening, she taught Stephanie how to kill someone by slamming the heel of her hand up into the base of the nose, pushing bone and cartilage directly into the brain. Before leaving in the morning, Stephanie tried it out again, shoving her wrist high.

"What's that?" Tina asked.

"Self-defense," Alexandra said quickly.

"In case Halifa gets rough," Stephanie said as she grabbed her bag.

"You're not hitting anyone," Tina said, serious. "Hear me?"

Flipping through Nexus messages, Stephanie said, "I hear ya."

Once she was gone, Alexandra apologized, but Tina blew it off. "Milo's already showed her plenty. If she wasn't so well behaved, she'd be in jail for murder."

As much as she liked Tina, Alexandra found her enigmatic. How could she have stayed with Milo, particularly through their New York years, when she learned that Milo had hidden his entire history from her? The best she could figure was that Tina maintained an intensity of loyalty bordering on the psychotic. She'd even given up a career as an administrator in an actual library in order to live obscurely in one of Europe's duller banking capitals, where the uptight young men had taken to proto-fascist haircuts—long on top and shaved around the sides.

"I never thought I'd like it in Zürich," Tina said over coffee. "But I do—it's calm, you know?"

"Not boring?"

"I used to dream of boredom."

Boredom as the big dream. But wasn't that the kind of life Alexandra, too, loved most? Predictable, repetitious. Her little ODI office and men she never kept long enough to fuck with her schedule.

"It wasn't always easy," Tina said reflectively. "You know, I read this interview with Simone de Beauvoir. The paradox of life, she said, is that you spend all your time trying to *be* rather than just exist. But eventually, you look back and realize that you never actually succeeded. All you did was exist. Life isn't some solid thing that builds up behind you. It's just a series of days that vanish one after the other."

"Jesus," Alexandra said. "That's depressing."

Tina raised her coffee cup and smiled. "No, Alex. It's freeing."

The conversation was interesting enough for Alexandra not to hurry to the office, instead settling in for a long talk that shifted to the framework of feminism that Tina had grown up with. "Is it wrong," she asked, "that I'm only really at peace when I know my daughter is safe and healthy? No," she said, answering herself. "It's not."

"And when she leaves home for good?"

"Then I guess I find something else."

It was midday when Alexandra finally drove across the Limmat, the conversation still swirling in her head even as she reached the building in Escher Wyss and typed her code to get inside. She made her way up the narrow stairs leading to another keypad-protected door, behind which she found Noah clambering out of his overpriced desk chair and hurrying over to her.

"We just got a report in from Algiers," he said.

"Something wrong with Milo?"

"Uh, no," Noah said. "But he needs to hear about this."

6

Milo had nearly drifted to sleep in the gloom of the fetid apartment, half dreaming of Leticia's belief that it was up to them to change the course of history for the better, and his own conviction that neither of them deserved that kind of power, when his ringing phone shocked him awake. It was Alexandra.

No hello or greeting, just "Emergency. Exfil."

"What?" Milo asked, sitting up. "Why?"

"We just learned Kirill Egorov is dead."

A chill went through Milo. "How did he . . . ?"

"Unknown. Next flight out will take you to Tripoli. From there you can make New York."

Milo was on his feet now, snatching his shoulder bag and heading for the door. "Any sign anyone knows about this place?"

"Unknown."

"Okay," he said as he stepped into the dark stairwell and slammed the door shut behind himself. "I'll check in from the airport." He hung up and trotted down the steps, where he pressed the buzzer to unlock the front door and stepped out into the blazing sunlight that momentarily blinded him. He paused, waiting for his eyes to adjust, and from the hot whiteness he was able to find shapes—a minivan among the cars, an old woman smoking, two men hurrying across the street toward him. Instinctively he turned the other direction, away from them, but faced a chubby white man in a wide-brimmed hat holding up his hands.

"Milo Weaver?" the man asked with a thick Russian accent, and once Milo had made sense of the situation the other two men had reached his side of the street and were stepping up behind him. Unlike the one who spoke, these two men were hard, their poorly fitting suits tight over a padding of hard muscle, not doing much to hide the bulge of shoulder holsters. With a parked car on one side and the old stone building on the other, there was no getting away. "Milo Weaver?" the Russian asked again.

Milo looked past him, to the cracked sidewalk beyond, and felt a rare longing to run.

"Ach!" the Russian said, his hands waving around. "Of course, you do not know who I am, yes?" He held out a hand to shake. "Maxim Vetrov, vice-consul of Russian Federation in Algeria. And now, I am sad to say, acting consul. I have bad news. Esteemed Kirill Egorov is dead by heart attack. Only one hour ago. But before he dies he asks me to keep meeting with you, Mr. Weaver."

His hand remained in the air between them, and, knowing that the two young goons behind him would be able to outrun him in five seconds, Milo took the hand and shook. "Heart attack?"

"Doctor's opinion. Kirill was old man. Drinker."

"He died at the consulate?"

"Home."

Milo nodded, wondering. Coincidences did exist; they were everywhere. But this one strained credulity. On the very day Egorov was to meet him in order to ask for the kind of protection he could not trust with his own people, he had died. And according to Maxim Vetrov, acting consul, with his last breath Egorov had instructed the people he didn't trust to come and meet Milo. "So you were with him when he died?"

"In last moment, yes." Vetrov rubbed his thick hands together. "Kirill, he insist I come here and meet you."

"What did he say we would discuss?"

A blankness crossed Vetrov's face, then left it. "He says you tell me. That it is very important secret."

Then why don't you get your people to protect him? Milo had asked Egorov.

Your father never would have had to ask that question.

"Listen, Mr. Vetrov, I'm afraid I don't know anything. Kirill Egorov requested the meeting but didn't share any details."

Pursed lips, then: "I do not think you come all the way to this hot place without details."

"I'm very gullible."

Vetrov sighed loudly through his nose, shaking his head. "This is stupid," he said in Russian, then nodded at his men. Milo felt two sets of hard hands grip his arms and pull him back, then off to the right between cars. They were dragging him across the street to a minivan with diplomatic plates. He fought back, but these young men had been trained to grab things and hold them still. They were black belts in it.

Milo said, "I'm a United Nations official. You'd better let me go."

Maxim Vetrov didn't seem to care. It was apparent that Vetrov wasn't your run-of-the-mill diplomat; he was one of many GRU embassy plants, a military intelligence officer who didn't flinch as he watched his men throw Milo into the backseat of the van and climb in with him. Milo looked at each of their blunted faces, wondering which one he might be able to go through, then heard the sound of shouting.

Outside the driver's door, three dark-skinned men, their suits tailored a size too big, ran up to Vetrov and spoke rapidly to him. Though it sounded like French, he couldn't make out their words, but the two men on either side of him looked concerned. The one on his left got out of the minivan to check on it while the one on his right grabbed hold of Milo's arm with both hands.

After a moment of conversation, Vetrov flashing his diplomatic papers and looking very put out, it was done. Vetrov and his goon stepped aside while a dark mustached man pulled open the door of the van and said in Berber-tinted English, "Mr. Weaver, you will come with us."

The grip on his arm only tightened.

"Who are you?" Milo asked.

"I am an officer of the Algerian government, and we wish to have a conversation with you."

Through the window, Vetrov made a sign, and the grip on Milo's arm finally loosened. Milo got out to join the mustached man, and as they headed for an unmarked car parked in the middle of the street Vetrov said, "Good-bye, Mr. Weaver." The Russian was trying to look smug, as if all this had been part of his master plan, but he wasn't pulling it off very well. Kirill Egorov would have done a much better job.

7

The mustached man was named Mustafa Rahmani. He was small and damp-looking, with dark eyes and tufts of oily black hair hanging down to his thick eyebrows. He was a colonel in the Département de Surveillance et de la Sécurité, he explained patiently as his two associates walked Milo into an office building in some residential neighborhood they'd reached by driving inland. Only when they entered did Milo spot crayon drawings of families under happy suns and realize that it wasn't an office at all but an elementary school. Only Rahmani and Milo entered the small first-floor room with the lazy ceiling fan and a view of a green courtyard.

Milo made sure not to look too put out by his second kidnapping of the day. Even though Algeria was one of the twelve countries that secretly contributed to the Library's budget, he doubted that the DSS would have been happy to learn that its own politicians didn't consider its intelligence sufficient to keep the nation in step with the West.

They'd already been through his carry-on, which only held his clothes, and Milo placed his UN identification card on the desk at the front of the classroom. Rahmani examined it closely, then smiled up at his guest. "This is very good."

"You don't doubt it's real, do you?"

"Why would I?" Rahmani shrugged and leaned back. "Tell me, why were our Russian brothers pushing you into an automobile?"

"What did they say?"

He raised his hands, waving away the question, then spoke at length. "Understand me, Mr. Weaver. We are not interested in angering the Russians. We are a people under threat. These Islamists, they don't see Algeria on the map. They see the larger Maghreb, and they want to turn all of the countries in the Maghreb—us, Libya, Morocco, Tunisia, Mauritania—into a single caliphate. Crazy, yes? They do not believe in sovereign national borders. We have been fighting the Islamists since 1991, long before the West even noticed the threat. We cannot afford to make enemies." He shook his head. "Now we look to Syria and see how well those Russian weapons perform, and we sign a billion-dollar arms deal with Moscow. The battle tanks—they're so good. Really. And the Russians—they don't want to anger us either. They spent the Cold War throwing money at Africa for ideological reasons, but now they do it for market reasons. Geopolitical reasons. They want our warm-water ports to park their ships, maybe even warships. And if they position themselves in North Africa, then that keeps France and America out. It is win-win."

"I'm very pleased for you," Milo said, then gave him a smile for good measure.

"Thank you," said Rahmani. "But then you show up. On the same day the good Russian consul, Mr. Egorov, dies of a heart attack in his home. You, an esteemed representative of the United Nations, come to our city and go to a little apartment in the middle of Bab El Oued. Then the Russian vice-consul comes to harass you." He opened his hands. "Surely you see that this is odd."

"I thought it was odd as well. Were you following me, or the Russians?"

A tight-lipped smile. He raised an index finger and wagged it at Milo. "I will tell you something, Mr. Weaver. I will let you in on a secret. While I love our Russian brothers, I cannot say that I trust them all the time. No one is perfect—I understand this. Your own countrymen, too. Americans send mercenaries to fight your wars, and what do they do? Slaughter civilians. We all see it on TV."

Milo considered answering but found he had nothing to say.

"Of course, no one is perfect," Rahmani went on, "but the Russians . . ." A shrug. "I suspect that they want to control us the way they control places like Armenia, like Georgia, like Ukraine. So I keep an eye on them. I note strange behavior. For example, the dear departed Kirill Egorov—I met him, you know? A good man. But we watch him, as we must. And a few weeks ago, when he gets back from Paris, his movements, they go crazy! He no longer goes to his neighborhood café for coffee and biscuit each morning. He instead goes to the *other* side of town for coffee and biscuit. His mistress, who used to come to his house once a week—now she joins him for coffee, and they perform their lovemaking at her home."

"Is that so strange?"

"When he then dies on the day you magically appear, yes."

Milo wondered about that as well but didn't have enough information to understand anything just yet. "When did this start?"

Rahmani tilted his head, examining Milo, who suddenly worried he'd shown too much interest. "August twenty-two. Does this mean something to you?"

Milo shook his head. "Do you know why he was in Paris?"

"A security conference—the usual. Can you tell me why *you* are *here*?"

"Egorov wanted to talk to me. I don't know what about."

"It was something he could not mention over a telephone?"

"I got that impression."

"And do you, Mr. Weaver of UNESCO, often fly to North Africa when elderly Russians call you?"

"He was a friend of my father's, long ago." That was true, but the next was not. "I thought that it might have had to do with him."

"Yevgeny Primakov."

"Yes," Milo said, realizing that Rahmani knew a lot more than he was saying. Did he know about the Library? Maybe. But that, at the moment, was less important than what else Rahmani was telling him. Kirill Egorov's patterns had abruptly changed four weeks ago, after his return from Paris. Was that when his mysterious ward had shown up, the person he wanted Milo to protect? Milo leaned closer. "Where did Egorov go to get breakfast?"

A smile flickered on Rahmani's face. "El Kahwa El Zarka, over in Dar El Beïda." He blinked at Milo. "But before you become too excited: He never met with anyone of interest there. Only his mistress."

"Who is she?"

Rahmani smiled but said nothing—he'd shared enough.

"Then I suppose Kirill found better coffee," Milo said, even though he didn't believe it. Neither of them did.

There were more questions, but by then the purpose of the interrogation had been satisfied. Rahmani tried to poke holes in his story, but only half-heartedly, then returned to the subject of his Russian brothers and Algeria's precarious position in the world. Eventually, Milo explained that he needed to fly to New York. "UN Headquarters," Rahmani said, nodding somberly.

"Are you going to let me go?" Milo asked.

Rahmani raised his hands, energy flowing back into him. "Let you go? Let you *go*? Have you not been listening to a word I am saying? Algeria cannot afford to make enemies. And to hold you here and anger our great friends in America and the United Nations? Perish the thought!"

Milo was surprised that Rahmani personally brought him to Houari Boumediene and walked with him to the ticket counter. He'd missed his Air France flight so had to settle for an Air Algérie–Turkish Airlines ticket that would stop in Istanbul on the way.

At security, Rahmani raised a hand in farewell. "Please, Mr. Weaver. Next time you come to Algiers, do give me a call. We can try that excellent coffee."

8

Leticia Jones was angry with herself. They'd had a room for two days, under Mr. and Mrs. Gary Young, and it wasn't like she hadn't noticed the only other non-Japanese guests in the Sun Hotel. Yet she hadn't figured it out. Age, maybe, or the distraction of Milo Fucking Weaver. What a piece of work he was. Sweeping in a decade after their last good-byes, as if she'd been in Wakkanai just waiting for him. No, not for him. The developer. That's who she'd been waiting for, and now she had a tail.

She *had* seen them down at the harbor before Milo arrived at the hotel, one of those couples that was not a couple, and her senses had begun to tingle. Brown guy, five-ten, late forties, walking shoulder to shoulder with a younger white woman with thick eyebrows who spoke quietly to the man who was clearly not her man at all. But Leticia had also been followed back in Tokyo by Milo's ham-fisted librarian, and she'd assumed these were more of the same. Then Milo stumbled out of town, and in the evening when Leticia headed down to the harbor to wait for the ferry from Korsakov, she spotted the white woman fooling with a rental bicycle.

Why were they still here? Why hadn't Milo taken them with him when he left? Did he really think he could continue to keep tabs on her?

The answer only occurred to her the next morning at the docks, when the brown guy appeared again, meandering past the lines of fishing boats, talking on his phone, and she kicked herself for not realizing it earlier: They weren't Milo's people.

That tingle returned, the one that had kept her alive more times than she wanted to remember. It told her the time had come to move on.

She had everything she needed—the three IDs she switched between, money, credit cards—but unless she went back to the hotel she was going to lose the robe she'd picked up in Tokyo, which was a damned shame. She'd never found one as soft, and probably never would again.

She walked inland, through the industrial wasteland, and predictably the man—Mr. Young—followed for a while before realizing where she was going, at which point he hurriedly made a new call. But he stayed with her, crossing the road to pass the bright orange Yumeshokukankita Market and around it to reach the big, airy station, where she bought a train ticket to Asahikawa. Her Japanese was good enough to earn praise from the old woman behind the counter, who explained that she had just missed the 10:21, but there were two more leaving at 12:55 and 5:40. Then, when Leticia followed her purchase with a ticket for the bus to Sapporo, which wouldn't leave until 6:30 the next morning, the old woman asked which trip she was going to take.

"I just can't decide," Leticia told her. "What do you think?"

"Sapporo," she advised. "Definitely Sapporo."

"Thanks."

Tickets in hand, she went out and flagged a white taxi, noticing Mr. Young now getting into a little Mazda with the not-his white woman at the wheel. "Airport," she told her driver. As he headed east, she glanced back to find the Mazda keeping a safe distance. She used her phone to buy an All Nippon Airways ticket for the 1:15 flight to Tokyo.

It took less than twenty minutes to reach the little airport, which only ran three flights a day, and when the driver let her out she could see the Mazda coming around the curve behind them. Beyond the road lay the expansive parking lot and then an open field of green parkland heading inland for half a mile until it reached a line of roadside trees at the park's entrance. Inside the airport, she headed straight for the bathroom, where she closed herself in a stall and checked her watch.

The Tokyo flight didn't leave for another hour, the train to Asahikawa in forty-five minutes. The bus ticket to Sapporo was backup, in case everything fell apart. And if she didn't time this just right, it would.

She waited twenty minutes. Though she took the opportunity to pee, the rest of her time was spent listening to Japanese women come and go, gossiping and whispering to one another about troublesome men and children, and work, which was also troublesome. At one point someone entered silently, then left again without doing anything. It might have been Mrs. Young; she didn't check.

At exactly twelve thirty, she flushed the toilet and left the stall, washed her hands quickly, and left the bathroom. She spotted the man right away, on a chair near All Nippon's Festa shop. He saw her, then averted his gaze clumsily to find his friend, waiting at the top of the stairs to the second floor. Leticia didn't bother showing them anything. She just went back outside and walked to the first taxi in the queue and hopped in. "Train station," she said in Japanese.

As they started to pull away, she turned to see the man and woman bolting at full speed out of the airport, across the street, and to the big parking lot, where they'd been forced to leave their Mazda. She leaned close to the driver's seat and, in her kindest voice, said, "I'd like to try something, if you don't mind."

"Try what?" he asked, eyeballing her in the rearview.

"You know that park over there?" she asked, pointing across the open field.

"It's for the kids," he said as he turned onto the main road. "Horses, goats, rabbits."

"Sounds great. I'd like you to drive me to the entrance to the park, let me out, but keep driving to the train station. Can you do that?"

"Why? Am I picking someone up?"

"No. But you'll earn another five thousand yen."

An extra forty dollars was enough to brighten him up. "What do I do when I get to the station?"

"That's up to you, but I need you to go all the way there. Can I trust you?"

"You obviously don't know me."

"What does that mean?"

"I'm a Jehovah's Witness. There's no one you can trust more than me."

"I'm very lucky to have found you, then," she said, and started counting out thousand-yen bills, placing them on the armrest. "But it has to be fast. I jump out and you keep going."

"Do you want to tell me why?" he asked.

"I'd rather not."

"No trouble, though?"

She shook her head and gave him a brilliant smile. "No trouble at all."

By the time they followed the road's curve to reach the entrance to the park, they were hidden by trees, and when she jumped out and sent him on his way she quickly dropped into the overgrown grass. She lay flat, waiting, and after three cars passed she warily raised her head and started to jog back, heading across the field.

She guessed that by the time she reached the airport the taxi was only halfway to the train station. She showed her e-ticket and went to the small lounge to wait for her Tokyo flight. It was all about timing: Her shadows couldn't get from the station to the airport in less than fifteen minutes. By the time they figured out what was going on and made it here, she would be in the air.

9

Milo hadn't set foot in the United States for nearly six months, and while he and his family had once lived not so far from JFK Airport, over in Park Slope, when he stepped outside to join the busy taxi queue, he didn't have the feeling of returning home. There was something off in the cacophonous hustle that typified New York City, the feel of a threat hanging in the air.

He supposed it was a hangover from Algiers, because, even trading calls with Alexandra from Atatürk Airport, they hadn't gotten any closer to discovering why Kirill Egorov had been killed by his colleagues—because by now Milo was running with the most straightforward explanation. Nor was there any way to figure out who Egorov had wanted him to protect. Did Paris have anything to do with it? Alex promised to check. But that was a long shot, and now, with Egorov dead, it was beginning to look like he would never learn who the old man had been hiding.

Or maybe the feeling that had overcome him had nothing to do with Egorov and was instead deeper, born of the creeping worry he'd been carrying for months. That the world was leaning at too dangerous an angle, and that if they didn't watch out it would topple.

No. He knew what it was: Leticia had been approached to join a resurrected Department of Tourism, and he had just landed in the city where its headquarters had once been. And he knew, because he was no longer the man he used to be, that if they wanted to, any Tourist could walk right up to him and end his life before he even knew they were there. Everything, now that he'd landed in America, was a potential threat.

Alan Drummond, whose cheeks were starting to bloom with late-life rosacea, was in a perfectly silent Tesla sedan idling at the curb. Milo threw his bag in the backseat, and as soon as he got into the passenger seat and pulled the door shut, Alan pressed the accelerator and they were off, the Tesla's big navigation screen charting the gridlock traffic in their immediate future.

Other than the red face, Alan looked undeniably fit. After a mild heart attack eight years ago, he'd become a fitness nut, and now haunted Tribeca gyms and blended esoteric smoothies in his kitchen—and the results were startling. His cheekbones stood out, his skull was clearly defined, and his pink skin glowed with health. As he drove, eyes on the road, Alan tapped a clear plastic cup that sat in the cup holder, full of green liquid. "Made that for you."

Milo eyed it suspiciously. "What is it?"

"Almond milk, protein powder, lecithin—"

"Lecithin?"

"For the brain."

"Why's it green?"

"Spirulina," Alan said. "Algae. Crazy healthy."

Milo had no intention of drinking the mixture, so he changed the subject. "You heard about Algiers?"

"Alex told me. She even called Said Bensoussan for help."

Milo nodded; Alexandra had told him this back in Atatürk. "I want to drop in on him before the meeting."

Once, their roles had been reversed; Milo had worked for him rather than the other way around. Alan Drummond had been the Department of Tourism's final director, his short tenure ending abruptly with the end of the department itself, a disaster that had arguably shaped them both.

As Milo recounted his Algerian adventures, Alan absorbed it all without comment until the very end, when he said, "We can put someone on it, but it doesn't sound like a front-burner worry. Not with the patrons grumbling."

"You know what the meeting's about?"

He shook his head. "But I've got suspicions. You didn't give them that Jordanian intel. You passed it to Israel instead."

"They needed it first."

"Israel isn't paying our bills. And our patrons don't want to learn things from the papers. Particularly when those things are happening in their own country."

Milo looked out the window at the traffic and the ugly expanse leading from the airport to the city. These decisions—choosing which country got what information, and when—were as close to manipulation as the Library ever got. The Lebanese intelligence, dealing with the movement of certain known terrorists through Beirut, had been entirely time dependent, and if he'd given it to Lebanon first the Israelis would have lost their chance to catch the person in question. "The Lebanese didn't want him in their territory anyway."

"Of course they didn't. And of course they were secretly happy the Israelis took care of it for them. But it serves them better not to admit that."

"Well, we'll see," Milo said, and stretched himself out in the seat.

"I saw a preview of the IPCC report."

Milo didn't have to ask what the IPCC was—Alan kept constant track of the UN's Intergovernmental Panel on Climate Change, and the IPCC's report, which had been ordered in 2015, involved ninety-one authors from forty countries, many of whom Alan was by now on a first-name basis with. He'd sometimes show up at Milo's home in Zürich after sitting with IPCC scientists at their headquarters in Geneva, just so he could vent his frustration at the world's blindness to the encroaching disaster. When America had pulled out of the Paris Climate Agreement a year ago, it took Alan three full hours of yelling to finally exhaust himself.

"Tell me," Milo said.

"It's not good. We're looking at a one-point-five centigrade rise by 2030 at the current rate. At *least* one-point-five. And that's the average—it'll be two or three times higher in the Arctic."

"Translate that for me."

"Bad shit. Melting ice will raise the global sea level by half a meter. And it'll keep rising, even if we keep it to one-and-a-half degrees—which doesn't look fucking likely. Say good-bye to the Maldives and Solomon Islands. Say good-bye to New Orleans, Miami, and Atlantic City. Boston's underwater. Bergen. Half of Baltimore."

"I'm guessing the West Coast is not much better."

"Not if you're in Seattle, Madera, Silicon Valley, or the LA coast. No, you're screwed. It's not just people—you can forget about the coral reefs. Seventy to ninety percent of them are toast."

Milo looked ahead at the gridlock leading into Manhattan. If ever there was an iconic image for human destruction of the planet, it was this—thousands of cars driving through packed, desolate-looking neighborhoods toward huge, energy-wasting skyscrapers. "Well," he said, "I guess everyone moves inland. Problem solved."

"You're jerking my chain."

"Just trying to be a problem solver."

So Alan took a breath and gave him a dissertation on the ills that awaited middle America: extreme weather patterns, tornadoes, hurricanes, floods and mudslides, and new diseases immune to antibiotics. Wildfires. "The melting ice caps lower the salinity in the oceans, which means the nutrients at the floor of the ocean can't move to the surface and produce plankton algae, which fish live on. And so do we. Seventy percent of the atmosphere's oxygen is produced by marine plants. We're killing ourselves, and not enough people are panicking."

Though Milo agreed with Alan's assessment, he had listened to this, or permutations of it, plenty of times before. "Want to hear about Japan?"

Alan hummed an okay.

"She's not signing up."

"What a shame," he said unconvincingly. Alan disapproved of recruiting Leticia. He, not without reason, considered her reckless, but unlike in the old days in the Department of Tourism, Milo's decisions prevailed. "Were you not convincing enough?"

"She wants more."

"Money?"

Milo shook his head. "Utility. She wants to change the world."

"We talking about the same Leticia Jones?"

"She's gone through an awakening," Milo said as they slowed for traffic. "By the way, they've opened the department again."

Alan eyeballed him as they came to a stop behind a large truck. "Wait, you don't mean—"

"Tourism."

Alan exhaled. "I'll be damned."

"We'll all be damned."

"But it's not surprising. You're not surprised, are you?"

"A little."

As the traffic finally opened up, neither said a thing, the pile-on of memories burying their words. Eventually, Milo said, "Can you talk to your old contacts about it? We can't afford not to know what they're doing."

"Sure. But maybe we're too worried. The department lasted for decades. It did good work. And look around—you think Tourists wouldn't be useful right now? Jesus, just think about what they could do in Ukraine or North Korea. Gather ten of them, and the Russians would never touch our elections again. They're effective."

It had always been the most persuasive argument for Tourism—its effectiveness when diplomacy was shot. But Milo knew too well the other side of the argument. "They're too powerful to be a permanent fixture."

Alan shrugged, then nodded ahead at an enormous billboard advertising a TV show—a spy drama set in Berlin, attractive actors in dark outfits, looking intently at the camera. Someone had used a ladder and red spray paint so that the image was covered in two enormous characters: M3.

"And are *they* too powerful?" Alan asked.

10

It was after one when Alan let him out in front of the slab of the United Nations Headquarters, which many of its employees called Turtle Bay after the neighborhood. Milo only made it a few steps before he heard Alan shouting at him. He turned to see his deputy holding out the plastic cup of green liquefied health. "You forgot the smoothie!" he shouted.

"Keep it," Milo called, then hurried across UN Plaza and up the stairs to the entrance. Security took a moment to examine his scuffed, laminated ID before waving him on. In the elevator, he got a few looks from the other employees rising with him, and that was when he realized he should have changed, because the dust of Algiers was still all over him. Again, he wasn't the man he used to be.

He got out on a high floor and wandered down the narrow corridor until he'd reached a door with a plaque: DEPUTY AMBASSADOR TO THE UNITED NATIONS, ALGERIA, SAID BENSOUSSAN. He knocked once, waited, then knocked again. Finally a slim secretary with hair up in a bun opened the door. A flash of familiarity, but only slight, for he rarely visited the patrons' offices. He put on a smile. "Milo Weaver. I'd like to speak with the deputy ambassador, please."

She stepped back and gestured to the chairs across from her desk. "I will see if Mr. Bensoussan is available." She disappeared behind another door, gave him a moment to collect himself, then stepped out again and opened her hand for Milo to enter.

Said Bensoussan was just shy of forty, as slim as his secretary, and more stylish than his job required. Immaculate suits, a perfectly coiffed goatee, and manicured nails gave him a fussy look that always impressed Milo, for whom vanity felt like one thing too many to keep track of. Bensoussan was also much smarter than the ambassador he served.

"Sit down, sit down," he said, rising to shake Milo's hand. Once his secretary had closed the door, Bensoussan went through the pleasantries. "When did you get in? Have you rested? What can I get you?"

"Listen," Milo said, "I wanted to thank you. I'm told you made a call on my behalf."

"My pleasure. However, no one I talked to admitted knowing anything about you. I'm not sure I was any help."

"For the effort, then."

Bensoussan opened his hands and settled back behind his desk. "Perhaps you'd like to tell me about it."

Milo told the Egorov story just as it had happened, fighting his natural instinct to hide details from a patron. He knew that Bensoussan in particular was adept at catching loose details and holding on to them, patiently waiting for other puzzle pieces to fit, until he could eventually create entire pictures of things you never wanted to share. But in this case, Milo hoped that openness would encourage Bensoussan to react in kind.

By the time he finished, Bensoussan had taken a cigar from a box and begun rolling it in his fingers, a cue that he was deep in thought. "You don't believe the official story? Heart attack?"

"Do you?"

Bensoussan shrugged. "Whether or not Egorov was murdered, it doesn't answer the question of who he wanted to hand over to you. You said he had changed his movements?"

"Last month, after a trip to Paris."

"And the DSS found nothing at the café. Did they speak to his mistress?"

"I don't know. Can you ask?"

"Who questioned you?"

"His name's Mustafa Rahmani."

Said nodded severely. "I'll let you know whatever he decides to tell me."

"Are you worried they won't tell you?"

"These days, one never knows," he said, opening his hands. "I haven't seen my president for months. In this world, everything is a question mark."

"Wasn't it always?"

Said smiled and rocked his head. "We'll see you in a few hours, correct?"

"Both me and Alan."

"Good."

"What's it about?"

A smile twisted the corner of his lips but didn't spread any farther. "A month ago you sent in the preliminary fiscal year 2019 budget."

"Ah," Milo said, instantly annoyed.

Bensoussan picked up on this. "We pay a lot of money for the Library's services, Milo. You have to expect your customers to ask for improvements now and then."

"What kind of improvements?"

Bensoussan blinked at him, then shook his head. "Nothing too egregious, I'm sure. We'll talk this evening."

After the Algiers safe house, the Hilton room that had been reserved for him to freshen up in felt like decadence. He took a long shower, pulled on a thick robe, and drank coffee while looking out at the UN building from his thirty-ninth-floor window. Beyond lay the East River and Long Island. It was a clear day, the sun sinking behind his building, and as he stared he listened to American news playing on television.

Anthony Halliwell, head of Northwell International, was in Congress defending against news reports of the massacre of Afghan citizens by his private soldiers. This was what Rahmani had been talking about: America farming out the defense of its empire to contractors who lacked discipline. Stories like the Northwell massacre were the bread and butter of North African politics, used as a cudgel during campaign speeches to the wound-up masses.

There was a lot of talk about Donald Trump, Special Counsel Robert Mueller, and the upcoming midterm elections. Trump was on-screen, shouting about a caravan of Central Americans marching north in order to justify his promised border wall. His words sounded familiar, the same sort of rhetoric he'd heard in Hungary, Poland, France, and Britain about Syrian refugees escaping war. And if Alan's scientists were right—and after three years of research by hundreds of scientists checking one another's work, he didn't doubt they were—then refugees would be the new reality, fleeing natural disasters, wars over water rights, disease, and starvation.

Just thinking about it gave him a headache.

A well-known, mustached commentator named Sam Schumer came on the screen to discuss the Massive Brigade's three-month burst of violence earlier in the year, the explosions in shopping malls, a kidnapped CEO, the brief hacking of the DC electrical grid, and the numerous bank robberies. Then President Trump was there again, in the Rose Garden, declaring that the Massive Brigade, like ISIS, had been defeated. "I don't think any previous administration could have taken care of it so quickly," he said.

There followed a blurry photo of a middle-aged woman with dark hair, a baby in her arms, sitting in a dilapidated living room with young people who all looked to her with something approaching adoration. It was an odd photo, with the feel of a Virgin Mary re-creation.

Schumer said, "Their new leader, Ingrid Parker, seen here living underground with her Massive Brigade comrades, is still on the loose. The silence these last months is not defeat. We know this—even the president knows this. It's only the calm before the storm. Stay vigilant."

He met Alan at Sakagura, a moody Japanese restaurant hidden beneath an office building on East Forty-Third. Around them, in other dim booths, customers talked animatedly but quietly, as if the very design of the place had lowered their volume. Architecture as mood control. He and Alan followed suit, talking quietly about regular business and making plans to distribute recent intelligence that had come in from Brazil concerning the popular right-wing presidential candidate Jair Bolsonaro. After Milo talked him through the report he'd sent in on the Philippines, Alan started complaining about DC. "It's a cesspool of Chinese, Saudi, and Russian spies."

"More than usual?"

"Absolutely. Everybody knows the Oval Office is full of venal, easily manipulated peacocks running the country like their own piggy bank. So the charm offensive arrives with suitcases full of money. This country's going to spend the next twenty years unraveling all the intelligence lost and compromised these four years."

"It's sad," Milo said.

"If only there were an organization that could do something about it," Alan mused theatrically.

"Don't start," said Milo.

"Why not?"

"Because that's not what we do."

"But if we did we would do it best," Alan said, smiling. His phone bleeped a Nexus message from his wife. "Pen wants to know if we can take you out for drinks."

Milo shook his head. "My flight's at eight-thirty."

Alan nexted back a negative and said, "It's all right; she's just being polite."

"You mean she doesn't like me?"

"I guess you'll have to have a drink with her to find out."

Milo smiled, then thought a moment. "What do we know about Egorov besides the obvious?"

"I checked his file. Nothing really out of the ordinary. For a few years he was close to Putin, but four or five years ago he started pulling away. Which, I suppose, explains being posted to Algeria."

"He was in Berlin before?"

"Sounds like a demotion to me," Alan said.

The mystery of Egorov hung on Milo's shoulders, but he knew from experience that he probably wouldn't find an answer. And if he did, it would come years later, when an unrelated situation revealed the truth. Which was why the reference librarians and their enormous, deeply encrypted database were the backbone of the Library. They kept track of everything, cross-referencing and finding connections that Milo was just too human to be able to make.

"Do me a favor," Milo said. "Get word to Berlin that I'd like to have a talk. I'll have Kristin reroute my flight."

"Because Egorov was stationed there?"

"And because he was friends with my father. So was Erika Schwartz. They were all the same generation."

"And Erika's been out of the picture three years."

"Oskar Leintz isn't."

"Really?" Alan shook his head. "You hate that guy."

"I work with you, don't I?"

11

The Abdul Rahman Pazhwak conference room was a hermetically sealed space on the thirty-eighth floor of the UN with cracked wood paneling that had been installed in the midsixties. With the gathering darkness outside, the windows acted as mirrors until Alan lowered the blinds.

Collecting all twelve wasn't unprecedented, but it was rare. Invariably a few patrons either bowed out or chose to join through video chat. Even the elusive Beatriz Almeida, assistant deputy to the Portuguese ambassador, sauntered in chatting quietly with Said Bensoussan. Milo approached them and welcomed Almeida, a small woman with a perpetual smile, then caught Said's eye. Together, they stepped into the bland corridor.

"So?" Milo asked. "Egorov's mistress."

He frowned, rocking his head. "She spoke for two hours with your friend Colonel Rahmani, but I'm afraid nothing came of it."

"What's her name?"

Bensoussan hesitated, then said, "Gazala Mokrani. But it appears she knows nothing. Nor, I'm afraid, does Colonel Rahmani. He's one of our better public servants, you understand, and Egorov's death troubles him. The Russian acting consul has declined an invitation to enlighten us."

"Did Gazala Mokrani explain why she and Egorov changed their daily pattern after Paris?"

"She only said it was Egorov's wish. Otherwise, their liaisons remained the same. From what I understand, Ms. Mokrani is a singer. Worldly, a sophisticated woman. Rahmani believes she is telling the truth. I'm sorry I don't have more information for you, Milo."

By the time they returned to the room, everyone was seated and waiting. Bensoussan took his place beside Almeida, and Milo settled in a chair at the head of the table, Alan to his right.

Looking over his dozen patrons, he wondered again if he'd made a fatal mistake when, soon after taking over, he'd expanded the patron count from seven to twelve. At the time, he'd discovered too many holes in their globe-spanning intelligence network of forty-two librarians. They needed more staff, and a bigger support budget, but in a world where a global recession had been brought on by a toxic mix of fiscal and real estate malfeasance, demanding more from the seven his father had assembled—Germany, Luxembourg, Iceland, Kenya, Bangladesh, Ghana, and Portugal—was out of the question. So he'd gone hunting, and in consultation with the original patrons settled on five more—Algeria, South Korea, Lebanon, Botswana, and Chile.

That had solved the immediate budgeting problems, and with the larger staff he'd had to alter his father's organization by creating a stable head-quarters, the office in Escher Wyss, which was how he preferred it. He had no interest in the nomadic life his widowed father had led. But by nearly doubling the patrons he had doubled his political headaches. Building consensus among all twelve was like playing Whac-A-Mole, and the possibility of insurrection was an ever-present threat.

"Before we get started," Milo said, "I wanted to share some information from Manila, where I recently came from."

Eyes lit up around the table. It was rare when he shared intelligence with them as a group, which was why he'd chosen to do it now. To put them off their guard. The political unrest that he described to them would be of particular interest to Katarina Heinold, the German patron and the largest power at the table, whose country traded heavily with the Philippines. Yevgeny had brought on Germany at the start the way an American mall brings on a Macy's to anchor the entire enterprise, and all the others noticed the way she leaned in and focused on Milo's words.

When telling them about the incidents of piracy, he posed the same question he'd put to the UN lifer and his lover in Manila: Why would pirates sink vessels? The point of piracy was booty—how else did you pay for your enterprise? "This is what I find most disturbing. We know how to deal with piracy, but not a group that is willing to sacrifice both lives and profit."

"Competition," Almeida said. "It's clearly for the benefit of competing transport companies."

"Possible," he said, "but no competing companies made a bid on their shipping lanes. Apparently, they're all terrified of the same thing happening to them. They ended up being bought out by a company on the other side of the world, Oman."

"Islamists," Katarina Heinold suggested. "The Bangsamoro terrorists set off a bomb in Isulan two weeks ago. Or Abu Sayyaf."

Milo was impressed by her breadth of knowledge but said, "No one has claimed responsibility."

She accepted that with pursed lips, and as he wrapped up his disclosures Milo tried to read the patrons' expressions. It was impossible, though, for these diplomats had spent their entire adult lives learning how to mask their feelings behind the shell of their faces. Some of them, he knew, were under significant pressure from home; some were at the end of their careers; others were eagerly vying for power on the home front. Some were backstabbers, others fatalists. Many were eyeing upcoming elections, populist challengers biting at their parties' heels, and didn't know if they would have a job next year. Which was another way of saying that whatever they did to him tonight was not personal; he just happened to be in their way.

"We hear you were in Algiers," said Alfred Njenga, the Kenyan representative. "To meet Kirill Egorov?"

"The *late* Kirill Egorov," Katarina Heinold corrected.

Milo wasn't sure how they'd come across this information so quickly—either the Algerians or the Russians had let it out. He glanced over at Bensoussan, who gave him a very faint shrug, feigning ignorance.

"So, what was that about?" asked Beatriz Almeida, smiling.

"I don't know," Milo said. "He asked for a meeting, but we never got a chance to speak."

Katarina Heinold looked over at Alfred Njenga, a subtle communication. Almeida looked at some papers she'd brought with her, while beside her Bridgette Tlhabi of Botswana checked her watch. That was when Elias Kanaan of Lebanon cleared his throat, brought his hands together on the shining surface of the table, and said, "We have gone through the new budget."

Milo straightened in his chair, waiting for it. Waiting for the arguments over each item on the list—the travel expenses or the computer budget or the librarians' per diems—preparing himself to fight for each euro.

But to Milo's surprise, Beatriz Almeida said, "You'll have your money."

Though he should have felt relief, he didn't, because her expression only hardened. Milo said, "Thank you," and waited as she looked off to the side, at Hilmar Jonsson of Iceland sitting with Sanjida Thakur of Bangladesh, then back.

"There is, however, a caveat. We need to change the distribution method."

Milo blinked. "Go on."

"We need complete access."

Beside Milo, Alan leaned back in his chair and sighed loudly.

"What does that mean?" Milo asked.

"It means you give us the files," Hilmar Jonsson cut in, his face pink.

"The database," said Pak Eun-ju of South Korea. "Give us our own access. We no longer wish to receive piecemeal information from you."

"*Christ,*" Alan muttered.

Milo opened his hands. "Let me be sure I understand this. You want unredacted access to the entirety of the Library's files."

"Yes," Almeida said.

"I'm afraid I can't do that."

"Of course you fucking can," said Jonsson.

Alfred Njenga raised a finger for patience. "Milo," he said. "Every penny you spend comes from us. There are no other countries in the world that would be stupid enough to make a deal like the one we've made. Yevgeny—he convinced us. Some of us here, some of our predecessors. But after sixteen years we believe it's time to renegotiate the terms of our support." He exhaled through his nose. "It's an entirely reasonable request."

Milo scanned each of their faces, seeing in their expressions that they were of one mind. While he'd expected something like this, he had underestimated their unity. So he took a breath, thought, and said, "Do you know why my father set up the Library this way?"

"Because he wanted control," Almeida said, a smile on her face.

"Sure," Milo said. "He always liked control. But that wasn't the reason. He didn't trust any of you."

Silence. Jonsson frowned deeply, and even Almeida's smile faded away. The rest settled back into their diplomatic cocoons, watching.

"Yevgeny knew that if you had complete access to the files, the Library would die within a year, possibly its employees, too. The Library, he understood, could only exist if it was secret. It can't exist if anyone outside of this small circle knows it exists. It *can't* exist in the outside world."

"You think we don't know this?" Jonsson demanded.

"If you knew it," Milo countered, "then you wouldn't ask for this. If you *knew* it, you would understand that as soon as you had open access to the Library, and put that intelligence to use, people outside this small circle would grow curious. How did you learn this, or that? America would start peeking into your files, start triangulating intelligence, and realize that you're getting your information from a third party. Then the big nations add two and two and realize that all of you are using the same organization. Where on earth would all of you have come to the same trough to drink? Well, maybe on the thirty-eighth floor of the United Nations Headquarters—maybe there? And then . . ." Milo shook his head. "And then America and Russia and France and the UK—they figure it out. And they shut down the Library before you can say 'It's your world.'"

Milo leaned back and crossed his arms over his chest. Ending with the UN motto was a rhetorical flourish, but he didn't care. The important thing was that their faces, that wall of unyielding expressions, had cracked. Said Bensoussan, maybe the smartest of the bunch, had taken on a reflective pose. Jonsson had had the wind knocked out of his anger, but he was still bubbling inside. Almeida pursed her lips, staring at the surface of the conference table. Pak Eun-ju, though, wasn't ready to be dissuaded.

"We appreciate your concern, Mr. Weaver. Frankly, though, we'd hoped that you would have shared less of your father's paranoia. After a lifetime in the KGB, he could be excused for it. But you grew up in a different time." She sniffed. "The fact is that this isn't a negotiation. We are your investors, and we expect more from our investment. I understand that this might be a shock to you, though I don't know why it would be. And you don't have to answer yet. Take a few days to think it through. See it from our perspective."

"I've done my thinking," Milo told her. "The answer is no."

"Jesus, Milo." That was Gaston Majerus of Luxembourg, speaking for the first time. "You have no oversight. No transparency. You give us chicken feed for the millions we invest, and you don't even share the information evenly. You can't just say no."

Milo focused his next words on Majerus, speaking slowly so that he would understand. "In 2008, a foreign power discovered not only the existence of my CIA department, but also the identities of its field officers. They killed almost every one of our field agents." He snapped his fingers. "Like that. If anyone got access to the Library database, we would be open to precisely the same kind of violence. I'm not putting my people in danger. The answer is no. Tomorrow it will be the same."

"Fine," Majerus said, still calm. "Then I'm afraid we have to reject your budget in its entirety."

"What?" Alan said, leaning forward, hands on the table. "You don't fucking know—"

He stopped because Milo had held up a hand. This was Alan Drummond now, quick to anger, the polar opposite of the administrator he'd once been.

Milo said, "I suggest you rethink your position."

Gaston Majerus's eyes narrowed, noticing the easy confidence Milo was trying to display.

"You're right about my father—he *was* paranoid. In the deepest recesses of the Library he set up a small section devoted to patrons. It's automatically updated every month. It was his protection against a coup. Since 2002, we've never needed to use the information."

Milo stopped. He could have gone on, because he had looked at those files, which chronicled misdeeds and crimes by not only the patrons themselves but the presidents and prime ministers of the countries they represented. But he didn't need to go into all that, because each of these people knew their own weaknesses better than he did. Beside him, Alan had calmed again, an impolite grin spreading across his face. He was enjoying this.

"Wait," said Jonsson. "You're *blackmailing* us?"

Milo looked back at him, feigning surprise. "Didn't you just blackmail me? I'm not sure what you expected." He turned to look at Majerus. "Don't tell me this is a surprise. Don't tell me anyone here is surprised."

But they all were . . . except, perhaps, Said Bensoussan, who was fighting back a smile of amusement.

"You don't have to answer yet," Milo said, rising from his chair. Alan followed suit. "Take a few days. Think it through. See it from our perspective."

12

"Got more in the godown, you want to wait," the vendor told Leticia as she turned the used phone over and popped the lid off to examine inside.

"No," she said. "This will work. Charger?"

He handed over a plug and cable. "You want SIM?"

"What do you have?"

"I got jetso for you."

"You got what?"

"Discount."

"Just tell me what you have, okay?"

The Temple Street Night Market was full of the noise of Hong Kong hagglers and the heavy aroma of fish frying. Her eyes ached from the intensity of the fluorescent stall lights. Above her head red globe lamps shone down on crowds hunting for cheap electronics.

This was the third vendor she'd talked to, having walked away from the first two, and her head was starting to hurt from all the haggling. But she knew the routine, even if her Cantonese wasn't good enough to catch all the nuances. She was hungry, too. The little rat-infested dump she'd found in Wan Chai had no kitchen, but that was the trade-off for fifty dollars a night and no record of your visit.

The vendor ducked behind his table and came up with an international SIM in plastic packaging. "Coverage?" she asked.

"Excellent."

"I bet," she said, and turned the package over to read the networks it used. "Tell me about your jetso."

She assembled the phone while waiting in line to order a plate of *shumai*, wondering where she would go next. Hong Kong was just a pit stop to get her bearings before she found a better place to hole up; she wouldn't stay long enough to have to bother with the stress of black-market gun shopping. Tomorrow, then, she would move on to Phnom Penh, or she could stay in Kowloon with an old lover, if he hadn't broken down and gotten himself married.

Her second concern—no less important than the first, but slightly less imperative—was who the hell her shadows were working for. She had ideas, more ideas than she could wish for, but if she didn't narrow it down, she would never figure out how to neutralize the threat.

The only things she really knew about them were their legends, Mr. and Mrs. Gary Young of London. While it turned out they weren't working for Milo Weaver, they worked for someone, and that someone had been tasked with keeping an eye on her.

Had that been their aim? Just keep tabs on Leticia Jones? Or had they been waiting for a chance to do something to her? Age and wear might have dulled her wits, but at least she'd been smart enough to not hang around and find out.

A pretty girl in a chef's hat passed her a steaming paper plate and throwaway chopsticks, and she slowly ate the pork dumplings as she walked back through the market, eyeing stalls for other items that might make her travels a little easier.

This had become her life in the last year, wandering cities at night, picking up things she'd left behind. *A disposable life* was how she described her existence when the dark mood came over her, usually after midnight in some dead-end motel where her grasp of the language was tenuous. For a while, she'd fought the darkness by drinking herself to sleep, and it usually helped, at least until the dawn showed up. It had gotten bad in Tromsø, Norway, in January, when she'd been following up a lead, and the polar night meant that the dawn never came. That was when she'd been visited by the woman who called herself Joan, who'd sat across from her at the Bastard Bar and told her she was wasting her life. Leticia had drunk a lot by then, and at certain points she wondered if Joan was a mirage, an echo of her old job wrapped in the cloak of Joan of Arc, her childhood hero. That blend of faith and stupid brav-ery had been the only thing young Leticia Jones had been able to look up to.

Might Mr. and Mrs. Gary Young have been sent by Joan to keep tabs on the ex-Tourist who didn't want to come home? Maybe, though it seemed like a lot of expense just to know where Leticia was. More likely, they were from some country that she'd pissed off over the years.

And *how* had they found her? The same way Milo had, through the Cabinet Intelligence and Research Office, where people weren't known for their ability to keep secrets? Or had she exposed herself while working her personal project, the job no one was going to pay her for? Had they caught her tracking payments to Boko Haram via the global banking world? Were *bankers* on her tail?

No, it was something old. That was the problem with living so long. All you ever did was add to the army of enemies who were pissed off at you. Jesus, she was past forty, having collected fifteen years' worth of enemies—it could be anybody.

She passed through the market gate, and the crowd, now relegated to the narrow sidewalk, grew claustrophobic along Jordan Road. She'd done it again, been distracted by too many thoughts, and had headed the wrong direction. She ate her last dumpling and turned abruptly around to work her way back against the press of locals and tourists and . . .

Oh, shit.

There, maybe thirty feet ahead of her, was Mr. Gary Young himself. Dark skin, blunt North African features. Their eyes met, and though he turned to look away in a fluid motion, betraying no surprise at all, they both knew the ruse was over now.

Over the space of the next second, Leticia debated which way to go. Turn back around and run? Where to? If they'd found her here, they cer-tainly knew about the Maai Fei Fat Inn. Mrs. Gary Young might already be there, discovering that Leticia hadn't left anything in her room, because she'd learned her lesson in Wakkanai. Move forward, and see if Gary ran away? Maybe, but what if he didn't? Was Leticia ready to deal with whatever he was packing?

As the second ended, she turned back and pushed ahead toward Shang-hai Street, where she would head left, across the street, and work her way to-ward China Ferry Terminal to find out what bus or boat could take her where.

It was a plan, and not a terrible one—a doable one—but it quickly fell apart when she saw Mrs. Gary Young not ten feet ahead of her, wearing a baggy jacket, the kind women wear to hide curves or small armaments.

Leticia spun left and threw herself into the six-lane road, a wail of horns and bumpers bearing down on her as she sprinted toward the other side. A truck nicked her left heel, but she let the force of it spin her 360 degrees and just kept going, hopping over the potted plants in the median and galloping through gridlock on the other side.

A quick glance back told her that the surprise of her escape hadn't done much to help her. The missus was jumping down from the median, while her old man was halfway across the far lane.

No worries. She pounded down the sidewalk, around the corner 7-Eleven, and went at full speed, swerving into the road to avoid the slow-moving crowds. Bookstores and clothing outlets and aromatic restaurants and parked scooters flashed by, and when she eventually turned right on Austin Road her lungs were on fire. At the next corner she snuck another glance and saw that both of them were still there, maybe five stores back. And they didn't look like they were hurting. She was only halfway to the terminal. She wasn't going to beat them to it.

So she ran past three narrow storefronts and leapt into the alleyway next to the brick façade of Park Tower. She threw her back against the filthy wall and swallowed air. When they emerged onto Austin, in her direction, they would be faced with two possible routes—one down Austin, passing her alley, the other across the street and up Scout Path. They would have to either make a decision or split up. This was her Hail Mary pass.

She still held the crumpled paper plate and chopsticks; she dropped the plate and gripped the sticks in her fist, watching the alley's opening, waiting.

How much time passed? She didn't know. Just as she had fit an entire argument into one second of panic outside the Temple Street Market, the adrenaline that sustained her warped time, and it seemed as if she stared at the alley's opening forever, the sticks gripped in her sweating, trembling fist, watching locals saunter by, the tangle of their Cantonese like unsettling music to her ears.

Then Mrs. Gary Young, one hand beneath her oversized jacket, stepped into the opening and looked to the right, directly into her face. Leticia's fist was already swinging sharply toward the woman's throat, and it was a testament to her training that the woman parried Leticia with her wrist at the same moment she removed a small automatic from her jacket. As it rose—time, again, was so damned slow—Leticia kicked high at the gun arm, hitting the woman's elbow hard; the elbow cracked, but the woman's face didn't betray any pain. The missus couldn't, however, seem to point her gun anymore, and she looked surprised by this fact. She tried to grab the gun with her other hand, but Leticia was already back: One hand caught the woman's free hand while the other swung the chopsticks at her neck.

Then three things happened at once: Leticia's chopsticks struck the underside of the woman's chin, knocking her head back and piercing deep into the soft flesh; Leticia pulled Mrs. Young's wrist up and back, knocking her against the wall; and the woman's gun hand twitched, pulling the trigger and firing once, wildly, into the alley. At the sound of the shot, people jumped and ran. The woman, now run through, perhaps to her brain, slid down the wall. Blood was everywhere, pumping out of her neck. Someone screamed. Leticia removed the pistol from the limp hand and patted at the jacket until she found something hard. Inside pocket: a phone and a clip of cash and credit card. She pocketed it all and peered out to Austin Road. Gary himself was running toward her at full speed, pistol in his fist, veering around cars, eyes full of malice.

Without thinking any further than the next moment, Leticia rose and pointed the pistol at him. Instantly, he threw himself to the side, behind a slow-moving car, and Leticia turned and ran up the alley. The sight of her pistol terrified shoppers, who crouched against the wall and put their arms over their heads, waiting for her to pass. When she heard the gunshot, it sounded like it was very far away. But the bright, burning pain in her left arm was right there, right on her. She nearly dropped the gun, but quickly caught it with her other hand and took the next corner.

Keep moving, baby, she told herself.

13

After the long flight from New York to Berlin, he was struck by the anticlimax of standing at the curb of Tegel Airport, chilly under the muted afternoon sun. When the black BMW finally pulled up in front of him, he'd spent twenty minutes watching taxis and families pick up other arrivals, trying not to fall asleep. He put his hands on his knees in order to look through the rear window and found a small, pinched face and toothbrush mustache glowering back at him. He hadn't seen Oskar Leintz in three years, and that had been for the funeral of his boss, Erika Schwartz, director of the Bundesnachrichtendienst, or BND, Germany's federal intelligence agency. Three years, and it still didn't feel like long enough.

"Not dead yet?" Oskar asked in his thick Leipzig accent.

"I can never tell one way or the other with you," Milo answered.

The driver, a woman with a severe bob and lavender lips, smiled with her eyes.

"Inside, Milo."

Milo reached for the door handle to get in and join him, but it was locked.

"The front!" Oskar called, and Milo found the passenger door open. He got in, sinking into the musty warmth, and the woman began to drive very slowly. "You could thank us," Oskar said after a few uncomfortable seconds. "A civilian like you, a UN bureaucrat? I don't have to meet you at all."

Milo might have shown some appreciation, but he and Oskar had never liked each other. Oskar considered Milo an entitled American, while Milo couldn't quite forgive him—or Erika Schwartz—for their first meeting, a decade ago, when they had tortured him. He knew it was pettiness, but still.

"How is the family, Milo?"

"In good health."

"Still in Zürich, on Hadlaubstrasse?"

Oskar still knew how to irritate him; anyone who pinpointed his family's whereabouts could pull it off. "Yes," Milo said, then twisted himself to look into the pinched face. "And your health? Not drinking yourself to an early grave, like Erika?"

Oskar was devoted to Schwartz, even now that she was living in the Black Forest, having faked her death. But Milo hadn't poked at him for fun; he'd done it to see if the driver knew Schwartz was still alive. Apparently not, for Oskar's mouth twitched uncomfortably, and he directed his next words to the driver: "You remember Milo, Lana? I told you about him. This man was once part of the infamous Department of Tourism. A man to be feared. A man to be reckoned with. But now? A minor UNESCO official. I wonder what he wants from us."

Lana took a left turn, looping back toward the airport, but seemed pretty entertained. She said, "Maybe Mr. Weaver is back to his old tricks."

"Terrifying," Oskar judged. "Lana, I think the fear has made me weak."

"You're a comedy duo," Milo said, but the funny thing was that while Oskar knew about the Library, and that Katarina Heinold was a patron, he was still making a show of ignorance. Which twisted the situation on its head. Lana thought she and Oskar were teasing Milo, when in fact Oskar was making Milo complicit in fooling his assistant. Not funny, no, but it had the feel of something like a joke, one that was in bad taste.

Finally, Oskar's smile vanished, the fun over. "Milo," he said, "please do tell us what's going on. Your time is running out."

Perhaps, if this had been someone other than Oskar Leintz, he would have told them that the Department of Tourism had been resurrected. That kind of information wasn't really his to share, but it was an alarming development that should be known. But it *was* Oskar Leintz, so he just said, "You heard about Kirill Egorov?"

"You went to Algiers to meet with him."

"You have ears everywhere."

Oskar nodded slowly. "I do, Milo. I do."

Milo told him of Egorov's request, and what few details the old man had shared during their one conversation: His ward was connected to the death of Anna Usurov and had fled Moscow last month for Germany but must have continued to Paris, "because that's where Egorov found him."

Oskar leaned back, pursing his lips, looking very interested. Then he caught Lana's eye in the rearview mirror. Something unspoken passed between them. To Milo, he said, "There was an uptick of activity in Budapest."

"Budapest?"

"The GRU's unofficial European headquarters. Viktor Orbán will let the Russians do as they like in his town. Just before Egorov was reported dead we picked up a lot of coded communication between Algiers and their listening posts in Buda, another burst when you were taken into custody by the Algerians. We could not decrypt the messages."

"But you can guess."

"We don't like to guess. You know that."

Lana drove past the spot where they'd picked up Milo and kept going. She said, "Maybe *you* have a guess."

Both looked at him expectantly.

"My guess is that it has to do with Egorov and his mystery guest. Which is why I'm sharing this with you—I suspect you know who the mystery guest is. He or she came through your territory."

Lana looked at Oskar in the rearview again. It was clear they both knew who Egorov had been protecting, but with his hard frown Oskar removed any possibility that they would share this information with Milo.

"If we do find out," he said finally, "we will be sure to get in touch with you."

Despite the ache in his twisted neck, Milo pressed on. "I assume you knew Egorov when he was consul in Berlin?"

"Erika knew him well. Long time, from the old days. They watched each other from across the Iron Curtain. Like she did with your father."

"I'm told Egorov was on his way out with the Kremlin. Do you know why?"

Oskar cocked his head. "Egorov grew up in Ukraine, near Crimea, and some of his family was killed in the fighting four years ago. In an interview with *Stern* magazine he called Russian involvement another step toward the end of Russian greatness."

"That would do it."

In his pocket, one of Milo's three phones vibrated. He checked it, saw Tina's name, and disconnected it.

"Don't let us stop you," Lana said.

"I'll be home in a few hours anyway."

"So soon, Milo?" Oskar asked, sounding hurt. "What is the hurry? UNESCO business?"

Milo finally turned to look forward again, giving his neck a rest. "A parent-teacher conference."

"Ah, children," said Oskar. "Lana, did you not tell me they are delightful?"

"Never," Lana said.

14

Frau Pappan, whose bony, frown-prone face never quite fit her Stevie Nicks–inspired wardrobe, shook everyone's hands when they came in. The children weren't to be part of the conversation—they were waiting in the anteroom—and Milo and Tina were introduced to Mustafa and Tazeen Abi, whose accents Milo found soothing until Mustafa began to shout at them.

"Halifa came home in *tears*! This is not why we left Lebanon, to have our child bullied by an American princess!"

"Who's bullying who?" Tina demanded. "Maybe Halifa has a problem with Americans—a problem she learned from her parents?"

"Now, please," Frau Pappan cut in, trying her best to sound gentle. "We're here to solve problems, not create new ones."

Unlike her husband's, Tazeen Abi's eyes remained on Milo and Tina throughout the meeting. She said little, but her gaze felt like a lengthy, accusing lecture. Milo tried to appear nonchalant, because nonchalance seemed like the right play here, and when his phone began vibrating in his pocket he crossed his legs and tried to ignore it. Trying—that's what he spent the conference doing, though never quite successfully.

He also hadn't caught up on his sleep yet. When he'd returned her call in Berlin, Tina had informed him that she'd moved the meeting to seven o'clock, so he'd taken a taxi home and sat with Alexandra in the living room to get a rundown of intelligence that had trickled in during his absence, and then listened to her complaints about Kristin and Noah. "I don't know how you work with them."

"They get the job done."

They discussed the patrons' discontent, Leticia's refusal to join the Library (which Alexandra, like Alan, considered good news), and Oskar Leintz's reticence. "He knows who Egorov was hiding, I'm sure of it. But he's not going to tell me."

"Then we let it go," Alexandra said.

She was right. There were too many other things to keep track of to halt Library business for one little mystery. "I'd just really like to know what the Russians are up to."

Over dinner, Tina explained what their strategy would be at the conference: Milo would have to take the lead, because she was sure that if she did she would let her anger take over. Sullenly, Stephanie picked at her chicken and sent Nexus messages to school friends, likely complaining about her parents. "What do you think?" Milo finally asked her, and she shrugged.

"Whatever."

"No—I mean really. What *do* you think?"

Stephanie sighed. "You guys are doing this to make yourselves feel good. Fine. Do what you like."

And then he was here, faced with a couple who had probably also worked out a strategy that, like theirs, had immediately fallen apart.

"Your daughter," Mustafa said, "called Halifa an anti-Semite. Perhaps you do not realize how cutting those words are."

"It was a judgment call," Tina replied.

"I believe," Milo said, "your daughter called ours a cunt. That, in America, is pretty cutting as well."

Tazeen finally spoke up. "She certainly did not say that."

"What we have," Frau Pappan said, "is a she-said-she-said conflict. Neither can be proven beyond doubt. In essence, they nullify each other."

Tina turned on her suddenly. "This isn't *math*. We're discussing two young women, not formulas."

"Yes," Mustafa said, his temper rising again. "What are you talking about?"

And that was how it happened. In her effort to mollify two pairs of outraged parents, Frau Pappan had succeeded in becoming the focus of everyone's rage. That, in its own way, solved the problem, uniting the parents against her, and when Mustafa shook his head and stood, saying, "This is no help," Tina stood as well.

"You're right," she said.

With an apologetic look at Frau Pappan, Milo stood, followed by Tazeen. By then, Mustafa had opened the door, allowing them all a view directly into the anteroom. All four parents froze. On the bench, Halifa and Stephanie sat close to each other, their phones out, sending Nexus emojis, laughing together.

"You were useless," Tina said as she drove them home through the darkness.

"Well, it worked out anyway," he said, then yawned into the back of his hand. He glanced into the rearview, where he could see Stephanie focused on her phone, typing. "What do you think, Little Miss?"

She shrugged.

"Who are you on with?"

"Halifa."

Milo and Tina looked at each other but said nothing. Then Milo's phone hummed again in his pocket. He took it out and saw a Berlin number—the same number that had called during the conference. "Hello."

"Weaver," said a familiar male voice, thick with *ostdeutscher* contempt.

Milo sighed. "Lovely to hear from you, Oskar."

"Are you back home safely?"

"Yes, thank you."

"But not at home."

"How do you know?"

"Are you heading home?"

"What's this about, Oskar?"

At that point, Tina turned onto their leafy street, and he saw exactly what it was about. Parked across the street from their apartment building, just outside the ring of streetlamp illumination, was a black BMW with Berlin plates. Oskar Leintz leaned against it, phone to his ear, saying, "Let's have a talk."

15

Milo didn't want Oskar anywhere near his family, but there was nothing to do about it now. When they parked, Oskar raised his hand to them, and Tina immediately crossed the street to meet him. "Mrs. Weaver," he said, offering a hand, "I am so happy to finally meet you. Oskar Leintz."

"You've known Milo a long time?"

"We are old friends."

"He's not a friend," Milo cut in, hurrying to join them. "Professional acquaintance. Sort of."

With a sudden expression of mawkish sadness, Oskar said, "Milo, that hurts."

Stephanie showed no interest in any of this, only focused on her Nexus chat with Halifa.

"We'll go to a café," Milo said.

Tina shook her head. "Do you like *Totenbeinli,* Mr. Leintz?"

"Who does not?" he answered with a smile. "And please: Oskar."

"Then come in, Oskar," she said, and led him to their building. After a moment to collect himself, Milo followed.

Totenbeinli, or "legs of the dead," were hard almond cookies that went well with coffee, and Oskar praised the batch that Tina had baked the week before. "You should open a restaurant," he said.

"I like your acquaintance," Tina told Milo.

As Oskar ate, Milo climbed upstairs to find Alexandra in the guest bedroom and told her of their visitor. Together, they came down to the kitchen and hovered, waiting for Oskar to finish flirting with Tina. Eventually, the three of them ended up in the living room. Stephanie was already up in her room, and Tina stayed behind in the kitchen as Oskar settled on the sofa, cradling his second cup of coffee.

"You live well here, Milo."

"I do."

"Better than you deserve."

Milo sat in a chair across from him as Alexandra kept sentry at the wall. "Why are you here?"

Oskar sniffed and set down his cup. "Erika always had a soft spot for you. I do not know why."

"She still does," Milo said.

Oskar's expression stiffened, and his eyes shot over to Alexandra.

"She knows," Milo said.

Oskar shook his head, disgusted. "We had a deal, Weaver."

Indeed, they had made a deal. The year 2015 had been a busy one in the West, with Brexit and the American presidential election looming, the continuing Ukrainian crisis, and Syrian refugees pouring into Europe and changing the political landscape. The Library had found itself at the intersection of all those power struggles. The BND had, too, and in a series of moves that soon passed beyond anyone's control, Erika's office had been responsible for the murder of three Russian agents. The Kremlin demanded her extradition, threatening to cut off Germany's natural gas, and as under-siege politicians inched toward giving her up, Milo had helped to stage Schwartz's quiet death in her suburban house in Pullach. The "deal" Oskar referred to had been a pact of silence that protected Schwartz's continued existence and quiet retirement in the Black Forest, as well as maintaining the secret of the Library, which in 2015 was nearly revealed to the general public.

"Only three of us know," Milo told him. "I couldn't keep it from Alexandra or Alan."

"*Typisch,*" Oskar muttered, then raised his head. "Anyway, Erika asked me to tell you about Joseph Keller."

"Who?"

"The man Kirill Egorov was protecting in Algiers."

Interested, Alexandra moved to a chair and sat down.

"He is a bookkeeper," Oskar said. "British. Worked for Sergei Stepanov."

"The head of MirGaz?" Alexandra asked.

Oskar nodded. "Two years ago, MirGaz absorbed its two largest competitors to become the world's largest natural gas producer. Joseph Keller moved from London to Moscow, and he helped make Stepanov richer than he already was. Certainly richer than he needed to be. Arguably richer than he deserved to be."

"But it didn't work out," Milo said.

"Oh, it did. He was there for a year, with a wife and two little boys, in a gated community outside Moscow. Living well, by all accounts. Until a month ago, when he boarded a plane and flew to Düsseldorf. It is a three-and-a-half-hour flight, and two and a half hours into the flight the Russians requested an Interpol Red Notice on him. Capture and send back home. We noticed it and called the Russian embassy. Asked what was going on. No one knew, and they said they would call us back. A half hour later, the Russians changed it to a Blue Notice. Just locate and get information on him."

"Weird," said Alexandra.

"We thought so, too. We suspect someone panicked and sent the Red Notice, then realized it was drawing too much attention and changed it. The story was that Keller had embezzled government accounts. But why were they afraid of the attention?" He opened his hands in an expression of ignorance. "So we used some Interpol contacts to slow approval of the notice, just by another half hour, so Joseph could make it through passport control. Then we put a team on him. We watched him max out his card to buy as many euros as he was allowed—about six thousand. Then he took a taxi to the train station and boarded the very next train, as if he didn't care where it was going."

"Where was it going?" asked Milo.

"South, to Cologne. From there he changed trains to reach Brussels, then Paris. We put one of our irregulars on it. He shared a hostel room with him, then took him out to a club. That is where it went wrong. Quite unexpectedly, two men threw him into a van and drove off. It was the last anyone saw of him."

"What do the French say?"

Oskar scratched at his cheek, uncomfortable. "Well, we did not inform them of our presence."

"Really?" That was Alexandra, surprised.

Oskar glared at her. "In the heat of the moment, we sometimes do lose track of protocol."

Alexandra nodded, understanding, and Milo closed his eyes, trying to picture the sequence of events. "Luggage?" he asked.

Oskar cleared his throat, now looking even more uncomfortable. "Apparently, yes. Not luggage, but a plastic bag with documents."

"What documents?"

"Pages. Our agent didn't know what they were."

Again, Alexandra let her surprise show. "You're saying he didn't *look*?"

Oskar shook his head sadly. "As I said, he was an irregular."

Though it was disappointing, Milo wasn't surprised. As much intelligence is gained as lost by stupidity. "So how does this connect to Kirill Egorov?" he asked.

"At that time, Egorov was in Paris for a conference on African security. Though no one saw Keller again, one of the two kidnappers was later spotted with Egorov. They were his people."

"Did anyone follow up with Egorov?"

"We had someone approach him in Algiers, but he claimed ignorance."

Alexandra settled deeper into her chair, frowning.

"What did the Russians do after that?" asked Milo. "Is the Blue Notice still active?"

Oskar smiled. "No—but it was followed, within hours, by Red Notices from the UK, USA, China, and Israel."

"Why?"

"Different reasons. America connected the accountant to the Massive Brigade. Britain to computer hacking. China to money laundering. Israel to something else." He waved a hand. "I forget."

"All that for Joseph Keller?"

"Unlikely, isn't it?" Oskar said. "But even more unlikely is this: Within two or three days, all the Interpol notices were canceled. Until you told me about Egorov's request, I had assumed the Russians had just killed Keller in Paris. That, I think, is what everyone believed. But if Egorov was being straight with you, everybody was wrong."

Milo nodded, seeing it now. "Egorov cheated his bosses. He let Keller live."

"That is our working assumption," Oskar agreed.

Even Alexandra seemed convinced.

"What about Anna Usurov?" Milo asked. "Egorov said she was connected."

Oskar shrugged. "Maybe. Once you told me that, we looked into the records. Usurov's body was found the morning of August 16. That is the same morning Joseph Keller boarded his plane to Germany. Further investigation revealed that the night before, both Keller and Usurov attended a gala party for MirGaz at the Moscow Ritz." He smiled and opened his hands. "That is everything I have to share."

"Thank you," Milo said. It was perhaps the first time in history he'd thanked Oskar Leintz without irony. "Erika isn't your boss anymore—you could easily have ignored her request."

Oskar shrugged.

"Why didn't you?"

Oskar rocked his head, musing on that. Then he said, "Because you are stupid, Milo. You go around asking too many questions. You are no longer protected by the American government, and your Library is no protection at all. Yet you keep asking. Eventually, you are going to be killed just for being a nuisance. And at least for now, neither Erika nor I want you to die. Maybe you will be useful one day. Stranger things have happened." He smiled at his own joke, then got serious, leaning forward. "So take this answer, but then forget it. Rest assured that the adults will take care of it."

16

Alexandra walked Oskar out, and Milo called Kristin to ask for Gazala Mokrani's phone number in Algiers. When he hung up, he found Alexandra in the doorway, arms crossed. "You're not leaving me here again, are you? I do have a life elsewhere."

"It'll be fast. Either I get answers or I don't."

"Why not let the Germans look into this? If Oskar wants it, let him have it."

Milo ran a hand through his hair. "They approached Egorov, and he rebuffed them. He didn't trust his own people, and he didn't trust the Germans. Maybe he had good reason to come to me."

"Okay," she said, resigned.

"And while I'm gone, can you get someone to follow up in Moscow? Background on Anna Usurov and Keller's office at MirGaz."

"Leonberger's there," Alexandra said, worry in her voice.

Milo sighed—he'd been planning to retire Leonberger as soon as they found a Moscow replacement. A holdover from his father's days, the old man was no longer as dependable as he would have liked, and his drinking habits were growing worse. "He shouldn't have to do much. Just ask some questions."

"Remember last year?" Alexandra asked. "When I got him out of jail, the police told me he was suicidal."

"How did he seem to you?"

"He seemed reckless."

"Anyone else in Moscow?"

"No."

Milo opened his hands. "Well, then. Leonberger in Moscow. Me to Algiers."

"I believe there are some Russians in Algiers who want to get their hands on you."

"I'll be careful."

Alexandra wasn't convinced. "Don't get yourself killed, okay? I don't want to be left running this operation."

"Who's getting killed?" they heard, and turned to see Tina in the doorway, frowning.

Milo came over and kissed her. "No one. I have to take another trip in the morning. Be back before you know it."

She looked him in the eyes. "What's going on?" Then, to Alexandra: "One of you needs to tell me."

Alexandra left Milo to deal with it alone, and he told Tina the whole story, which, seeing as he knew so little, wasn't much at all. What he left out—the attempted kidnapping by the Russians and the successful kidnapping by the Algerians—would only have worried her.

"Fine," she said, shaking her head. "If you're not going to tell me everything, then don't say a thing." Then she turned on her heel and left.

He called Gazala Mokrani. The first time, she didn't answer, so he waited a half hour, pouring himself a vodka, and tried again. When she answered, he spoke in French. "Ms. Mokrani, I am Milo Weaver. I was a friend of the late Kirill Egorov."

She said nothing.

"I will be in Algiers tomorrow. May I buy you a coffee?"

"Why do you want to speak with me?" she asked, her French waxy with Algerian intonation.

"Because I'm sad he is dead, and because he spoke highly of you."

"I don't know anything," she said.

"I'm not asking anything, just to speak with you about him. How he was."

When she paused again, he wondered if he should have tried a different tactic. He could have told her that Egorov had left her money and that he was supposed to deliver it. But Bensoussan had described her as "worldly, a sophisticated woman," and he worried that an implicit bribe would make her suspicious. So he'd chosen sentimentality.

"Do you know Algiers?" she finally asked.

"A little."

"We can meet at his favorite café, El Kahwa El Zarka. It's in Dar El Beïda."

"I'll find it," Milo said. "Thank you."

Before heading upstairs, Milo searched "Joseph Keller" on the Interpol site. As Oskar had told them, there were multiple listings that showed his name and date of birth, but no photo or list of crimes. He turned to Google to find a picture, but that, too, was limited. There was a shot of his stern face on his MirGaz employee page and the same shot on his profile Nexus page. Otherwise, there was nothing. No Facebook, no Twitter, no LinkedIn. While a couple of industry articles mentioned his move to MirGaz, none were accompanied by photos. All he had was a single shot of a plain-looking accountant smiling mildly at the camera.

He found Tina in bed, reading glasses low on her nose, scrolling through news on Facebook. She ignored him as he undressed, and he finally said, "I'm not hiding anything. I'm just trying to find out what an old friend of my father's wanted help with before he died."

"Not your friend. Yevgeny's."

"Yes."

She looked up from the screen. "And what makes you think he was trust-worthy? You're handing your safety over to a stranger."

Stripped down to his underwear, Milo sat on the bed and settled a hand on her uncovered ankle. "Because at some point you have no choice but to trust. Otherwise, you're frozen in place. Every step is a risk."

"Then send someone else."

"The man asked for me."

"And he's dead."

Milo squeezed her ankle. "No one's going to kill me."

"How do you know?"

"Because even killers are rational, and I'm too ignorant to be a threat. Certainly too ignorant to be worth the effort of killing."

She set aside her computer, took off her glasses, and looked at him a long time. Finally, she said, "Come here, dummy."

17

Leonberger took off his weathered dockworker's cap and sat across from the young accountant with the smooth cheeks. ALEXEI BERIDZE, the nameplate said. Georgian stock. He'd been surprised when he finally reached this Mir-Gaz satellite office, a glass edifice on the Frunzenskaya embankment; it was huge, particularly given that its sole function was financial—payroll and investments for the enormous energy company.

"So," young Alexei said in his barely disguised Tbilisi accent, "you were interested in one of our employees."

"That's right," Leonberger said. He wove his blunt fingers together over his growing stomach. He was a big man, and when he was younger his size was its own kind of weapon, frightening people into submission. "Name's Joseph Keller."

The young man blinked at him, stiffening. "I'm afraid he no longer works for us."

"Really?" Leonberger pursed his lips, as if this were a surprise. "I saw him just last month."

"It was last month when he left."

"Did he go back to England?"

A shrug. "I don't know." When Leonberger let the silence go on, Alexei said, "Why are you looking for him?"

"Ah!" Leonberger leaned his mass closer to the edge of the desk. "Joseph rents a little place from me in Kitay-gorod, and he hasn't paid the last three months."

"Are you sure?" the young man asked. "He lived in Pokrovsky Hills with his family."

Leonberger grinned mischievously and wagged a finger at him. "I didn't know about the family, but I guess he didn't want me to know. He brings girls up there sometimes."

"Joseph?" Alexei said, flabbergasted yet interested. "Unbelievable."

"Not my type, you understand—*skinny*—but pretty enough. I don't know if he pays them."

"Joseph *Keller*?"

"All men are dogs," Leonberger said, then rapped the tabletop with his nails. "Tell me—how could I get in touch with Joseph?"

"I wish I could tell you. He walked out one day, no explanation, and we never saw him again."

"Last month, you said?"

"August sixteenth."

"Girl trouble. That's my guess," Leonberger said as he rose to go.

"If you *do* find him," Alexei said, "we would love to know."

"Would you pay off his rent?"

"Look around. I think that could be arranged."

In the enormous parking lot, he checked for shadows, then climbed into his Golf and drove south for a while before doubling back on himself and heading back into Moscow. He'd clocked the accountant's anxiety when he'd first brought up Keller's name, and had known from that point that he wouldn't get anything out of him, not even if he reached over and dragged the man across his desk and beat him to a pulp; within minutes the beefy security he'd seen floating around the place would have descended on him. Besides, Leonberger wasn't quite so formidable anymore—a fact he often forgot.

In the late eighties he'd been a welterweight champ in rough-and-tumble Kapotnya, then in greater Okrug District, until getting knocked out in the Moscow finals. Good enough to land him some respect, though, and while Yeltsin fought against the old guard, Leonberger had bruised his way through street fights against the still-devout Communist youth. After 1991, he'd found himself a field agent for the FSB, watching out for counterrevolutionaries (his phrase, not his bosses') and putting muscle where muscle was needed. He'd made it to lieutenant before, in 1996, being kicked out for assaulting a superior who had ordered him to organize an attack on a gypsy encampment outside town. At the same time, Elena divorced him and took Nadia away. A bad time. That was when old Yevgeny Primakov showed up at his apartment block and asked if he'd like to do the occasional odd job for him. It had sounded good to Leonberger. Anything to keep his mind off his life.

Those odd jobs hadn't been what he'd expected. His fists turned out to be of little use. Instead, he'd had to develop new skills like patience, observation, and deduction, as well as the occasional use of a camera on government officials Primakov told him were ripping off the Russian people. Leonberger was, he insisted, part of the vanguard of the effort to clean up the New Russia. Which was good enough for him.

Of course, he and Yevgeny had failed in this endeavor. He'd snapped photos of politicians in metaphorical bed with bankers and foreign tycoons and intelligence officers who were expanding their reach, but the fact was that he and Primakov were only witnesses. By the time Yevgeny sat him down in 2002 to explain that his job would change, Russia had become a different place. The crimes they had painstakingly documented were no longer secret. They'd become common knowledge, but it was too late. The intersection of the intelligence apparatus, the banks, the politicians, and the police meant that what was once illegal was now only illegal if you were poor.

"You'll be part of something bigger now," Yevgeny had told him. "But you'll have to learn how to live in ignorance. Because what you'll be working on will be so big that one man cannot keep it in his head. It won't be Russian; it will be global."

"What's the job?" Leonberger asked.

"Saving everything."

Which wasn't an answer Leonberger was ever able to really understand, but he trusted the old widower who had by then left the FSB and moved to Western Europe, working for the United Nations. And when orders came through to surveil some player in the larger game, to break into an office and photograph documents, to meet someone and pretend to be someone else . . . whenever he was asked to do something, he reminded himself that it was for a larger good that only Yevgeny Primakov fully understood. All he needed to understand was his orders.

This was why Yevgeny's death, a decade ago, had been such a ground-swell. The news had spread through Moscow before he heard it from the Library itself: The great Yevgeny Primakov had been found killed in an apartment in New York, in a place called Park Slope. What was he going to do? When he got the call from a soft-spoken woman whose Russian smelled of other lands, he demanded to know who was taking over his command. "For the moment," she said, "I am."

"And who are you?"

"I'm Yevgeny's daughter."

"I didn't know he had a daughter."

"He has two," she said, and when she called again a few months later, it was to tell him that management had changed again. "To his son."

"He has a *son*?"

Despite the shock and the momentary sense of dislocation, when the Library returned to regular operation, Leonberger's life remained much the same. Elena still didn't speak to him, and Nadia, now married to some bureaucrat in Sochi, hardly knew him. So he was available to make sudden trips to St. Petersburg, or the other side of town, in order to gather this or that and send it to an encrypted server located somewhere in the world, other times to a post office box in Zürich, which was the only physical address he had for the Library. And when he wanted to, he could imagine Yevgeny Primakov still at the helm, somewhere in the world, reading his messages.

There had been troubles, of course. A man left on his own really is a dog, him no less than others. Last year, he'd taken it into his head to put down a cheap bottle of Dobry Medved and rush a trio of Moscow policemen hassling some queers in Vin Zavod, breaking one arm in the process. When she arrived, he'd seen in Yevgeny Primakov's daughter's face a kind of disgust that filled him with the desire to drink six more bottles of vodka and go for a swim in the Moskva.

In fact, it sounded like a good idea to him now.

But that would have to wait until he'd given Primakov's children what they needed. Joseph Keller and Anna Usurov. At home, he used his computer to look up Usurov. *A pretty girl*, he thought, and though her blog, *RESIST,* had been shut down he found plenty of her articles reprinted on other sites, proving that she'd been a thorn in someone's side. Probably Putin's. That was when he found one of Usurov's pieces on a website called *Старайтесь!*—or

Endeavor!—run by someone who claimed to have been Usurov's friend: Sofia Marinov.

This was interesting: In her last post, dated August 18, Marinov claimed that the security services had killed Usurov. The official report, that Anna Usurov had stuck her head in her gas stove and suffocated herself, was ridiculous, she said, because no one had been as happy to live as her friend.

Not a convincing argument, but a heartfelt one.

Leonberger found Marinov's number in the public records, but when he called he got her voicemail. "Ms. Marinov," he said, "my name is Anatoli Kedrov. I'm writing an in memoriam about Anna Usurov. If you could spare me some time, that would be great. You can call me back at this number anytime."

He hung up and wandered into the kitchen, where the refrigerator revealed bottles of water and a half-empty Dobry Medved. He took one long swig from the bottle, just one, then put it back in the fridge and closed it. He thanked God every day that he wasn't an alcoholic.

18

Once Milo laid eyes on El Kahwa El Zarka, it was obvious why Colonel Rahmani had noticed the change in Egorov's schedule. Though the tiny café was pleasant enough, it was in a strange spot, the ground floor of an apartment block, the kind of place frequented only by people who lived in the same building. Glass doors led to plastic chairs on concrete tiles, a twisted tree, and, inside, little black tables around a counter. Why would the old man break his routine in the upscale center of town for this?

"No good reasons," Whippet said.

Whippet, the Paris librarian, had joined him during his layover in Charles de Gaulle's tubular concourse, where they drank macchiatos and he filled her in on the situation. She was almost self-conscious in her focus, a thin, dark-haired Frenchwoman in her forties who had once worked for the DPSD, France's military counterespionage outfit, before taking an early retirement. Retirement hadn't worked out, though, and Milo's recruiters had found her looking for work in Vietnam when they talked her into expanding the scope of her loyalty. On the plane, she gave him an update on the Chinese plastic guns she'd reported on before: Her source said that, despite never solving the weak barrel issue, the Sixth Bureau had decided to order a thousand of them for test use throughout the world, each preloaded with a single reinforced-plastic bullet. Which, Milo thought, was the kind of forward thinking that had helped Xin Zhu and his Sixth Bureau wipe out Tourism.

It had been Whippet's idea to wait outside the café. "Never know when the Russians might sniff you out."

"How will you recognize them?"

"I can tell Russian tailoring a kilometer away."

As soon as Milo stepped inside the cool, shadowy café, he felt the weight of Gazala Mokrani's cool judgment from her large dark eyes. She was in her late fifties and had a noticeable tendency to bring her cigarette within a millimeter of her lips, move it quickly away as if it had burned her, and then bring it back for a long drag. There was something hypnotic in that movement, and how it translated into scorn. She had been asked too many questions by too many men in too short a time since losing her lover.

"You're just like them," she said.

"Them?"

"The new Russian consul, and Colonel Rahmani."

"Not really," he told her. "I'm the one Kirill called. I'm the only one he trusted."

"Why?"

"He and my father were friends."

"That's a terrible reason to trust someone."

"I agree."

She brought her cigarette to her lips, jerked it away, then took a drag.

Milo said, "Kirill wanted me to protect Joseph Keller."

She exhaled smoke at him, then glanced past him to the bar. "I don't know anyone with that name."

"I think you do," Milo said.

Again she looked at the bar, so Milo turned to look for himself. The bartender, a huge bald man with hair coming out of his ears, watched them both. Maybe waiting for a signal. And Milo had come inside alone and unarmed. He was beginning to regret that decision.

"Ms. Mokrani," Milo said, "you have a choice. Either you let me take over the protection of Joseph Keller, or you keep him yourself. But for how long? You know that you're being watched, right? Colonel Rahmani is very curious, and smart, but I don't think he's your real problem. The Russians— they killed Kirill in order to get to Keller. And they will not give up."

Gazala knitted her brows, as if hit by a sudden pain. "You are sure they killed him?"

"Pretty sure."

"Why would they?"

Milo shook his head. "I won't know until I speak with Joseph Keller."

Gazala brought her cigarette to her lips, pulled it away, then took a drag.

Whippet was still in the doorway across the street when he and Gazala left the bar together. Milo caught her eye, and she nodded that the coast was clear. For once, luck was on his side.

As Whippet crossed the street to join them, Gazala looked frightened, so he introduced them, but called Whippet Mary. Together, they followed a winding path through narrow streets surrounded by high apartment buildings. "He never liked my place," she said.

"Egorov?" Milo asked.

"He said a woman like me should live on the water. He was that way. A charmer. But not a fool. He had been hurt, and had learned from pain."

"Who had hurt him?"

Gazala Mokrani raised her chin, just a little, in the way of a natural-born performer. "He told me that he had devoted his life to a political system that had failed him. It wasn't until he grew old that he realized his only responsibility was to himself, and to me."

"So you wouldn't describe him as a patriot?"

She narrowed her brow, considering the question. "Countries, he told me, mean nothing. They are just masks. Money is everything."

"Did he convince you?"

A mild shrug. "Kirill Egorov was a very convincing man."

The foyer was chilly, with iron stairs wrapping around an ancient elevator that looked like it hadn't functioned in a long time. The walls were coarse and occasionally marked up by graffiti—but it was always low, no more than four feet up, which made Milo think that little children were the culprits. At the third floor, Gazala pressed a button on the wall and the landing lit up, the bare bulb buzzing. She used another key on her heavy door, and when she pushed it open they could hear the sound of a television playing English-language news. She waved them inside, then shut and dead-bolted the door.

"I am back," she called in English as she unwound her scarf. "Not alone."

A male voice said, *"Fuck."*

Gazala looked at them and shook her head in annoyance.

Milo followed the direction of the voice and in the high-ceilinged living room found a white, barefoot man in a dirty shirt and slacks, scrambling to his feet in front of an old television bled of most of its color. He smoothed his unkempt hair, then wiped at his bristly cheeks. His eyes were bloodshot, but he was fit, his arms wiry with muscle. Not what Milo had expected from an accountant, but it was the same face from the MirGaz website and Keller's Nexus page.

"Joseph Keller," Milo said, "Kirill Egorov sent for me."

"Name?" Keller snapped, his accent more working-class than Milo would have expected.

"Milo Weaver."

Keller thought about that, tilting his head. "Prove it?"

Milo handed over his laminated UN card. "And you?"

Reading Milo's details, Keller used his other hand to reach into his back pocket and take out a worn British passport with his name and photo in it. Slipped between its pages was a business card: JOSEPH KELLER, SENIOR CONTROL-LER, MIRGAZ, with an address on the Frunzenskaya embankment in Moscow.

When Whippet entered the room and raised an eyebrow, Keller took a step back. "Who's she?"

"The only way you're getting out of here alive," she told him.

Keller's shoulders sank, and he handed back Milo's ID.

"I will make tea," Gazala said as she passed the doorway.

"What's going to happen now?" Keller asked.

"We're going to sit down and drink some tea. You'll talk. After that, we'll arrange for you to be moved someplace safer."

"Where?"

"Europe."

Keller thought about that, then nodded. He went to the television and turned it off.

"We need to hear it all," Milo said. "Okay?"

Keller held his eye for a long moment. He had the look of someone who had lost everything. A barren look. Milo had seen that look before, years ago, in the face of Martin Bishop. He'd also seen that look further back, when his days smeared into the next in a constant blur of cities and languages and hotel rooms and sudden, brutal acts in service to his nation. It was the face he'd seen in the mirror.

19

Before telling his story, Keller asked if Milo knew anything about his family in Moscow. "Are they all right?"

"I have someone checking on it. We should know soon."

Keller nodded. "You're CIA, then? FBI?"

Milo shook his head. "But I'm in a position to help."

That answer seemed to bother him. "Then, uh, what's your relationship to Egorov? You're not . . . *Russian,* are you?"

"No, I'm not," Milo assured him. "I'm not CIA, MI6, or any of them."

"Who *do* you represent?"

"Does it matter?" Milo asked. "I'm the only one here offering to keep you safe."

As Keller considered this, Milo wondered if their negotiations were going to break down here and now. Because there was no way Milo would admit, at this stage at least, the secret of his organization. Eventually, Keller wiped at his lips with his thumb and said, "I didn't know. I mean, if I had known I wouldn't have touched it. I don't *enjoy* knowing things like this."

"I don't doubt you."

Keller looked around, unsure, and Gazala entered with three cups and a steaming teapot on a tray. When she set them down, Whippet came over to fill the cups. Gazala gave Keller a look—neither kindness nor hatred—then disappeared.

Milo said, "Why don't we work through who you are first. Okay?"

Keller blinked at him. "Well, Joseph Samuel Keller."

"Married, obviously."

"Yes. To Emily Thompson, we have two sons—Jeremy, six, and Daniel, eight."

"You're an accountant, I understand."

"CPA. Successful, too. I was. That's how Sergei heard of me. Through my clients. Sergei Stepanov, CEO of MirGaz. You've heard of him?"

"I have."

Keller gratefully accepted the cup Whippet offered, but Milo only set his on the coffee table and focused on Keller. Watched him take his first tentative sip, place the cup back on the table, and say, "This was a year ago. MirGaz, you understand, is the world's largest natural gas producer. So Sergei's job offer wasn't a small thing. I moved my family from London to a gated community outside Moscow, and . . . well, we did well. I did good work for Sergei, skirting the bleeding edge of international financial law."

Milo remembered how Oskar had put it: *He helped make Stepanov richer than he already was. Certainly richer than he needed to be. Arguably richer than he deserved to be.* "Did you like the work?" Milo asked.

"Sure. People usually like the things they're good at, and this is what I'm good at."

"You made Russian friends?"

He shook his head. "We weren't social, not with them. We had our English school, a nice circle of Protestant expats—I suppose we lived in a bubble, but it was *our* bubble, and we were happy. Sergei and his political friends lived their lives while we lived ours. By last month, a year into it, we were still happy enough. And then I got the invitation. To a gala party at the Ritz-Carlton."

Milo raised his brows to show he was interested. "This was Sergei Stepanov's party?"

Keller nodded. "He put them on all the time, oligarchs and Duma members getting drunk with high-class prostitutes, but it was the first time I'd been invited."

"Why were you invited?"

Keller shrugged. "I didn't know. I just knew I wasn't up to it. So I declined the invitation, and was surprised the next day when Sergei walked into my office to insist that I come. I mean, I'd been there a year but had only been in the same room as Sergei Stepanov maybe four times. And here he was, coming out to the office just to see me. He told me my 'countrymen' would be there, that I would make them feel more comfortable, and, well, to come for *him*."

"Hard to say no to that."

Keller nodded. "He'd rented the entire ground floor. It was—it was *enormous*. Hundreds of people, the social and political stratosphere. Everyone said Putin was going to show up, but I never saw him. Drinks flowed, and sometimes camera crews squeezed through, because the press had been invited, too. To show off what Russian success looked like. I didn't know anyone, of course, and Sergei was busy entertaining others, so all there was for me was to stand around and drink. Not too much, but enough to relax a little, and that was when this Russian woman, Anna, struck up a conversation. At first, I thought she was flirting, and then I worried she was a prostitute. She was young and pretty, and the party was full of them. But she wasn't a prostitute, and her English was quite good. Anna, it turned out, was as much of an outsider as me—not sickeningly rich, and not screwing any of these rich men. She ran a cultural blog, and she'd gotten into the party with her press pass. It turned out she also knew a fair amount about finance, and I was happy to talk about what I did . . . until she started asking uncomfortable questions, questions about Sergei. What kinds of financial interests did Sergei have in London? How close was he to Putin, really? And, more specifically, was it true that Sergei had close personal contact with Diogo Moreira?"

"Diogo Moreira?" Milo cut in. "Who's that?"

"I didn't know. Not yet. But Anna did—the name really meant something to her, and more importantly she'd come to the party to follow up on a connection between Sergei and Moreira."

"She doesn't sound like a cultural blogger."

"Even I was starting to figure that out. I demanded to know what she was, really, and that's when she admitted that she ran a dissident blog that published a lot of political exiles. *RESIST*. Her full name was Anna Urusov."

"She was a well-known journalist," Milo said. "No one figured this out when she showed up at the door?"

Keller shook his head. "The thugs at the door weren't the cream of Russia's crop."

"Sure."

"Still, I was just as ignorant. I didn't know the name Anna Usurov from Anne of Green Gables. But I knew that anyone who ran a dissident blog and was asking questions about Sergei could only mean bad news. So I started to extricate myself from the conversation, and that was when Sergei appeared again, drunk. He introduced himself to Anna, who he didn't recognize, and kissed her hand. But he'd come for me, wanted to introduce me to my countrymen."

"Did you tell him about Usurov? About the questions?"

Keller took another swig of his tea, as if he might need it. He flexed his arms, the muscles and tendons taut. He said, "Look. Though I did try to close my eyes to these kinds of things, I knew where Sergei's money came from, and where it went. Mostly. I knew Sergei was not someone to fool with, and when he asked me about Anna, I didn't say a thing. I didn't want anything to happen to her, but more importantly I didn't want anything to happen to me or my family. Guilt by association, you understand?"

Milo did.

"Sergei brought me to meet a group of English businessmen. Told them I was the cleverest accountant he'd ever seen, that I could rub two stones together and make money appear. Nonsense like that. But it went over well enough. Eventually, I went to get another drink and in the lobby saw Anna again—she caught my eye as two big goons dragged her out of the hotel. Her eyes seemed to be pleading. Really. Pleading. I felt sick. I got my stuff from the coat check and left."

"No one stopped you?"

"Why would they?"

"Sure."

"And I drove home. Slowly, worried I'd have a wreck. I just felt so filthy. You know? I told Emily, and told her that I'd sworn off things like that. Never again. I was going to visit the office, home, church. That was it. Emily surprised me by disagreeing. But it shouldn't have surprised me. My success is entirely her doing. If it wasn't for her, I'd still be shuffling numbers for bloody Oxfam. But she pushed. Just like she did that night. *This is how you move up the ladder, Joe,* she said. *You endear yourself to the boss.*" He shook his head and asked Milo, "But at what cost?"

Milo felt like Keller needed an answer, but he didn't have one to give.

20

"I couldn't sleep," Keller said. "I couldn't stop thinking about Anna Usurov and her questions. Who was Diogo Moreira? What was his connection with Sergei? Looking back, it was stupid of me. If I'd been like my wife, I would've known it was in my best interests to just forget about it. But I'm nothing like Emily. I'm too curious. So I lay there, wondering, and decided to check on it in the morning."

"In the office?"

"Yes. It's a forty-minute drive, door to door, and on the way I listened to Moscow FM. That's the English-language station. News and cultural pieces, mostly, and news from London, which I like. I get to the office, hello to the guard on duty, and up a floor to my office. I ignore my emails and get right to it—Diogo Moreira. And it was quick. A simple Google search. Moreira's an officer in Portugal's intelligence agency."

"Serviço de Informações de Segurança?"

"Look, I'm not naïve—I know MirGaz has shady connections to some European governments, but Portugal? That's what I don't get. MirGaz's European interests are in the east, where natural gas pipelines run into the EU. Portugal isn't even on MirGaz's radar."

"NATO," said Milo.

"What?"

"If Moreira is Portuguese intelligence, then he has access to NATO documents."

Keller stared a moment, as if this were news. Milo doubted it was, though, for even if it hadn't occurred to Joseph it would have occurred to Egorov, who would have told him. Or maybe not.

"Anyway," Keller said, "that's not my wheelhouse. MirGaz is. So I plugged his name into the company's intranet, just to see, and was surprised to find a hit. A document—thirty-two pages—detailing Diogo Moreira and about sixty other names, along with payments to each of them."

"What kind of payments?"

"I don't know. And even as I send the spreadsheet to my printer, I'm already starting to worry that what I'm doing might not be the best idea. I don't know—maybe it's Emily's voice in my head. I take the pages and leaf through them. Payments to banks all around the world, small banks I've never even heard of. Monthly, quarterly. Tens and hundreds of thousands of euros at a time."

"How much are we talking about in total?"

"One-point-two billion euros."

"Jesus."

"Yeah. And the thing is, all this is being paid out to people I've never *heard* of, names that have never been noted in the accounts. At first, like I said, I was a little scared, but when I realize this, I think that, no, I *have* done the right thing. I'll take the document upstairs to get to the bottom of this. Maybe right to Sergei. Because if I don't it might come back to bite me in the ass later on. Right?"

"That's a reasonable assessment," Milo said, but knew he wasn't convincing. "Is that what you did?"

"I didn't get a chance. My door opened, and one of my co-workers comes in. Alexei. Little guy, twenties. No one likes him. He walks in, poking at his phone, as if he expects the room to be empty, then stops short when he sees me. He's stunned, but I don't know why he would be. *You're here?* Alexei says. *You came* in? Like he can't believe it. Then he holds up his hands and starts to back up. *Wait. Okay? Don't move. Stay right here. I have to get the others.* Then he runs off."

Keller reached for his tea and took a drink, his hand trembling. When he set the cup down again, it clanked against the saucer.

"Now I'm the one who's stunned. It's weird, right? But before I can think it through, my phone rings. It's Emily. She wants to know why Grigory,

MirGaz's head of security, an old man we dealt with when we first moved, is parked in our driveway. I ask what the old man is telling her. *Nothing,* she tells me. *He's not even getting out of his car. I'm scared.* And—well, that's enough for me, isn't it? The morning is sliding into really weird places quickly. So I tell her I'll be home as soon as I can, and I walk out of the office. Downstairs, good-bye to security, and when I'm almost at my car I realize I still have the document under my arm. All thirty-two pages. Fine, it'll be safe with me, and I'll deal with it later. And as I'm getting in the car I hear my name being called. It's Alexei, and there are five others with him. One of them a guard. They're all calling for me to come back. But I . . ." He hesitated, thinking back to that moment. "Look, I'm worried about my wife, and everything just feels too strange and uncomfortable. So I get in my car and drive off. Back on the highway, heading out to the suburbs. And that's when it happens. The radio's still on, and I find out that the police have just discovered the body of Anna Usurov in her apartment, dead from asphyxiation."

As Milo watched, Keller reached for his tea, but then changed his mind and took his hand back.

"There it is, you see? Anna asked me about Diogo Moreira, and now she's dead. Every inch of the Ritz-Carlton was covered by security cameras, which meant that all anyone had to do was look through the footage to find that Anna had been speaking to me, and for a long time. Why else would the head of security be sitting in my driveway? And right next to me, on the passenger seat, was a stack of payments with Moreira's name on it."

He exhaled loudly and shook his head. "This story—it's a story of stupidity. Me making the wrong choices, one after the other. I'm a numbers guy. Give me spreadsheets and I'm happy. Give me people and my calculations crumble. That's why I've always depended on Emily. And really, I didn't understand any of it. What I had was a terrible ache in my gut and this ominous feeling. Frankly, I was terrified. And sick. Which was when I looked ahead and saw a road sign pointing in the direction of the airport."

Milo leaned back, nodding. "You ran."

"Straight to the airport. First flight out of the country."

"Düsseldorf," Milo said.

Keller sighed, nodding. "Once I was on the plane I sent a message to Emily. *I'm sorry, but I have to go. I'll be back as soon as I can.*"

Keller rubbed his face, and Milo wasn't surprised to see that tears were slipping down his cheek. Could he understand what Keller had done? Maybe, in some loose, abstracted way, but he couldn't imagine abandoning Tina and Stephanie when some kind of forces—underworld or governmental— were moving in on them. But he wasn't Keller, was he? Milo had had self-preservation trained out of himself during his Tourism years. Keller had never had that aspect of his humanity scrubbed clean.

Keller sniffed loudly, and a manic, hysterical laugh popped out. He clamped a hand over his mouth and shook his head. As if reading Milo's thoughts, he said, "It hit me, you know. Once the plane took off, it hit me right in the face. What I'd done. I was sick. I wanted out. I cried—made a scene, actually. And then . . ." He shook his head again. "Hours later I was landing in Düsseldorf. It was enough time for me to collect my thoughts. Running hadn't helped anything. Sergei, I knew, had government friends, and I fully expected guys from the embassy to be waiting for me at arrivals. And if they weren't waiting there, they would track my credit cards and any tickets I bought. I know how easy it is to track money. I wouldn't last long before someone showed up to drag me back home."

"There was an Interpol warrant out for you. Did you know that?"

Keller frowned. "Then why wasn't I arrested?"

"Because the Germans didn't want to hand you over to the Russians. They wanted to watch you instead."

"They were watching me?"

"Of course. They saw you go to an exchange office and buy about six thousand euros, then take a taxi to the train station. Did you know where you were heading?"

Keller, stunned, shook his head. "I just got on the first train out."

"Cologne."

He nodded. "But I thought I should get out of Germany. So I went to Brussels and then Paris."

"Where you stayed in a hotel."

"*Hostel*. The Saint Christopher. I needed to make my money last long enough to figure out what I was going to do."

Milo considered telling him that his roommate in that hostel had been a German agent but decided against it. No reason to sharpen his paranoia.

A wry grin crossed his face. "Then I made another stupid mistake. I called the office. Spoke to Grigory, and he—you have to understand, I was desperate. He told me I was a hero for uncovering these payments. He said I'd uncovered thievery."

"You told him where you were staying?"

Keller nodded. "He told me they would come get me. I believed—I *wanted* to believe. But then, a couple of hours later, out on the street, two guys threw me into a van." He shook his head. "No, I wasn't a hero."

"That was Kirill Egorov's team."

He just blinked.

"What about the list?"

"I'd kept it on me. Under my shirt. It was uncomfortable, but Grigory had told me not to let it out of my sight."

"And you gave it to Egorov."

"Immediately. I was scared."

"Why didn't he send you back to Moscow?"

"I don't know. They took me to some warehouse, somewhere out of Paris, and Kirill sat with me, alone. He asked me to tell him everything. Asked me to explain all the numbers to him. I didn't have the guts to lie about anything."

"How long did this go on?"

"Two days? Something like that. Then he left me alone, under guard, for another day. When he came back, he explained that I was coming with him to Algeria. I didn't want to go to Algeria. He said, *Do you want to live? Then go to Algeria.*"

"So you went."

"So I went."

"How?"

Keller frowned. "What do you mean?"

"I mean, by boat, plane, car and ferry? How did you get through customs?"

He shook his head and raised his hands. "I don't know. There was a car. There was a boat, and then another car. And then I was here."

They all looked up as Gazala entered, but she wasn't carrying food. Instead, she held a clear plastic folder filled with bent and soiled sheets of paper full of names and numbers, which she handed to Keller. "Go," she said. "Give me back my peace."

21

Leonberger stood in front of a narrow old apartment building in upscale Zamoskvarechye, looking up to the third floor, where, a month ago, Anna Usurov had either put her head in her oven or had it forced in. He'd already made some calls and learned that Usurov's place hadn't changed hands after her death—a distant brother was trying to get ownership, and it was going to court. Sofia Marinov still hadn't called him back, so all he had to go on was this apartment. Afterward, he would drive out to Pokrovsky Hills to check on Joseph Keller's family.

Getting inside the building wasn't hard. The front door's lock was broken, and as he walked up the concrete stairs, keeping an eye out for the old women who always guarded buildings like this, he wondered if the lock had been broken the same night Anna Usurov fell asleep in her oven. At the third floor, he passed a heavy woman in a smock carrying a mop bucket downstairs, and when he greeted her with a smiling *"Zdrávstvujte,"* she rolled her eyes at him.

"You're heading upstairs, I guess," she said.

"Am I?"

"That's where the whores are. Fifth floor."

"Then I guess I am. Thank you, darling."

She grunted, shook her head, and continued down the stairs. A small-time prostitution ring wouldn't stay hidden in a building like this with that old battle-axe on the prowl. Leonberger gave it a week, maybe two, before the cops arrived to demand their cut.

Once she was out of sight, he knocked on Usurov's door and waited. Nothing. He took his tools out of his jacket and unwrapped them. He knocked again, waited, then crouched and got to work on the lock. It was an old Soviet model he knew well, because it secured most of the doors in this neighborhood, barely. In a minute and a half he was inside.

He had to fight the urge to air out the place; it was humid and stank of something putrid. In the kitchen, all signs of death had been cleaned away, and the oven was closed. So he got to work in the other rooms, opening drawers and rifling through papers. Her computer, unsurprisingly, wasn't here. Nor were any phones.

He tried not to rush, but so much here was junk—bills and ticket stubs and an unopened pack of Marlboros that he pocketed—and when he reached the bathroom he discovered the source of the smell. A cat had been trapped inside and died of starvation. The rats had taken pieces away, but enough remained for him to make a positive ID.

He started at the sound of a ringing phone before realizing it was his own. He cursed himself for not putting it on silent, then answered with a whisper. *"Allô?"*

"You called me," said a woman's voice.

It was Sofia Marinov, he realized. "Yes, thank you for returning my call. I'm interested in speaking with you about Anna Usurov—she was a colleague of yours."

"Why?"

"I'm writing an article on journalists who have . . . well, you know."

She was silent for a moment, then: "Let's meet."

Her acquiescence surprised him. He'd expected to have to talk her into opening up to him, and the hope of a face-to-face conversation had been beyond his expectations. "That would be great," he said.

"Do you know La Bohème? It's a café on Tito Square."

"If there's only one, I'll find it."

"It's next to the pharmacy. Can you be there tomorrow morning?"

"Sure. Nine o'clock?"

"Yes," she said, her voice sounding pinched and strained.

"Are you all right?" he asked.

"Yes," she said. "Yes, I'm fine. How will I know you?"

"Big, old, and ugly. I saw your picture on your website, so I'll find you. Thank you for your help on this. I appreciate it."

"Okay," she said, and hung up. He took a moment to stare at the phone, wondering about Sofia Marinov, the young journalist who was willing to meet a complete stranger. She was either brave or incredibly stupid. Or perhaps she had something that she really needed to share—one could hope.

He searched in vain for a couple of hours before starting to tidy up, and that was when he saw that the power outlet under the desk had slipped half a centimeter out of the wall, as if it had been removed and put back poorly. He got on his knees under the desk, his back aching, and gave it a tug. It came out smoothly, leaving a rectangular hole in the wall. Though his hand was big, he was able to squeeze it inside and feel along the inside of the wall, touching wood frame, wires, rat turds, screw heads, and . . . what felt like a flash drive. He caught it between his index and middle fingers and withdrew it. He blew off dust and turned it over in his hand. Red, with a single white stripe down the side. In marker, someone had written the letter *P*. Whether it was a Latin *P* or a Cyrillic *R* he didn't know. What he did know was that it was important.

He slipped it into his pocket, checked to be sure the place looked untouched, and out of morbid curiosity looked inside the oven. Other than a few spots of old, burned sauce, it was clean. Only as he was closing it did he register the most striking detail: It was an electric oven, not gas.

22

They were back in the Abdul Rahman Pazhwak conference room, and as they settled in Milo wondered if the patrons understood how many miles he'd traveled for them. With Whippet and Keller, he'd reached Mallorca by way of night boat, taken a private plane to Barcelona, and then a train to Lyon, where Alexandra had waited to drive him and Keller home, while Whippet returned to Paris. By the time they got to Zürich, Kristin and Noah had spent hours scouring photos of Keller's list and trying to understand it. Office workers, bureaucrats, and political figures paid through Sergei Stepanov's company. Half of them made a sort of sense—NATO suboffices, intelligence contractors, energy-industry specialists—but others didn't. Why would Stepanov pay a lump fifty thousand to a waste collection official in Bangladesh? Or a hundred grand to a Lebanese dock manager?

Joseph Keller didn't have answers. They had put him in the office bedroom, where he'd looked around and asked if he was a prisoner.

"You're doing it again," Alexandra told Milo.

"What?"

"It's Martin Bishop all over again."

He waved her away and went to sit with the reference librarians.

"Each of these names could make sense on its own," Kristin explained. "A Russian company wants to bid on Bangladeshi waste, or they're trying to smuggle something—weapons, maybe—in and out of Lebanon and need someone to destroy the paperwork."

"But *all* of these things on the same accounting document?" Alexandra countered. "What's Sergei Stepanov up to?"

Noah sighed loudly enough to get everyone's attention, then said, "Maybe nothing. Maybe none of this is real."

"False flag?" Milo asked doubtfully.

"Sure. The Russians plant a document hoping that some dope will dig it out. I mean, he did make it to the airport, didn't he? No one was waiting for him in Düsseldorf—though they would've had time to put that together."

"It's a stretch," said Kristin. "Besides, Egorov's team was sent to find him."

"And Egorov decided to change plans. Maybe he knew the list was nonsense." When no one replied, he said, "We're looking at a list that as a whole makes no sense. Which suggests that this avenue of payment is a catchall for different Russian operations—private companies, government ministries, intelligence. But who does that? Who runs a whole country's clandestine monies through a single stream? It's unheard of."

"And therefore," Milo said, "none of it is real."

Noah raised his hands. "It's something to consider. Okay?"

"We need to know what Anna Usurov was investigating before she died," Kristin said. "Why was Diogo Moreira so interesting for her?"

"Let's hope Leonberger comes up with something," Milo said, but no one looked hopeful.

Then it was the next day, and Milo, exhausted, was faced again with his patrons.

From his shoulder bag, he took out twelve sealed envelopes, each labeled with the name of a country, and passed it to his left to Aku Ollennu, from Ghana. "Take yours and pass it on, please."

Like good schoolchildren, they did as they were asked, a couple even waiting to rip theirs open. Most, though, got into it immediately, the tearing sound filling the room as they unfolded their single sheets to find one or two names typed there, along with an account number and a dollar amount. No one understood anything, which was how he liked it.

He said, "Each of you has one or two names that come from an accounts list taken from MirGaz records. I've given you the names we've identified as being one of your nationals."

Sanjida Thakur wrinkled her nose at the Bangladeshi waste official on her page. "Where did you get this?"

"New source. As far as we know, Stepanov doesn't know the list is in any-one's hands, and we don't want him to know until we have a better handle on what he's doing. So it's imperative that no one pick up any of these individuals."

"He's trying to expand internationally," said Pak Eun-ju, who had only one name to deal with. "He's been trying that for years."

"It may be more complicated than that," Milo told her. "Which is why we would appreciate it if your governments would surveil these people. As you know, we don't keep staff in your countries, as a courtesy, so we depend on you."

Said Bensoussan, who was one of the few with two names before him, scratched his lip. "But you have a theory, yes? An idea?"

"Nothing worth sharing yet," Milo said. "Maybe it is simply an attempt to expand MirGaz's reach, though we don't yet understand the logic behind it all. Few of these make sense for the energy sector. What we do know is that this is a major expense for Stepanov, or whoever is using his pipeline—in the billions."

Exhales all around. Katarina Heinold said, "It's Putin's money. Stepanov is one of his deputies."

"Maybe. But it's early. We're following up in Moscow and elsewhere, and when I know more I'll share."

Bensoussan raised a finger. "Does this have to do with your escapade in Algiers?"

Milo hesitated, considering a bald lie, but reconsidered. He suspected Bensoussan knew the answer already, and perhaps he'd shared his concerns with the others. "Kirill Egorov was protecting this new source from his own government. We think he was killed when he tried to pass the source off to me."

"So the Russians already know you have this," said Beatriz Almeida, whose memo listed only Diogo Moreira, of the Serviço de Informações de Segurança.

"Not necessarily," Alan cut in. "All they know is that Milo was in town at Egorov's request. Anything beyond that is speculation."

"And they won't," Milo added, "unless someone in this room tells them. Or if any of these people are picked up. So, please: surveillance only."

Silence fell, and Milo's eyes found Alfred Njenga, representing Kenya, who was still staring at his paper. Two names faced him, but they were both known politicians, and their payments were exceptionally large. His expression was bleak. Milo said, "Is there any other business we should discuss? I know we left off in an awkward place a few days ago, and if anything needs to be settled we can take care of it while we're all together."

Hilmar Jonsson, who had been so angry last time, looked off balance now. He glanced over to Gaston Majerus, who cleared his throat and said, "Milo, I think you know what kind of a position you put us in. On the other hand, we know what kind of position we put you in. So we feel that it's best to table any changes in procedure for another three months. Hopefully you understand our position better, as we understand yours. Let's try to build toward a compromise that we can settle on by the end of the year. Is that agreeable?"

"Extremely," Milo said.

After the meeting broke up, Milo found Beatriz Almeida in the corridor, waiting for him. She peered at him as he approached, then waved her envelope. "This is not good, Milo."

"Agreed," he said. "But your name in particular—Moreira—we want to look more closely at him."

"Why?"

"A Russian journalist was investigating him specifically. And now she's dead."

Almeida frowned at this. "Then come to Lisbon with me. You and I can interrogate him together."

"No," Milo said. "Please don't. Just watch him. And if you come across anything interesting, please pass it on to us."

Almeida hesitated briefly before lighting up with a smile. "Of *course*, Milo. Of course." Promises, after all, were only words.

23

It was turning out to be a pretty lousy week. Leticia had spent a long night on a dirty blanket in an abandoned abattoir in Cheung Sha Wan, near the Rambler Channel, that she'd rented from a weaselly meth addict for 120 Hong Kong dollars, about 15 US. The meth addict, with big, bloodshot eyes, told her the story of a water buffalo that had literally cried for its life upon arriving there for slaughter, disturbing the workers so deeply that they set it free to live with the monks at the Tsz Wan Kok temple. Since closing twenty years ago, the ugly building had fallen into decay, concrete cracking and water seeping through the roof.

But it had been a place. A place for her to sleep and heal from the bullet that had grazed her in that alley. She'd met the other abattoir residents—six in all, hooked on meth, heroin, or GBH, and one of them, maybe fifteen, kept a paper bag with him at all times for huffing glue. They smelled of urine and smoke. That first morning, she paid the huffer to go to the pharmacy and buy bandages and alcohol. After cleaning and wrapping her wound, she settled on a dirty blanket and went through the clues she'd taken from Mrs. Gary Young: a small bundle of cash, a credit card under the name Sharon Young, and a phone. She powered it up and found that there were no phone numbers in its contacts, and the only nonsystem app was Nexus Messenger—which, given its famous encryption, made sense. When she pulled it up, there was only one contact, labeled "DC."

Ah, shit.

As she toyed with her options, the huffer, eyes alighting on the phone, asked if he could touch it. She said no and sent him on his way. She pressed the button to connect with "DC" and heard the tinny *wah-wah* ring of all Nexus calls. Then it was picked up, and a wary female voice said, "Hello?"

"Want to tell me why you're trying to kill me?"

"Leticia," the woman said, and Leticia felt a pang of familiarity. "You're well?"

"I've been better. How's Sharon Young?"

"She's at Queen Mary, intensive care. They say she'll pull through. But you *did* hurt her. Bad."

Leticia closed her eyes, the familiarity of the voice suddenly coalescing: It was Joan, the recruiter for Tourism. From that drunk eternal night in Tromsø. *Fuck.* "Listen, Joan," she said, "I'd like to know why you've targeted me."

"Have I?"

"Yours is the only number in Sharon's phone."

"Yes," Joan said. "I guess we have targeted you."

"Why?"

"You must have stepped on someone's toes."

"Come on, Joan."

"You remember how it used to be, don't you? You get an order, you follow through. Doesn't matter why. It's just Tourism, Jake."

Was she really making jokes? "Then let me talk to someone who does know."

"Afraid I can't do that," Joan said, then went silent a moment. "Tell me: When did you start working for Milo Weaver again?"

"I'm not working for Milo Weaver. He tracked me down in Wakkanai. Wanted to talk to me. That's it. A conversation."

"About . . . ?"

"None of your business."

Silence again, and Leticia wondered what Joan was doing in DC. Was she in the bath? Sitting in a parking lot? It didn't matter, did it?

"What I need," Leticia said, "is for you to keep your hands off of me. We don't have to be friends, but there's no need to be enemies."

Joan hummed reflectively. "Well, that's not really up to me." She cleared her throat. "How about this: How about I make some inquiries and see what's possible?"

"How's that going to help?"

"Well, I can make the argument that we tried to recruit you, and that what you did there in Hong Kong proves you've still got it."

"So you're offering me my life if I reconsider your offer."

"Now you're getting it."

"Fuck you."

Joan laughed. "I'll do my research over here, you have a think, and then call me back in twenty-four. How does that sound?"

"Sounds like a shitty deal, Joan, but I'll call."

After hanging up, Leticia had a think, then called to the huffer. He grinned stupidly, showing off his missing teeth. "I've gotta go," she told him.

"Okay."

"I'm going to Macau," she said. "Can you remember that?"

"Macau," he answered, grinning.

To make sure he remembered, she asked the huffer for detailed directions, then got him to walk her all the way to the bus stop at Kwai Shing West Estate. She even followed the path, only deviating at Mei Foo Station, where she hailed a taxi to reach Hong Kong International. If it worked, when Gary Young reached the abattoir, the addicts would send him to Macau. The question was: How soon would they realize she'd flown out of Hong Kong with her last clean passport, Wanda Kumalu of South Africa?

It didn't really matter—her course was set. She didn't want to cross to the mainland; since limping out of China ten years ago, she'd successfully avoided returning to Xin Zhu's domain. In Europe she could cross borders without anyone being the wiser, and that was something she needed now. She was able to get the last seat on a KLM flight, and she purchased a connecting flight from Amsterdam to Budapest just in case they decided, over the thirteen hours she was in the air, to plant someone at Wanda Kumalu's destination.

Her seat was in the rear, where the engines were noisiest, but she didn't mind. She changed her bandage in the bathroom, then curled up and fell quickly asleep.

In Amsterdam, she checked for shadows, though she didn't know if she had it in her to discover them anymore. Hong Kong had nearly killed her, after all. Well, so be it. At the Enterprise counter she chose a Suzuki Vitara SUV for 150 euros a day, and only by the time she was on the road heading south toward Düsseldorf was she finally able to relax her aching shoulders. And that, of course, was when she realized it was time for her to make another call. Her twenty-four hours were up.

She powered up Sharon Young's phone. Opened Nexus, tapped "DC," and put it on speaker. The tinny *wah-wah*, and then:

"Leticia, so glad you called back."

"Of course, Joan."

"You're not in Macau."

"You're just saying that to make me feel good," Leticia told her, and listened to a full five seconds of silence until:

"I have good news."

"Do tell."

"First, I need to know something."

"Shoot."

"What were you doing in Wakkanai?"

Leticia hesitated. This was the question she had been waiting for, and there was only one right answer. But which was it? To know that, Leticia needed to know why they had latched on to her. Did it have to do with Wakkanai? If so, was it about the Chinese developer she'd never found, or was it about Milo Weaver? Had they known, before she did, that he would come recruiting? And if Milo was their real target, then why had they let him go? A chill went through her as she realized she didn't actually know if they had let him go. She'd watched him leave the hotel from her third-floor window, but maybe they'd gotten him before he reached the airport.

So the question was: Which excuse for Wakkanai was the one they were looking for?

She said, "I told you already."

"Milo Weaver, yes. But is that why you went to Wakkanai in the first place?"

"He wanted to talk, but I didn't want us to be seen. Obviously I'm not as good as I thought, because you were already onto me."

Silence. Not long, maybe four seconds, but enough to know that Joan didn't believe her.

Motherfucker.

"Okay, Leticia. Thanks for that. Let me tell you the good news now."

"I'm on the edge of my seat."

"Well, we have decided that you should live."

"That *is* good news, Joan."

"Caveats, of course."

"Of course."

"We'd like you to reconsider joining. Did you have a think?"

"I did. And I have to admit I'm curious now."

"Is that so?"

"But I'll have to hear more."

Another brief silence, then: "How about this: I'm flying to Zürich tomorrow. Can the department buy you dinner?"

"That sounds terrific, Joan. It's a date."

Once they'd settled the details of a seven o'clock dinner at the Kronenhalle restaurant, Leticia hung up and pulled over to the side of the road. She took a breath, trying to steady herself. Joan, and the Department of Tourism, hadn't cared about Milo. His appearance had been interesting, sure, but for some reason it was *her* they'd been watching. Little Leticia Jones, who had come to Japan to track down a Chinese businessman connected to Boko Haram and hundreds of disappeared schoolgirls. And their date at the Kronenhalle, she felt sure, was nothing more than a way to get Leticia to a known place, so Joan could finally finish what she'd started.

Nothing was going her way this week. What the hell was she going to do?

Zürich, then. She powered down the phone and removed the SIM card. The fastest route lay straight ahead, through Düsseldorf, but Joan had already tracked her direction. So she took out the Enterprise atlas and charted a new route, westward through Eindhoven, just in case Joan had already sent someone to lie in wait for her.

24

Milo was seven miles above the Atlantic when the light above his head told him that it was safe to take off his seat belt. He left it on, though, unlike the woman beside him in coach, who unlatched hers and stretched her arms out in front of herself, tapping her fingernails against the entertainment screen. "Last leg," she said.

"Where from?"

"Hawaii."

"Hawaii to Zürich?"

"Vacation. When you already live in paradise, a European city sounds inviting."

"Wait until the cold sets in."

She laughed at that, a big throaty sound, then stuck out one of her manicured hands. "Jane."

They shook. "Milo."

He'd slept little in New York, Alan dragging him to a celebratory dinner after the patrons meeting, but it had been good to see Penelope, who was still the sharp-witted woman he had met many years ago, when both he and Alan were in the Department of Tourism. She was focused on raising money to help the legal challenges against the US administration's draconian immigration policies, and the work seemed to have filled her with purpose. Still, they talked for too long, and Alan had to speed him to JFK to make his flight home.

While waiting at the gate, he'd called Zürich and learned that Joseph Keller was becoming problematic. He'd demanded internet access, and after they'd refused they'd discovered him trying to get into Kristin's computer. Only the fingerprint recognition stopped him from getting to his Nexus account. "Confine him to his room," Milo said. "I'll talk to him when I get back."

His new friend, Jane, made sleep impossible. At first it irritated him, but it turned out that Jane had excellent entertainment value. Her chatty nature belied her seriousness; she was an astute follower of politics and a seemingly devoted family doctor, volunteering regularly to help the poorer segments of Hawaii's native population. Milo knew so little about Hawaii, as compared to more obscure parts of the world, that he even welcomed her history lessons, which chronicled the systematic abuse that typified colonialism. He imagined Martin Bishop would have liked Jane, and he even brought up his name to gauge her reaction.

"They're the future, aren't they? The Massive Brigade. The young people are going to set things straight."

"You've seen what they did, right? People died."

"Sure. But *why*? Ingrid Parker is smart, you can tell. You could argue that she's the one who *stopped* the bloodshed once she took over. But either way, sometimes the ends do justify the means."

"Well, that almost sounds optimistic," he said.

"It's not optimism. I just know that if I don't believe it I'm going to slit my wrists, because what's the point?"

When dinner came around, she asked the stewardess for a half bottle of red, then convinced Milo to share it with her. She served his elaborately, joking that if the doctoring didn't work out, she could become a sommelier. The wine was a little off, but he drank it anyway.

By the time they were descending toward Zürich, he felt as if he knew everything about Jane: childhood in Alabama, a failed marriage, a brief youthful career fronting an emo band in Austin, and an even briefer stint in rehab when the touring lifestyle got out of control. Med school in Honolulu had been a way out of a lot of things, and a way into a new kind of balance.

"Balance," Milo said. "It's a good thing."

"Tell me about it."

"I hear medication's pretty good, too."

She laughed.

As enjoyable as it had been, he knew when he stood to join the exiting caravan that powering through his fatigue had been a bigger mistake than he'd imagined; he was dizzy. He held on to the seat, and Jane looked back at him, concerned. "You okay?"

"Fine," he said. "Enjoy the vacation."

"I will," she told him, and flapped a hand above her head. "Swiss Alps, here I come!" Then she was gone among the shuffling passengers.

Milo let more people pass before joining the line, and by the time he reached passport control he was starting to feel better, and even cracked a smile at the border guard, who just handed back his stamped passport and sent him on. He worked his way through the crowded baggage claim and spotted Jane in the distance, waiting for her luggage, but she didn't see him.

A crowd of expectant faces looked disappointed to see him exit to the main concourse, and that was when he felt a rush of heat to his face, as if all the blood in his body had surged to his head. He stumbled slightly, skirting around the waiting crowd, and made his way to a small shop, where he bought some water. The suspicious cashier pouted at him as he laid down a five-euro bill. "Are you all right?" she asked in German.

"I don't know," he said, then took the water out of the store, where he tried to open the bottle, but his hands were shaking too much. His heart pounded loudly in his ears, and his vision grew spotty. Pinpoints of light floated in the air, shifting and forming halos. He had no idea what was going on; he just knew that everything was wrong. And when he fell to the hard floor, he heard a shout in the distance. But he couldn't see well enough to know where it had come from. The water bottle rolled away as a shadow came over him. A face—it was Jane.

"Milo? How are you—" She turned away and shouted at someone, "I'm a doctor!" Then she turned back to him, face twisted in something like concern. "Breathe. Okay? We'll call—"

And then she was gone. Not disappeared, but *thrown* to the side. Someone had tackled her. Who the hell would do that? Jane was a doctor, and he needed her—

A new face entered his fading vision along with a wave of nausea.

Oh. It was Leticia Jones.

"She's a doctor," Milo whispered.

"No, fool. She's the one who tried to recruit me for Tourism."

She wasn't making sense, but nothing, really, was making sense.

Leticia shook her head, a sly grin appearing. "Don't die, handsome." She looked up at something and began to rise. "I'll find you."

Then she was gone, and in the gathering darkness he saw two Swiss cops. One of them, a pale woman in a peaked cap, crouched, and as her face came closer the darkness enveloped him.

25

Josip Broz Tito Square was an uninspiring intersection southwest of the center with tower blocks as far as the eye could see in the hazy morning light. Leonberger parked along Ulitsa Profsoyuznaya, then sauntered across the six lanes and grassy median of Nakhimovsky Prospekt to reach the pharmacy Sofia Marinov had mentioned. Yesterday, he'd run to an internet café in order to take a look at the contents of Anna Usurov's flash drive and found himself utterly confused by the gibberish of what was clearly an encrypted file. So he headed over to the FedEx office on Ulitsa Shabolovka and mailed the drive to the Library's post office box. Afterward, he'd driven up to Pokrovsky Hills to track down Joseph Keller's family. Their neighborhood was gated, with a fat security guard he could've knocked out in no time at all . . . but that was the old Leonberger. The new one, the one who served the *world*—he knew better than to cause a scene. So, responsibly, he picked up a couple of bottles of Dobry Medved and some takeout minced-meat *chebureki,* and went home to refuel, smoke Anna Usurov's Marlboros, and drink himself to sleep. He still felt a little fuzzy this morning.

Even standing in front of it, he might have missed the sign for La Bohème beside the pharmacy. It was a small watering hole with large windows obscured by blinds. He looked around out of instinct—anytime he entered an unfamiliar place it paid to take the temperature—but nothing seemed out of the ordinary. He pushed through the door and found himself in a simple bistro. A black-haired woman was playing a game on her phone behind the corner counter, and two guys who looked like regulars—blunt features, maybe thirty, in faux-leather bomber jackets—slumped in the corner with beers in front of them. And no one else.

The bartender smiled, and he ordered a beer. She set down a glass and a can of Baltika 3, and after taking his money without comment returned to her game. He took the can over to the blinds and peered out as he drank, but he couldn't focus. Two things were wrong with the men in the corner. First, they were utterly silent, just watching him from behind. Second, their glasses were full. Two Russian men can't sit for more than a minute without at least one of them swallowing half his beer.

So Leonberger drank, sucking down most of the can, belched loudly, then gave it back to the bartender and thanked her. As he left, heading for the sidewalk, he realized how lucky he was that they didn't know his face.

But was he making the right move? What if Sofia Marinov showed up as soon as he drove off? He guessed they would sit watching her until, eventually, they gave up on him and put Sofia Marinov into the back of their car.

He stopped at the corner, waiting for the light, then turned to look behind himself. No one had left the bar yet. The light changed, but he didn't cross; instead, he turned back and took a position at the corner of the apartment block, leaning against the wall and lighting one of Usurov's Marlboros. In this area of town, there was nothing strange about an old man smoking on a street corner, waiting on nothing in particular.

It took ten whole minutes and two cigarettes for it to occur to him that something was indeed wrong. Sofia Marinov had not arrived, but two more men had. Hands shoved deep into their bomber jackets, so like the others', they'd looked around as they went into the bar. No one came out. Then his phone rang. He checked—it was Marinov's number.

"Are you lost?" asked Sofia Marinov.

"Um, running late. You said La Bohème, right?"

"Yes. The corner of Nakhimovsky and Profsoyuznaya."

"Are you there?"

A pause, then: "Yes, I'm there."

A chill went down his spine as he imagined her in some small room with more of those guys in bomber jackets, maybe tied up, the phone held to her ear. He said, "Five minutes," and hung up. He pocketed the phone and hurried away, not waiting for the light to cross the big road and find his car. His mind whirred away, thinking through what *they* knew. They had his phone number, which meant they had his name. Which meant they had his car tags and, probably, his location. How did they not know his face yet? Luck, probably. Sometimes you got it.

So. What to do?

Shed everything.

He halted a couple of meters from his car and looked around. Up Profsoyuznaya, he saw the red *M* of the metro. Behind him, the door of La Bohème opened and one of the bomber-jacketed men stepped out to light a smoke.

Leonberger walked toward the metro station and disassembled his phone, pocketing the pieces. He didn't look back again—that bar was dead to him now—and trotted down the stairs to take the long, narrow tunnel back again to the Profsoyuznaya subway platform, passing old grannies and chattering children as he wondered where he'd made his mistake. *Had* he made a mistake? Maybe this was a trap that had been laid last month, as soon as they killed Anna Usurov. Kill her and wait for people to come ask questions.

He needed to get out of town. South, ideally, to Bryansk, where he knew steelworkers who would keep him safe for a while. Long-term plans were beyond him; he only needed to find a place to hole up.

He caught the southbound train, which would take him to the end of the line at Novoyasenevskaya, where he would hustle over to the Butovskaya line at Bitsevsky Park, then ride to the terminus at Buninskaya Alleya. A lengthy walk north to the MSK rental desk, and with luck he'd be driving down the Ukraine Highway by five o'clock.

Easy, right?

It seemed so. He made the transfer to the Bitsevsky Park station, where a colorful mural of people with horses stared down at him, and by the time he reached Buninskaya Alleya he was quite sure that no one on his train was even aware of his presence. It wasn't even ten-thirty yet, and he walked the half hour to the MSK desk without breaking a sweat. There was the pleasant stretch of green beside the highway, then the forest of tower blocks that reminded him of his youth, of growing up in concrete suburbs that, back then, were new and exciting and devoutly Soviet. Now they were how everyone lived in a city that had burst out of its seams and spilled all over the neighboring countryside. He picked up a bottle of Borjomi water from a kiosk and offered a Marlboro to an attractive woman buying a magazine. She laughed but otherwise ignored him. He didn't care. The sun was bright over Bulevar Admirala Lazareva, and he was almost out of Moscow.

He had to wait behind an out-of-towner with a Petersburg accent, but not long, and the clerk who served him, a girl in her twenties, found him another Volkswagen Golf. When she asked, he lied, telling her he would be taking it to St. Petersburg. He hesitated when she asked for his papers, but only briefly, and as soon as she typed in his information he began running a mental clock. How long before that information was processed through the system and available to whoever was looking for him? Because he had to assume they were government. If they weren't, then he had nothing to worry about, but it paid to assume the worse.

He was behind the wheel by eleven-thirty, and he drove back down Admirala Lazareva, passing the towers full of families. Ten minutes later he was on the Ukraine Highway, plotting where he would exit to reach the smaller access roads. He was fine. Everything was fine.

Then he heard the siren and saw the lights. A militia car was speeding up the highway from behind. He pulled to the slow lane to let it pass, and caught his breath when it pulled up beside him. There were two cops inside, and the one in the passenger seat—just a kid, really—pointed at him and signaled for him to pull over.

Leonberger smiled grimly at him, understanding everything.

The people after him were not private individuals; they were representatives of the Kremlin. When they took him away, he understood, he would never see the outside of his cell. He would not be told why—even his curiosity, by now raging in him, wouldn't be satisfied. By now they would have taken a hard look at his bank accounts, and someone would have noticed some funny little Swiss account that he'd unadvisedly tapped a couple of years ago to put a down-payment on his overpriced apartment in Arbat. And of course by now they'd noted Elena and Nadia. Of course they had. Which meant they had something to hold over him.

He'd spent his whole life serving these people, and when power changed hands he'd endeavored to maintain his loyalty. But they'd changed too much, and he'd done the best he could and still failed. No, he didn't want to pull over and let those children in their uniforms take him away.

He smiled and nodded at them but pressed hard on the accelerator. He could see the young cop shouting. The little boy's window was down now, and his red face puffed up as he shouted and pointed. Leonberger gave him a wink, then turned sharply left, colliding with the police car at high speed. The cops spun off to the left, out of his field of vision, but so did he. The little Golf skidded and, as he tried to regain control, it hit something in the road and flew through the air, high and true, spinning.

26

When Milo woke, cotton mouthed and weak, he was surrounded by women. Tina and Stephanie and, behind them, Alexandra and Leticia Jones—who, it turned out, hadn't been a fever dream. He should have been surprised, but this somehow felt right, that all of them would be there. His head hurt, but the pain had been pushed some distance away by whatever drugs he'd been filled with.

"Hey," he said, and smiled.

"Dummy," said Tina.

Stephanie shot her a look. *"Mom."*

"He promised he'd stay out of trouble. Milo, you promised."

Alexandra pressed forward. "How are you?"

"I hurt."

"Good," Tina said, then leaned close and kissed his forehead.

"Leticia," Milo said. "Thank you."

"Don't be nice to me," Leticia said. "If it wasn't for you, I could have gotten her. Now I'm stuck here, watching over you and your family."

"You don't need to," Alexandra said over her shoulder. "We have people."

"Then why weren't they waiting at the airport for him?"

Gradually, that mellow feeling of being surrounded by women faded. He was having trouble keeping track of the back-and-forth, and when the doctor came and told them to keep it down it felt like protection. Only Stephanie remained above the fray, gripping his hand and looking silently at some point over his head, her mind moving through whatever emotions were taking hold of her. He squeezed her fingers and gave her a smile that she returned, but sadly.

The doctor explained what everyone else already knew—he'd been poisoned with aconite.

"Wolfsbane," Stephanie blurted. "It's what they used to kill Emperor Claudius."

"We were lucky to discover it," said the doctor.

Once the doctor had checked his vitals and proclaimed that he would live, Alexandra followed her out to take calls, and Leticia went to the chair to watch over him from a distance.

"You going to tell me?" Tina asked him.

"A woman poisoned me."

"*She* told me that," Tina said, nodding at Leticia. "That's why she won't leave the room. But I want to know why. I want to know who she is."

"Little Miss?" Milo said. "Can you give us a minute?"

"No," said Stephanie, squeezing his hand tighter. "I'm seventeen, Dad. I'm not a little anything."

Milo looked to Tina, who arched a brow as if to say, *Don't ask.* "Okay, then," he said after a moment. "She works for my old office."

"Tourism?" Tina asked.

"Yeah."

"I thought that was history."

"Apparently not."

Stephanie shifted, eyes on him, but she didn't look confused. Just curious.

"Why you?" Tina asked.

"I don't know." Milo raised his head an inch to see Leticia looking at her phone. "How did you end up there?"

Not looking up from her screen, Leticia said, "I wasn't there for you. I was there for her. Then you went and collapsed, and I lost her. Thank you very much."

"Sorry."

Leticia shrugged.

To Tina, he said, "She saved my life."

Stephanie looked over her shoulder at Leticia, her expression softening slightly. She was impressed by Leticia Jones, as well she should be.

"So what do we do now?" Tina asked.

The enormity of what had happened was only now dawning on Milo, though Leticia had seen it immediately. The Department of Tourism had decided to target him, and if the department was half as ruthless as it had once been, then that meant that the full force of the American machine was bearing down on him and would not let his wife and child stand in its way.

"We hide," Milo said, and in Tina's face he saw what those two little words meant. Flashbacks to worse times, to paranoia, fear for her child's safety, and a time when she didn't completely trust her husband.

Leticia was already standing up, pocketing her phone. "No. We go after them. You've got the staff."

"We're ignorant," Milo said, trying to sit up. "All we would do is make things worse."

She didn't like that answer, he could tell. Unused energy, a by-product of fury, coursed through Leticia. She wanted an object to point all that energy at. Instead, she pointed at Milo. "You better not get me killed, old man."

It was a long night. Alexandra called for two nearby librarians—Dalmatian and Samoyed—to take Tina back to the house to choose what couldn't be left behind, while Stephanie and Leticia remained in the hospital with him. His daughter had questions, and Milo tried to stay awake in order to answer them. It was a strange feeling, opening up to her for the first time about things that she'd never shown an interest in, even though, more than once, they had altered the course of her life. Stephanie listened quietly to it all—Tourism, his secret UN department, working off the grid, gathering intelligence, the Library. "It sort of makes things make sense," she said.

"What things?"

"You know. Like the guy who shot you."

She'd been six when a distraught man had arrived at their Park Slope apartment and, in a rush of anger and tears, shot Milo point-blank. "I'm still so sorry you had to see that."

"I see everything," she said.

"You do."

Unexpectedly, she grinned. "Does that mean I should become a spy?"

"Never."

They discussed the practicalities of going underground. Losing weeks, or more, of school wasn't a tragedy—Frau Pappan could be talked into some compromise—but Stephanie was more worried about losing her friends, even Halifa. What would they think of her sudden disappearance?

"Why don't you call them?" Milo asked.

"I can do that?"

"Just don't tell them what's really going on. Let's come up with something better."

If she didn't already know, Milo taught her how to lie.

By midnight Tina had returned to the hospital, the back of their Mercedes station wagon so full that the rearview no longer showed the road behind it, and Leticia joined them on the four-hour drive south to Milan, where they maintained an acceptable safe house in Brera. The whole way, Milo remained hunched in the backseat with Stephanie, fighting nausea and trying to keep his eyes open. He was surprised that his daughter had so few concerns. After the initial shock, she seemed to have been energized by this onrush of danger and sudden movement. As if she'd been waiting for something to break through the crust of her boring life. Or maybe Milo was reading her that way because that was how he wanted to see her. Excited, and not terrified.

27

When they arrived at the safe house in the predawn hour, and a dour old Milanese man opened the door for them, Leticia felt a grudging respect for Milo's organization. Not the details necessarily—as far as she could tell, their security wasn't much at all—but the unity. Where Tourism, and the life that she'd followed afterward, had been about solitude, the Library felt, even during her short exposure to it, like a team effort. Each person had taken a role without really having to ask Milo what to do, and their roles felt instantly complementary.

Still, though, she searched the apartment and then checked the surrounding streets as Tina helped Milo up the narrow stairs and to bed. The girl, Stephanie, was a surprise. She'd seen kids whose lives had been turned upside down, and more often than not they broke quickly. Mute shock, and then a meltdown. But Stephanie wasn't in shock. Surprise, yes, but fascinated surprise. When Leticia returned from scouting the neighborhood, the girl asked her if she'd ever killed anyone.

"Yes," Leticia told her.

"Many?"

"What's many?"

Stephanie's wry smile told her all she needed to know about this girl—she was going places.

While the Weavers took the two bedrooms, Leticia lay down in the living room and set the alarm on her phone so she could take twenty-minute power naps. After the second one, which was interrupted by a call from Alexandra back in Zürich, she decided to stay up. With late-morning light streaming in through the lace curtains, she brewed coffee and looked through the meager bookshelves, finding a copy of Dante's *Inferno*.

> *Nel mezzo del cammin di nostra vita*
> *mi ritrovai per una selva oscura,*
> *ché la diritta via era smarrita.*

Poor Dante went astray of the straight road. Hadn't they all?

She heard someone moving in the back of the apartment and stiffened, but when the bathroom door opened and closed, followed by the sound of a man peeing, she relaxed again and waited until Milo stumbled out and headed to the coffee machine. He saw her and smiled.

"How's the head?" she asked.

"Better," he said as he poured himself a cup. She waited for him to add some milk, then work his way over to one of the chairs in the living room. He settled in and took his first sip.

"So," she said.

"So," he answered.

"Your sister called."

"Anything?"

"Everyone's safe. Your . . . reference librarians?"

"That's right."

"Joseph Keller, too." In answer to his look of concern, she added, "Alexandra filled me in before we left Zürich."

He looked surprised. "On everything?"

"I think so. Keller is a refugee from MirGaz with a list of international payoffs."

Milo nodded, apparently accepting his sister's breach of security.

"She says there's no sign of anything at your apartment. No one skulking around."

"There wouldn't be," he said. "If they saw Tina packing, they know we're gone."

"Alexandra's wondering if all this is overkill."

"What do you think?"

"Compared to how we were, back in the day? This is *not* overkill."

He nodded, agreeing, then stretched his legs out and yawned. She knew what he would say next, but she would make him ask the question. When he did, though, she didn't like the way he formulated it: "A week ago you were in Wakkanai, waiting for me," he said. "Then you're in Zürich. Are you stalking me?"

"You really think the world revolves around you, don't you?" She shook her head. "I wasn't in Wakkanai waiting for a job offer, that's for damned sure. I was there because I'd gotten a lead from a contact in Tokyo."

"The Cabinet Intelligence and Research Office."

"Yeah."

"I thought you were there to sell them information."

"It was a trade. My information for theirs."

"What kind of information?"

She looked at her hands, which still held the *Inferno*. She tossed it on the coffee table. "Chibok, remember? It bothered me. All those girls, just gone. Forced to convert to Islam, forced to marry militants, forced into slavery. Even after the negotiations and the escapes, there are still more than a hundred unaccounted for. And I'm not just talking about these girls, understand. In 2014 alone Boko Haram kidnapped about two thousand people."

Milo nodded. Of course he knew this; the UN had stacks of reports on it.

"I wanted to do something," she said.

"In Japan?"

"I couldn't walk into the Sambisa Forest, where they had dragged those girls, and singlehandedly rescue each one of them. Now, could I?"

Milo shrugged.

"But others could do it," she said. "The UK, for example, tracked the Chibok girls soon after the kidnapping and offered to go in and rescue them. Nigeria said no—it was an internal matter. They were afraid, I suppose, of looking weak beside their old colonial masters. As long as the government thought that way, nothing was going to happen. So I saw a possible solution: Convince the government to accept foreign help."

She knew what this sounded like to someone like Milo: a shockingly naïve proposition. His expression didn't make her think she was wrong. "How would you do that?"

"Did you know that during Goodluck Jonathan's administration twenty billion dollars of government money went missing?"

"That's a lot."

"For you and me, yes. But for an economy like Nigeria's? It's ridiculous. So I began with the cabinet and worked my way down. Gathered evidence. I charted where their money came from, which accounts it was laundered through, and whose pockets it went into. And that's when I stumbled across it."

Leticia got up, walked to the kitchenette, took a bottle of water from a cabinet, and returned, cracking the top open. Milo watched her the whole distance, and when she returned to her chair she said, "This world we live in—we put border checks everywhere for people, but money? Money is the freest thing that exists. It can vanish and reappear anywhere on the planet like *that*." She snapped her fingers. "And in the space of forty-eight hours one cabinet member's account rose to a million dollars and then fell to twenty dollars."

"Cashed out?"

"Yeah. Three days before the Chibok attack."

Milo's face twisted; he was clearly confused. "Wait—are you saying . . . ?"

She held up a finger. "I didn't know, did I? So I followed the money in reverse. It had been laundered through a Senegalese shipping company, a Malaysian textile firm, and a Chinese economic development company."

"How did you track all these accounts?"

"Friends. I have friends."

"But this," Milo said, sounding pained. "Look, the Library's good, but even with all our resources it takes months for us to track these sorts of things, and we're not always successful. But you have a few friends who can pull this off?"

"The difference," she told him, "is that my friends, even the ones working for Maastricht, aren't worried about a little breaking and entering." She winked and gave him a smile to make him feel better. "But this *did* take years, Milo. I started looking in 2014, after the Chibok girls were taken. Didn't put it together until last year. In July 2017, I was working on the other side of the world when my friends told me that over a two-day period, that same bank account had been filled again and emptied."

"And you thought . . ."

"I didn't know. But if it was true . . . ?" She shook her head. "I dropped everything and went. But I was too late." She hesitated, then went silent, remembering landing at Murtala Muhammed International and finding the news already full of another Boko Haram attack. A hundred and twenty girls, gone. She felt the emotion building in her, just as it had then, and cleared her throat.

"So you knew," Milo said, sinking deeper into his chair, his expression bleak. Maybe he wasn't a bad egg after all.

"I spoke with the local cops," she went on. "I even went out into the bush for a week, talking to villagers who were too afraid to answer my questions. Then I came back to town and ran into a guy, Karim Saleem. Moroccan, or so he said. Accent? British, and not just from school. I'd seen him three years earlier, in Chibok. Worked for some NGO—Literacy Across the World. LAW. Focus on education in the third world. Over drinks he told me he'd been studying the effect of unrest on education trends, which was adorable, but utter bullshit. I didn't believe anything he told me—it sounded scripted. So I lifted his wallet and found three names on three different credit cards. I had Maastricht run the names. There was nothing on the name he used with me, but another one—Walid Turay—came up in a police report from Thailand. He'd been arrested as the fence for an armed robbery of—get this—land title deeds from a distant relative of the king."

"Strange."

"Stranger still, his outbound flight from Nigeria had been paid for by a company called Tóuzī."

"What's Tóuzī?"

"The Chinese developer that laundered the Boko Haram money. I also had the name of the person who authorized that million-dollar transfer—a man named Liu Wei."

"Are you honestly telling me some Chinese company was paying Boko Haram to kidnap these kids?"

She opened her hands. "I didn't know. That's why I was in Wakkanai—to find out. Tóuzī's headquartered in Shanghai, but Liu Wei was working on a big project on Sakhalin Island. He has Japanese family in Wakkanai that he visits once a month. I didn't want to deal with Russian security in Sakhalin, not alone, so I was going to wait in Japan and hold him down and ask him some questions."

"Did he show up?"

She shook her head. "I'll lay odds he's back in Shanghai by now."

Milo frowned at her. "So what happened?"

She looked squarely at Milo, licked her teeth behind her lips, and told him the rest of the story. Mr. and Mrs. Gary Young. Fleeing to Hong Kong. Fighting back. To remove any doubt, she unbuttoned her shirt and slipped it off her left shoulder to show him the bandage on her arm. "I got nicked." Then she described fleeing to Amsterdam, and that call with Joan—or, to Milo, Jane.

Milo looked stunned. He rubbed his hands on his thighs, finally asking, "So you came to us for help?"

This was getting tiring. "Really, Milo. You've got to do something about your ego. I came to Zürich looking for the bitch. She told me she was flying into Zürich from the States, and we made a date. I had no intention of meeting on her terms, so I tracked all the flights coming into Zürich from the US and stood around waiting. I saw you first, watched you stumble around, buy a bottle of water, and pass out. Honestly? Seeing you pissed me off—I was there to deal with Joan, but there you were, dropping like a drunken fly. To help you, I was going to have to break cover. And then . . . well, you know the story. There she was, crouching over you, something in her hand. A needle, maybe? I don't know. But I wasn't going to wait to find out. I launched. She ran off. I bolted when I saw the cops coming. Afterward, I saw her in the parking lot. She'd been picked up by a white van. It was two car-lengths away, in the other lane, and she rolled down her window and pointed at me like this." Leticia made a finger-pistol and pointed it at Milo.

He looked like he had finally woken up. She hoped he appreciated what she'd done by changing her plans, and what kind of a mess she was in now.

He said, "This woman—Joan, or Jane—she's after both of us."

"Yes."

"I wasn't attacked until I took Joseph Keller into safekeeping and shared names from his list with our patrons. To protect, one assumes, MirGaz."

That sounded right to her, so she gave him the solution: "Give him up."

Anger flashed through Milo's face. "What?"

"Alexandra says his list isn't helping anyone, and the guy doesn't know enough to be of any use. Give him to the Swiss; let him be their problem. Won't help me, but it might get them off your back."

He shook his head. "He'll be dead inside of a week."

"It's not your problem. Your problem is keeping your people alive, not him."

"Enough, Leticia."

She shrugged, leaned back, and crossed her legs. "You know what we need? Some of those Chinese guns."

He frowned, still looking a little pissed. "What?"

"Those plastic guns you told me about. Something untraceable. Something to bring through security. I'm sick of leaving my hardware behind."

"I don't—" he began, then paused, seeming confused. "I *told* you about those?"

"The one-shot wonders from Beijing? Sure."

He rubbed his forehead, and it gave her a measure of satisfaction to hear him say, "You really must have gotten me drunk."

"Hell yeah I did."

After a moment, he nodded and leaned back, accepting his incompetence. "So. We know why they're after me. But what about you?"

Leticia rubbed her lip, letting the air go out of the room. "I didn't know before, but I do now."

"How?"

"At the airport. The man at the wheel of Joan's van was Karim Saleem, or Walid Turay. They've been on me since Nigeria."

Milo rubbed his hands through his graying hair, as if something terrible had occurred to him. "No," he said.

"What, no?"

"Boko Haram in Nigeria, Tóuzī in China, MirGaz—they all connect to a single CIA department. *How?*"

"Elephant," Leticia said.

He looked at her, waiting for an explanation.

"We're each looking at parts of the same elephant."

"But what is the elephant?"

Leticia didn't have an answer, and neither did he. Then Milo's phone buzzed on the coffee table. He answered it with a "Weaver," then listened for a full minute. His shoulders sank, and he closed his eyes. "Jesus." Whatever he had heard was seriously bad news. He pinched the bridge of his nose and finally said, "Thanks. Let me know how it goes."

When he hung up, he pressed the heels of his hands into his eyes. "What is it?" she asked.

"Leonberger, one of our librarians, is dead."

"What is with these names?"

He ignored her. "But he did his job. He sent us a flash drive. They're decrypting it now."

"What flash drive?"

"Anna Usurov's."

Leticia got up to pour herself another coffee—she was going to need it.

28

Five days later, Alan stared out the window of the Acela Express, watching the landscape of New York turn into New Jersey, Pennsylvania, Delaware, and Maryland until it reached DC, flipping idly through a discarded *Washington Post*. It was the third time he'd taken this route in the past two weeks. First time, he'd gone to meet Helen, his CIA contact, to find out who in the US government had sent Interpol the Red Notice request for Joseph Keller; once she'd agreed to that, he slipped in the more dangerous question about the Department of Tourism. She'd pouted at him as they walked together through Dumbarton Oaks park, not far from her Georgetown apartment, and told him that he'd be better off not dredging up ghosts. "I'm asking if it really is a ghost, Helen."

"What would make you ask that?"

"Things that are hard to explain. Bumps in the night."

"You've been listening to ghost stories."

He didn't deny it, just said, "Can you check on it?"

His second visit had been with Penelope, when she'd insisted on going to the Museum of African American History and Culture because she'd heard there would be an exhibit on James Baldwin. When they arrived, though, it turned out that it wasn't an exhibit but a discussion of Baldwin's only children's book, *Little Man, Little Man*, with a panel including the actor LeVar Burton. As Penelope sat listening, Alan had wandered through the museum, eyeing artifacts of slavery and oppression, feeling the echo of all that horror in the news he'd been reading lately: black people killed by police, black neighborhoods losing access to the voting booth, white supremacists crawling out of the woodwork and staging torchlight parades. His mood darkened.

Bad days in America and, always, the cloud that hung over all human endeavor: climate change. As world temperatures crept steadily upward, people remained resolutely distracted by the crimes humans committed against one another. Everyone was dancing to the wrong tune, and dancing toward a cliff.

And now he was back on the Acela, alone this time, sipping an antioxidant smoothie he'd picked up at the Penn Station Jamba Juice. Helen had given him no preview of what she would say, only a note in the drafts folder of their shared Hotmail account: *Monday 1345 Lincoln.*

Yes, even this—even the possibility of a resurrected Department of Tourism—was nothing in the face of global disaster. But it was the only thing that, for now, he could have an effect on.

As the train was nearing the station, he looked down at the *Post* in his hands to see a headline on the fifth page: PORTUGAL ARRESTS SUSPECTED RUSSIAN SPY. He began to read, then cursed silently to himself. Against their instructions, the Portuguese had picked up Diogo Moreira. Fucking Beatriz Almeida. Milo, hiding out in Milan, was going to blow his top.

It was a little after one when he tossed his empty cup and hustled out of Union Station for the twenty-five-minute walk down chilly Massachusetts Avenue to Lincoln Park. There had been a time when he would have balked at the idea of going by foot, but he'd been younger and stupider back then; self-destructive, too. A heart attack turned that around, as did Penelope, who cut through his self-pity with a line in the sand: *Cut it out, or I'm gone.*

He waited by the statue of Mary McLeod Bethune handing a copy of her educational legacy to two children. Farther down the park, Abraham Lincoln stood holding the Emancipation Proclamation, as if with a simple piece of paper America could be cured.

"Good, you're early," he heard, and turned to find Helen smiling at him, her blond hair curved around her face and flowing into the raised collar of her black trench coat.

"You are, too."

"How's Pen?"

"Saving immigrants. It keeps her busy."

"Good for her," Helen said, and he joined her slow walk toward the six-teenth president. "The request for the Red Notice," she told him, "started at Justice. You've heard of Gilbert Powell, I believe?"

"Founder-of-Nexus Gilbert Powell? What does he have to do with it?"

"Well, Powell plays his senator like a fiddle. My source says after a boozy lunch with Powell, the senior congressman from Kentucky came out all cyl-inders firing, demanding a talk with Justice."

"What was his reasoning?"

"National security."

"So the request was pushed through by Gilbert Powell."

"Yeah, I know. Doesn't make sense to me, either." She opened her hands. "But that's all I got."

Alan wasn't sure what to make of this revelation, so he just said, "Weird," and, "The other thing?"

"The ghost?"

"Yeah."

Helen rocked her head. "That took longer than expected."

"But you found it?"

"Indeed I did."

"So it does still exist?"

"It does not."

He was taken aback by her unequivocal reply. "What did you find?"

"A story," she said. "Remember 2008?"

Alan did. Alan would never forget 2008. "It was the end of Tourism."

"It was also an election year," she reminded him. "Did you vote?"

He hadn't—he'd been too far gone for that—but said, "Of course."

"A lot of people did, and a young politician with a weird name won. Democrats got control of both houses. There was a lot of talk during the cam-paign of the crimes of the previous administration. Iraq's weapons of mass destruction. State-sponsored torture. Outing CIA officer Valerie Plame. The Democratic base wanted Republicans behind bars. This ring a bell?"

"Vaguely."

"Well, imagine the feeling in the White House in the weeks before inau-guration. They didn't know what the new administration would do. So they started cleaning house. They sent people into all the departments to find dirty secrets and either shred or move them, so the Dems couldn't bring them to a grand jury."

"And among those dirty secrets . . ."

"Tourism. Exactly. It had been around for decades, but all the administration worried about was what it had done during *their* eight years. As you know, not all of it was pretty. And the way it ended—that's a story no one wanted out. So it was decided to erase Tourism from the archives."

"*Erase* erase?"

"Erase from the server. Hard copies put into cold storage, off-site."

"Where off-site?"

"There's probably no more than five who know where. I'm not one of them."

"Do you know who those five people are?"

"I'm not even one of the people who can find that out."

Alan understood. "When were the records erased?"

"Sometime in December 2008. But the point is that there's no way in hell anyone has revamped the department. Not without the records. Without them—without the blueprint for putting it together—you can't create the department. You can create *something*, but that would just be a shadow of Tourism, which had been honed over half a century to perfection."

Not perfect enough, Alan thought as they reached Abraham Lincoln.

"You going to tell me?" she asked. When he didn't answer, she said, "Those things that are hard to explain—do they really look like Tourism?"

He almost told her that, yes, they did look like Tourism, and, further, it called itself Tourism and even used the go-codes of the original Tourists—Leticia had verified that. He almost told her all of this but stopped himself. "It's doubtful," he said. "Just wanted to be sure."

Helen looked like she didn't believe him. "It's a good thing," she said with a shrug.

"What?"

"Imagine what the current administration would do if they had those files."

"Or if those files ended up in Moscow," he said.

She let out a short, sharp *ha!*, then winked at him. "Take care of yourself, Alan."

29

"Give me a few days," Milo said into the phone, sitting on a box of printer paper in a back closet of the Milan safe house.

"What does it matter if you're there or here?" Tina asked. She and Stephanie were only two hours away at a safe house across the Swiss border, in the mountains just north of Locarno. It was tempting to get in the car and, at the very least, spend the day with them, but he could hardly do that and still demand Kristin, Noah, and Joseph Keller remain trapped in this claustrophobic apartment.

"It's not an option right now, okay?"

"Bring everybody," she suggested, obviously reading his mind. "The Wi-Fi here is great."

"You know I can't."

"You really think we're safer without you around?"

She knew the answer to that, so he changed the subject. "How's Dalmatian treating you?"

"I don't think he's used to being around women; he always looks embarrassed."

"But is he being careful?"

"Very. He confiscated Stef's phone on the drive here."

"She must be pissed."

"You can't imagine."

Milo had confiscated her phone plenty of times in the past; he could imagine. "Just a few more days. Then I should have a better idea what's going on. I'll come then."

"Sure, Milo," she said doubtfully.

When he came out to the main room, Noah and Kristin were working opposite each other at a long table, their computers surrounded by printed pages, portable hard drives, and multiple burner phones they'd brought from Zürich. "Anything from our guest?" Milo asked.

Noah shook his head, only half listening, and Kristin said, "He doesn't like the coffee. And he doesn't want to help."

"What about Usurov? Still no connections between her information and his?"

Kristin shook her head.

"Strange," he said.

"More than strange," Kristin told him. "Why isn't Diogo Moreira on her flash drive? That was her obsession when she went at Keller."

With each new discovery, the questions only seemed to collect. "Give me his list?"

Without looking away from his computer, Noah held up a stapled copy of Keller's list. Milo took it to the bedroom, where Joseph Keller was sitting at a table by the window, writing in a notebook.

"Hey," Milo said.

Keller looked over his shoulder and turned to face Milo.

"Want to go through some names?"

Keller shook his head. "What did I tell you? I don't know them. They weren't part of my job. I dealt with organization-level finances—the macro, not the micro. The question is: When are you going to let me go?"

Milo had to remind himself that Keller had lived more than a month in captivity. Paris, Algiers, Zürich, and now Milan. He'd twice been smuggled between Europe and Africa. It was only reasonable that he would react unreasonably, his mood swinging from self-pity to anger and vindictiveness. Understanding, though, didn't make him easier to live with. "We're all stuck here," Milo told him.

"Really?" Keller snapped. "What kind of protection can I expect when *you're* too scared to go outside?"

It wasn't just the claustrophobia of captivity, Milo told himself. Keller had spent the last month despising himself for leaving his family behind.

They were fine—while Leonberger had been unable to get eyes on them, Kristin had tracked down Daniel Keller's Nexus account and showed Keller that his son was still posting happily about his school days—but that didn't negate the fact that Keller had abandoned his family. When he snapped at Milo, it was a way to shift the blame elsewhere. Milo understood that, but Keller was close to becoming more trouble than he was worth. Not just him, but his thirty-two pages as well. Nothing in them shed any light on the elephant they were hunting.

The worst thing, though, was how useless Milo himself was starting to feel. Leticia had flown to Shanghai, where she and Poitevin would follow up on Liu Wei, the developer who signed million-dollar checks for Boko Haram. Alexandra was back in London to run down the UK's Red Notice against Keller, while Alan was trying to get a handle on the extent of Tourism in America. Kristin and Noah were working to tie together Keller's list and Anna Usurov's just-decrypted flash drive. *Everyone* was accomplishing things, while Milo was stuck protecting an unhelpful and unappreciative man.

"You know what?" he said, and Keller cocked his head, noting the change in tone. "Go."

"What?"

"You need money? No problem. I'll ask Kristin to book a plane ticket. Where to? Back to Moscow?"

Keller's mouth fell open, and he shook his head.

"London, then."

"Wait," said Keller.

Out in the main room, Milo grabbed Keller's jacket from a wall hook, then opened the lockbox and took out two thick bundles of twenties. Noah and Kristin stared but said nothing. He returned to the bedroom and tossed the money and jacket on the unmade sheets. Keller looked confused.

"No need to wait," Milo said. "You're obviously not happy here." When Keller didn't move, he said, "What's the problem?"

"You know I can't go," Keller said. "They'll kidnap me."

"No, Joseph. They'll *kill* you. That's what they'll do."

Keller sank deeper into his chair.

"But the question," Milo said, "is: Who are *they?* Who wants you dead, Joseph? Because as a result of my decision to protect you, *I* have to hide out, away from *my* family, and send *my* people off on jobs that might get them killed. Did you know that one of my people already died in Moscow, trying to find out what happened to you?"

Keller looked surprised. "What?"

"This is no picnic for us either, Joseph."

Keller rubbed the side of his neck, as if something hurt. Milo sat across from him on the bed. "If you ever want to get out of this situation, you have to help us. The list you took is so important that people are willing to kill to get it. Russians, Americans. Maybe others. Now they're trying to kill us, too. If we don't know why the list is important, then we'll be stuck in this apartment for the rest of our lives."

Keller stared, and for a moment Milo sensed tension. Keller flexed his fists, the tendons in his wrist rising. Then he relaxed and nodded. "Okay," he said as Noah looked into the room.

"It's Alan."

Milo followed him out and picked up the satellite phone from the table. "Alan?"

"It's not the US of A."

There was relief in that news, and as he listened to the story of how the Tourism files had been placed in storage a decade ago, he found himself struggling with the question: If Tourism wasn't American anymore, then what was it? "What's your feeling?" Milo asked.

"My money is on Moscow."

"Mine, too," Milo said. "Particularly after Leonberger."

"But it may be more complicated than that," Alan said, then told him about the influence of Gilbert Powell on the American Red Notice for Keller.

"Nexus?" Milo asked. "You're not making this any simpler."

"Sorry about that. And to make matters worse, did you see the news from Portugal?"

Alan told him about the arrest of Diogo Moreira, and together they cursed Beatriz Almeida.

When he hung up, Kristin handed him a folder of reports. "Preliminary assessments of names."

"From Keller's list?"

She shook her head. "Anna Usurov's. I'm building another document from Keller's list, but it hasn't led anywhere yet."

Milo nodded, weighing the hefty document in his hand, not looking forward to reading it all. "Headlines?"

"I filtered out the Putin hit-pieces, and a lot of what's left is obvious—people bribing, people getting paid. What's weird, though, is that a lot of them seem to be shooting themselves in the foot. Look." She took the file from his hands and turned to page 16, a single-page report on Philippine shipper Eduardo Ramos, paid 250,000 euros by MirGaz.

"MirGaz?" Milo asked.

"Yeah. But Ramos isn't on Keller's list, just here."

As Milo scanned the page, something nagged at him. Then he saw it: Asia-Wide Transport. "This is the company that went bankrupt after pirates sank their ships."

"That's right. Ramos had hidden the damage from his shareholders, and once it became clear the company was tanked, he came to the table with a buyout offer from Salid Logistics."

"From Oman," Milo remembered from his time drinking in Manila as Typhoon Mangkhut raged outside.

"Exactly," she said. "The shareholders had no choice but to accept the offer, and Eduardo Ramos was hired by Salid Logistics to run their Western Pacific region. Essentially, he got a bigger job after ruining Asia-Wide."

Milo frowned, trying to see how everything connected. MirGaz pays a Philippine shipper to . . . what? Hide the damage pirates were doing his company? That would only make sense if MirGaz then swooped in to buy them out. But they hadn't; Salid Logistics had swooped in. "What does Sergei Stepanov have to gain from this?"

"That's the question."

"Could Stepanov have been paying Ramos to do something else? Something we don't see?"

"Maybe," Kristin said, "but for a quarter million I'd expect to find something that benefits either MirGaz or Russia in a big way. MirGaz doesn't ship anything down there. There's nothing."

"Are there a lot like this?"

"Enough of them. It's creepy. Now look here."

She turned to page 30 in the dossier: In 2017, Skorost Endeavor, a Singapore-registered shell company that Noah had identified as a cutout for

MirGaz, had bought twenty-two acres in Lekki, Nigeria. "This parcel of land is right on the Gulf of Guinea. Beachfront property in the free trade zone. MirGaz walks in and, with government approval, purchases half a kilometer of waterfront property."

"Oil?"

She shook her head. "They haven't filed for drilling rights, even though the Niger Delta is peppered with rigs. No one knows what's going on at the site. But what's interesting," she said, turning to the next page, which was a photostat of a patent application with drawings of cylinders and propellers, "is this. Skorost bought this patent back in 2015."

"What is it?"

"An industrial-sized drone with some new kind of propeller. Look here." She pointed to a column on the top right, listing Nexus Technologies as the primary applicant for the patent.

Milo rubbed his face, thinking back to Alan's intelligence on Gilbert Powell, founder of Nexus. "So MirGaz and Nexus are using the same cutout. One for beachfront property in Africa, the other for patents?"

"Yes."

"Any other companies using Skorost?"

"Not many," she said. "MirGaz, Nexus, the shippers from Oman—Salid Logistics—"

"Tóuzī?" he cut in, remembering Leticia's investigation.

"Yes, actually. They used Skorost for a land purchase on Sakhalin Island."

"Okay," Milo said, and for the first time in a while felt like things might be coming together. They were dealing with transactions on a global scale, run through a handful of cutouts like Skorost. It was a start. "Fill in Leticia— she'll want to know about Tóuzī and the Nigeria angle."

"I did that hours ago," Kristin said, making him feel even more useless than before.

To his surprise, Milo found Keller still at the desk, but now looking over his list, carefully going through names. Discarded on the bed was the notebook he'd been scribbling in earlier. He'd been drawing caricatures of Milo, Noah, and Kristin. They were very good.

"Do you have something?" Milo asked.

"No," Keller said. "But I'm trying."

"Thanks." Milo sat on the bed. "Tell me—have you ever heard of Skorost Endeavor?"

Keller furrowed his brow. "Skorost? What's that?"

"A Singapore-based company doing things for MirGaz, Nexus, and a couple of other companies."

"Nexus? You mean the social media company?"

"Yes."

"But my kids use that."

Milo raised his hands. "I don't know what it means, but both companies are using Skorost. Nexus for patents, and MirGaz is buying land in Nigeria. Any idea why?"

Keller shrugged. "Oil?"

"Maybe, but they haven't asked for drilling rights. Not yet, at least. We're also finding MirGaz is paying out money that seems to benefit companies that MirGaz has no stakes in. Oman, for instance. A shipping company called Salid Logistics."

Keller thought a moment. "Where did you get this?"

"From someone who was collecting information for years."

"Who?"

"Anna Usurov," Milo said.

Keller's face stuck, the muscle in his jaw tightening, and Milo feared the memory of that night at the Moscow Ritz might throw him into another funk. After a moment, Keller whispered, "But she's dead. Isn't she?"

"We found her research."

Keller only nodded.

"Why would Sergei Stepanov pay out this kind of money to benefit other people?" Milo asked. "What's the connection?"

Keller looked down at Milo's fist, which still clutched Usurov's information. "Let me see."

"Just tell me, Joseph. What's the connection between Stepanov and Nexus and Salid Logistics?"

Keller folded his hands in his lap, raising his eyes from the file. "MirGaz is global. Okay? Sergei goes to Davos every year. Drinks with titans of industry from all over the world. They make deals. It gets complicated. You're just missing the connections. Maybe I can find them."

"Poitevin," they heard, and turned to see Noah in the doorway gripping the satellite phone.

Milo came over and put it to his ear. "Yes?"

On the staticky line from Shanghai, Poitevin sounded out of breath. "It's Kanni."

"What about her?"

"Trouble."

30

Leticia cleared border control at Shanghai Pudong International, which proved that the German passport Milo's people had scrounged up was good enough to get her into China . . . but would it get her out once she'd dealt with Liu Wei? A question for later. For now, she sailed through customs and found Poitevin waiting at arrivals, looking small and wired in his heavy coat. She remembered him from Tokyo, hovering on the periphery of her meeting with the Cabinet Intelligence and Research Office. When she approached, he said, "Where is your luggage?"

"They lost it in Seoul," she said, and saw him relax.

"I'm looking forward to working with you, Kanni," he said, using the Library cryptonym Milo had handed her before she left; she hated it.

As they stood in the taxi queue, the cool night breeze off the Yellow Sea washing over them, Poitevin whispered to her that Tóuzī's office was located in Lujiazui, on the eastern bank of the Huangpu River, where new skyscrapers grew wildly.

Leticia knew Lujiazui; it was the new China, built up since the nineties to overshadow the old financial district of the Bund, that reminder of foreign domination on the western side of the river. As they climbed into an overheated taxi, her phone rang. It was Kristin, calling to tell her about the link between Skorost Endeavor and four companies: MirGaz, Nexus, Salid Logistics, and Tóuzī. "What does that mean?" she asked.

"We don't know. But MirGaz purchased twenty-two acres of Nigerian coastal land using Skorost."

"Why?"

"Again, it's a mystery."

"I'll put it to Liu Wei," Leticia said, then hung up.

As the taxi worked its way north, she gazed out the window at the modern city full of afternoon activity. She'd been to Shanghai plenty of times before—any serious Asia work seemed to bring her through Shanghai's golden streets—but she'd never loved the place. She'd once spent weeks in Xi'an, inland, and compared to that austerity Shanghai was a gaudy whore that had nothing to do with the Chinese culture she'd been fond of.

The Mandarin Oriental, a block off of the Huangpu, was right in the thick of the action. They were a quick walk from the Times Finance Center, Foxconn, China Minsheng Bank, Huaxia, and, on the fifth floor of the China Development Bank Tower, Tóuzī.

"I'm going to need a nap," she admitted as they got out. "It was a long flight."

Poitevin shrugged. "I'll look around some more. See what I can find."

"Whatever suits you," she said, then went inside to get her key.

Her room was expansive, with a view of the Huangpu and the watercraft of the rich lazily floating by. She hadn't stayed in a posh place for nearly six months, and the sheets reminded her why she missed it: the smell. Large-screen TVs and fully stocked fridges didn't do much for her, but the smell of overpriced soaps and linens made the cost worth it. "I'll have *you*," she told the enormous bathtub, suddenly feeling the exhaustion of the long flight that she'd been pushing back ever since landing.

When she woke, it was after midnight, the city now a firmament of lights through the window, and the bathwater had gone cold. Someone was banging on her door. She threw on her robe and found Poitevin in the corridor. Looking at his wild eyes, she first thought he was loaded, but he was only excited. "Yanlord Garden."

"What?"

"Yanlord Garden—that's where he's staying."

It turned out that Poitevin was less inept than he appeared. He'd left the hotel and headed straight to the China Development Bank Tower, where he'd ridden up to the fifth floor and talked his way inside with a story about scouting investments for a Chinese-American billionaire.

"Did it work?"

"No. They're not interested. I just wanted to get inside and note names and faces. There are only three people in their big office—the secretary, a mainlander who kicked me out, and a Pole named Kowalczyk."

"A Pole?"

"Strange, yes? And lucky—he wasn't hard to pick out of a crowd. So I waited downstairs for him to leave. Followed him over to the riverside, all the way to the Paulaner Bräuhaus, where he met at one of those wooden tables with . . ." His dramatic pause was a little too self-conscious.

"Liu Wei," Leticia said dryly.

A big smile. "I had a beer, and when they split up I followed Liu Wei back to Yanlord Garden, West Gate. Huge place."

"Do you know which apartment he's in?"

Poitevin smiled and opened his hands. "Right on the buzzer."

"So you're not just a pretty face."

She dressed quickly, and they walked the half hour down the Yincheng Middle Road to reach Yanlord Garden. The midnight cold bit, and the streets were empty save for early-morning workers trickling out of busses. Poitevin was upbeat and eager, and she asked how much time he'd spent in China.

"I've only been here once for the Library," he told her. "Courier job."

"Is Milo afraid of China?"

"Just careful," he said, then lowered his voice: "Guoanbu."

Xin Zhu, Leticia thought. That's who Milo was afraid of. "Was anyone following you?" she asked.

"What?"

"The Pole stood out, but so did you. Were you *followed*?"

"I don't think so."

It was as honest an answer as she could expect, and as they made their way across the enormous park reserved for Yanlord's residents she thought she could hear in the cold stillness the aperture shift of surveillance cameras and the wet movement of eyes watching them.

Poitevin brought her to a high tower on the southern end of the estate. Once they reached the foyer, she told Poitevin to stand down. "We don't need to both go up there."

"What am I going to do?"

"You're going to keep an eye out."

He sighed, as if he weren't getting the respect he deserved for all he'd done, but then he shrugged. "Milo told me to follow your lead."

"He did?" she asked, surprised.

She left Poitevin in the foyer, and in the cramped elevator pressed 16. It was a long, slow ride, and Leticia wondered how many crappy elevators, in how many cities, she'd ridden. Sometimes, like now, she rode them to interrogate people; a handful of times she'd headed up to kill someone. Other times she rode aspirationally, to collect payment for work done.

As she passed the twelfth floor, her phone vibrated. She answered it and heard gasping, the sound of someone running. "What?" she said.

"It's a trap," said Poitevin. "Get out of there."

Leticia slapped the emergency-stop button, but it was too late. She'd arrived at the sixteenth floor, and the elevator lurched to a halt with a loud bang. She took a breath as the doors opened, and she found herself looking into the face of a young Chinese man in a black turtleneck gripping an automatic pistol in both hands, pointing somewhere around her stomach. Behind him stood two more men, also in turtlenecks, as if they were members of a boy band, but one that only played death metal.

"Gàn," Leticia said, which was as close to "fuck" as she knew in Mandarin.

31

Alexandra's apartment smelled musty, and when she went to open the window she needed to bang on the frame to shake it loose. She'd lived there for nearly twenty years, having bought it with the bonus that had followed her work on the successful defense of a TransBank CEO for insider trading. "Ill begotten," her father had called the place when he visited on a rainy afternoon and made the offer of a job. It was wrong, he told her, that a banker could walk for financial crimes, while a teenager from the estates could spend a year in jail for smoking a blunt. "Don't you want to be on the right side of history?" he'd asked in his high-bred Russian.

"I want to be on the right side of my bank account," she'd answered, but that was just her wanting to get one over on the old man.

A decade and a half later, she put on some tea to brew and opened up her computer on the kitchen counter. She closed a tab for the RSPCA, where she'd been looking at a particularly adorable Shiba Inu, and did a quick search for Conservative MP Catherine Booth, age thirty-nine, narrow-gauge glasses and severe dark bangs. She'd been representing Sheffield Hallam since 2015, when she'd run on bank deregulation and the review of the National Curriculum. After winning, she aligned herself closely with the Brexit camp. Her office, Alexandra found, was among the overflows in Portcullis House. And there was a telephone number.

It took her a while to get through the Westminster switchboard, but eventually she was speaking to a soft-sounding young man who took the

MP's calls. She caught a whiff of tension in his lower octaves when she said she was writing a series on the history of the Brexit campaign for *The Guardian.*

"Hasn't that been beaten into the ground?" he asked.

"We've uncovered a fresh angle."

"Yes?" he asked. "Not the Russians, I hope."

"No," she told him. "Worse."

That earned her a respectful pause. Then: "What could be worse?"

"Many things. But I'd prefer to speak about it with the MP."

"*Guardian,* you said?"

"Yes, but I'm freelance."

"And what did you say your name was?"

She hadn't, but she had a name ready. "Vivian Wall." It was a legend that she had used now and then when they wanted to get information out to the public quickly. And when Booth's soft-spoken gatekeeper Googled the name—which she guessed he was doing at that very moment—he would find two recent pieces, one in *The Telegraph,* the other in *The Times of Israel.*

There—a quick intake of breath. He now knew from the sensational by-lines that Vivian Wall wasn't someone to brush off. "Yes, well. I do have an opening tomorrow morning. Can you be at Portcullis by eight-thirty? Twenty minutes, then she needs to be in a meeting. Will that do?"

"Why, yes, it will. Thank you very much."

She went out for sushi and had a nice chat with a Bolivian banker she would have taken home, were it not for her morning meeting. Instead she went for a half bottle of rioja in front of the telly, absorbing the news of the world. A far-right candidate was set to win the presidential election in Brazil. Nigerian pirates had kidnapped the crew of a Swiss cargo ship. In the States, a Supreme Court nominee was being accused of sexual assault, while over in Afghanistan a protest against Northwell International soldiers had turned violent; three Afghans had been killed.

She thought of wily Leticia Jones, whom she'd spent a few hours speaking with in that Zürich hospital. She still didn't entirely trust the woman, but felt like she understood her a little better. Leticia was, as Milo used to be, an action-oriented human being, but unlike Milo, Leticia felt obligated to take responsibility for things that weren't her fault, or even her business. Alexandra disagreed. The world was as it was, and to think she could change it was hubris—which was the perfect word to describe Leticia Jones, and, before life had knocked him down a few pegs, her brother, Milo.

In the morning, she disembarked from the bus in front of Portcullis House fifteen minutes early. Across busy Great George Street, Big Ben was covered in scaffolding, looking like a half-undressed monster. On the ground floor, she showed a clerk her Vivian Wall press papers, had her photo taken for security, and was asked to wait in the large glass-ceilinged atrium. She took a seat at one of the scattered tables, looking up at the muddy sky, then eyed young people sipping coffee and communing with their phones. She checked her own. Nothing from Milo. So in preparation for her conversation she started a recording app that ran in the background, then switched over to her email.

"Ms. Wall?" asked a thin voice. She looked up to find the bangs and narrow glasses of Catherine Booth. An unsure smile and an outstretched hand.

Alexandra rose and took the hand. "Ms. Booth, pleased to meet you."

Though she'd assumed she'd be whisked upstairs to an office, she was wrong. Catherine Booth sank into a chair, touched her fingertips together, and looked into Alexandra's eyes in the manner of a born politician: *I'm hearing you.* "Nigel mentioned something about the Brexit vote?"

"Yes," Alexandra said, then touched her phone on the table. "Do you mind?"

"I'd rather not," Booth said without hesitation.

"Of course." Alexandra pushed the phone to the side but still near. "I'm actually not interested in Brexit."

"No?" A hint of surprise, but only a hint.

"I'm working on a story about Joseph Keller. A British accountant who worked at MirGaz in Moscow until he disappeared a month ago. An Interpol Red Notice was issued for him."

Booth's face, smooth from a lifetime of creams and shade, did not reveal a thing. "Yes?" she asked.

"My understanding," Alexandra said, "is that the request for the Red Notice came from your office. From you, in fact."

Finally, Booth's face changed, but it was so well trained that Alexandra could find no irritation in it. "Your story," she said. "It's not about Brexit but about Joseph Keller."

"Correct."

"And what, specifically, about him?"

"The charge against him has to do with computer hacking. However, I can find no one in law enforcement who has any record of it. No complaints. No warrants. Nothing."

There—a momentary hesitation, a decision being made. Booth nodded, pursing her lips, then spoke gently. "Well, there wouldn't be. The intelligence on him didn't come from the Met."

"Who did it come from?"

"From the intelligence services."

"Special Branch? MI6?"

"I'm afraid that's all I can tell you, Ms. Wall. Official secrets and such."

"Then perhaps you can explain why the notice was withdrawn only a couple of days later. I'm unable to track the original notice down, just a record that it existed. Was Keller found?"

"It was taken care of, Ms. Wall. That's all I'm at liberty to say."

"I understand," Alexandra said. "But the notice *was* a public document, and as such it calls for some sort of explanation. Is there someone from the intelligence services I could speak to, who would be cleared to say *something* on the record?"

Catherine Booth drummed her nails on the edge of the table, just once, then nodded. "I'll have my people check on that and get back to you. Do we have your number?"

"Nigel does."

"And an address?"

Alexandra almost hesitated. "I'm staying at a friend's now."

Booth nodded again and rose, sticking out her hand. In the distance, Alexandra noticed, a young man with a sad mustache and an iPad was looking on expectantly—Nigel, she guessed. As they shook hands, Booth said, "A pleasure, Ms. Wall. I don't suppose you're one of my constituents, are you?"

"If I lived in Sheffield Hallam, I wouldn't be getting up this early to chase leads."

Booth let out a full, throaty laugh. "Well, fortune favors the bold. And if it weren't for Oliver, I wouldn't be able to live there either."

"Oliver Booth?" Alexandra said, only now making the connection that she should have made long ago. "Of TransBank?"

"You know of him," Booth said, then shrugged. "My husband has always been more recognizable than me, sadly."

"He's in London?"

Booth frowned. "Berlin, I'm afraid. Do take care."

Alexandra watched Booth join Nigel, and as they walked away the assistant glanced warily back at Alexandra. He had the expression of someone who was being scolded for putting a nutter onto his boss's busy schedule. But she didn't care. She remembered Oliver Booth very well. The bonus she'd gotten from helping represent his business partner, Sir Edward Acton, had bought her a lovely old flat in Hampstead.

32

"What?" Alan called, then shut off the noisy blender, opened it, and added two tablespoons of protein powder to his morning mix.

"Can you make it?" Penelope called from the living room.

"To what?"

"The Met."

Right, the gala charity dinner, five hundred dollars a plate, all proceeds going to a legal fund for Honduran refugees stuck in southern-border cages run by private prison companies—it was boom time for the incarceration business. "Thursday, right?"

"Tomorrow."

"Sure. Okay. But I can't stay long."

Penelope appeared in the doorway, her clothes looking slightly off. "You *have* to come."

"Why?"

"Because we just got the best news—Gilbert Powell confirmed he's coming."

"*The* Gilbert Powell?"

"Is there any other?"

What were the chances? Gilbert Powell had only come to their attention in the last forty-eight hours, and now he was showing up at Penelope's charity evening?

"See?" she said. "I deal with important people, too."

He came close, eyeing her, then reached out and adjusted a shoulder strap on her complicated blouse—a mildly S&M mix of sheer fabric and dark straps. Half an inch to the right, and everything settled into place. "Very nice," he said, then kissed her on the lips.

"You're diverting," she said. "I know you don't like these people, but they're no worse than UN diplomats."

"That's not a compliment," he said, "but I'll be there."

Once she left, Alan drank his smoothie and looked through the news. It was all hell in a handbasket, but he was still optimistic. Despite insurgent patrons and a temporary headquarters move, the Library remained solid, and the fact that Washington hadn't revived the Department of Tourism was stellar news after having lived the previous week looking over his shoulder, always expecting to find one of those dead-eyed monsters on his tail.

He had changed into sweats for a morning jog when the buzzer rang. A familiar woman's voice said, "Mr. Drummond, may I come up?"

Beatriz Almeida was one of the less diplomatic diplomats he worked with, but she had never crossed the line by appearing at his home. Just as he would never consider heading over to the Portuguese complex of apartments on Madison. But he said, "Of course," and buzzed her up.

He was waiting at his open door when she stepped out of the elevator and looked around hesitantly before finding him. Noting his old sweats, she gave him an awkward smile, and when he asked if she'd like some tea her wary expression suggested she'd never been offered a drink before.

"No, thank you. I'll only be a minute."

"Have a seat, then," he said, motioning her to a chair.

As she settled in, Almeida crossed her hands on her knees and gave him a stiff smile. "Alan," she said with finality. "I have come to ask you about Joseph Keller."

He and Milo had never revealed that name to the patrons. "Who?"

"Please, Alan. We are not stupid. Milo Weaver gives us information, we compare notes, and we realize that he has found Egorov's man in Algiers, and his name is Joseph Keller."

Alan wondered how he should reply. Play dumb? He'd done that plenty of times, but in this case he sensed it would be self-defeating. Milo had gotten Keller's name from the Germans, and Almeida had probably gotten it from Katarina Heinold. So: "He's being kept safe."

"Where?"

"I don't know," he lied.

"Is he with Milo?"

"Like I said, I don't know."

"Then where is Milo?"

Alan blinked slowly at her. "There was an attempt on his life."

"Yes," she said, impatient, "but where *is* he?"

"In hiding."

"And you don't know where."

"I don't need to know," he said, then switched gears. "But one thing I do know is that you have made our work far more difficult."

She touched a hand to her chest, all innocence. *"Me?"*

Christ, but these people could be trying. "You picked up Diogo Moreira. We were very clear—none of those people should be taken into custody. You just raised the stakes unnecessarily. You've increased the danger to Milo, to myself, and the entire Library."

The accusation didn't have much of an effect. Almeida lowered her hand to her knee and said, "Are you sure about that?" When Alan didn't reply, she went on. "Yes, we took him. We were afraid of what NATO secrets he had given, and could still give, to Putin. We interrogated him. We searched his home and office. Brought in his wife and daughters. Went through every bank account associated with anyone in his family. And do you know what we found?" She didn't wait for a guess. "Nothing."

"These people are good," Alan told her.

"Not that good. We left no stone unturned." She sniffed. "Perhaps there was a mistake?"

It didn't make sense to Alan. Certainly they would find evidence of payments to Diogo Moreira—you can't just hide the three quarters of a million dollars Keller's list documented. Sistema de Informações da República Portuguesa, or SIRP, knew its job. "I don't know what to tell you," he said, which was true enough.

"It turns out Mr. Moreira is actually very upstanding. He takes a strong stance against the tide of chaos spreading across the globe."

"Then I suppose you made a mistake, didn't you?"

She glared at him, then glanced down and picked something—lint?—off her knee and flicked it away. "How can Mr. Weaver run the Library if he's in hiding?"

Alan tried for a nonchalant shrug. "It can be done."

"But not well," she said, as if she knew. "Shouldn't you take over for him? As his deputy that would be natural."

"When it becomes necessary, I will. But it's not necessary yet."

She nodded with satisfaction. Everything, apparently, was clear now. She raised her chin, looking down her broad nose at him, and stood. Another stiff smile, and then she headed back to the front door. He followed. She paused at the door and looked up at him. "The next time you speak to him, let Milo know that the patrons are worried for him. We offer all our resources to help. Do not hesitate to ask us."

"We won't," he assured her.

He opened the door. After giving him one more stiff smile, she took the hint and left. Alan sighed. His morning run was now out of the question.

An hour later, he watched two high school groups, one from Harlem and another from Queens, fill the UN lobby with chatter and cell phone alerts. Four teachers tag-teamed, running around the students, pointing forcefully and demanding a silence they would never get. Alan grinned at the sight as he showed his ID to the guard and headed through to the elevators.

While Milo had an innate fondness for Said Bensoussan's sense of style, that very quality made Alan wary. He'd spent much of his early career working with politicians from the Midwest, where slick old men learned how to charm you to the gills while laying traps that sprang to life as soon as you left their Capitol Hill offices. The sweeter they were, the more you had to fear, and in Said Bensoussan he sensed a North African twist on the same thing, from the compliments upon his arrival—"Look at you! You really have been taking care of yourself"—to the obsequious way he offered a drink.

"No, no," Alan told him, holding up a hand.

"Well, then," Bensoussan said, settling in his chair and giving him an *I'm-very-serious-now* expression, "what can I do for you?"

"You can tell me what's going on with Beatriz Almeida."

Bensoussan arched a brow. "How do you mean?"

"She showed up at my home this morning. She's trying to talk me into staging a coup against Milo."

"A *coup*?" Utter shock. "Did she *say* that?"

"Without saying the words, yes. What's going on?"

Bensoussan leaned back in his chair and pinched his lower lip. "Well, Beatriz is famous for her impatience, yes? And you're not the only one she bothers. She was in that same chair yesterday. Impatient."

"Tell me."

"She wants to go back to the budget fight. Demand Milo come to New York so that we can present new arguments." He pinched his lip again, thinking. "Strangely, though, she doesn't have any new arguments."

"But she knows his life is under threat."

"That she does."

"And that forcing him to come to New York would be extremely risky."

"She knows all this."

Alan nodded—they understood each other. "What did you say?"

"I told her I would take it under advisement."

"And have you?"

"Not yet," Bensoussan said. "I'd like to see where things go before committing myself to rash action."

Did this mean that Almeida was actually trying to get Milo killed, or was that just his myopic way of looking at it? Was she angry about the arrest of Diogo Moreira, which had probably cost her some goodwill back in Lisbon? Or was it really just impatience? "Who else?" Alan asked. "Are other patrons on board?"

"I'm not sure," Bensoussan said. "She *has* been lunching with Hilmar and Aku, Katarina as well. Are they discussing Milo? I don't know. But one question I would ask: Who was in her envelope?"

"How do you mean?"

"I just want you to understand," Bensoussan said. "When I received my two names, I was surprised. I knew one of them. He was an old friend, many years ago. No longer. But if I'd been given his name five years ago, when things were better between us, I don't know how I would have acted. Would I have tried to protect him by any means necessary?"

Bensoussan left that question unanswered, and Alan wondered, as he often did, about this patron's motivations. Had Bensoussan told him this in the interests of full disclosure, or was it a play of his own, something to throw suspicion on Beatriz Almeida, to weaken her position?

That was the problem with diplomats and politicians: Nothing they said could be taken at face value. They were worse than spies in that regard, but it was Alan's cursed fate that he would forever work with them.

When he reached the lobby, the children had cleared out, and he was wondering what kind of threat Beatriz Almeida represented. That she *was* a threat wasn't a question—she was. But what kind? It was still so hard to say. Crossing UN Plaza, he called Heeler, one of six librarians who roamed North America. Last he'd checked, she was upstate. "How fast can you get to Manhattan?"

"Three hours, give or take."

"Good," he said. "Check into someplace out of the way and keep an eye on Beatriz Almeida."

"She's a patron."

"I know."

"But the—"

"I *know* the rules, Heeler. But we're moving into uncharted territory."

33

Both Milo and Noah had packed pistols—a SIG Sauer and a Taurus Millennium, respectively—and driven a fast hour and a half from Milan to Turin, where they showed their IDs at the front desk of UNICRI, the UN's Interregional Crime and Justice Research Institute. The low, broad headquarters was old, like a lot of other UN buildings, and they took the stairs to the second floor's rarely used secure communications room. At one end a monitor was bolted to the wall, and its controller was in the center of a long conference table. Noah lowered the blinds as Milo fooled with the controls, trying to pull up a signal.

"Where do I type the conference code?" he asked, puzzled.

"Let me do that."

Noah brought up the menu on the monitor and worked at it, finally pulling up a screen that said WAITING FOR REMOTE HOST and showed, in the lower corner, an image of the two of them in the room.

"Want me to wait outside?" Noah asked.

"No need for him to see your face."

As Noah exited to the corridor, the screen flickered, then lit up with a wide view of a similar conference room in Beijing—similar because it was also a UN space, the Development Program for China. At the Beijing conference table, with a teacup in front of him, sat an old Chinese man, bald and enormous, a man who had once been the most terrifying thing in the world to Milo.

Xin Zhu was the closest Milo had to an enemy. There had been competitors, and there were always threats, but the history between him and the Chinese colonel from the Ministry of State Security was particularly fraught. If given the chance, he knew, Xin Zhu would crush Milo, his family, and the entirety of the Library. By wiping out the Department of Tourism he had proved himself uniquely dangerous—which was why, once he took over the Library, Milo had put every effort into finding a way to neutralize the old man. After initially blackmailing Xin Zhu, he'd meticulously documented each of their interactions. By now he had an entire book of evidence that, were it slipped to Beijing, could only result in the harsh interrogation and swift execution of the old Chinese colonel. It was the best protection Milo could manage.

"You have not slept," Xin Zhu finally said, his accent thick.

"I've been busy."

"Bad idea," he said. "Rest before negotiations, not after."

"I'm not here to negotiate. I'm here to ask about Leticia Jones."

"Ms. Jones?" Xin Zhu said. A smile.

Xin Zhu was playing with him, and he wasn't sure why. Noah had already communicated the topic of conversation. Still, this was Xin Zhu, who never made things easy. Milo leaned closer. "Leticia Jones has been taken into custody."

"By whom?"

"I was hoping you would know."

Xin Zhu blinked languidly at him, not wanting to fill in the silence. Finally, he sighed and said, "She was in Shanghai. Correct?"

Milo nodded.

"Yanlord Garden. Breaking and entering."

"She wasn't taken by security guards, was she?"

Xin Zhu smiled again, broader now. "Leticia Jones taken by security guards. Imagine!" He shook his head. "No, of course not."

"Your people? Guoanbu?"

Xin Zhu cleared his throat and leaned back, regarding Milo warily. "From what I can tell, no, we do not have her. Nor does the Ministry of Public Security—I called Pudong precinct myself."

"Do they know anything about her?"

Xin Zhu didn't answer. He reached for his tea, took a sip, and replaced the cup in the saucer. "Do you know of the International Defense Institute?"

Milo did. "Private military training school outside Beijing. Run by Northwell International."

"Their graduates are not only Chinese," Xin Zhu said casually. "They are Japanese, Indonesian, South Korean. More. They are so successful they are building another school on Sakhalin Island, across the border in Russia."

"Sakhalin?" Milo asked, surprised by the coincidence before realizing that it was no coincidence at all, and a new connection was made. He said, "Tóuzī, the development firm, is building it."

A smile. "So you do know something about it."

Not much, Milo thought, but returned to the matter at hand: "So Leticia's been taken by graduates of the IDI?"

"You tell me what she was doing in Yanlord Garden, Milo, and I'll find the answer to your question."

"I'd rather not," Milo said.

Xin Zhu shrugged theatrically, as if to say, *What can I do, then?*

Milo suppressed an urge to shout. He lowered his voice: "I have a book, Xin Zhu. With the press of a button it's published for the world to see."

"It's been ten years, Milo. You don't think I've come up with ways to talk my way out of trouble by now?"

"And each of those ten years you've been helping me. Each year adds a dozen more pages to the book. You'll never be able to talk fast enough."

Xin Zhu frowned, as if this hadn't occurred to him. But of course it had. He never entered a meeting without knowing precisely how it would end. Milo imagined that for a man like Xin Zhu, life was dull and without surprise, but it was also safe.

Milo said, "Sung Hui wouldn't last long without you."

Xin Zhu winced at the mention of his wife, a surprisingly naked emotion from the old man. "I know the names of your family, too, Milo."

"I'm well aware of that."

Xin Zhu sighed. "You do realize, don't you, that one day everything will flip? Black will be white. Victors will be defeated."

"You're nearly seventy, Xin Zhu. You'd better work faster."

Another smile slipped onto the colonel's face. "So. You want me to find Leticia Jones."

"I want you to get her safely out of China."

He opened his large hands. "Do you think that would go unnoticed,

Milo? Northwell has friends in the Central Committee. I will be asked very serious questions."

Milo had considered this on the drive to Turin and had called Kristin to prepare for it. He took a slip of paper from his pocket and said, "I'm going to read you an IP address. It'll give you the excuse you need."

"What is it?"

"A rundown of weaknesses in Japan's domestic intelligence apparatus."

Xin Zhu raised his eyebrows. "You're handing me Japan?"

"A carefully curated list. It will be good enough to justify your help. But not good enough to cause serious trouble."

Xin Zhu sighed heavily. "You must really want Leticia Jones back." When Milo didn't answer, he said, "And that, Milo, is how I will get you in the end."

34

She didn't know if Poitevin had escaped, and this was what troubled her most. The armed boy band shoved her back into the elevator, all three of them squeezed in tight with her, wordless, and pressed the button to return to the ground floor. Their stink filled that cramped space—one of them had an abiding affection for patchouli, while the other two preferred the musk of anxious sweat—and when the doors opened on the ground floor it was a relief to escape the smell, even though each step brought her closer to her destination.

Years ago, when she'd been more impulsive—when she'd been a Tourist—Leticia would have done something. Either in that tiny elevator, where the walls might have worked to her advantage, or along that short walk to the glass front doors, where another armed boy watched—presumably the one Poitevin had spotted. But she'd lost that impulsiveness somewhere along the way, in Nigeria or maybe before. So she let them take her across the park to the white van she hadn't noticed before, and when she looked across the grounds, trying to pierce the darkness with vision that had never, despite rumors, been superhuman, she saw no evidence that Poitevin was out there.

Of course he wasn't. If he hadn't been captured, then he'd gotten his ass the hell out of Shanghai. It's what she would have done, probably.

Maybe.

In the windowless van the stink returned, and they rocked with the bumpy road, taking hard turns that she could only imagine on the knotted map of Shanghai in her head. Certainly they had left Pudong, but had they gone east, or west? Or maybe south, toward Hangzhou Bay? Were they just traveling in circles?

Did it matter? It didn't.

When they finally did stop, the boys sprang to life, hauling her out. They emerged into a basement parking lot, and her fragrant captors hustled her to another elevator—bigger this time, fluorescent bright, with numbers that went up to 72—and it rose so quickly that she felt it in her stomach.

The corridor on the sixty-third floor was white and gray, and they passed office doors with Chinese characters until they reached a door marked with Latin characters: NORTHWELL INTERNATIONAL, LTD. Patchouli opened the door. Together, they entered a dark space full of low cubicles, all empty. Through floor-to-ceiling windows Shanghai glittered, and for a moment she was mesmerized by the beauty, almost forgetting her escorts.

"Sit," Patchouli barked.

He was pointing at an Aeron office chair near the windows.

"No, thanks," Leticia said. "I'd rather stand."

Patchouli looked exasperated by her. He took a step closer. "You sit. You no sit, you go," he said, pointing at the high window.

It was a long way down, so she walked over to the Aeron, sat down, and crossed her legs at the knee. It was as casual a pose as she could find, but it was quickly ruined when Patchouli and the others hurried over with white zip-ties. They bound her hands behind the back of the chair, then crouched and tied her ankles to two of the rollers. Then they spun her around, and Leticia was not happy to see Patchouli holding a syringe in his dirty hand. He roughly pulled the sleeve of her left arm up to her elbow and gave her the injection.

Then he stepped back, eyeing her, and went to join the others, who had settled into chairs around cubicles. One cleaned his fingernails with a knife. It wasn't nice to look at, so Leticia turned to the side to look at the lights of Shanghai as, one by one, they slowly twinkled out.

When she was slapped awake, it was light outside. All those pretty lights had been replaced by the ugly tangle of a modern metropolis, and even more disappointing than that sight was the man who had hit her. A white man of the sort of indeterminate age only wealth allows. From the shape of his shoulders and his buzz-cut scalp above old-acne cheeks, she could tell he had once been a soldier.

"Leticia Jones," the man said, straightening. His accent was American, and his smile wasn't bad. "Nice to meet you. I'm Ted."

"Ted, huh?"

"You feel all right? It was just a mild sedative, until I could get over here. Not sick?"

She shook her head but said nothing.

"Good," he said, taking a step back and glancing out the windows. "Okay, then. Tell me, please, why Milo Weaver is interested in Liu Wei."

"What?"

"You and your partner are working for Milo Weaver," he said, swinging his fingers around as if finding a rhythm in his own words. "You broke into Liu Wei's apartment building with the intent of getting to him. But why? Why does Milo Weaver care about this man? Why does the Library care?"

Leticia tried to hide her surprise. Milo's precious Library was supposed to be a closely guarded secret, so why did this asshole know about it? And despite the stupid canine code name, she didn't work for the Library, but Ted assumed she did. It couldn't simply be because she and Milo had met in Wakkanai, could it? Or was it because they knew who Poitevin was and had seen him with her? Given the poor quality of his spycraft, so easy to spot back in Tokyo, that could be it. Really—what kind of half-assed operation had she allied herself with?

She said, "I don't work for Milo Weaver. Coming here was my idea."

"*Your* idea, huh?" She was struck by the way Ted said those words. That doubtful tone—it was a tone she knew well. All her life she'd heard it. "Where'd you get a big idea like looking into someone else's business?"

Yes, that was the tone all right. This was what she'd meant when she'd used the word "racism" with Milo a week ago. This Caucasian, like others before him, had misjudged Leticia, and she'd made a career out of using that to her advantage. She said, "Borno, Nigeria."

Ted straightened, looking surprised, so she went on.

"I followed a money trail from Boko Haram to Liu Wei."

Ted chewed his lower lip, concerned. "How much of this does Milo Weaver know?"

"Why are you so worried about Milo, Ted? Big guy like you, you've got everything under control."

The answer stunned him briefly; then he cracked a grin. "Yes, Leticia, we do. But when this much money is involved, you have to have it more than under control. You need to have it locked up."

"And you don't? You've got the power of Northwell International behind you. That's no small thing. And I . . ." Leticia stiffened, a sudden realization dawning on her. "Oh, shit," she said, and almost laughed.

"What is it?" Ted asked.

She shook her head and told him something she knew he would believe: "I'm stupid."

"Don't tell me that, now."

But she *was* stupid, she now saw. It had taken her too long to make the obvious connection. Milo hadn't made it either. She said, "A woman named Joan tried to get me to work with you. She said she was from DC, but she wasn't. Not at all. Not the Bureau, not the Agency, not Homeland. No, she was Northwell all along."

Ted scratched the side of his neck, but from the calm expression on his face she knew he didn't care what she'd put together. Because he'd never planned to let her leave this office alive. That was bad news, but here she was, and, tied up, there was nothing she could do about it. So she filed that fact away for the moment and decided she might as well satisfy her curiosity.

"Tell me, Ted. Why is Liu Wei sending money to Boko Haram? How does kidnapping little girls help Tóuzī?"

Ted shrugged. "That's beyond my pay grade."

She smiled at him. "And here I was thinking you were the captain."

She heard movement and looked over to see Patchouli straighten suddenly, put a finger to his ear, and leave the room in a hurry. Ted either didn't notice or didn't care. He stepped right up to her, and when he leaned close and gently reached out to her face she steeled herself. With a thumb, he wiped some sweat from her cheek. Very seriously, he said, "Leticia, it's time to talk. It's time for you to tell me everything."

"I don't know much, Ted. Remember, I'm stupid."

He smiled, then walked slowly around the chair until he had disappeared behind her. "Milo Weaver and the Library aren't worth dying for."

Ted was right. But Ted and Northwell International weren't worth dying for either. The dilemma now wasn't how to survive this office. It was how to die with the least amount of embarrassment.

"So you think you know about Northwell?" his voice said.

"Sure. Rent-a-soldiers."

He leaned close, his breath wet and warm on the back of her ear. "We're much more than that, Ms. Jones. People hear us coming, they run."

She stopped herself from laughing—that was how Tourists thought of themselves, back in the day. "You're not magic."

"Magic," he hummed into her ear. "Maybe you've got some of that black girl magic I've been hearing about. Think I'd find some if I—" In a remarkably fast move, he grabbed the hair at the base of her skull, squeezed it tight, and with his other hand brought a knife to rest against her cheek. Her hair follicles ached, and the knife, which was cool at first, quickly warmed to the temperature of her hot skin. He whispered into her ear: "If I dig deep, will I find some magic?"

Despite her fatalism, and her conviction that she would never leave here, Ted's ham-fisted threat was disheartening. She could make peace with death, even find some dignity in it, but *damn*—she really didn't want *this* asshole to be the one who finally took her out.

Then she heard—heard because she couldn't turn her head to look—the door open and a group of people enter. Among them, she smelled Patchouli. The grip on her head dropped away, and she turned to see Patchouli with two more Chinese men and a Chinese woman, who snapped in Mandarin at the American. Her accent wasn't easy, but Leticia made out *This isn't your country*.

"Who gives a shit about countries anymore?" Ted asked in English. "Who the fuck *are* you?"

35

Alexandra had to drive north two and a half hours to reach Salperton in the Cotswolds, where Sir Edward Acton lived in semiretirement on farmland that had been in his family for three generations. Lord of the manor, so to speak, though she was struck, as she drove up the pitted, wet road to the mansion, by how the English seemed to take dilapidated as a model design choice. How much would it cost to bring a bricklayer in to fix the crumbling walls and lay down a bit of asphalt so visitors' transmissions didn't prematurely expire?

But it wasn't an aesthetic choice, not really. It was the fear of having a home that looked new, the fear of looking like new money, a crime far worse than the insider trading Alexandra and her colleagues had defended Sir Acton against those many years ago.

Though he was in his midsixties, he looked much as he had nearly two decades ago. The only sign of those extra years was the care in his movements. Almost wariness. The same could not be said of his speech, which had become blunter.

"I didn't like your defense. I told Freddy as much. Demanded he take you off of the team."

This wasn't news to her. Frederick Berg, the Berg half of Berg & DeBurgh, had passed Acton's complaints on to Alexandra with one of his *Freddy's-feeling-guilty* expressions. Of course, the defense had been a group decision, and Freddy had brought her in at the last moment, but because she was the only woman on the team, Acton had zeroed in on her for blame. "You didn't serve any jail time," she reminded him. "We considered that a win."

"Some things are worse than jail."

They were sitting on the cracked stone veranda, bundled in coats, and a young man in a white shirt brought them biscuits and hot tea that quickly went cold. Their view of the hills was obscured by an ancient barn that had partially collapsed. As far as she could tell, the Actons had no animals. She said, "But you *were* guilty, Sir Edward."

"So?"

"And you'd done a lousy job covering up for yourself. The only other option was to attack the investigators who'd uncovered it, and TransBank didn't want to play dirty."

Acton shook his head. "What a difference time makes, eh? Manners have gone out the window."

"You got off with a fine," she reminded him.

"There were *protesters*." He pointed. "Right out by the gate. Labour communists. Angry at me for not moving to prison. Did they come after you?"

She shook her head.

He frowned as if she'd made his point and said, "It looked *bad*."

She wanted to say, *It made you look exactly as you were,* but held her tongue.

"I read your piece in *The Telegraph*," Alexandra told him. "About Oliver Booth. You called him a traitor for his position on Brexit."

"Oliver Booth was a traitor then, and he remains one."

"But he wasn't the only person in favor of leaving the European Union."

"Of course not. But he was one of the few who would willingly take that public position and represent it as the position of TransBank, when he knew Brexit would destroy the company. The shareholders were beside themselves."

"Then how did he justify it?"

"The same way everyone did—invented statistics and made-up facts. But the board wasn't made up of the rabble, you understand. And Oliver wasn't some backwoods nationalist. Every year he goes to Davos to brush shoulders with the foreigners. The man made no sense."

"You could have voted him out."

He rocked his head. "Yes, of course. But we didn't think the referendum would go the way it did, did we? No one did. And if the referendum failed, we would have had an enormous public fight for no good reason. You see? When the market smells blood, it attacks. No one wanted their shares to plummet."

"And then the referendum did pass."

Acton rubbed his forehead, now looking as if the years had finally caught up with him. "Yes."

"And?"

He sipped his cold tea. "Many of us wanted to vote him out. Others felt this would be rash. Again, in all honesty, they were driven by short-term fear for their shares' value. Maybe the effect of leaving the Common Market wouldn't be as drastic as we'd feared."

"Which camp were you in?"

"It doesn't matter," he said, waving it away, and she felt like she had her answer. "The important point is that the effects of the referendum passing *were* as bad as we'd imagined. Our European clients began pulling out, as did the Americans, Russians, Chinese, Japanese. The UK's banking laws are some of the most welcoming in the world, and for decades we've been the world's access point to the Common Market. That was going to end, and so they simply moved to the mainland."

Alexandra had heard plenty of stories like these. The looming deadline for Brexit, set for the coming March, was like a curtain hiding the future. No one knew for sure what post-Brexit Britain would look like, and there wasn't a business on earth that liked uncertainty.

"So," he said with a sigh, "we finally gathered everyone at headquarters and voted Oliver out."

"Really? I didn't know."

He smiled thinly. "No, I'm sure you didn't. The problem was that we had waited too long. When presented with the vote, he put his lawyers in motion to stall us, and at the same time he presented to the board an offer from a German bank to buy us out." He shook his head. "*Germans!* Bloody travesty."

Alexandra had spent last night looking through all of this and at least had the public history down. She said, "Investition für Wirtschaft."

"Investment for Economy," he translated. "IfW. There was an uproar. Then Oliver produced a preliminary outlook he'd commissioned. At the rate our clients were leaving us, within six months our shares would drop by half.

IfW, he told us, did not have access to these numbers, and if we acted quickly they would never see them until it was too late. Either sell now and keep our shirts, or wait and lose them."

"And that worked?" she asked.

"It was close," Acton said, rubbing his cheek as he remembered. "One-vote margin. Within a month the Germans owned us."

"A month? That's fast."

"Indeed. The bastard had been laying the groundwork long beforehand. Within a week he was on the IfW board." He grunted. "What Hitler hadn't been able to do by bombing us every day for eight months, IfW accomplished in days, with the help of their own Lord Haw-Haw. If you'll excuse me."

She'd thought he was excusing what he'd called Booth, but he was rising from his chair.

"Bloody age," he said, and left her, assumedly to empty his bladder.

Alexandra gazed out at the barn. The collapsed half looked as if it had been hit by a meteor, but no—it had fallen apart because it had been ig-nored, the same way people like Acton had ignored the British economy. They hadn't bothered with the structural supports that kept strangers above water; people like Acton only fretted when the economy stopped working for them and their small circle of friends.

The thing was, all those backwoods nationalists, the ones he derided—they weren't stupid. After being ignored for generations, they'd risen up even while the wise men in tweed advised against it. They didn't vote leave despite the wise men in tweed advising against it but *because* the wise men in tweed advised against it.

And now the collapse was gaining steam, and hard truths were coming to light. Men like Acton, once respected on the global stage, were discovering that the rest of the world looked at them the way he looked at that barn—useful not for its structural integrity but for ease of access, for the clout it gave them. Now that the UK economy was crumbling, the world was leaving in a hurry, before the roof collapsed on their heads.

Why did it never occur to anyone to stay, to raise a fucking ladder and climb up and replace the rotting wood?

"So you wrote an editorial," she said when he returned and settled down. "And that's why you were voted out?"

Acton shook his head. "No bloody reason to be on the board anyway.

Decisions are made in Berlin. Oliver spends half his time there, making decisions for the London office."

Alexandra closed her eyes, a thought coming on. Then she opened them. "Tell me—the companies that left TransBank. Where did they go?"

"To the Continent. I said that."

"To IfW?"

Acton shrugged, eyes big, looking momentarily silly. "Some, yes. That American mercenary outfit—*Northwell*. That was his oldest client, more than ten years. A few others."

"MirGaz?" she asked.

He nodded. "Yes, I believe so." He thought a moment. "Yes, actually. It was Oliver who had brought both accounts to TransBank in the first place. Them and . . . what's that social media company . . . ?"

"Nexus?" she asked.

"That's it."

"And then they *all* went with him to IfW?"

Acton squinted at her, raising his chin. "Not *with,* exactly. They moved to IfW after the Brexit vote, before IfW purchased TransBank and promoted Oliver."

"All in the space of a month," she said, "the Brexit vote happens, Booth's clients move to IfW, and IfW buys out TransBank." Alexandra was in awe of that timing. Acton, too, seemed stunned, as if this were the first time anyone had laid it out so simply. She looked at him a moment, then said, "Oliver really had been laying the groundwork for a long time, hadn't he?"

Manor living had done a job on Sir Edward Acton, distancing him from the realities of the modern world, but it hadn't quite broken him yet. He sat up and leaned against the wrought-iron table. She finally had his full attention.

36

Heeler was one of Alan's recruits, a thirtysomething Indian-American who had worked for the FBI's SWAT team until July 2017, when she'd taken part in the well-publicized attack on a Massive Brigade safe house in Watertown, South Dakota—an attack that had gone pear-shaped quickly, resulting in the deaths of nine young people. She'd watched all this with growing disgust, blaming herself for taking part in the raid, and after six sessions with a Bureau therapist decided to resign.

Alan had gotten her name while at dinner with an old colleague who had entered the Bureau with the new administration. He was a weathered Army veteran who had brought up Heeler in the most scathing terms. "What's this new breed? Who do they think they are? In my day, you put your nose down and you *marched*. These days—if I give them orders they'll have to clear it with their shrinks first!"

Unlike his old colleague, Alan had a more complex view of the Watertown raid, and the idea that someone had made the hard choice to leave her chosen career was a sign of rare independence in a section devoted to unblinking compliance. So he tracked her down at a job fair in St. Paul, Minnesota, where they spoke for an hour. He probed her psychological and ideological framework, slipping in the interview questions Alexandra had developed years before. Satisfied, he'd given her a phone number to call. "Wait," she'd said. "I don't know who you are. Who do you work for?"

"Everyone," he'd said, using the reply that he'd grown fond of even if it was wildly inaccurate. "I work for everyone."

"What the hell does that mean?"

"It means that if you're interested, you'll call that number."

A week later, she had, and she now moved fluidly across the continent, taking care of the intricacies of working for *everyone*.

Alan was last-minute shopping for a new jacket to wear that night to the Met when, around two, Heeler called. "Big lunch at Sardi's, private room in the back," she told him.

"How big?"

"Five including her. I sent in photos."

"Do we know names yet?"

"Other than Almeida, I recognized Katarina Heinold and Gilbert Powell."

Portugal, Germany, and Nexus Technologies? "Did Katarina look like she'd been convinced of anything?"

"No idea. But there was a lot of hand-shaking."

"I don't like this," Alan said.

"You don't have to. I'm staying with Almeida."

Alan sent a request for Noah to forward Heeler's photos to him once everyone had been identified, and by the time he had paid for his new blazer and found a taxi on Fifth, his phone pinged with the photos of the sidewalk outside Sardi's. There was Beatriz Almeida chatting with Gilbert Powell, then Katarina Heinold alongside a woman in a faux-fur coat and glasses, who Noah had ID'd as Grace Foster, a former CIA administrator. With them was a well-dressed and tough-looking man in sunglasses who was "unidentified"—a bodyguard, maybe, or even a Tourist.

Alan called Milo, and as he talked through the photos, Milo pulled them up in the Milan safe house. "Look, I'm going to see Gilbert Powell at Pen's event tonight."

"He'll be there?"

"Signed on last minute. I don't know if he just happened to be in town, or if it has to do with me. I suppose I'll see."

"Careful," Milo said, then: *"Oh."*

"What?" When Milo didn't answer, Alan said, "Everything all right? Keller okay?"

"Yeah," Milo said, his voice oddly subdued. "It's not that."

"Well?"

"This photo," Milo told him. "Grace Foster."

"What about her?"

"That's Jane, the woman who poisoned me. Or Joan, who tried to recruit Leticia for Tourism."

Alan felt a cold tingle cross his scalp. He wasn't sure what to say.

"Really, Alan," he finally said. "Be careful tonight. Keep Heeler around you."

"Yeah," Alan said. "Good idea."

37

Alexandra was talking, but he was having trouble listening. He kept turning to the screen of his laptop, where Grace Foster stood outside Sardi's, smiling, with Gilbert Powell. But he couldn't focus on that either, for he was worried about Leticia. Finally, he walked over to the kitchen, the phone pressed hard to his ear, and started a pot of coffee. "Sorry, Alex. Say it again."

"Okay," she said, then took an audible breath. "Oliver Booth campaigned for Brexit, knowing what it would do to his company, and when Brexit passed he convinced his big accounts, MirGaz and Northwell and Nexus, to move to IfW. Got that?"

"Yeah."

"Then, once the bank was in trouble, he brought in IfW's offer to acquire TransBank. He painted the board into a corner and gave them a deal they couldn't refuse. Now Oliver Booth is running TransBank from his IfW office in Berlin."

Milo was back now. "That's what happened with Asia-Wide and Salid Logistics."

"Exactly what happened. But instead of Brexit, it was piracy."

"Pirates who never took anything."

"Sure," Alexandra said. "And guess where Salid Logistics banks."

"IfW."

"Exactly."

"Okay," Milo said, then sighed.

"What?"

"There's something else."

He told her about Grace Foster meeting with two of their patrons, along with Gilbert Powell. Foster, once of the CIA, who had tried to kill him on a plane flight to Berlin and tried to recruit Leticia to join this new outfit called Tourism.

She exhaled loudly. "Alan said the Agency hadn't started up Tourism again."

"Maybe he was wrong," Milo said. "Catch a morning flight to Zürich, and I'll pick you up."

"I'll just fly to Milan."

"No," he said. "We don't need to draw attention to this city."

"Oh," she said, a note in her voice as she got it. "Say hi to the girls for me."

She had him. The path to Zürich would take him past Locarno, close enough to Tina and Stephanie to make a visit obligatory. He would leave soon and spend the night.

As he was looking for milk for his coffee, Noah came in and placed a sheet of paper on the counter. On it was a page from *The Punch,* a Nigerian daily newspaper, from August 2017.

NEW RUSSIAN FACTORY PROMISES JOBS was the headline, and below it was a photo of the Nigerian interior minister shaking hands with a man in his forties identified as Yuri Kozlov, regional manager of MirGaz.

"That's the land purchase?" Milo asked. "The twenty-two acres?"

"Forget about the land," Noah said, and pointed to the Russians and Nigerians crowded in the background of the photo-op. He touched his finger to an old man, sad looking, a big gray face he'd only met once but could still identify immediately.

"That's Kirill Egorov," Milo said.

"Gold star."

They moved to the kitchen table and sank down. "Part of his official duties?"

Noah shrugged. "Maybe. Maybe he was ordered to head south to assist the deal. Happens all the time. Or maybe Egorov was connected to MirGaz in a way we don't yet understand."

Milo sighed heavily. Why couldn't anything just be simple? He took the information to Keller's room and found the accountant sitting at the desk with a book, Stephen Hawking's *A Brief History of Time*. "It takes me away from here," Keller said. "Makes all this seem small."

Keller knew nothing about Egorov and MirGaz and Nigeria, and his ignorance no longer frustrated Milo—he'd made peace with the man's uselessness. "I'm going to leave in a while. I'll be back in the morning. Want me to pick up anything?"

"Decent coffee," Keller said.

Milo grinned. "Thank you, by the way."

"For what?"

"For not going really crazy. I know captivity is hard. But we're close to figuring things out."

Keller shrugged. "Are you really close?"

"I think so."

He closed his book on the bedside table. "Did you want me to look at Anna Usurov's information? Maybe I'll see something."

"Sure," Milo said. "That might be helpful."

As he left Keller's room, Kristin waved him over to her computer. She'd done a background check on Grace Foster and laid it all out on a spreadsheet. Born 1974, raised in Minnesota, Vassar College, Harvard Law, divorced, no children, a stint in a Boston firm before a post-9/11 move to Langley for eight years until returning to the private sphere in 2009.

"What am I focusing on?" he asked, feeling as if the fatigue of so many hours looking at words had made him stupid.

"Ex-husband," said Kristin.

His gaze returned to the marital data and stopped. Married for six years to Anthony Halliwell. Halliwell, founder of Northwell International.

"Jesus."

Noah looked up from his computer and asked something that, in that moment, felt like a non sequitur: "What did Foster do in the CIA?"

Milo's eye moved to the relevant paragraph. "OIG."

"Office of the Inspector General," Noah said. "They would have been responsible for getting rid of the Tourism records."

"Oh," said Kristin.

For a moment, no one said a thing; then Milo looked at Kristin's screen, searching for something. He said, "Alan told us the files were cleared out in December 2008. Foster resigned the next month."

"Wait," Kristin said, holding up a hand. "Are you suggesting she took the Tourism files and . . ."

". . . and gave them to her ex-husband," Noah said. "To Northwell."

Milo covered his face in his hands, the world suddenly shifting beneath his feet. Was it really that simple? That clear? The only way to know was to say it aloud and see if Noah and Kristin could poke a hole in it. "This was never about one country reviving Tourism," Milo said slowly. "Northwell *is* Tourism. It's a private enterprise."

"An international enterprise," said Noah.

Milo felt like he needed to sit, to let the idea sweep over him, but he feared that if he sat down he would never get up. Northwell as the new Tourism. And MirGaz? "MirGaz is its client."

"Its patron," said Kristin. "So is Salid Logistics."

"And Nexus?" Milo asked.

Kristin nodded.

"And its banker," Noah said, "is Oliver Booth at IfW."

Kristin was pacing, tapping a ballpoint pen against her chin. She said, "If you were running a private army of Tourists, what would you fear most?"

"The same thing we fear," said Milo. "Exposure."

"But the risk to them isn't as great as it seems," Noah cut in. "CIA pays attention to anything that threatens US security. The GRU does the same for Russia. MI6, MSS—all the same. Their operations are spread so thinly across the globe that any single intelligence agency isn't going to put together the big picture."

"Exactly," said Kristin, excited now. "That's *exactly* it."

Both men looked at her.

"National agencies aren't a threat," she said. "But if Northwell was aware of the Library—an organization that looks at the world holistically—then we would be perceived as its biggest threat."

"You gave the patrons Keller's names," Noah said to Milo. "One of them—maybe more than one—passed this on to Northwell. Northwell realized you had Keller, which is why Foster tried to kill you."

"I think we know which patron," Kristin said.

Milo exhaled. "Beatriz Almeida."

It was a lot to take in, and Milo had trouble sorting through the ramifications of it all. He would have to leave it to his two geniuses to distill it all into a report for little minds like his own. He gulped down half of his coffee. He was trembling, but not from caffeine.

"One more thing," Kristin said as he gathered his keys. "Outside the US, Nexus is the most popular messaging app in the world. They advertise absolute anonymity. But what if they put in a back door? What if these new Tourists have access to the largest tracking system in human history?"

"Then we're fucked," said Noah, and Milo couldn't find a reason to disagree.

38

"I am from the Guojia Anquan Bu," the small Chinese woman said, her voice sharp.

Ted didn't bother to hide his fat knife, still warm from Leticia's cheek. "And?" he asked, unafraid. "What the hell are you doing here?"

What Leticia found shocking about this exchange was that the American acted as if he were the put-upon one, when he was on Chinese territory, faced with the authority of Xin Zhu's Ministry of State Security. He was either a fool or backed up by some powerful people. The woman said, "She has information we need."

That took some of the air out of the American, and he shook his head. "I'll need her back afterward."

"Of course," she said. "But first I take her."

He looked like he was going to fight this, but the woman's hard stare convinced him to step back and raise his hands, the knife still in one, as if he had nothing to do with Leticia. She approached and looked Leticia over once, seemingly disgusted, then nodded at her two men, who used their own knives to cut her free.

It was only in the elevator, when the woman made a call, that she began to understand. Leticia made out fragments—

. . . can't be allowed to do this . . .

. . . I don't care if Wu is allied with—

Of course not. The plane will leave soon.

Then they were exiting to the parking garage, hustling Leticia into the backseat of an old Mercedes, the woman joining her. When they drove out to the bright street, in what looked like the Pinghu neighborhood, the woman hung up and looked at Leticia. "You are stupid, you know?"

"Am I?"

"But lucky. Tell Milo Weaver this is what generosity looks like."

"You work for Xin Zhu."

"I work for China."

Leticia looked out the window. "What kind of information do you need from me?"

"From you?" She barked a short laugh. "You have nothing for us. Milo Weaver already gave it to us."

Now she understood—Milo had traded to get her out of China. She couldn't help but appreciate that. "Why are you letting Northwell walk all over you?"

The woman crossed her hands over her knee, considering her answer. "Northwell has friends in the Foreign Bureau."

Of the many Chinese bureaus, the Second Bureau, aka the Foreign Bureau, was a good place to invest in friends. "Come on," Leticia said. "You're the Sixth Bureau. Nobody fucks with you."

A faint smile passed across the woman's face, then disappeared. "These days the Central Committee is more enamored with the Second."

Realpolitik, Leticia thought, *and in real time.* "Can you tell me anything about Tóuzī? What they're doing on Sakhalin Island? Why they're messing with Nigeria?"

The woman tilted her head curiously, then: "On Sakhalin, they are building a new school for Northwell. Those boys who took you are from the local Beijing school. International Defense Institute."

"They study hard," Leticia said. "So arrest them."

The woman shook her head but didn't elaborate. Anthony Halliwell's Second Bureau friends were really making things hard for the Ministry of State Security. It was difficult to imagine how a Western company in China could be considered more important than the MSS. How much money had to exchange hands for that to happen?

"You mentioned Nigeria," the woman said.

"They're funding Boko Haram."

The woman blinked rapidly, as if the gears in her head had suddenly started moving at light speed. "Where?"

"Borno district."

The woman spat a violent Chinese curse, then, in English: "The pipeline."

"What?"

"CNPC—China National Petroleum Corporation. We are preparing to build a pipeline from Niger to Chad."

"And?" Leticia asked, not getting it.

"Look at a map," the woman said, her face very serious.

Leticia sighed, trying to see the map of Nigeria in her head, but they were approaching the airport, and she didn't know how much time she had left. She said, "MirGaz bought twenty-two acres on the Gulf of Guinea, but not for drilling."

The woman waved a hand. "It is the same as on Sakhalin. Training camps. More soldiers."

"They're expanding."

"Everywhere," the woman said as the car approached the terminal. "I believe your friend has your ticket. They are holding the plane for you."

"Friend?"

She rocked her head but only said, "Do you need anything else, Ms. Jones?"

Leticia grinned. "How about one of those plastic guns?"

The woman did not find her amusing at all. "Just leave, okay?"

They let her out at the curb and drove off, but Leticia didn't fool herself into thinking she'd been left alone. In addition to the cameras, the Guoanbu certainly kept a few full-timers at Pudong International. The Second Bureau, of course, had its own people, too, and all of them, no doubt, watched her search the big hall until she spotted Poitevin leaning against a café counter, lighting up when he saw her. And they certainly took a photo or two as she sidled up beside him and said, "Why the hell are you still here?"

"I wasn't going to leave you behind."

"I would have."

"You've been working alone for a long time, haven't you?"

"What does that mean?"

He shook his head. "Come on."

They were waved through security, and as they hustled through the terminal Poitevin told her that after calling Milan he'd made it back to the hotel just in time for Xin Zhu's men to pick him up. Like her he'd been packed into a van, but unlike her he hadn't been asked anything. Just held on ice for a long time as they drove slowly through town until, finally, his captors received a phone call and brought him to the airport with instructions on which flight to take—Swissair direct to Zürich.

Once they were seated in economy, Leticia called Zürich and appreciated the relief she heard in Noah's voice. Milo wasn't in the office, but he would get word to him. "He'll be here when you get back," Noah said. "Stay safe."

As they reversed out of the gate, she looked out the window and remembered what Xin Zhu's agent had said. She pulled up a map on her phone. She found Nigeria and looked around it, to the east, where Niger and Chad lay. She shook her head. Why hadn't she seen it before? The CNPC's oil pipeline running from Niger to Chad went right by the Nigerian border—right by Borno State.

"Disruption," she said aloud.

"What?" asked Poitevin.

She yawned into the back of her hand. Outside, the earth was starting to move. All those girls, their fates sealed by people willing to ravage them in the hopes of disrupting someone else's oil business. She shook her head. "I thought I was cold. Jesus."

39

He was in a swirl of black and white, of tuxes and gowns and jewelry that half the thieves in Manhattan would have given their right arm just to touch, and a live quartet's bright classical music that helped everything glitter, yet the only thing Alan really noticed was the skinny man with the sun-dried face who stood awkwardly in a white suit that Penelope had picked out for him. Occasionally the preternaturally tall bankers and financiers stepped up to loom over him and shake his hand and speak rapidly to him before breaking off and returning to their own kind, leaving him again looking entirely out of place, even though, as Penelope had said, all of this was *for him*.

His phone vibrated in his pocket, and he saw Heeler's number. "Hey."

"His limo just pulled up."

She was stationed outside, on the other side of Fifth Avenue, watching out for Gilbert Powell. "Got it," he said. "Any sign of others?"

"Just a bodyguard."

"That's fine. I'm not going to give him trouble. Just need to be available in case he wants to talk."

"Well, call if you want backup."

"Thanks, Heeler."

He hung up and looked around the vast foyer, but Powell hadn't made it inside yet, so he turned back to the guest of honor. Alan had heard Manuel's story many times as the plans for the gala had been made in his living room. Manuel Garcia, born in Tamaulipas, had come to America as a child in the seventies, part of the migrant underclass that kept America's farms work-ing, and when his parents eventually became citizens, he did as well. He also worked the land, marrying and raising two daughters, both in their early teens, and together they would visit Tamaulipas yearly so that his children could see another way of living. The previous summer, his wife and daugh-ters went on their own so he could finish the harvest season, and when they returned his wife's papers were flagged. She, too, had arrived as a child in the seventies, but her parents had never become legal, and a previously forgotten charge for buying alcohol with a fake ID at sixteen had suddenly appeared on the ICE computer. Manuel's wife had been redirected to a holding facil-ity in an old Walmart in Brownsville, Texas, and since their daughters were minors they had been detained, too, but elsewhere.

"They won't let Manuel speak to them," Penelope had told him as they dressed for the evening, him pulling on his new jacket. "He can't afford a lawyer. There's a pro bono guy down there, and he's not even sure ICE knows *where* they are. Can you believe it?"

He could. And this, tonight, was what it came to: a sad man in an un-comfortable suit whose family had been taken from him.

Alan set the glass on a table and headed over to speak to Manuel. If nothing else, maybe he could help the guy relax.

He was halfway through the crowd when he noticed a tall fortysome-thing in a blazer and crisp T-shirt talking with Penelope. He stopped in his tracks. Gilbert Powell, who had lunched with Beatriz Almeida and Kata-rina Heinold and Grace Foster. The man whose social media service, Kristin theorized, gave a new breed of Tourists the power to track almost anyone—a power that in his day Tourists could only have dreamed of.

As he approached, he heard Powell saying, "The platform is already wildly popular in Costa Rica. I don't see why we can't tweak it for the other markets."

Penelope looked mildly buzzed, or maybe it was the intoxication of standing so close to a billionaire. She said, "That would be *terrific*. People like Manuel could get a lock on their families."

"Isn't that the opposite of what you do?" Alan asked, stepping into the conversation. They both looked at him, blank; then Penelope introduced "my husband," and the two men shook hands. "Alan Drummond," Alan clarified.

He couldn't tell from Powell's expression if the man knew who he was—

how much did they *really* know about the Library? He only smiled and said, "Sure, our model is anonymity, but it's a matter of adding a switch in the settings so users can choose to share their locations. We're working on versions of this. But what's really interesting is pushing it further—we've developed algorithms that can *predict* location."

"Those are in the app?"

He shook his head. "But they could be added in an update. Imagine— your family can know where you *will be* at any particular time with, say, eighty percent accuracy."

"That's amazing," Penelope said.

"Dictators of the world will be very happy," Alan said.

"No," Powell came back quickly, shaking his head. "You misunderstand. This wouldn't be automatic, and if it were added you would choose who has access."

Alan didn't trust himself to speak. He felt a strong desire to grab Gilbert Powell and shake him and demand answers. This was out of the question, of course, but the feeling didn't go away. Powell was connected to a dark, dangerous world that threatened people he cared for, but that wasn't the only reason. There was also jealousy, seeing the attention Penelope bestowed upon him; was *that* why he wanted to slap Powell across his smug face? He almost pulled Penelope close, to show his ownership—

No, not ownership. Protection. Because this guy wasn't the Silicon Valley darling he pretended to be, and she had no idea.

Alan said, "I read a report that the Honduran military uses Nexus to communicate, so there'll be no record of its atrocities."

Powell surprised him by smiling. "There's a rumor the Massive Brigade has started to use it, too. Going to blame us for their attacks?" He took a step closer, seeming incredibly confident. "Mr. Drummond, I'm just trying to level the playing field. Governments already have the technology to cover their tracks. Privacy should belong to everyone."

Penelope's features twisted, looking anguished, and she said, "People like Manuel over there don't care about political considerations. They just want their family."

"How do you know, honey?" Alan asked, now feeling inexplicably bitter. "Did you ask him?"

"No, I—"

"I'll bet Manuel's a pretty smart guy. He's certainly politically savvy enough to know that showing up at a party in Manhattan makes better sense than being where he wants to be—back in Texas, looking for his family."

A little grin played in the corner of Powell's lips. "You *know* that, huh?"

"No, Gilbert, I don't. But I'm going to find out."

He looked around the room and had just spotted Manuel, still on his own, when his phone vibrated again. Heeler. He nodded apologetically to Penelope and turned away. "What's up?" he said, but the music was too loud, her voice too quiet. He veered left through the crowd, toward the exit, and spotted Powell on his own now, frowning directly at him, the mask gone. Yes—*there* was the real Gilbert Powell, and Alan decided that when he came back he would have to face him; there was no other way.

He continued past the burly security guards out into the cold, where the columns and shadows dominated, lit from below.

"Heeler?"

A woman's voice replied, "We've got an offer."

Heeler's phone but not Heeler. He felt a chill. "Who is this?"

"Cross Fifth, and we'll talk."

"Who?"

"Who do you think?"

"Where is the owner of that phone?" he said, suddenly worried for Heeler.

"She's fine."

"I'm not going anywhere."

Silence. Then: "Take a look across Fifth. I'll wave to you. So you see I'm alone."

Alan stepped from behind a column, looking down the wide stairs and across Fifth at the familiar park-view buildings he'd seen all his life. Occasional stragglers wandered by, but he didn't see . . . there. Standing in a long coat, head uncovered under a streetlamp, her left hand raised in greeting. "Grace Foster," he said.

In the silence, that cool tingle spread across his scalp again. He'd made a mistake, maybe, revealing that he knew who she was. Then he heard footsteps behind him and turned to find a beefy security guard approaching. "Sir?" the guard said.

"I'm with the party," Alan said. He looked for Foster, but she was gone now. As his eyes focused on the other side of the road, he felt the guard come near, very near, so close that he felt his hot breath. When Alan began to turn to face him, he felt a sharp pinch in the middle of his back, behind his ribs, and only after he'd turned to look into the guard's eyes did he realize he'd been knifed. His knee buckled. He raised his arms instinctively against the flash of the blade, but the guard was a big man, and too close already. A second jab caught him in the chest, running through to his lung, a searing, bright pain, and the guard's free hand clamped his throat and shoved him against the column. It was all so fast that Alan couldn't quite register that he was being killed. And by the time he did, it was too late.

40

When he looked out of the upstairs window at the picturesque field dotted with little mountain cottages leading straight into the base of Cardada Mountain, Milo thought that in spite of the cynicism and horror that humans visited on one another, there were places where you really could find peace. Like here, in a safe house north of Locarno, outside Avegno, in the Italian part of Switzerland.

"It is a great view," Tina said behind him.

"Not tired of it yet?"

She put her hands on his shoulders. "I think even Stephanie's warming to it."

He grunted doubtfully. When he'd arrived last night, he'd listened to Stephanie's complaints about the solitude. "That guy won't let me go into town."

"It won't be for long," he'd told her, even though he still had no idea how long it would be.

"Tell him to give me back my phone."

"Who do you want to call?"

"I don't make *calls*. No one makes calls anymore. I Nexus."

"You can't," he'd told her seriously, trying to make himself heard. "Nexus most of all."

Milo kissed his wife, and together they went down to the kitchen.

Dalmatian had brewed a pot of American coffee before stepping out for a security check. Last night, the librarian had walked him through the area, pointing out places he considered hardest to defend. Up the street was a Catholic church that got traffic on Sundays.

They'd just poured their cups when Stephanie appeared, looking groggy. He kissed her forehead and watched her piece together a ham sandwich. She was quiet until after she took her first bite.

"I don't get it," she said, then sighed. "I mean, I *get* it. Someone tried to kill you. You're trying to make sure they don't come for us."

"That's right."

"But who are they?"

"It's hard to say."

"Well, *try* saying," she said. "Is it Russia or something like that? Is Vladimir Putin trying to get rid of you?"

"I don't think so. I don't even think it's a country."

"The *mob*?"

"Something like that," he admitted, because it was as good a description as one could give of the sprawling network of companies that was threatening the Library. Not just the Library but everything it touched—other companies, countries, people just trying to live.

"Jesus, Dad."

"Yeah."

"And you're going to put them in jail?"

That was an excellent question. "I don't know yet."

She took another bite. "Well, hurry up, okay?"

After coffee, Milo said his good-byes, checked in with Dalmatian, and drove south through winding roads to Via Cantonale, where he turned north to reach the A2, which brought him most of the way to Zürich. He called Milan and spoke with Noah, who had decided to look deeper into Kirill Egorov. "Last July, he went to the Aspen Security Forum."

"They don't usually invite Russians," Milo said.

"They didn't invite him," Noah said. "He sat in the audience for a panel called 'The New Reality of Private Security and Intelligence.' The main guest was Anthony Halliwell."

"Oh."

"Maybe just another coincidence, but I did an image search. I've got five photos of them at the forum together. Drinking, talking. Different outfits, so different days. It smells."

"It does," Milo said. "Did you talk to Keller about it?"

"I will when he wakes up."

Road work added a half hour to what should have been a three-hour drive, but he still reached the airport with twenty minutes to spare before his sister's eleven-thirty flight landed. Carefully, he packed his SIG Sauer under his jacket and joined a sparse crowd of waiting families. Alexandra was the first to exit, and together they left the airport. As he merged onto the highway that would take them back to Milan, he took her through the expanse of connections that had been made in her absence.

"Jesus," she said, sounding like Stephanie.

"We stay together now," Milo said.

They had passed Locarno and were near the Italian border, only an hour from Milan, when Milo brought up the connections between Kirill Egorov and MirGaz in Nigeria and Anthony Halliwell in Aspen. Alexandra went silent, watching the mountains pass in the bright afternoon light. Milo assumed she was on to thinking about other subjects when she turned and said, "What if?"

"What if what?"

She hesitated before speaking again. "What if Egorov actually was working with MirGaz and Northwell? Could that even make sense?"

Milo thought about it. "I don't think so. Why sacrifice himself to get us Joseph Keller? Why contact me at all?"

"I don't know," she said, then looked at the mountains again. Eventually, she turned to him, eyes squinted in thought. "Egorov knew about the Library. Dad told him. And he knew you were running it."

"Which is why he knew I could protect Keller," Milo said. "And don't forget that he kept the Library a secret all those years. Otherwise, we would've had trouble."

"We have trouble now," she said.

Silence fell again, but the idea kept revolving in his head, and he knew he had to follow it through. "Say he *was* working for Northwell. He calls me when I'm in Japan, going to meet Leticia. What's Leticia working on?"

"The Nigerian money trail."

"Which leads eventually to Tóuzī and to Northwell."

Alexandra looked at him. "He thinks Leticia's working for us. That she's tracking the money trail for the Library. Which would explain why Grace Foster tries to hire her—right?"

"Maybe."

She took a breath. "Okay, so Egorov calls you, thinking you're investigating them. But—"

"Yes, but," Milo cut in, feeling inexplicably irritated. No, not irritated: defensive. "*But* he smuggled Joseph Keller to Algiers rather than kill him. *But* he wants to give me Joseph Keller and a list that could be a blueprint for all of this. And he dies trying to do that."

"*But,*" Alexandra said, her voice suddenly deeper, and when she didn't go on he turned to look at her. Her mouth was moving, just a little, as if she were trying to form difficult words. Finally she turned to him. "But what if none of that is true?"

"What?"

"All those *buts* assume a lot. That the list Keller brought us is real. That Joseph Keller is the same Joseph Keller who stole the list. What if Egorov *did* kill Joseph Keller and replaced him with someone else, who he gave to you?"

Milo suddenly felt cold. His fingers tingled.

She said, "Keller's list—have we gotten *anything* actionable from it?"

Milo opened his mouth, hesitant. "The one piece from it that was acted on—Diogo Moreira—the Portuguese found no evidence at all. Everything we've learned has come from Anna Usurov's flash drive."

"Milo," she said, her voice quieter now. "How do we know that's Joseph Keller? The Red Notices were taken down before we ever found him, so we didn't have that to go by. Passport?"

"The passport he had on him," he said, nodding. "And one more photograph. From the MirGaz website, and his Nexus account. Nothing else."

For a moment, they only breathed loudly in the car, and Milo pressed down on the gas. Without having to be told, Alexandra took out her phone and made two calls. Neither Kristin nor Noah picked up.

"Kristin says the Library is Northwell's biggest threat," Milo said, his breaths shallow. "At least, it would be perceived as the biggest threat."

"Which means they'll do anything to bring us down."

Forty minutes later, they typed the code to get inside the building, and in the foyer Milo took out his pistol as they quietly ascended to the third floor. At the door, he motioned for Alexandra to stay back as he typed the second code into the keypad and, pressed against the wall, reached around and pushed the door open. They waited, listening, as a nauseating stink wafted out; then Milo moved around the corner, pistol drawn, and entered.

Noah was in the main room, sprawled bloody across the big table. One of his index fingers, Milo noticed, had been cut off. Kristin was in the bathroom, folded inside the bathtub in a deep puddle of red. Milo crouched, staring at her frozen face for a long time, until Alexandra put a hand on his shoulder and quietly said, "Come look at this."

He followed her back to the main room, trying and failing to avoid seeing Noah. Alexandra took him to the kitchen and opened up Kristin's laptop computer. She had brought up the security footage from the street. There— from above, they saw the man they knew as Joseph Keller walking calmly out of their building. In his hand was Noah's laptop. Following him out was a man neither recognized—tall, dark-skinned, and carrying a pistol he slipped beneath his heavy coat. The two men walked calmly down the street and out of view.

"You with me, Milo?"

"Yeah," he said.

"He has our data. Encrypted, but we don't know for how long. Our people are exposed."

Milo rubbed his scalp with both hands, a feeling of vertigo coming over him. He remembered that horrible night a decade ago, when he'd watched on a computer monitor Tourists around the world being killed, one after the other, and he'd been powerless to stop it. Thirty-three murders, and all he could do was watch.

41

As the plane descended toward Zürich, Leticia listened with her eyes closed to Poitevin take out his phone and power it up. For most of the twelve-hour flight he'd slept like a baby, leaving her alone to puzzle over the intersection of Northwell, a Chinese developer, a Russian energy company, an Arab shipping conglomerate, and an American social media behemoth. She knew English bankers were involved, as was China's Second Bureau. Jesus, but it was big.

Theories spun in her head, the tentacles of her imagination spreading across the atlas of what she knew. Nigeria, at least, she understood. Xin Zhu's agent had pointed her to the answer: disrupting the CNPC's Niger Chad pipeline by supporting Boko Haram. When she'd worked the mining deal in Nigeria in 2014, she'd researched energy on the continent and still remembered a list of the top ten oil producers. Number one? Nigeria. Numbers nine and ten were Chad and Cameroon—through which the Chinese pipeline would run to the sea.

The chaos of a well-funded terrorist organization would keep oil exploration at bay, but it would do more. She imagined Boko Haram, flush with money and successful in Borno State. Beyond the establishment of a caliphate, what would that mean? What would their leader, Abubakar Shekau, want to do next?

Expand.

Yes. Like all successful revolutionary leaders, he wouldn't be satisfied with a slice of a single district in northern Nigeria. He would want to expand his organization's footprint and secure his territory by growing right into Niger, Chad, and Cameroon. And then, to support a growing empire, he would want to get his hands on oil—the Agadem field in Niger would be within reach.

But wouldn't Boko Haram oil be competition for MirGaz? No. Even if Abubakar Shekau got the pumps working and trucked the oil out, no one would buy it—no large market, at least. It wasn't about benefiting MirGaz directly; it was about hurting China via the suffering of thousands of innocent Nigerians.

Everything was interconnected. The work of Tóuzī in Nigeria benefited MirGaz; MirGaz payments to the Philippines benefited Salid Logistics; influencers in four different countries put out Red Notices to find Joseph Keller to help MirGaz find their escaped employee; and Northwell was working hand in hand with Tóuzī as it expanded on Sakhalin Island and in western Nigeria, training new field agents they called Tourists.

But these details were just the tip of the iceberg, weren't they? Everything under the surface was enormous and hidden because the system they'd established was secret. Or virtually secret. The facts she and the Library had discovered were the result of mistakes, and from what she could tell Northwell didn't make many of those.

She opened her eyes, and the sun shone brightly through Poitevin's open window. He was staring silently out of it, at the land rising to meet them. Swiss houses rolled underneath, and in the distance a runway was laid out to greet them. The wheels groaned as they lowered in preparation, and in as few words as possible she explained her thoughts to him. When she finished, he chewed the inside of his cheek.

"Hundreds of stolen girls," Poitevin said, "on the off chance that it'll boost their bottom line?"

"They're not girls to them. They're numbers. They're statistics. Trend lines."

Poitevin, disgusted, shook his head as the plane touched down. Brakes squealed, and the cabin trembled. Then his phone beeped an incoming message. He read it, squinting; then his eyes widened. He looked at her. "Check your phone."

"Why?" she asked as she powered hers up.

"Just check it."

The screen came up quickly, and it vibrated a new message. A single sentence from an unknown number: *Your book is on hold*. She showed it to Poitevin, who had received the same message. "I've never gotten this before," he said.

"What does it mean?"

"It means we disappear."

"What do you mean, disappear?"

His cheeks were flushed now, and he began to disassemble his phone. "It means security has been compromised. It means we've all been exposed."

She, too, began to disassemble her phone. Milo Fucking Weaver. She'd been part of his crew for a grand total of . . . what? A week? And already it had gone to hell.

"What are you going to do?" she asked.

"Get far away from here."

"Japan?"

He thought a moment, then shook his head. "Not for a while. Easier to move around in Europe."

This was all going too fast. "But . . . how do you reestablish contact later?"

"He didn't tell you?"

"We had other things to worry about."

He nodded. "I'll write down the IP address for you. You don't come in until the recall message appears."

Leticia didn't like this at all. Just when she felt like she was close to understanding things, the rug had been pulled out from under her. All those years she'd spent on her own, she hadn't made a dent in the mystery of those girls in Borno, and now real answers were within reach.

"You know where he is, right?" she asked. When he frowned at her, she said, "Milo. There's only one place he'll be."

"Yes," he said, "but I'm going in the opposite direction. I suggest you do the same."

"That's how we get picked off one at a time."

Poitevin shook his head. "I'm following my orders."

When they left the airport, she regretted not talking him into coming with her; despite his lousy tradecraft she enjoyed Poitevin's company. Or maybe it wasn't him but company in general. She'd forgotten how much she

enjoyed the back-and-forth of human interaction. People didn't suck quite as badly as she generally believed.

Before leaving the airport, she bought a new SIM card and plugged it into her phone, then used her Wanda Kumalu credit card and South African driver's license to rent a BMW. It was the one ID she hadn't blown yet. Maybe.

42

"Someone's coming," Dalmatian said, trotting down the stairs. "Just over the hill."

Milo looked across the kitchen table at Tina, whose eyes were damp and red. He'd made a mistake telling her about Kristin and Noah. She'd known the reference librarians, had made dinner for them on occasion, and on other occasions they'd gotten drunk together in the living room on Had-laubstrasse, and now she'd been asked to accept their murders with a swift-ness that she wasn't built for. Better to just walk in, say, "We have to leave now," and get into the details later. He'd tried that, of course, but failed. Tina was done being the uninformed one; it was a role that had never suited her. And here she was, sitting frozen at the table, dealing with the consequences of knowledge.

"Who?"

Dalmatian checked his old Makarov pistol. "No idea."

Milo grabbed his SIG Sauer from the living room, and out front he and Dalmatian waited on either side of the wide gravel driveway until the front end of a BMW slowly rolled forward. Sun glinted off the windshield, then passed, and he could see Leticia sitting inside. He lowered his gun and nod-ded at Dalmatian, who approached, still wary, as Leticia parked.

"So?" she asked as she opened her door and got out. "What the hell's going on?"

When Milo told her about the betrayal, she raised her head to look down at him, as if she were going to dispute the story, but said, "So what does he have on that computer?"

"We don't know everything Noah kept on there. Certainly our codes and legends—that's the first thing he would look for. Maybe safe houses. It's why I sent everyone away."

"Library files?"

"It can get to the database, but without the passcodes no one can access it."

"How good is the encryption?"

Milo opened his hands. "The best we could buy."

"Just a matter of time, then," she said, and rubbed her temple, clearly frustrated. "Still, though. One asshole, and you throw everything away?"

"Do you remember 2008?" Milo asked, and she straightened. Of course she did. She was lucky to have survived. They both were. "I'm not letting that happen again," he told her.

As they entered the cottage, Alexandra was trotting down the stairs, her face red as sunburn. She nodded at Leticia; Leticia nodded back. In the kitchen, Milo used Kristin's laptop to pull up the security footage from Milan. At 11:12 a.m., the tall, dark-skinned man approached their street-side door, entered a code, and walked into the building. Twenty minutes later, he exited with Keller—but a different Keller than Milo had known. Not irritable or scared. Relaxed, satisfied, at peace.

"That's Gary Young," Leticia said, pointing at the other man. "From Wakkanai and Hong Kong."

When Dalmatian hurried into the kitchen, no one looked at him until he pointedly said, "We have to go." They looked up, and at the phone he was holding out. On its screen was Milo's face, the old photo he'd used for his UNESCO documents, and his name. Then: *Wanted by China, Russia, United Kingdom, United States*. Pasted at the corner of his picture was the Interpol logo in red above the words *RED NOTICE*.

But Leticia didn't want to be hurried. She settled into a chair, then slowly took them through what she'd learned in China. She described the interconnectedness of the companies they'd been tracking, and seemed surprised that no one in the room disagreed with her. They'd all reached the same conclusions by different paths. "Now that we know who they are," she said, "how do we take them down?"

It was almost quaint, remembering his state of mind only a few weeks ago, his fear of turning the Library into an active-measures organization. Now that it was their only option, he'd waited too long. There was no Library to activate.

"What about the patrons?" Alexandra asked.

"We don't know who we can trust. Portugal is a no, and maybe Germany, too. I don't know about Said Bensoussan."

"Any contact is going to be a risk," Dalmatian pointed out.

Tina was standing in the doorway, quietly listening. How long had she been there? He didn't know. She said, "There's nothing you can do, is there?"

Milo considered this seriously, then shook his head. "Not by ourselves."

"No," Leticia said, stiffening. "We get your family safe, and then we go after him," she said, nodding at Gary Young, frozen on the computer screen. "Or we go after Grace Foster. There are a lot of people we can get our hands on."

Alexandra disagreed. "What makes you think any of these people are the head of the snake? They built it like this on purpose; the organization is diffuse. One link won't bring down the edifice."

"Then we go after two, then three. Until it *does* start to crack."

"I'm with her," said Dalmatian. "Enough hiding."

Milo leaned against a counter, because the exhaustion—the real exhaustion, the psychological exhaustion—was taking hold. Every time they took a step forward, they were knocked back five steps. Things might be clearer, but not better, not for any of them. He wondered what the point was of moving forward. He'd disbanded the Library, and by doing that had made his family even less safe.

His pocket vibrated; it was his encrypted phone. He took it out and checked the screen: Alan's number. Even Alan had known. Back in New York, he had pestered Milo to make the Library more active—*we would do it best*. Everyone had understood this, but not him. He'd been led by his fears, and that fault was going to be their downfall. But when he answered the phone, Alan wasn't on the other end. Penelope was, and she was crying.

PART THREE

MERGERS AND
ACQUISITIONS

7 8 9 0

FRIDAY, JANUARY 18, TO FRIDAY, JANUARY 25, 2019

1

In those first moments after he stopped talking, as the ferry groaned around us and we rocked our way toward the Spanish coast, I had trouble putting it all together. This wasn't the first time he'd stopped. Hours ago we'd broken for a meal that Leticia brought from the galley—at which point I realized the seasickness I'd been feeling was only hunger. But while eating ravenously I made a conscious choice not to judge anything until the story had reached its conclusion. Now it had, or at least it seemed as if it had, Milo falling silent and reaching for a bottle of water.

"So you went to Laayoune," I said.

"Yes," he answered. "Eventually." He sipped at his water and looked expectantly at me.

So there we were; I had my story.

Could I believe him? Maybe, yes. Because while our industry is full of talented storytellers, few dig into such detail, such intricate interconnection, and it struck me that if Milo Weaver really was spinning a lie, such a convincing delivery could only mean that I was in the presence of a true psychopath. And that, at least at this point, didn't seem right.

So, yes, I did believe him, which led to the next question: What did I take from the story? Were there other ways to interpret the data he'd presented, some less insidious analysis he'd been too narrow-minded to see? Maybe he was attributing everything to one organization when it was really a Venn diagram of separate actors who overlapped just enough to look like a single entity. I'd seen that in studies of war-torn areas: The simple among us would attribute all bombings to a single party, when that was seldom the case.

But Milo had a through-line, the enigmatic Grace Foster. She had appeared to Leticia and to Milo, and her marital connection to Northwell was stronger than circumstantial. It was certainly good enough to hang a hat on.

"And in Laayoune you hid," I said. "For three months. Without even your family. Then you called me."

"Not you, Abdul. I had no idea who you were. I still don't."

Who *was* I? In the grand scheme of all this, I was a nobody. A stenographer to the stars. And so far out of my league that I wondered how I was still alive. Luck, and a good dose of protection by Milo Weaver and Leticia Jones.

"Why, though?" I asked. "What good does it do for you to get your story to the Agency?"

Milo scratched the back of his neck, and Leticia got up, saying, "Excellent question, Abdul. Milo?" Without waiting for an answer, she pulled open the heavy door and looked outside the cabin. "Spain ho."

Milo got up, and I followed suit. The three of us watched the Spanish shoreline grow in the distance, a mess of beaches and ships and buildings and harbors in the evening light. She turned back to us. "I'm going to keep an eye out as we pull in."

"Good idea," Milo said.

She departed, and I went back to check the recorder. Fifteen hours of story. Jesus.

"Unlike her," Milo said, following me back inside and pushing the door shut, "I don't think CIA is a cesspool of cynicism. I think it's an organization full of decent, if flawed, human beings, with no more bad apples than any other place. I think that if they understand that there's an intelligence organization representing only business interests, weaponized far beyond the usual muddle of private contractors, one that exists entirely in the shadows with zero oversight—I think in that case your employer will have no choice but to act against it."

"You want us to help you bring it down."

"Bring it down. Expose it. Cripple it. Whatever works. Think about it, Abdul. No one knows it exists, yet it's active all over the globe."

"Like the Library," I said.

He opened his hands like a patient father dealing with a know-it-all middle schooler. "And not like it. Ask those drowned Filipino sailors, the slaughtered Nigerian schoolteachers and their students. Ask Collins. Ask Kristin, Noah, and Alan. Ask Leonberger. Ask Griffon." He shook his head, momentarily emotional, then kept going. "Look, we got it wrong, and we kept getting it wrong. All of us. After 1990, we thought history as we knew it was over. The last big competing superpower had imploded, leaving only the US to oversee the final move into a liberal democratic world order. Not everyone agreed. Rwanda, Yugoslavia, Syria, Afghanistan, Iraq . . . yes, superpowers were done, but they had been replaced by a hundred brush fires, too many for one country to put out. Factionalism. So we all started adjusting our policies to deal with this. But history kept shifting. Russia and China rose and Europe began to fracture, which brought us back to the start: Superpowers were back."

"Yes," I said. "That's how we look at it, too."

"Because we don't think the way they do," Milo said. "The rest of us—the Agency, Pentagon, State, even the Library—we're taught to see the world in the old terms. Ethnic groups. Nation-states. Languages. But those aren't the source of power anymore. Money ignores borders. Corporations are the new nation-states. It's why your own analysts never saw any of this. Nigeria, the Philippines, Nexus, what's going on in China—they don't fit into your models of the world. You couldn't look at these events and trace them to a single country, because no countries benefit. Only the members of this consortium."

He was right, of course. It would have never occurred to us to look to a Chinese development firm to explain Boko Haram. It was like pointillism: Stand too close, and it makes no sense. Step far enough back, and you can see it. Maybe.

"We've missed this for a decade," he said. "Ever since Grace Foster gave the Tourism files to her ex-husband. I don't know whose idea it was, and it doesn't matter, but Halliwell and Foster went to Davos together in 2009 for the World Economic Forum. That same year the CEOs of IfW, Nexus, Mir-Gaz, and Salid Logistics also attended. Each year since, none of them have missed the Forum."

I scratched the back of my head, imagining snowcapped mountains and a lot of whisky. I stood up again, but now my legs felt tingly. Weak. I said, "Okay. What do you want?"

"I want your help. The Agency's."

"Do you even trust the Agency?"

"I trust it to follow its mandate. If a private army is ignoring national sovereignty, causing mayhem around the world and, yes, cutting into American profits overseas—don't tell me that's not a national security issue."

I could see that, but I could also imagine how Paul, Mel, and Sally would react to this story. "They don't trust you."

"And you, Abdul? Do you trust me?"

"No," I said without hesitation.

"What about the story I've told you?"

I blinked at him, unsure how to answer. *Did* I believe it all? There were parts that I found hard to swallow, but overall . . . "I'm still digesting it," I told him.

He nodded curtly. "Fair enough."

"Do you have a plan?"

He said, "There's only one place for us now. We're going to Davos. The Forum starts in four days. That's why I told you we were running out of time."

"And then?"

"We're still putting it together."

"So you don't know what you're going to do."

"We have ideas," he said.

"But you don't trust the Agency enough to tell me."

"Let's just say it hasn't been finalized yet." He leaned closer and tapped the recorder. "Who will you give this to?"

"My boss, Paul Williams. He'll pass it on to Mel and Sally—I don't know their surnames. The ones who sent me to you."

"And what do you think? Will they act? Or will they bury it?"

"I don't know."

He worried over my answer, then checked his watch. He rifled through Leticia's bag until he found a satellite phone. "Do you want to call home?"

"What?"

"Your wife. Tell her you're okay. That you're coming home. We're putting you on a flight out of Madrid for tomorrow morning. Eleven a.m."

I blinked, surprised. Though he'd told me as much, I couldn't imagine stepping onto a plane and getting back to my family. "Yeah," I said. "Thanks."

He powered up the phone and handed it to me, and while I dialed he went to the door and stepped outside to give me privacy. Laura picked up on the third ring—it was seven in the evening where I was, one in the afternoon in DC.

"Hello?" she asked warily, not recognizing the number.

"Laura, it's me."

"You back?"

"No. I'll get on a plane in the morning. Should be home late tomorrow."

"Okay," she said, and yawned, and I realized that only three days had passed since I'd seen her last. In her mind, I was calling after a series of meetings with powerful men, probably sitting in a hotel with room service and a few drinks in me. But then, in the silence, she seemed to pick up on something. "You all right, Abdul?"

"Sure," I said, then said it again: "Sure. Just wanted to let you know. How's the monster?"

"Doesn't like being back at school."

"I bet," I said, then realized I was weeping. I didn't know why—or, I didn't have a specific reason. It was just the convergence of everything. I took a deep breath to distract from the sound and said, "All right. See you tomorrow. Love you."

"You, too," she said, then hung up.

The ship groaned, and I stared at the satellite phone in my hand, drying my eyes and thinking of my brother. About a year before he died, he told me, "There is nothing special about the powerful. They're only a bunch of assholes trying to get one up on each other."

"That's why we have checks and balances," I countered.

"Did you read that in a book?" he asked, grinning. He'd just gotten back from Yemen, where Houthi Shia insurgents, he'd had to admit to his clients, had made foreign investment a nonstarter. "That's the problem with education—you're taught that the systems we have in place actually work. What they don't admit is that everything is falling apart in slow motion."

We were in a DC bar where my co-workers often met after hours, and I even saw a couple of them by the window, glancing curiously at the big, tough-looking man I was drinking with. "In Yemen, sure," I said.

"I'm not talking about Yemen. I'm talking about right here—the West. Each year a little more washes away. The tide of history eats at it. Just look around. Open your eyes."

It was my job to look around, to see threats where no one else saw them. It was Haroun's job, too; we just had different employers. "My eyes are open," I told him. "I see reports you'll never see."

"The Agency?" he asked. "What do you think you're doing there? Your job isn't to push back the tide. Your job is to make sure no one notices what's going on."

I was growing insulted by his condescension; over the years his expansive travel itineraries had made him vain. "That's bullshit, Haroun."

He flashed that charming grin and took a swig of beer. "Listen, brother. In places like Yemen, I see the West's future. I can handle it because the future isn't really my problem. I don't have kids. But the plebes out there? If they saw what I see, they would lose their shit—total panic. Social norms would be a thing of the past. Laws just words on paper. And you, in the Agency, would have to throw up your hands and give up. Which is why you hide the truth. I don't blame you—everybody does it: the government, the media, the church, the mosque. Every mommy and daddy in the world. Because without the illusion of security there *is* no national security. The most important thing you can do is make sure no one sees the world for what it is."

"You're an idealist," I told him, the realization just then dawning on me. "To you, what's not perfect is a complete failure. But that's not the world. Those reports I read? They show me how messy *everything* is. Ironically, that makes me optimistic."

"See?" Haroun said, as if I'd proven his point for him. "In the face of the impending disaster you're *optimistic*. Face it, Abdul: The CIA will never make a difference."

"And you?" I demanded. "Are *you* going to make a difference?"

"Of course not. But I'm not the one fooling myself."

He'd pissed me off, but for days I couldn't shake the argument. I'd go to the office, read reports, and send analyses up the ladder, and I started wondering what the point of it all was. Later, after Haroun died and Rashid was born, this question became more imperative. I had a son now, one who would have to survive in the world I was leaving him. It was no use telling myself that the world wasn't my responsibility, the way Milo Weaver had done. And after the 2016 election, I thought that Haroun, had he lived, would have seen that moment as a milestone in the dissolution of the West. In newspapers and the blogosphere, pundits questioned the foundation of

American democracy. It was one reason the Massive Brigade had been able to gain so many followers so quickly, and why its members felt that setting off bombs in shopping malls was a valid way to express themselves. They were expressing the hopelessness that Haroun had predicted. Idealists like Haroun and Ingrid Parker couldn't stomach the imperfections that defined us as human beings.

And what was I doing about it? Reading reports and writing analyses that vanished into the bureaucratic abyss, while Rashid grew older and his mother and I grew further apart. Haroun's vision of the world was coming to fruition. For me personally, for my country, and even for this organization that called itself the Library.

2

Our nearness to the Spanish coast was an illusion, revealed by the hour and a half it took to reach Huelva as the sun disappeared behind the Atlantic off to our left. Along the harbor were crowds, some waiting for arrivals, others waiting to board outgoing liners. I stood with Milo and Leticia, and together we looked down at hundreds of faces. Who were we looking for? Grace Foster, or the Tourists themselves, like the relentless Gary Young who had come at Leticia in Hong Kong, and after all three of us in Laayoune, then helped the fake Joseph Keller kill their colleagues? I didn't know those faces; the only face I'd seen was the second man in Laayoune, who had walked calmly, pistol outstretched, and fired with the steady rhythm of an automaton. The memory still chilled me.

But would I have even recognized that face in the crowd? I doubted it. Disorientation had crippled me, making me useless. Milo Weaver's story, the threat to my life, the sudden shift in my understanding of how the world worked. All of that, mixed with the sound of Laura's voice and the prospect of surviving long enough to be with her again—these things undermined me entirely. My joints tingled; my vision kept going spotty. I was weak and strong and tired; I was exultant to return to solid earth. And my thoughts were a mess, but I would have time to sort through them on the long flight back to DC. For now, I allowed myself to walk down the gangplank with my protectors and not think about anything. I had given myself over to them and was free to let myself be pulled through the crowd. Women, young and old. Grizzled fishermen and sharp businessmen from Barcelona. Traders and tourists in so many shades. The throb and hum of humanity and life.

"Come on," Weaver said.

I followed him to where a slender black man stood next to an Audi SUV, speaking with Leticia. He shook Weaver's hand and then mine. "Dalmatian," he said.

From the other side of the SUV a woman appeared, and seeing her hard dark eyes and the look on her face I tensed, imagining that this was Mrs. Gary Young or Grace Foster—but, no. Milo hugged her tightly, then introduced her to me. "Abdul, this is my sister, Alexandra."

She shook my hand and looked me up and down, her judgment quite apparent, then turned to Leticia. "Thanks for keeping them alive."

Leticia shrugged. "Griffon's family?"

Milo Weaver's sister nodded seriously. "Safe."

Weaver, Alexandra, and I rode in the back, Leticia in the passenger seat, and Dalmatian drove us through the evening crowds and traffic out of Huelva and down the *autopista* through dark farmland, deeper into Europe. I had the strange desire to be back on that ferry, where all I had to focus on was the sound of Milo Weaver's voice. Here, on land, everything moved and vibrated, and I had the nasty feeling my senses were lying to me.

An eye on the speedometer, Dalmatian said, "Papers in the glove compartment," and Leticia took out an envelope and passed it back to Milo, who passed it to me. Inside was a plane ticket in my name from Madrid-Barajas to Dulles, direct, departing at 11:15 a.m.

"It'll take us six hours," Dalmatian said.

"All of us?" I asked, which provoked a laugh from Leticia.

Milo said, "Abdul, you're our messenger. We're not leaving you alone until you're safely inside that airport."

In coded language that was just beyond my understanding, Alexandra updated Milo on his family, who were apparently secure somewhere in Europe. Then she gave a rundown of the most recent Davos confirmations. "Oliver Booth just reserved his room at the Intercontinental. For Thursday."

"At the end of the Forum," Leticia said. "Which means we were right—they are meeting on Friday. We just need to find out what time, and where."

By the time we passed Seville and turned north toward the rugged heart of Spain, low shrubs flashing in our headlights, it occurred to me to return to the most obvious question: "What exactly are you going to do there?" They all looked at me, maybe irritated, but I didn't care. "You don't have authority to arrest anyone. I don't think you're planning to kill them—you aren't, are you?"

"I consider that an option," Leticia interjected.

"No," Milo said. "It's not being considered."

"Then what? You pull up to the meeting, and those people, those Tourists, cut you down. You die for nothing."

"That's why you're important," he said. "I don't know why the Agency chose you, but I'm glad they did. You know how to listen."

Was that my magical ability, the one that made me perfect for this particular job? What a sad superpower.

Alexandra focused on my face in the darkness and spoke to me for the first time. "What's the alternative, Abdul? Let them do what they like? Say that this is just the way the world is, but at least we've got full refrigerators and nice cars?"

She was trying to shame me, and I let her do it because she was right.

"Once Keller returned to them," Milo said, "they knew how much we'd put together. They're never going to leave us alone."

"Hello," Dalmatian said, and the tenseness in his voice made us all look. He was squeezing the wheel and looking straight ahead along the dark country road to where two pale pickup trucks were parked, forming a V that blocked any passage. Dalmatian brought us to a stop fifty yards short. Leticia, Milo, and Alexandra already had pistols in their hands. I suddenly remembered I had one as well. I floundered, tugging it out of my jacket pocket.

"I don't see anyone," Leticia said, squinting through the windshield.

"They'll be in the fields," Milo said. "Let's get out of here."

Dalmatian was already switching to reverse, and we roared backward down the road until a pair of headlights switched on behind us, another pickup truck rolling forward.

Leticia pressed the button to lower her window and said, "Put me on that side."

Dalmatian spun the SUV and screeched to a halt as Leticia turned and, with both hands, aimed her pistol out the window. She only fired twice, two ear-piercing *booms*, straight into the truck's windshield. Glass cracked, and then from the rocky landscape there was a cacophony of pops and little flashes in the night as hidden people began shooting at us. I ducked to the floor. Dalmatian punched the gas. We sped away, past the single pickup, and back into darkness. We'd left our attackers behind, but the car shook violently. I raised my head. Everyone seemed to be all right.

"Tire?" Leticia asked.

"Front, right," Dalmatian said.

Calmly, he pulled to the side of the road and parked as Milo, Alexandra, and Leticia got out and watched behind us. I finally climbed out as well, but my knees were rubbery, and I felt nauseous. I went to help Dalmatian with the spare tire, but all I could manage was to crouch with him in the cold, balancing the replacement tire and holding the flashlight. From our side I couldn't see the road, could only hear the other three pushing through underbrush. They were taking positions silently, like people who have known one another all their lives and no longer need to speak.

"Pass it," Dalmatian whispered, and he traded my tire for his blown one. He was incredibly fast, setting the fresh one in place and picking up nuts, spinning the wrench like a professional. Which, I supposed, he was.

As he finished we heard a truck engine approaching.

"You wait here," he told me, looking straight into my face. "Don't move. Okay?"

I nodded.

He took the flashlight from me and walked around the front of the SUV to the road, the flashlight above his head. I was confused—was he signaling to the people who had just shot at us? Did this mean . . . was he betraying Milo? Then Dalmatian shouted in Spanish, some long stream of what sounded like angry abuse. The truck was so close. I heard it come to a stop and idle.

A new voice—female—asked him something in Spanish. He answered. Then a door opened and closed. I guessed the woman, or someone else, had exited the truck.

I saw movement in my periphery, off to the left. Leticia Jones rose from a shrub and fired twice into the road. Other shots rang out—a battle suddenly raged as Dalmatian appeared, running full speed back around the front of the SUV to me. He threw himself into the dirt and fumbled at his side, breathing so loudly that I could hear him above the gunfire. I saw what it was—a bullet had gone through his side, and blood, black in the night, streamed onto the dirt.

The firing stopped, but I wasn't thinking about that anymore. I ripped open his jacket and found the hole gushing blood. I pressed on it. Blood spilled between my fingers, making them slick, and I had trouble holding on. Dalmatian moaned deeply and miserably. From somewhere, I heard Milo Weaver shout, "Keep driving and we'll let you live!"

Who the fuck was he talking to? I shouted, "Dalmatian's been hit!" Off to my left, Leticia looked over, but she didn't come to join me. I supposed she had more important things to deal with.

"Milo Weaver!" a male voice called. "You have *got* to finally die."

Who joked at a time like this? Psychopaths and Tourists. I pressed harder, but I didn't think I was doing any good. Dalmatian's hand came around and pressed on top of mine.

"Move on, Gary!" Leticia shouted.

"Is that Leticia Jones?"

"Five seconds and we open fire," Milo called.

"He's *dying* over here!" I shouted.

"Four seconds!" Milo called.

"You never made a difference, Weaver!" the man called back, and that was when I realized it was a voice I knew. I would have known it immediately if he hadn't been shouting. If he'd been speaking in a cool, measured tone. But he hadn't been. He'd been trying to make himself heard.

Beneath my hand, Dalmatian jerked violently. I couldn't leave him. I couldn't go and look. Was I right? No, I couldn't be. The man finally put his truck into drive, and I heard it rolling forward, crunching rocks. I looked up to see it emerge, very slowly, from around the front of the SUV. The driver was hunched over the wheel, his head turned in my direction, maybe wanting to get a good look at whoever was dying. His face was lit by the dashboard lights. Our eyes met. And I was shocked beyond measure. From the way his eyes grew and his mouth fell open I was sure that he was, too.

Then my dead brother, Haroun, drove on, deeper into the no-man's-land of Spanish countryside.

Shook.

My son's favorite word felt right.

I was shook when Milo and I pulled Dalmatian into the SUV, and when Leticia took the wheel and we sped off. I was shook when Alexandra and Milo tried to get everything out of me. I was shook when Milo announced to the vehicle that of *course* this was why the Agency had sent me. They had noticed these new Tourists—had come across some leads—and one of those leads had been Haroun Ghali, a dead man who was not dead, a man whose own brother worked for CIA. Who else *could* they send?

"But it tells you they're shooting in the dark," Leticia said as she drove. "If they knew anything, they wouldn't have sent him. They sent him on the off chance that the brothers would cross paths and Abdul would recognize him."

"Desperation," Milo said. "They're running blind. Which means they're going to want what we're giving them." He turned to me. "That story they told you about us supporting the Massive Brigade? They knew it was bullshit. That was just a way to frame it for you. They're interested in the same thing we're interested in."

I had nothing to say because I was shook.

Leticia found a late-night clinic in Monesterio, and I used its bathroom to clean most of Dalmatian's blood off me, though my clothes would never be clean again. The nurse on duty was horrified until Leticia took her aside for a conversation that somehow mollified her. I joined Alexandra and Milo outside in the cool night while Spanish doctors worked on their friend.

"I don't understand," I finally said.

Milo heard the wobble in my voice and spoke softly. He said, "A Tourist is an identity, and in order to be untraceable, in the old days we would often stage a death so they could be reborn under a fresh identity. That's what happened to your brother. He didn't die in 2009. He got a job. A job that required he drop contact with everyone he knew."

"But . . . why?"

"Why did he take the job? There's never only one reason."

That wasn't the question my *why* referred to, but not even I knew what I was asking. Why was Haroun chasing us? Why was this happening to me? Why had my brother become a monster? My *why* was all questions and none.

Leticia came out after an hour to tell us that Dalmatian had been sewn up but that they wouldn't let him leave until he'd had at least six hours in their bed. "What about the police?" Milo asked.

"We have a deal," she said, rubbing her thumb and index finger together. Then she looked me over critically. "Get him changed before his flight. But don't come back here. Dalmatian and I will meet you there."

I nearly passed out during the four hours it took to reach Madrid. We stayed on the outskirts, in Carabanchel, and Milo checked the size of my clothes and went into a men's outlet that had just opened, eventually coming out with a complete suit. It was a good fit, but my shoes, beaten by their trek out of the Sahara, were permanently scuffed; once I got home I would have to throw them out.

We arrived at the airport with time to spare. In the car, Milo gave me my phone back. "It's Saturday now. I'll call your number on Wednesday. That should be enough time for them to make up their minds."

"Okay," I said, then handed him Collins's gun. Not because of airport security but because I wanted nothing to do with it. I wanted nothing to do with anything, because I was shook.

Neither got out of the car with me, but when I entered through the automatic doors and looked back they were still in the idling car, both Milo and his sister watching me.

At check-in, the woman behind the counter gave me a bright smile and pointed me to the security check. After a long wait, I put my phone and filthy shoes into a plastic box, and on the other side of the X-ray machine took them back. I took a seat at the gate, surrounded by tired travelers. I was still so fucking shook.

Yes, I would have time on the plane to figure it out, to assemble my thoughts and outline what I would tell Paul, but I desperately wanted to understand it right then and couldn't. Nothing quite connected. I had been filled with a story from the dark side of capitalism. Yet it still didn't make sense to me, and making sense of things was what had given my life value. I was faced with a convoluted tale of excess that had suddenly become a ghost story that could only be cleared up by speaking directly with the ghost.

I heard my name over the PA system and saw that all the seats around me were empty. The stewardess at the Lufthansa gate was asking where Abdul Ghali was, because my flight was about to leave. She looked across the empty seats to catch my eye and turned off the mic. "Abdul Ghali?" she asked me.

I shook my head. "No, sorry," I said, then got up and left.

3

After Madrid Airport, Milo and Alexandra drove north, diagonally through France, and all the way to the Black Forest. In total, it took eighteen hours, the two of them taking turns behind the wheel, stopping only to buy gas with euro bills and eat a long lunch in Bordeaux, where they spoke haltingly of the days ahead. When that conversation began to feel hopeless, Alexandra told him how well Tina and Stephanie were doing, which was encouraging, but eventually they wound their way back to failures.

"Where did we go wrong?" Milo asked, and Alexandra smiled wryly.

"Now it's *we*, is it?"

"It's always been we," he said.

In Freiburg im Breisgau they stopped at Jacques' Wein-Depot, where Milo searched the shelves and picked up an expensive bottle of Riesling from the Mosel region; then they entered the Black Forest, where snow-adorned branches closed in around them, dimming their path. As the sun set, they arrived at the small city of Schramberg, cut through with mountain streams, shop windows celebrating its famous Junghans watch factory.

It was an attractive city, but they didn't linger, instead pushing north, back into the mountains and eventually turning onto an unmarked gravel driveway that snaked at an incline through the trees, lit only by their head-lights. Milo drove slowly, foot on the brake, then stopped midway down the winding road when a man stepped out of the snow-covered foliage in a heavy white coat. He held a Heckler & Koch MP7 submachine gun in one hand and showed them the palm of his other. A white coiled wire grew from behind his right ear and disappeared into his collar. Milo rolled down the window, kept his hands visible on the wheel, and waited for the suspicious guard to approach.

In German, the man said, "You took a wrong turn. Back up."

"Please let her know that Milo Weaver is here."

"I don't know who you're talking about," the guard said, shaking his head. "Put the car in reverse."

"Tell her Milo Weaver needs to speak with her."

The guard frowned, seeming very pissed off. "Your name is Milo Weaver," he finally said, speaking very clearly. "Who is your colleague?"

"She's my sister. Alexandra."

"Alexandra Weaver?" the guard asked.

"Jesus," Alexandra muttered. "We've been here before."

"Alexandra Primakov," Milo told the guard.

"Alexandra Primakov," the guard repeated, enunciating each syllable for the benefit of whoever was on the other end of his earpiece. And while that person figured out what to do, the guard held still, his eyes sweeping across the windshield to eye Alexandra, and then he looked behind them, along the driveway, in case they had brought friends. Though of course he would know already, since the woods were littered with cameras. Eventually, the guard lowered the gun to his side and said, "Slowly. If you speed you will be killed."

Milo rolled up his window and continued around two turns to reach a large wooden house that, in the traditional style, was three-quarters sloping roof. Untraditionally, most of the roof was covered in solar panels, and a pair of spotlights illuminated the parking lot in front.

Two more figures in heavy coats approached their car, a man and a woman, their Heckler & Kochs fitted with forty-round box magazines and long suppressors—he guessed they didn't want the neighbors to be disturbed by any late-night mass murder. When he and Alexandra got out of the SUV, leaving their pistols behind, Milo grabbed the wine bottle and held out his arms as the soldiers patted them down. They were taken around the side of the house to a door of reinforced steel. The woman knocked, and the door was immediately opened by the white-haired, enormous woman who, many years ago, had been a senior official in the Bundesnachrichtendienst and had, along with her deputy Oskar Leintz, tortured Milo in her basement in Pullach, just south of Munich.

"Milo," she said, her accent thick and coarse from too much abuse. "You have survived."

"As have you, Erika."

Erika Schwartz's skeptical gaze took in Alexandra for a moment, and she said, "You know, darling, you're looking more and more like your father."

Alexandra smiled cryptically.

"Are they here?" Milo asked.

Pointedly not answering him, Erika said, "Is that wine?"

The soldiers sauntered away as Erika Schwartz stepped back so they could enter. That was when Milo noticed she was using an aluminum quad cane, which she hadn't had back in October, and when they followed her through the narrow dark-wood corridor he saw how difficult walking had become for her. Her weight had always been an issue, but the drinking certainly hadn't helped.

"Are they here?" he asked again.

"Soon. You can open that bottle in the kitchen," she said, then led Alexandra into the living room.

Milo searched through stuffed drawers to find a rusting corkscrew and blew out three dusty glasses. When he got to the living room, he found Alexandra standing close to the wall, looking at old photographs as Erika relaxed in her large comfy chair, narrating them. "Helmut Kohl was much smarter than people knew—one-on-one, he was formidable. But, as with any truly intelligent person, talking to the masses was an issue. And there—1969, with Willy. Now that man, he *made* the SPD." She shook her head. "And now they're gone—Willy, Helmut the Older, and Helmut the Younger. And what are we left with? *Technocrats.*"

"Angela Merkel?" Alexandra asked.

"Ha!" Erika spat, plainly disgusted by the advance of history, so Milo served her the first Riesling, then Alexandra, who sipped it and made a face.

"What's wrong, dear?" Erika asked. "You prefer red, I suppose. For the *heart.* Healthy drinking is an oxymoron. Come. Sit."

"How *is* your health?" Milo asked.

"My doctor won't let me eat Snickers anymore. The fascist." As Milo settled into a stiff chair, she turned to him and changed her tone: "You were right."

"About what?"

"Katarina Heinold reserved a room in Davos for Thursday."

Milo sighed, one turncoat patron now unmasked. It was why he'd stayed away from all of them, even Said Bensoussan. "Has anyone questioned her?"

"Not yet."

"What about Beatriz Almeida?"

"No sign. Yet." Erika sipped her wine, savoring it. "Foster and Halliwell reserved two rooms in the Belvédère."

"For Thursday?"

She shook her head. "Apparently they want to attend the Forum itself. My question, however, is: What are you planning, Milo? They're gathering. Many will be there by Tuesday. Sergei Stepanov, like Katarina and Oliver Booth, arrives Thursday. But I still don't know what you expect. We cannot tell the Swiss to pick them up, and Oskar is refusing to breach Swiss sovereignty. Where does this go?"

"Did he set up our meetings?"

"Reluctantly. The first one is tomorrow. Britain."

"I'll take it," Alexandra told Milo. "You can stay a little longer."

"I don't want you going alone," he said.

"Poitevin's already there," she reminded him. "He'll back me up."

"China will be tricky," Erika said wearily. "We were unable to find Xin Zhu—he seems to have vanished. So we had to settle for a contact in the Second Bureau."

"Shit," Milo said, an involuntary snap. "The Second Bureau is in bed with Northwell."

Erika frowned. "Did you tell us that?"

"I told Oskar," Milo said, trying not to let his anger take over. "What happened to Xin Zhu?"

"We don't know. He has gone dark."

This felt like the worst news of all. Northwell had had three months to decrypt the Library's files, and while they'd never used Xin Zhu's name, the Second Bureau could have run down the clues until they found the common denominator. "He might be dead already," Milo said.

That earned a moment of silence, until Erika showed off a crooked grin, "Or maybe I'll have to make up a bedroom for Xin Zhu, too."

What had gotten into the old woman? The Erika Schwartz he'd known, all the way up to her staged death and secret retirement in 2015, had been one of the most reticent people he'd ever met. Gloomy silence, a cutting word, and then an order that had a fifty-fifty chance of spelling Milo's doom. This Erika was as curmudgeonly as the old one, but she was almost . . . joyful. Was this what retirement had done to her? Had losing the burden of daily responsibilities changed her that much? Or had she already dipped into today's bottle of Riesling before they showed up?

"We should get our hands on Katarina Heinold," Alexandra suggested. "She'll at least know the time and place of the meeting."

"Talk to Oskar about this—he is watching her," Erika said, then a vague smile entered her face as she watched Alexandra. "So much like Yevgeny." She held out her now-empty glass. As Milo refilled it, she said, "Do you know why your father invited Germany into the Library?"

Milo knew, or thought he knew, but wanted to hear her opinion on the matter. "Tell us."

"Because no one trusted him. Iceland, Kenya, Ghana? An old KGB hand asks them to trust him with their money. Promises new levels of intelligence. What would you think? So he came to me. Did you know that?"

"To you?" Alexandra asked; Milo, too, was surprised.

"He understood that even though the Library was to serve marginalized countries, it would never get off the ground if it didn't have a senior member already committed. At the time, you'll remember, the Americans had gotten us into Afghanistan and were starting to feed us questionable intelligence about Iraq. So the Library could be useful for Germany as well. That is why I met with Gerhard Schröder and convinced him to help your father. And once Germany was in, the others lined up." She drank, then pursed her wet lips. "You know, this situation is the same. You are trying to gather countries that do not trust you. They hardly trust each other. You need a senior partner, and as much as it pains me to say it, Germany will not do. If you cannot convince the Americans to join your crusade, then I do not expect the others to commit."

"We're working on them."

"You need to do more than that. China, Russia, Britain—they have listened to all the stories these last three months. While you have been in the desert, Northwell has been spinning tales. That Milo Weaver's secret intelligence organization is in lockstep with the Massive Brigade. There is evidence, too. Reference points that connect you to those bomb-throwing anarchists."

"They're spreading lies to justify going after us."

"Of course. But the lies are built on known facts. Facts that are not appreciated." She drank, closing her eyes to better enjoy the flavor, then smacked her lips and said, "There have been sightings. Did you know? Ingrid Parker in Europe. Security agencies on alert. We spotted her ourselves, briefly, in Berlin. There is a photograph of her with one of our own radicals. Everyone is looking for her, Milo, and for you."

"Germany, too?"

"Looking for you? Of course. We don't want to let our allies down. Unfortunately, we don't know where you are." That crooked smile again. Then it disappeared and she opened her hands. "If you want to survive this week, you must convince America to cooperate."

"I gave them the whole story."

"And what do they say?"

"I'll know on Wednesday."

She took a deep breath that raised her enormous body a couple of inches, then she exhaled and rubbed the rim of her glass with a blunt finger. "We have done as you asked, Milo. When will you do as we asked?"

"When this is over."

"You don't trust us."

"I can't afford to," he said. Whatever history he and Erika Schwartz had, he couldn't trust that she would follow through on anything after he'd paid for her assistance. She had been waiting, though, for three whole months. She'd sent Oskar to connect with foreign intelligence agencies, convincing them to come to Davos to meet with people they had already been charged with arresting on sight. And by doing so she was risking Germany's relationships with those countries. So back in October he'd had to promise the only thing he really had to offer: the Library's collected files, unencrypted.

She finished her glass and held it out to him. Obediently, he filled it. "Now tell me, Milo: What do you think these meetings will accomplish?"

It was a good question, and over the hour it took to finish the Riesling, then open and drain half of another, Erika Schwartz came up with points to consider. For example, they could not simply make a public accusation against the consortium, or against Northwell, because they had no evidence. All they could do was spin a story that had the whiff of bad conspiracy. New World Order. QAnon. George Soros. And, yes, Davos itself. Those stories were always relegated to the darker corners of the internet, where they nurtured their own fringe followings but never—or, rarely—became accepted reality. No—all they had was a scattering of events that, together, looked a lot like Northwell running an illegal army for the benefit of its paymasters, but little tangible to prove it. The through lines connecting the Department of Tourism to Anthony Halliwell and his ex-wife, Grace Foster, and on to MirGaz, IfW, Tóuzī, Salid Logistics, and Nexus, were circumstantial. Not even Leticia's chain of payments from China to Boko Haram could be used, because it had all been illegally obtained. They had nothing on the fake Joseph Keller who had murdered Kristin and Noah, the New York police had made no headway on Alan's murder, and Heeler, who had been helping him, had simply vanished. And once Milo disappeared back in October, an anonymous call to Paris police had led to the body of the real Joseph Keller, buried in the suburbs, and the caller identified one Milo Weaver as the killer.

"And we'll never know what evidence Keller had," Milo said in despair. "We'll never know what got him killed. Maybe in those pages there was everything."

Erika chewed the inside of her mouth, thinking perhaps of her own service's mistake. If the BND's irregular had photographed the pages when he'd had the chance in Paris, all of this might have been avoided. Or maybe she was only anticipating another glass of Riesling.

"What we need, Erika, is allies."

"Allies to do what? Kill them all?"

"Of course not. To stop them. To put them out of business."

"But *how*?" she pressed.

Before he could answer, voices grew in the entryway, coming closer. Milo recognized the tones instantly and was on his feet, eyes wet in Pavlovian response, even after three whole months, so that when they appeared in the doorway he was ready for them. Tina was shocked by his sudden tight embrace, a shopping bag slipping from her hand, and Stephanie looked stunned, watching her rough-cheeked, dirty father. She even wrinkled her nose when he grabbed her, but then she started crying.

4

The Spanish doctors had assured Leticia that there was no infection, and while warning her that Dalmatian shouldn't move too much, they had given her the green light to transport him by car. That worked out well until they crossed into France in their rental and his wound started to bleed again. Dalmatian fought with her, insisting he could make it the whole way, but he was being a fool, and as they passed the snowcapped peak of Le Peuil she spotted him gritting his teeth and clutching wet red hands to his wound. So she'd sped to the next town, Vif, just south of Grenoble, and taken him to the emergency entrance of the Alpes Isère Hospital Center. A befuddled French doctor found the broken stitches and bandaged him up, and when Leticia explained that he'd been impaled on a broken railing in Barcelona the doctor sighed and contemptuously said, *"Spain."*

Dalmatian was forbidden from traveling for at least forty-eight hours, and the doctor would only discharge him after Leticia made a reservation at an isolated lodge at the edge of the Parc Naturel Régional du Vercors. In the morning, she stepped outside to survey the grounds of what turned out to be a ranch stocked with horses, mules, rabbits, guinea pigs, goats, ducks, and other farmyard animals. She went for a short ride, taking a beautiful stallion named Deck of Cards up to the edge of town to look out for shadows that never appeared. A little before one, the call came, and she gave Milo an update on Dalmatian. He listened soberly, then told her that the meeting the

Germans had set up in Davos was not with Xin Zhu's people, but with the Second Bureau.

"Shit."

"Don't go," Milo said.

"Maybe they want a new deal," she said, thinking aloud.

"Or maybe they want to kill us, one at a time."

Anything, she reflected, was possible. "Either way, I've got to get to Davos."

"Be careful."

"You don't have to tell me," she said.

When she came back to the room, she brought Dalmatian food from the kitchen, and he ate ravenously, which was a good sign.

"I gotta go," she told him.

"Let's go, then," he said through a full mouth.

"It's a six-hour drive," she told him. "Follow me tomorrow, when you're ready."

"And let you have all the glory? Here. Help me up."

They were in the car within the hour, following signs to Geneva, where they skirted around the edge of the enormous lake and ascended into the mountains. For a long time they were silent—neither was much of a talker—until Dalmatian said, "So what do you think? We making it out of this?"

"Well, I am," she said.

He grinned at that, then: "There are a lot of moving parts. One or two things go wrong, and this boat sinks fast."

She looked into the rearview at a BMW that had been around for a couple of miles. "If we see the boat leaking, we know what to do."

"What's that?"

"Abandon ship."

He frowned at her, then peered out at the mountain peaks disappearing into the night. Finally, he shook his head. "Someone has to plug the holes."

"Look, you're a librarian," she said. "You've been one a long time. I'm not part of any club—I learned my lesson long ago. I don't let other people's mistakes take me out."

Dalmatian grunted, then turned away and said nothing more.

It had been dark for three hours when they finally reached the Hotel Terminus in Küblis, just north of Davos, and settled into a room with two beds and bare-wood walls. Dalmatian was holding together well, but sitting up for so long had exhausted him. He stretched out on his bed, and Leticia bundled up, went outside, and drove south. It took forty minutes driving through sporadic traffic and two very long, beautifully maintained tunnels to reach the parking lot on the outskirts, beside Lake Davos. In the strobe of passing headlights, she walked along the road and caught a bus down to snow-covered Dorfseeli Park, across from another parking lot with a huge tent where journalists registered their credentials for the Forum. She joined the crowds walking down the Promenade, Davos's shopping street, past yellow and brown apartment buildings and their brightly lit ground floor shops.

She had no real plan other than to take it all in, to get the scent of a place she'd never visited before. A sleepy town that, for one week a year, became the epicenter of the world's wealth, all under the theory that the collision of ideas and money could make the world a better place. Which was, she knew, a bit of a joke, even to the attendees who paid, at a minimum, $75,000 for an invitation. Many paid it not because they thought they could build a future utopia—few even attended the endless forums where earnest humanitarians prescribed solutions to the world's ills—but because in the space of a few days they could meet more powerful people than they could in a year of flights in their private jets. And here they were, all around her, shoulder to shoulder.

Or, no. Not really *here*—for up ahead, in front of the Congress Hotel, which was part of the Congress Center where the Forum took place, was a line of black-clad Swiss soldiers toting submachine guns. There, *behind* that line, was where the world's most powerful had wrapped up the Forum's first day and were sipping short drinks and glad-handing one another and discussing the maximization of profit. Among them, but kept at a distance, were invited guests like the environmentalists—sixteen-year-old Greta Thunberg and ninety-two-year-old David Attenborough. What did these idealists do among the financial elite? They guilted and cajoled, and the businesspeople smiled and told them what great work they were doing, then passed them off to others so they could get back to the real work of the Forum: mergers and acquisitions.

Or was she being too cynical? Probably. But a lifetime of ups and downs had taught Leticia Jones that cynicism was the only way to see the world for what it was. As an added benefit, cynicism left little room for disappointment, and quite often you could even be pleasantly surprised.

She was turning to leave when she noticed a face among the crowd, off to the left. Chinese woman. Xin Zhu's agent, who had saved her in Shanghai. A little shorter than she remembered, but just as stern faced. Standing under the flags of the Migros supermarket, hands deep in her pockets, watching. Leticia approached slowly, the way you approach a potentially feral dog, and looked out for her inevitable colleagues. She only spotted one, a man with a phone to his ear eyeing them from across the street.

"I had no expectation of ever seeing you again," Xin Zhu's agent said.

Leticia stuck out a hand. "You never told me your name."

Without hesitation, the woman took it with a firm grip. "Li Fan."

"How did you find me?"

"We knew you would come here," Li Fan said, her voice as sharp as it had been in Shanghai. "You and Milo Weaver and Alexandra Primakov. And whoever else is still alive. So we joined Vice President Wang Qishan's entourage and sent everyone out to wait. You were not *hiding*, were you?"

Leticia shook her head and began to walk back toward Dorfseeli Park; Li Fan joined her. "You know I'm supposed to meet with your people tomorrow, right?"

"Second Bureau," she said. "Not my people."

"Should I be worried about it?"

"You should always be worried," she said, and that was when Leticia decided she liked this woman. "We in the Sixth Bureau have to be careful. Why? Because of Milo Weaver's stupidity."

That surprised Leticia. Had Xin Zhu actually told his underling that Northwell held evidence that, if decrypted, would get him killed? "I hear Xin Zhu has disappeared," Leticia said diplomatically.

Li Fan shook her head. "He has stepped back, yes, but he is still very much involved."

It was a kind of answer, so Leticia focused on the matter at hand. "You told me before that Northwell's friends in the Central Committee hold a lot of influence over the Second Bureau."

"That is correct."

"Does that mean I'll be killed tomorrow?"

Li Fan shook her head. "You are not important; Milo Weaver is not important. His files are important."

"Northwell has his files. So, I expect, does the Second Bureau."

"They are unable to read them."

Ah, there it was—the answer to the most urgent question. And it was the first piece of good luck she'd heard in a very long time. "Are you telling me that after three months they still haven't decrypted them?"

"That is what we understand," Li Fan said, almost gliding by her side, her head tilted up to look at Leticia, small eyes very still. "Milo Weaver has very good hackers."

"Do you know the deal Milo's offering?"

"The files for help taking down Northwell." She frowned. "All of the files?"

"All but a very few exceptions," Leticia said.

"What kind of exceptions?"

"The kind Xin Zhu would appreciate."

Li Fan did nothing to suggest she understood what Leticia was getting at, but her sudden lack of curiosity seemed to speak volumes. She said, "You do not have to talk us into it. Did you look at the map as I asked?"

"I did," Leticia said. "They're trying to disrupt the Niger Chad pipeline before it's even built."

"We cannot let that stand."

"Then I shouldn't bother meeting with the Second Bureau at all."

Li Fan shook her head. "If you don't go, they will warn Northwell. Northwell will take precautions. And you will lose your chance."

Leticia nodded, appreciating her point, then told her where they would assemble everyone, and when.

"Who else is joining this?" Li Fan asked.

"We'll find out when we all meet."

"CIA?"

Leticia gave her a lopsided grin. "We'll know when we know."

"Okay," she said. "Just don't be stupid this time. I cannot save you here."

"I'm betting on the crowds to protect me."

"I do not gamble," Li Fan said, nodding, then turned and headed back into town, her colleague across the street abruptly turning around to follow. Leticia continued to Dorfseeli Park, and after the bus ride back to Lake Davos drove back to Küblis. In one of the long tunnels, where the lights flashed by in an endless sequence and she felt as if the world outside this futuristic tube had vanished, she called Milo. He agreed with Li Fan's assessment that there was nothing to do but to go through with tomorrow's meeting, but Leticia didn't like it. She'd risked her neck quite enough for the Library; she'd suffered months of grueling solitude with Milo in Laayoune, preparing for this day. And at the last minute she'd been thrown a curveball.

The tunnel ended, and she was back in the world again, and it was unfortunately the same as it had been before.

What to do? Stick to the plan as Milo wanted? Because no matter how it looked to others, she was certainly *not* a librarian, and she would make her own decisions, particularly when those decisions could decide how long she remained alive.

Back at the Terminus, Dalmatian was poring over maps of Davos, and when she told him what had happened he sighed heavily and said, "Well, we should have expected this."

Once again, she wondered why she didn't just abandon ship. It was a rule she'd maintained her whole life, to always know where the exit was. Without that option, she couldn't function. The same was true now. In her pocket were car keys; in the lot there was a car. She knew how to get her hands on money. Leaving was always an option.

5

After a night's sleep in Erika Schwartz's too-soft guest bed, Alexandra climbed into a Mercedes that the Germans had confiscated from Montenegrin smugglers. It stank of cheap cigarettes, so she cracked the windows, letting in cold mountain air during her three-and-a-half-hour drive that cut through the pristine, tiny kingdom of Liechtenstein on her way south.

She stopped short of Davos, in Serneus, and checked into a bed-and-breakfast as Vivian Wall. In her room she opened her laptop and streamed the World Economic Forum's pre-event: the International Monetary Fund's World Economic Outlook—and it was a gloomy one. The world economy was slowing, leading to higher volatility and heightened risks of sharper decline in global growth. One ripple effect was geopolitical: If vulnerabilities weren't addressed, the world could see an increase in the advance of authoritarian regimes. Milo, who was still reconsummating his marriage in the Black Forest, had been onto something after all.

She didn't leave until eight o'clock, about the same time Li Fan found Leticia on the Promenade, and before getting into the car she checked in with Poitevin, who was renting a room south of Davos. He was already in town, he told her, and was ready.

She parked near the Davos Platz train station on the southern end of town, and from there she walked up the lower Promenade, where some stores had been taken over by countries eager to show off their investment possibilities. Benetton had become a display for Saudi Arabia, which, only three months after they had butchered *Washington Post* columnist Jamal Khashoggi in their Istanbul consulate, was probably a tough sell. She passed camera crews for Deutsche Welle and Russia Today, and even spotted a man with a microphone speaking American English to a pedestrian—his clip-on name tag identified him as working for NPR. And when she looked up, she caught a glimpse of movement on the rooftops: white-clad snipers with long rifles.

The Chämi Bar looked like the front of a traditional village house that had been slammed against a modern apartment building, but Alexandra recognized it by its sign: a ladder and a top hat. She didn't go inside immediately, though. Instead, she continued on, peering into its unhelpfully curtained windows as she passed, then waited by the window of a clothing store called Blue Lemon.

Only now did she see Poitevin, on the other side of the Promenade, almost parallel to her. He looked tired, which she imagined he was. After trading boats with Milo, he'd piloted the old fishing boat north along the African coast to Ben Khlil, where he'd waited in vain for Griffon to pick him up. The next morning, he'd caught a half-day bus to Agadir, then waited a day in Al Massira Airport, sleeping outside on the curb, until a Lufthansa flight brought him to Frankfurt at about the same moment Alexandra picked up Milo, Leticia, and Abdul Ghali in Spain.

They met eyes, but only briefly, and once the pedestrians around her had moved on she entered the Chämi Bar, with its sloped ceiling, red walls, Christmas lights, and exposed beams. It was busy and loud with multilingual chatter and rock music. To the right, on one side of the bar, a three-piece band was setting up, and on the other side of the bar was the man Erika had told her was named Francis, identified by the copy of *The Daily Mail* on his table—probably the only person in Davos who would dare to be seen with a copy.

As she approached, she noticed he was eating a hamburger and drinking from a tall glass of pilsner, so she stopped to order an eighteen-year-old Chivas Regal on the rocks. By the time she reached his table, Francis was cleaning his face with a napkin, half rising, holding out a hand. "Hello, hello," he said. "Ms. Primakov?"

Friendly. Maybe a Home Office clerk giddy to be handed a plane ticket. But they wouldn't have sent someone like that, would they? He pumped her hand, then settled down. "Have you tried the burgers here?"

"No," she said, and sipped her Scotch. "How much have you been read in on?"

"Oh," he said, sounding disappointed they wouldn't discuss mountain cuisine. "Well, there was nothing on *paper,* understand. But this little mustached German came by the embassy in Berlin."

"Oskar Leintz."

"Yes, exactly. BND. Talked us through it." Francis hesitated, chewing the inside of his lower lip. "Hard to swallow, to be honest. Still, I did my due diligence, and everything he reported *was* confirmed. But my colleagues asked, did these facts really add up to his conclusions?"

"What about Oliver Booth?"

He raised his brows, rocked his head. "That *was* interesting, wasn't it? Nasty bit of insider trading. The feeling at home is that this is a case that can be pursued, and will be in due time."

"Due time?"

"Years, I'm afraid," he said, smiling with his eyes. "Have to separate the wheat from the chaff."

"And Tourism?" Alexandra asked.

He cleared his throat, his smiling eyes shifting to take in the people around them, then leaned closer. "*Very* interesting. Now, this was news to me, the American department. Not to the higher-ups, of course, and when the file was shared with me I frankly found it all hard to believe." He raised a finger. "At *first.* Again, our people were able to verify a lot of what Mr. Leintz reported."

"So you believe it," she suggested.

He leaned back again, opening his body with spread arms. "What's belief? The evidence does suggest, yes, that what he says is true. And so follows the question: What now? And why should the Home Office be bothered?"

"Mr. Leintz didn't tell you why?"

A short shake of the head. "He did not."

Now she was the one who pushed her Scotch to the side and leaned in. He followed suit. Their faces were close, and his breath smelled of overcooked beef. "For its bother, the Home Office would receive fifteen years of secret intelligence reports from all around the world."

"From this *Library*?" he asked in a high whisper.

"Exactly."

"And what, might I ask, must we do for this treasure?"

"Help us bring down these new Tourists."

He pursed his lips, as if preparing to kiss her, then sipped his beer. He began to count on his fingers. "Britain. Germany. And . . . ?"

"We're meeting with China and Russia."

"The United States?" he asked, his speech quick, as if it were a question he'd arrived ready to ask. She remembered Erika's warning.

"We are in discussions with them now."

"How are they leaning, if you know?"

"Oh, they are in," she lied. "We're just settling details."

He nodded approvingly. "Well, I can certainly put this to my people. How shall I get in touch with you? Through Mr. Leintz?"

She shook her head. "If you can help, then join us. Thursday night. A restaurant outside of town. I'll give you the address."

"Thursday?" he asked, frowning. "The Forum ends on Friday. Isn't that . . . cutting it short?"

"We want everyone to have enough time to consider the offer. The consortium's annual meeting will occur on Friday."

"Where?"

"We'll know by Thursday."

"Hmm," he hummed, then chewed his lip. "So this is an intervention, yes?"

"Something like that."

Out in the street again, Alexandra worked her way back down to the train station, and on quieter Tobelmühlestrasse Poitevin caught up with her. "Good to see you," she told him, which, after Griffon's unexpected death, was even truer than usual. A month after the Library disbanded, she'd posted the recall message at the IP address that each librarian had learned upon joining, but which had never been recorded in the files. It was a simple advertisement, the kind you would find in small, local papers, asking for volunteers for a study of transcontinental library classification systems. Sixteen librarians had replied, but in order to avoid exposing them all over again, she'd only brought in Poitevin, who, along with Dalmatian and Leticia, would suffice for now. The other fifteen had been useful in other ways, gathering intelligence and redistributing the Library's physical assets to safe spots all over Europe.

Poitevin, sounding a little out of breath, said, "How did it go?"

"I don't know," she told him. "I really don't."

6

When I left the gate at Madrid Airport, all I had in my wallet was a few Moroccan dirhams and about two hundred dollars. I had credit cards but wanted to wait before using them. I changed the dollars into euros at a counter, then took a taxi into Madrid, wishing that I had Laura there to translate for me. In broken Spanish I asked the driver for a cheap place to stay, and he took me to the Room007 Ventura Hostel, a place for travelers a decade younger than me—eclectic art on the wall, a communal bathroom, and a bedroom I had to share with a surly French backpacker. But it was only thirty dollars a night, and the Frenchman left me alone throughout the day.

For forty-eight hours, I wrote with my thumbs, directly into my phone. Everything I had seen, everything I had heard, and everything that I believed the Agency should follow up on. I even wrote about Haroun, because they knew about him already. And I told them that the only course of action was to send a team to Davos to assist Milo Weaver and his librarians. Which sounded like the name of a band, but I didn't mention that.

When I finished, having missed meals in my obsession, my thumbs cramped into claws, I passed out with the phone hidden under my stomach, and when I woke on the second morning I reread it, making few changes to the text file that ran over ten thousand words. I used the hostel's computer to attach it and four big audio files to a message addressed to Paul's Agency email:

Paul, I don't know what you're going to do with this, or what the others will say. But if the Agency doesn't act on the information, I will be forced to release copies. See you in Davos.

I didn't know who I would release the report to, so I didn't say. Paul would fill in that blank with whatever the worst option was. After pressing SEND, I took a taxi to the train station, where I scanned the departures board. I was presented with so many possible choices, all over Europe. But my destination was no longer up to me. I took out my credit card.

It was after midnight when I powered up my phone again and made the call. "Hey," I said when she picked up.

"Abdul—oh, God, are you all right? Where are you?"

For some reason the emotion in Laura's voice startled me. "I'm fine. Sorry I couldn't call before now."

"Where *are* you?"

"I'm on a train. I'm going to Switzerland." She was silent a few seconds, so I said, "How are you? Is everything all right?"

"Other than thinking you were dead?" she asked.

"Yeah. Other than that."

"Paul keeps calling me. Asking if you've gotten in touch."

I closed my eyes and sighed. Of course he'd been pestering her. "I'm sorry about that. I'll talk to him. He won't bother you anymore."

"But," she said, looking for words, "what's going *on*? Are you in trouble?"

How to explain it? Was I in trouble? Probably, yes, but sitting in that clean train it didn't feel like trouble. I said, "It's about my brother."

"You mean Haroun?"

"He's alive."

Another moment of silence, longer this time. "He's not, Abdul. You know that." She was starting to speak to me the way she did to Rashid when he was confused.

"I know it sounds crazy," I said, trying to sound as sane and as calm as possible. "But I saw him. He's alive, and he's in Europe."

"But your father went to his—"

"His grave. He flew to Mauritania and saw a marker in the ground. He never saw Haroun's body. None of us did. He didn't die."

"Then . . . then what did he do?"

This, really, was something I couldn't tell her. If the knowledge of these new Tourists had put a price on Milo Weaver's head, then I wasn't about to do the same to my family. "It's unclear," I told her. "But I know where he's going now."

"Switzerland."

"Yes."

When she spoke again, her voice was choked. "Abdul, can't you come home? Talk to Paul. He'll help you figure it out."

My heart sank. She didn't believe me. No—she believed that I believed what I was saying, but she didn't trust that I hadn't lost it. "I'll talk to him," I said. "How's the monster?"

"He misses his dad."

"I miss him," I told her. "I miss you."

We spoke a little more, but the sentiments felt empty. She was too scared to say too much, in case I was on the edge, and I was too scared to tell her what was really going on. She again told me to talk to Paul, then told me she loved me. "I really love you," I told her, as if it had ever been in doubt, which I suppose it might have been a long, long time ago.

When I hung up, it only took thirty seconds for the phone to ring. A part of me, as I picked it up off my thigh, thought it might be Laura calling back, but no, of course not. It was Africa section, and when I answered Paul said, "What's going on, Abdul?"

"Did you get my report?"

"It's a hell of a read."

"And?" I asked, wanting him to hurry up. "Are you going to act on it?"

"Because if we don't you'll share it with the press? Is that what you're saying?"

Fair enough. After two days holed up in that Madrid hostel, listening through headphones to the hours of interview, ruining my thumbs, the threat had felt necessary. Now I wasn't so sure.

"Something has to be done," I told him. "We can't let this go on."

"And you believe Milo Weaver?"

"My dead brother tried to kill us. Yes, I believe Weaver."

"Look," Paul said, sounding tired. Maybe he was. "I appreciate what you've done. We all do. But you send me a screed about a secret army of industrial spies and killers, and you expect the Agency to take action within hours? As admirable as your work has been here, this is the first time you've been sent abroad in the line of duty. I show this to the seventh floor, what do you think they'll say? You're not giving *evidence* here. You're spouting conspiracy theories."

"You already knew about my brother," I said. "It's why you sent me."

Silence. Then, patiently: "It doesn't matter what I know or don't know, Abdul. It'll look like conspiracies to them. How do you know Weaver isn't playing you?"

How did I know? I'd asked myself that until the very moment that Haroun's eyes had met mine. From that point on, I didn't need to be convinced anymore. "You'll find the evidence here," I told him. "They'll all be at Davos. Weaver, too. I'll arrange the meeting."

That was when he broke. "You'll do no such thing, Abdul, because your job is done. You understand? Get home now, or we'll issue a Notice for you. Understand?"

"But—"

"Enough, Abdul. Get Stateside."

A part of me had expected this, though the rest of me had hoped, unrealistically, that everyone could be swayed simply by the depth of my conviction. "See you in Davos, Paul," I said, then hung up and turned off my phone.

7

Three months were like forever. That was a thought that came to him when he saw Tina's bright eyes appear in Erika Schwartz's doorway. As they embraced, Milo flashed on that moment in 2001, in Venice, when he'd first stumbled across this beautiful, pregnant woman on the damp cobblestones, seizing up as labor pains shot through her.

Now, eighteen years later, these two strangers—the woman and the baby inside her—had become such a part of him that without them he was no longer fully himself. During those months apart he'd felt as if parts of him, some internal organs, were missing. He could function, but something somewhere deep in him had stopped working. It was why he'd started smoking again, and within that first half hour of their reunion Tina sniffed and called him on it. But now that he was with them, the urge for nicotine faded. He was whole again, and the infant born on that day in Venice was a grown woman with tears in her eyes, and into her ear he whispered, "It's almost over, Little Miss."

It was a gift, these two days in Schramberg. He was like a sponge, demanding stories from them, particularly Stephanie.

"I've been learning about nature," she told him. "A month ago I went into the forest and lived for three days without any tools."

"What? But it was freezing!"

She shrugged. "I had a coat. I ate rabbit and ferret."

It had taken weeks for Tina to be talked into allowing this wilderness survival weekend, and even though one of Erika's guards had been assigned to keep track of Stephanie from a distance it had terrified her. "But she's different now," Tina confided in him. "In a good way, I think."

Their shopping trips, sometimes to Schramberg, more often to far-flung towns to avoid notice, began in early December when Tina told Erika that if she didn't allow a change of scenery she would face an insurrection. Unlike Milo, who had arrived skinny and sunburned, his wife and daughter looked healthy and strong, and for that he was thankful to Erika Schwartz.

Two days were enough, just barely, to repair him. He shaved and cleaned himself and ate and spent every moment with them. And when the stories ran out he just watched them—"kind of like a creep," Stephanie noted. Then it was Tuesday morning and time to go. He kissed them, then walked with hobbling Erika Schwartz out to another smuggler's car, an Audi.

"You know where you are going?" she asked.

"The Arkaden."

"The Russians don't matter as much as the Americans," she said. "You cannot expect Germany to attack one of its largest financial institutions if America protects two of its largest companies."

Milo opened the car door. "They need time to absorb it. I'm going to call them tomorrow night."

"You are pushing it."

"If I call now, the answer will be no."

Erika looked at him a long time, and he had the sense that her face was a mask covering an Escher maze of conflicting considerations that he would never entirely understand. This old woman was probably the most complicated and inscrutable intelligence officer he'd ever had to face, and in the past he'd paid dearly for underestimating her. Then she nodded abruptly. "Go," she said.

During his long drive, he thought about how his life had changed. He could no longer fly to New York and sit in a conference room to calmly talk people into his way of thinking. Instead, he had to skulk from one meeting place to the other, crossing borders undercover and stopping in roadside stores to pick up amateur tools of the trade, as he did at the last gas station in Germany, where he bought four burner phones from four different manufacturers.

Nearer to Davos, he found a radio station relaying live coverage of the

Forum. Prince William was talking with David Attenborough about climate change. "We are now so numerous," Attenborough said with his familiar intonation, "so powerful, so all-pervasive, the mechanisms that we have for destruction are so wholesale and so frightening, that we can actually exterminate whole ecosystems without even noticing it."

He'd been unable to make Alan's funeral in Boston, and when he called Penelope after the ceremony she'd finally broken, shouting down the international line that Milo was the worst thing that had ever happened to her. He'd had to absorb that blow, because what choice did he have? Maybe she was right. Alan, Kristin, Noah, Leonberger, Griffon. Heeler, probably.

The Attenborough session ended with applause, and after some brief commentary, as he was rolling through the outskirts of Davos, seeing soldiers in the distance, Brazil's newly inaugurated populist president, Jair Bolsonaro, came on the radio. Milo turned it off.

He parked in the basement lot of the Rätia shopping center at the southern end of Davos, not far from the train station. He pulled on the hood of his coat and used sunglasses, knowing there were cameras he couldn't spot as he made his way up the Promenade to the Arkaden cinema, where he bought a single ticket. The audience was thin, most people in the center or up front, so Milo took a seat along the back wall and settled in. The lights went down, and a series of advertisements for upcoming films scrolled, but he wasn't paying attention. He was watching the aisles on either side, waiting.

When they finally arrived, the film had started. In it, one young asshole, on what looked like a New York street, videotaped another young asshole punching and knocking out a Chinese man. For YouTube likes, apparently. Back at their house, though, they were paid back by an unseen person, violently, and that was when Milo noticed a sliver of light to his right as the theater door opened and closed. Two men entered at the same time as, on his left, a third man entered. They let the doors shut behind them. Milo was surprised that Maxim Vetrov had brought the same two thugs he'd had with him in Algiers. Maybe they'd lobbied for the job, a respite from the relentless North African sun.

Vetrov removed his wide-brimmed hat and edged his thick body slowly along Milo's row to reach him. The other two worked their way to the center of the next row up. Settling into the seat beside Milo, Vetrov smelled of cigarettes. "Hello, Mr. Weaver," he said in his halting English.

"Thank you for coming," Milo said, but in fluent Russian, which earned raised eyebrows from Vetrov.

"Russian?" he asked.

"Half," Milo said, then smiled at the two thugs, whom he suspected would soon have a crick in their necks from turning to stare so ominously at him.

"I have to admit, I am surprised," Vetrov said. "In Algiers, you did not seem very happy to meet us. And now that we have a warrant out for your arrest, you invite me to Switzerland."

"In Algiers, I didn't understand. Neither did you." When Vetrov frowned, Milo said, "You thought I was working with Egorov against you. And I thought you were working with my enemies. In fact, both of us wanted the same thing, and Egorov made sure neither of us knew it."

"He was very clever," Vetrov said. "Clever old man."

"By then Joseph Keller was long dead. He'd been killed in Paris. And Egorov had destroyed Keller's list. But he pretended otherwise because he wanted to destroy me."

This seemed to disturb Vetrov, and he sighed, glancing up at the movie, then back to Milo. He said, "When Kirill came back to Algiers, he was supposed to bring Joseph Keller with him. But he didn't. He claimed that Keller had been killed by accident. But then he began to change everything. His daily movements, his meetings with his mistress. He began sending encrypted cables to Moscow—but not secretly, mind. He made a show of it. Very strange."

"He needed to create the illusion he was protecting Keller."

"Maybe," Vetrov said with a shrug. "So we monitored his phone. He called one Milo Weaver, of UNESCO, and told him that there was someone for him to protect." He raised a short finger. "Evidence! Clearly he *did* have Keller. Now, then, was the time to confront him."

"And kill him," Milo said.

Vetrov shook his head vigorously. "No, no. Talk. A slap and tickle, yes, but talking, mostly. Unfortunately, his heart was not up to a simple interrogation."

"So Egorov really did die of a heart attack?"

"I am afraid, yes."

"Another question," Milo said. "When he picked up Joseph Keller in Paris, whose orders was he following?"

Frowning again, Vetrov shook his head. "The Kremlin's, of course. And we wanted him alive. We wanted information on Sergei Stepanov's operations."

"But the Kremlin did kill Anna Usurov."

Vetrov held up his hands, as if defending himself. "Usurov—yes, maybe they did that. She was in Moscow, attacking Putin. She had to expect it."

"What about Boris Nikolaev?" Milo asked, using Leonberger's real name.

"Who?"

"He worked for us in Moscow. He was looking into Usurov's death."

Vetrov's expression darkened. "Nikolaev was *yours*?" He shook his head. "The man killed himself—our people only wanted to speak to him. He put two militiamen in the hospital."

This was what Milo had assumed after reading the police reports, but it helped to have it verified.

Vetrov shifted in his seat, looking uncomfortable. "So are you going to tell me? I hope I didn't fly to Switzerland just to make friends with you."

Milo told him, but slowly so that it wouldn't sound too unhinged, about Egorov's friends, the international corporations, and their weapon of choice: specialized Northwell agents working to advance their interests by whatever means necessary.

Vetrov's frown had deepened so much that he worried the man's face would collapse on itself. "A private army," he finally said.

"Not just any private army. This one is global, and it's expanding. They have no problem working against Russian, Chinese, European, or American interests. They're not interested in long-term stability. They're motivated entirely by short-term gain. But this," he said, tapping the arm of his chair, "is where they meet every year. To establish yearly goals, settle financing, and bring in new clients. This is the only chance we have to get them all in one place. But I can't do it myself. I need help."

"You need the GRU."

"I need the GRU," Milo agreed.

"You ask for a lot, Mr. Weaver."

"I have no choice. They're trying to kill me."

Vetrov stroked his mustache. "I will have to discuss with Moscow."

"Of course."

Vetrov's eyes turned to the screen, where a man with wild hair sat in a wheelchair, staring back at the audience. "Samuel L. Jackson," he said, smiling. "What an actor. You like him?"

"Doesn't everybody?"

"No," he said, shaking his head and slowly standing. "Not everybody. There never has been and never will be anyone in the world who everyone likes."

He nodded to his thugs, who also got up, and all three of them headed to the exit. Milo waited until they were gone, then took out his burner phone and sent a message to Alexandra: *Done*.

Again Leticia left her car by Lake Davos, where the afternoon sun glinted on the water, twinkling brightly. She took the bus all the way to the southern end of town, around the ring of black-clad soldiers, to Davos Platz, where she disembarked among business suits and heavy coats and walked up Talstrasse. Residents who hadn't rented out their apartments for exorbitant prices walked little dogs along the snow-scraped sidewalk and barely gave her a glance. For a week each year, Davos became wildly multicultural, and the residents no longer noticed.

It only took ten minutes to reach the hulking form of the Vaillant Arena, which like so many other buildings had been built with sloping roofs to emulate a ski lodge. As she crossed the empty parking lot, she saw along the second-floor balcony two heavily wrapped Chinese men looking down at her. The lot was cut in half by a high chain-link fence set up by construction workers, but one end had been left open for her. By the time she reached the glass front doors, there was another Chinese guard approaching it from inside and unlocking it to let her in. She expected to be patted down, but he made no move to do that, only led her through the wide, dark space to another set of doors that opened into the huge stadium that usually hosted ice hockey but was now in the midst of a lengthy renovation that wouldn't be completed for a few more years. When the Forum came to town, the workers were all sent on vacation, leaving an empty shell in the middle of town, ideal for a private meeting.

At the rink-side seats, another Chinese man—heavy, with a hairy mole on his chin—stood and shook her hand with a big smile. "Hello," he said in English, his accent strong, losing the *l*'s along the way. "My name is Chen."

"Leticia," she answered.

"Please," he said, motioning to the chair beside him, and they both settled down as his guard wandered away.

For a moment, neither spoke, only looked across the dry expanse in front of them, and up at the high rafters. She thought of Li Fan's warning: Leticia was sitting with the enemy now, one of Northwell's friends. She and Milo had talked it through, but actually being here, her plan felt weak and haphazard. Finally, she said, "Did the Germans explain what's happening?"

"They did."

"And I expect you have questions."

He nodded thoughtfully. "So to be sure I understand: You are proposing that we, together, take apart Northwell International. How?"

"That will be discussed once we're all in the same room, but there are options. You, for example, can go after their training school in Beijing and stop their expansion on Sakhalin Island."

"Yes," he said, as if that hadn't occurred to him. "It is a possibility. But we cannot go after their headquarters. Do you have the Americans' cooperation?"

"We will," she said. "But even without them each country can go after Northwell's clients. Tóuzī is under your jurisdiction. Without customers, this ends."

Chen smiled, perhaps liking the simplicity of her words, perhaps finding them ridiculous. "And I understand there is a carrot."

"Carrot?"

"A reward for taking part."

"Well, China gets to build its oil pipeline without having to worry about terrorists."

He rocked his head, as if that were no reward at all. "I mean the files."

"Yes," she said, noting the interest in his voice. For three months Northwell and the Second Bureau had been banging their heads against Library encryption.

"Question," Chen said, breathing loudly through his nose and squinting across the arena. "How do we know that Milo Weaver will hand this to us? That he won't pull a trick?"

"That's easy," she told him. "He doesn't want to die. He doesn't want his family to die. None of us, Chen, want to die."

"Very good," he said with a smile. "How do I get in touch with you, or Milo himself?"

"You don't. If you agree, then you meet us on Thursday. We'll contact you with the address."

"And that is all? We meet, discuss our options, and then put a plan into action?"

"Exactly," she said. "Unless you have a better idea."

He shook his head, that smile returning. "No, no. It is a wonderful plan."

Crossing the parking lot again, she felt their eyes on her, and she also felt the anxiety of a plan that wasn't quite as clear-cut as she would have liked. There were too many moving parts, and one of those moving parts—Chen— was under the thumb of their enemy. Li Fan had been right—the Second Bureau had no reason to kill her. Yet. But what about Thursday? Once the principals were together in one room? Would Northwell decide that the sim-plest move was to send in their soldiers and wipe out everyone? Reckless, sure, but so was funneling millions to Boko Haram, or sending Tourists out to sink Filipino ships.

It wasn't going to work. She felt this so strongly that, heading back to Küblis, she nearly kept driving north, to Zürich, where she could board a plane to anywhere. Instead, she called Milo and told him what she believed needed to be done to make this work. Otherwise, none of them would make it out of Switzerland alive. He didn't like it, told her it was crazy, but said he would think about it.

"You better think quick," she snapped.

9

Alexandra's rented room on the bucolic, rural edge of Serneus was airy and gave her and Milo a clear view down to the valley. The view was starting to fade as night emerged, and that was when Leticia called from her car and spoke to Milo. After he hung up, he sank into a deep silence that irritated his sister. She knew, after all these years, that Milo's silence didn't always mean deep thought; it often meant confusion. So she forced him to tell her exactly what Leticia had said.

Just as Northwell's annual meeting on Friday was where the consortium was most vulnerable, Leticia had argued, their own meeting, on Thursday, was where they were most vulnerable. And the meeting place, a seasonally closed restaurant on the side of a ski slope, chosen for its solitude, was also the perfect spot for a mass killing.

"She didn't give Chen the address, did she?"

"Of course not. But the Sixth Bureau knows it. And she thinks Chen has a line into them."

"What makes her think that?"

"Experience." When she frowned at him, he said, "He's too confident."

"So what does she want to do?"

"Change of location."

"That's easy enough."

"But that's not it," he said. "If we can't get the Americans on board, she wants to do something crazy to convince the others to join us."

"Sounds like Leticia Jones."

In the morning when Oskar pulled up in one of the BND's black four-wheel drive SUVs, guarded by two blond beasts, they told him about the change of location, and he shrugged. "Sure," he said. "I can tell everyone."

"But not Chen."

"Of course not," he said, then checked his watch. "Vice President Wang speaks immediately after Angela Merkel, at two o'clock. I will tell Li Fan personally, and she can decide who to share it with."

He reached into his jacket and pulled out a heavy manila envelope, opened it, and spread five laminated cards on the coffee table. Milo picked up one, and Alexandra followed suit. The card she held had Leticia's photo and identified her as a stringer for *Frankfurter Allgemeine* Zeitung. Milo handed over the one he was holding, identifying Alexandra as an employee of *Der Spiegel*.

"It's the only way to get inside the security ring," Oskar told them.

"Thank you," Milo said.

Alexandra placed hers back on the table. "I already have one."

Oskar smiled. "Vivian Wall?" He shook his head. "Three hours ago the British put out a warrant for Ms. Wall. I believe Mr. Booth's wife had a hand in that."

That was news. She looked down at the cards—Milo, Poitevin, and Dalmatian were also taken care of, each under assumed names. She sighed. "These are German publications. My German isn't very good."

Oskar sniffed. "You're in Switzerland. Their German is not very good either." Then he winked, looking remarkably confident given the haphazard schemes they were putting together. To Milo, he said, "And the Americans?"

"I'll call them this evening. They've had enough time to think, so I should get an immediate answer."

"Good."

"What about Katarina Heinold?" Alexandra asked.

"She lands tomorrow morning," Oskar said. "I will pick her up personally."

"Good," she said.

Oskar's expression changed, and the confidence bled out of it a little. He cleared his throat and took another envelope out of his jacket pocket. As he opened it and took out two small photos, he said, "In terms of potential issues, of which there are many, let me add another. Ingrid Parker was sighted in Klosters."

He handed over the photos. They were both distant surveillance shots of a woman, but in different locations. In the first, she was sitting with a young man in a Berlin square Alexandra recognized from Kreuzberg. In the second, she was getting into a car on a pretty little street that could only be in Switzerland. They weren't good pictures, the woman's face in shadow, but the height and short-cropped hair looked familiar from a thousand news stories. Milo passed them to Alexandra, who frowned.

"How long has she been here?" Milo asked.

"We don't know. The Berlin shot is two weeks old, the Klosters shot two days. We don't know what they're planning, but we've shared the pictures with our allies, and the Swiss know to watch out."

Alexandra didn't like this. A Massive Brigade action in the middle of the Forum wasn't just dangerous; it could undermine everything they were trying to do.

Alexandra passed back the photos. "Do the Swiss know what we're doing?"

"Why would we tell them?" he asked.

"Well, if we can't arrest these people, maybe the Swiss would be interested in doing it for us."

Oskar grinned broadly, almost laughing. "You really think that the Swiss will want to put handcuffs on billionaires who have come to their country to be part of the biggest networking event in the world? They make a hundred million dollars over the space of one week. No matter my opinion of them, the Swiss are not stupid." He shook his head. "The only thing we could expect is for them to arrest *us* for troubling their guests."

10

It had taken a full exhausting day of trains, buses, and subways to reach Klosters, a half-hour train ride from Davos. I would have gone the whole way, but there was no chance I'd find a room there during the Forum, and I even had trouble in Klosters, trudging through snow from hotel to hotel, eventually lucking out in the one-star Adventure Hostel.

I passed out in my little room, and when I woke it was late. I showered and wandered down to the restaurant and gobbled down cheese and fruits and fondue with tortilla chips. I wasn't alone in the restaurant—it was full of young people chattering in European languages. Journalists, I supposed. Hand-to-mouth scribblers come to find a new angle on the World Economic Forum's annual meeting. I wondered who they thought would speak to them. They were all hunched over phones and laptops, except for one table in the back where a woman about my age sat with a tough-looking young man; they, unlike the others, had a notepad in front of them. They passed a pencil between them, each scribbling something on the page. At first, I thought they were deaf—but no, they were talking quietly to each other the whole time. Then the woman looked up, and around the restaurant. A pretty, serious face with dark hair that had been chopped short—it was so familiar. Did I know her? Someone from the Agency?

A wave of paranoia came over me. Was I already cornered?

Then the recognition came together, because sitting with Laura in the evenings, I'd seen the face so many times that it was a part of my internal landscape. Ingrid Parker, the de facto leader of the Massive Brigade. Here?

Of *course* here. Where else could she best stab at the heart of the international capitalist system that made American injustices possible? Not only possible, but probable? Where else could she attack the very kind of thinking that had resulted in Northwell and its Tourists? I—

But then she turned her head to the side, and the nose, I saw, was too long. The cheeks too sallow. She was very much *like* the feared Ingrid Parker, and the way she leaned conspiratorially close to her friend certainly *looked* like what people imagined she would be doing. But, no—this was an unfortunate doppelgänger.

And then my relief cracked when this faux Ingrid Parker looked up, across the restaurant, and into my eyes.

Suddenly terrified, I turned away and waved for the bill.

Up in my room, I threw on my coat and went out for some air. I skirted around cut snowbanks and followed people down to the center of Klosters, which was bright with illumination. Vendors and well-dressed visitors filled the streets and looked into the windows of stores that made me think of gingerbread houses. It was a spectacle of capitalism, so clean after the places I'd been. The bright, quaint opposite of Laayoune, and a part of me—a small part, admittedly—wanted to be back there. I hadn't taken pictures and had nothing to show Rashid.

Was I really worrying about pictures to show my son? Yes. Because to worry about everything else, to worry about my dead brother, was too much to handle. Yet, by the time I found myself back at the train station, I realized that I hadn't put any of it out of my mind after all.

The train was full of people far wealthier than me, and, looking out the windows at Klosters falling away and the trees and mountains rising in the darkness, I kept flashing on violence. In Laayoune and on that dark Spanish road, and the violent realization that my brother was one of them. How had that happened? What had brought Haroun from our mundane childhood to that place? I thought back to our fights about the world, how differently he saw it from me. That unbearable cynicism, the world as a perpetual power game, one without room for love or hope.

What they don't admit is that everything is falling apart in slow motion.

It was late when the train pulled into Davos Platz, and the little station, like Klosters, was bright, scattered Swiss police milling on the platform. When I disembarked, I half expected them to ask for my papers, but they just watched us head through the cold, around the station to the square. That was when I finally saw a face I knew. He was standing by a black Mercedes sedan, scanning faces with the same expression as the cops on the platform. Then he caught my eye and jerked his head for me to come closer. I did, unsure what was going to happen next. Paul opened the back door and said, "Get in the fucking car, Abdul."

Mel was waiting in the backseat. She did not look happy.

Still, there was no shouting or hand-wringing. We drove, mostly in silence, slowing for swarming pedestrians in the brightly lit streets, and stopping for a security check, where a Swiss soldier looked at the World Economic Forum passes held by everyone except for me. After some consultation, he waved us all on, and we got out at the small, six-story Congress Hotel, right next to the long, modern Congress Center. Paul handed the car keys to a bellhop, and he and Mel brought me up to a small room on the top floor, where Sally was waiting with a bottle of red wine for all of us to share.

She was clearly the one in control, leading the questions, and I took them through my journey through Casablanca, Laayoune, Foum el-Oued, Arrecife, then to Huelva. It didn't seem to matter that I'd put it all in my report. She stopped me plenty of times, wanting to know more about Milo's librarians—the Japanese man, who I guessed had been Poitevin, and the angry, now-dead Griffon. They wanted to know about Milo's state of mind; my assessment that he was remarkably well adjusted, considering, seemed to disappoint them. They wanted to know about his sister, Alexandra. When they showed a lot of interest in Leticia Jones, I got the feeling that they had a history with her.

After taking them through the gunfight in the Spanish countryside, I finally turned the interrogation around. "What I need to know," I told them, "is why you didn't tell me about my brother."

Sally blinked innocently at me. "Your brother?"

"*Jesus,*" I muttered. "You grilled me about him before I left. Then it turns out he's working for them. He tried to kill us. Tried to kill *me*."

"Is that why you didn't come home, Abdul?" she asked. "Because of your brother?"

Now it was me who blinked. Rapidly, trying to get my vision straight. Tears had suddenly formed. "Why didn't you *prepare* me?"

Sally looked over at Paul, who said, "Given the size of the planet, and where you were heading, we didn't expect you to cross paths. Why burden you with more than you needed to know?"

"You knew who Haroun was working for."

"Don't give us omnipotence," Sally warned. "We knew things, yes. We'd seen Haroun around. We'd connected him to others, but we didn't know who they were working for. One of our better theories was that he was working with Milo Weaver. Particularly after we learned of the existence of the Library and its connections to the Massive Brigade."

"And now you know that's not true," I said. "He tried to kill Weaver. He works for Northwell. They all do."

Paul leaned back, chewing the inside of his mouth. Sally crossed her legs at the knee. And in the dark corner, by the bedside lamp, Mel's shadowy form didn't move at all. They didn't look surprised—none of them did. They didn't look angry or horrified or even, really, very *interested*. And that's when it started to dawn on me. Not the details, but the shape—a hulking, dark shape coming out of the fog. A shape that, in a way, scared me more than men in Saharan alleyways, or even my brother coming back from the dead.

I said, "I don't know how you're not seeing it. This isn't about the Massive Brigade. *They* aren't the threat. These companies—MirGaz, IfW, Tóuzī, Nexus—they're destabilizing the world for profit."

"Now listen," Sally said, looking deep into my eyes. "You're upset. We get that. But listen, okay?"

I nodded dumbly.

"You're bringing in all of this—this whole story—but you're getting everything from a professional liar."

"I've taken that into account," I blurted. "Each time—"

"Just listen, all right?" she said, a little less patient now. "Use your analyst skills. You're getting everything from a single source. We, on the other hand, have you, the rest of the Agency, allied intelligence, and more SIGINT than you can imagine. Sources in industry and in our enemies' camps. So when we tell you to bring it down a notch, it pays to listen."

Paul cleared his throat, and Sally looked up at him. He had a question in his face, and she shrugged in answer, so he straightened and said, "Abdul. There are a lot of pieces on the board. Things you can't be reading into. But I can tell you a few things. One: We weren't kidding about a Massive Brigade threat. The Germans reported that Ingrid Parker is in Klosters. This is serious."

"Klosters?" I asked.

They all noticed the tone in my voice.

"A couple of hours ago, I saw a near-perfect match for Parker. At my hostel, in Klosters. But it wasn't her."

Paul frowned. "You sure it wasn't?"

"Absolutely."

Sally said, "She was in Berlin, too. Your seeing someone else doesn't mean Parker isn't here."

Paul seemed to agree with that assessment. He went on: "Second thing is we have *multiple* sources telling us Weaver was the one who killed Joseph Keller in Paris."

"Of course you do," I cut in, not liking the patronizing tone. "Russia, UK, China, Germany probably, and someone in the States. The same countries where Northwell has clients."

Mel turned on the corner lamp, saying, "That doesn't make them liars."

"And what you don't know," Sally said, "what you don't *need* to know—is that we're not here to throw a grenade into things. Have you thought about what would happen if Milo Weaver's story got out? Forget for the moment if it's true or not. Think about the repercussions. Do you know how big Nexus has become? How much money they bring into the US economy? Last year, they posted a profit of over twenty-five billion. They're expected to reach forty this year. That's Apple and Facebook territory. What do you think this story would do to American innovation in the world?"

I just stared at her, unsure what to say. She'd turned the conversation around, made it into a discussion of profit and loss. "Wait," I said. "This isn't just about Nexus. Are you going to tell me *Northwell's* yearly profits are too good to step on?"

"We can talk to Northwell back home," Mel said from her corner. "That's not a problem."

"And what? Ask them to cut it out?"

"Maybe we absorb them," Sally said, but I didn't know if it was a real idea or if she was just thinking aloud.

"Don't you just want to go home?" Paul said with a sigh. "Come on, Abdul. Think about Laura and Rashid. None of this is really your concern. It's not your world."

He was lying, even if he didn't realize it. This *was* my world, but I hadn't figured that out until now.

Everyone jumped when the *ding ding* of a ringing phone filled the room. It was mine. From my pocket I took it out and saw an unfamiliar Swiss number. I looked at Sally. "You'll probably want to take this."

11

Milo was idling in front of a BMW dealership on the north end of Davos, at the intersection of four different roads. If they traced his location, he could quickly drive down endless side streets to avoid easy capture. One of the burners he'd picked up on the drive from Schramberg was pressed to his ear, and it rang four times before a woman answered with a hesitant "Hello."

"This is Milo Weaver," he said. "To whom am I speaking?"

A brief pause; then she said, "You can call me Sally."

"Hello, Sally. Is Abdul with you?"

"Yes, he is."

"And so you know everything now," Milo said.

"Everything is a big word," Sally told him, warming to the conversation. "What we know is what you wanted us to know. To claim we know *everything* would be silly. Why don't we meet in person and discuss this more?"

Milo imagined taking a flight to Washington and heading to Langley and . . . "You're already in Davos?"

"The Congress Hotel. If you like, we can come to—"

"May I speak to Abdul?"

Another brief pause, then: "Sure." He heard the hiss of background noise. He'd been put on speaker.

"Abdul?"

Abdul's tight voice said, "Hey, Milo."

There was something wrong. "Did you explain it all?"

"Yes. They also have the recording."

"And what do you think?"

There was silence for a moment, just the quiet hiss, and Milo imagined some sign language between Sally and Abdul and whoever else was in the room. "They're weighing cost and benefit," Abdul said.

"How are we doing?"

"Not well."

A man's voice said, "Come on, Abdul."

"Maybe," Sally said, "we're getting ahead of ourselves. Maybe you should tell us what you have in mind."

Milo hesitated, watching bundled couples pass along the sidewalk. Traffic chugged along, but no cops, and no one looked too hard at the car idling in front of the BMW dealership. "First," he said, "I'd like to know how much you already knew. You sent Abdul to find me, when his brother was working for them. That wasn't a coincidence. Therefore, you were either already investigating Northwell, or you were working with them."

"Why would we work with Northwell?" Sally asked him. "They are anathema to American national security."

"Because you thought you could control them."

"No," she said definitively. "In fact, we believed you were running all this. We believed Haroun Ghali was one of your librarians. We believed it was some unholy alliance between your organization and the Massive Brigade. The question we asked was: Why? Why would someone who was once a steadfast Agency officer take his skills to the dark side?"

"You should ask Grace Foster that question."

"I'm sure we will."

"Tell me this," Milo said, eyeing an old woman with a shopping bag. "Has any of my story come up false?"

"Well, we haven't had a lot of time to dig into it."

"You've had long enough to catch any whoppers."

"No," she said. "No whoppers."

"Tell him," he heard—it was Abdul. "Just tell him, for Christ's sake."

The other man said, "Shut—" and the static disappeared; Sally had taken the phone off speaker.

"Are you going to tell me?" Milo asked. "Something about cost and benefit?"

He heard Sally give a little breathy laugh of impatience. "I think you understand, Milo."

And then he did. It was what Erika had said—why should Germany bring down one of its major banks if the US wouldn't go after two of its largest companies? "But unless you do something," he said, "Nexus and Northwell will continue to undermine national security."

"We're just trying to understand before we commit ourselves."

"You're not going to help, are you?"

"I didn't say that."

"I can offer you fifteen years of intelligence files."

"The Library's?"

"Yes."

He heard the sound of a body moving, fabric against fabric; then Sally said, "If we help, it won't be for the Library's files. It will be for better reasons."

"Better?" he asked, surprised by how unenticing that amount of intelligence was to her. Was she really not interested? Or was there some way that *not* helping was more beneficial? Was she—

Oh, shit, he thought, then said those words aloud.

"Milo?"

He felt stupid. He felt like the innocent in this conversation, which was not how any spy ever wanted to feel. This was never going to work, he realized. "The only way you would turn me down is if you had a better source of intelligence that would be harmed by helping us."

"Elucidate," Sally said calmly.

"Something very good," he said. "Like, twenty-four-hour surveillance of one-seventh of the world's population."

Sally didn't say a thing.

"How long have you been in bed with Nexus? How long has their app been your eyes and ears?"

Her continued silence was a clear reply. The CIA had made a deal with Gilbert Powell, probably years ago. Of *course* they wouldn't give that up. Not even to stop a rogue army of killers.

Milo hung up.

It had gone off the rails so quickly, and he remembered Leticia's worries when she'd called earlier. She'd been right; this whole plan was held together with Elmer's Glue and Band-Aids. He put the car in gear and drove out of town, and when he called Leticia she was in Küblis, night-jogging. "I still think it's crazy," he said. "But okay. Do it."

"America not coming through?"

"No."

She either sighed or gasped from the exertion. "All right, then."

"Dalmatian up to it?"

"I hope so."

"Be careful."

"Always am," she said.

12

In the morning, Leticia left the car with Dalmatian and took the train to Davos Platz, and during that ride she sent a message to Chen with the original location for that night's meeting. In Davos, she walked the same path she'd followed before, up Talstrasse and then Kurgartenstrasse, but continuing past the Vaillant Arena. To her right, a media village had been set up in Davos Park, and journalists lined up to have their Dorfseeli Park credentials checked and their bodies scanned before crossing into the secure area. Police and soldiers were everywhere, along with the rooftop snipers, all watching over the foreigners who had invaded this provincial little town.

At the top of the hill she faced the white, ornate monstrosity of the Steigenberger Grandhotel Belvédère and its long line of flagpoles displaying the colors of ten nations. After a hundred and fifty years, it trumpeted its famous guests—Thomas Mann, Albert Einstein, Arthur Conan Doyle—and each year that list grew. The large front lot was full of limousines and expensive sedans, electric cars, and porters who looked calm but, to her jaundiced eye, were clearly ready for a breakdown. She passed through them without notice, headed inside, and looked around the busy lobby. Businesspeople from around the world stared at their phones or stood in private circles laughing. It had the feel of controlled chaos, which, it struck her, the Swiss were very good at.

As she waited for a free spot in the bar that overlooked Davos through high windows, she kept her head held high, trying to see and be seen. But she recognized no one.

She camped out for an hour and a half, working her way through two almond milk lattes and a small plate of almond cookies, reading news off her phone and learning more about the day's Forum panels—climate leadership, cybersecurity, the beginning or end of globalism, AI, the EU and the future of the transatlantic alliance, Venezuela, creating jobs for the "Fourth Industrial Revolution," and even the epidemic of loneliness. And the guests: the presidents of Afghanistan and Rwanda, the Jordanian prime minister, Germany's federal chancellor, the Saudi finance minister, the chief executive officer of Microsoft, and private equity giants. She'd been in plenty of important cities over the space of her career, but it struck her that if someone were to place a nuclear device in this little Alpine town during this week, it would have a bigger effect on the world than placing one on Pennsylvania Avenue.

She was watching a live special address by António Guterres, secretary-general of the United Nations, wondering if he even knew what had been happening in Milo's secret corner of UNESCO, when a female voice said, "Hello, Leticia."

She hesitated before raising her head, knowing that the lag would make her look suave and mildly uninterested, but in fact it was a way to prepare herself for what, if she were being honest, she didn't want to see. And there it was: Grace Foster standing beside her chair, looking fresh and upbeat. A light sprinkling of freckles across her nose made her look like a soccer mom. Standing a couple of feet behind her was the man she now knew was Haroun Ghali, not Gary Young.

"Hi, Grace. Fancy meeting you here."

The bitch smiled at that, then looked around at the full tables. "It's very busy here. Would you like to go someplace private?"

Leticia wanted to make a coarse joke but decided against it. She stood, pocketing her phone, and said to Haroun, "Nice to see you again, Gary."

He nodded. "Ms. Steele."

"How's your wife?"

He didn't reply.

As she led Leticia in a circuitous route to the elevators, Foster said, "I'm surprised to see you."

"Well, we have some things to discuss."

"Don't tell me you've reconsidered my job offer."

"Actually . . ."

Foster looked over her shoulder at Leticia with a wry, surprised smile.

They shared the elevator with three Brazilian businessmen chatting in Portuguese and got out at the third floor. The corridor was very long, and when they finally reached the deluxe suite at the end Foster unlocked the door and put a DO NOT DISTURB sign on the outside handle.

The living room was large and pleasant. Through French doors, two shallow patios overlooked the traffic on the Promenade and the mountains in the distance.

"So," Foster said, taking the desk chair. "What brings you here?"

Leticia settled on the sofa, while Haroun remained by the door to the foyer, leaning against the frame, arms crossed over his chest. "I fucked up," Leticia said.

"How?"

"I put my faith in the wrong person."

"In Milo Weaver?"

Leticia nodded but said, "Look, I'm not here to apologize. I've just had a chance to think about what Weaver's planning, and it doesn't add up. He thinks he can get other countries to do his work for him. He should know better, but he doesn't."

"What kind of work?"

"Burying you. Burying your ex's company, Northwell. Burying IfW and MirGaz and Nexus and Tóuzī. He's smart enough to know the Library can't do it—even if there were a Library anymore. But he's not smart enough to know that Germany, China, Britain, and Russia aren't going to do him any good. They'll do *something,* sure. They'll lean on you guys. But they'll just bleed you. There's a lot of money to be made in extortion."

Foster looked past her at Haroun, who pinched his lower lip in thought. She said, "What about America?"

"There's a seat at the table if they want it."

Foster tilted her head. "Weaver's not that stupid either. He must think he has a winning hand."

"Sure he does," Leticia said. "He's got Joseph Keller's papers. They're convincing, but they won't make his new allies do what he wants."

"He doesn't know they're fake?" Foster asked, then grinned.

"No. Not the fake ones. The originals."

The frown that cut a line down Foster's forehead was the first sign that Leticia's words were sinking in. "Joseph Keller's papers were destroyed."

Leticia nodded. "Sure. But the Germans had an agent on Keller in Paris. Some irregular. Keller left the papers in his room, so their agent photographed them."

"The Germans?" she asked.

"Yeah. You knew that, right?"

Behind her, Haroun exhaled loudly, and Foster rubbed her forehead, her cheeks coloring. Their reactions gave Leticia a moment of satisfaction, but she shook her head as if annoyed. "Come on, guys. Don't make me regret changing sides."

Foster straightened, getting a hold of herself. "No matter," she said. "The Germans have Keller's document and shared it with Weaver. Yes?"

Leticia nodded. "I haven't seen it, but he considers it a smoking gun. He'll bring it tonight when he meets with the others. Once they're convinced, they're going to coordinate themselves in order to bring you down. Like I said, though, it's not going to go his way. They will thank him for the dirt, then toss him aside. Or worse—probably worse. They know they can't trust Milo to stay quiet."

"You think they'll kill him?"

Leticia shrugged. "There's a strong possibility. If he'd been smart, he would have met them here, in town, but no. He chose the Restaurant Clavadeleralp. Up on the side of a mountain. Kill someone there, no one will know until the place opens again in June."

Foster stared at her contemplatively, then asked, "When?"

"Eight o'clock tonight."

Foster nodded approvingly, looking past her to Haroun. "That matches what we heard."

"Heard from who?" Leticia asked, though she knew.

Foster didn't answer, only said to Haroun, "Is the team assembled?"

"Yeah," he said, straightening. "The others are tracking from Zürich. I'll check on them."

"And ask Lance to come here."

Haroun nodded and turned to leave, but paused when Leticia said, "I met your brother. Abdul. He's a good guy."

"I know," Haroun said, turning to look at her coolly. "And he's here."

"Here?" Leticia asked, sounding surprised, though Milo had already told her. "In the hotel?"

"He's with his Agency friends. And that's on you. Whatever you said convinced him to come here." Then he left.

"He's not pleased with me," Leticia told Foster.

"Well, you did a job on his friend in Hong Kong. Now you've gotten his brother tangled up in this. Want a drink?"

"It's not even noon yet."

"C'est la vie," Foster said, and went to open a cabinet to reveal a mini-fridge. She took out two little bottles of brandy, cracked them open, and handed one to Leticia. They tapped bottles with a dainty *clink,* and Foster said, "To new beginnings."

Leticia felt as if she'd been handed her last drink before execution. But all she needed was to last until night.

"How did you get here?" Leticia asked. "You're pushing papers at Langley, and now you're running a new generation of Tourists. You were assigned to get rid of the files, weren't you?"

"You put that together yourself?" Foster asked.

"It was a team effort."

She rocked her head, as if impressed, and took another sip. "Sure. I was supposed to get rid of all of it. But there isn't a single volume on the shelf called Tourism that you throw in your bag and take to the vault. There were scattered volumes on specific operations—the old ones hadn't even been digitized. The digital files could be taken care of in an afternoon. But the paper files? I had to track down cross-references. A 1969 report on Chinese supply lines to North Vietnam references a file about a Tourist assigned to liquidate a Vietnamese colonel. So I'd track *that* down. And I couldn't grab them without reading through them. Every day, all day, for two months. That's when I realized what I was dealing with. It's in the details. Government is blunt. A hammer. But this—this was brain surgery. And the American government was trying to forget about it. Such a waste."

"There's a reason Tourism was shut down, you know."

"Because it lost a single battle," Foster said. "Because one Chinese colonel was too smart. And because the politicians were too scared to put it together again. All those decades of development, of carefully crafting the perfect secret army—all gone to waste. The problem was never Tourism. The problem was its paymasters. They didn't have the stomach for it."

"But Anthony Halliwell did."

Foster smiled at that. "Tony was a shitty husband. But this? This was why he got up in the morning. There was no one else in the world who could really understand it. So, yes, I brought him in. Together, we pored over the records. Together, we analyzed failings and came up with solutions. And it was simple, really: politicians. They were the problem. They're not interested in strengthening the nation's bottom line. They're interested in their own personal gain. But CEOs? They live and die by their bottom lines. In business, the strength of your organization is what defines your power. It's simple and, in a way, beautiful."

"But you needed clients."

"Of course. And where better to find them than Davos? Each year we gather our clients. Inform them of our progress. Listen to their needs, and they listen to ours. So far, so good. We're even expanding."

"Who?"

Foster shook her index finger coyly. "You just arrived, honey. And until we leave Switzerland you're staying right here, in this room." She held out her hand. "Phone, please."

As Leticia handed it over, there was a knock at the door. Foster said, "Come," and a chiseled blond with striking light-blue eyes stepped inside. Lance, apparently. He surveyed the room, his gaze settling on Leticia. Foster rose and prepared to go. "She's to remain here."

"I will take care of that," the man said, his voice colored with Swedish singsong.

To Leticia, Foster said, "Thank you, by the way. By tomorrow all this will be over, and we can take care of your contract. How does that sound?"

"Sounds great," Leticia said, though she didn't believe a word the bitch said.

13

From the glove compartment, Alexandra took the small Glock pistol she'd carried everywhere these last three months and slipped it inside her long coat, then got out of her car to take in the large wooden stables of a horse-riding school. The snow had been plowed into low white cliffs along the edge of the road, and when she walked through slushy puddles toward the stables, she wished she'd picked up some Wellingtons. Instead, she'd brought a pair of suede boots that wouldn't last these few days in Switzerland, much less the trip back to London to visit the RSPCA. Because, yes, there really was nothing else left for her. She'd ended a good career to join a secret organization that had, after fifteen years, imploded. And what now? Take her heavily redacted CV on the rounds of London law firms? She couldn't face being laughed out of that many offices. Better to call it quits. Go back to her little flat. Find a dog to take care of. Read a lot. And get the hell off the potholed highway that was the twenty-first century. She'd had quite enough of it.

She wasn't like Milo, who thought that geography could solve his problems. In the mountains around Avegno with his family, he'd seen a paradise of solitude, while Alexandra had seen a slow, moldy death. No, Alexandra could only live among people in the throb of a modern metropolis; hiding was anathema to her. Even this place—Davos Frauenkirch, just south of Davos proper—with its mountain peaks and clean air, stank of death to her.

She heard the faint sound of banging and followed it around the side of the stable, through the stink of hay and horseshit, where she discovered a woman and a man shoeing a large stallion's rear foot. The horse stood placidly as the woman huffed, gripping the horse's ankle, and the man hammered nails into the hoof. She watched a moment, then worked her way back to the front, where a large black SUV with tinted windows splashed through puddles to reach the building. When it stopped near the front door, Oskar got out of the passenger's side. He had a worried look—or what she interpreted to be a worried look, his silly mustache twitching—as he came over to her.

"So?" she asked.

"Yes," he said, and turned back to the car. Two of his young thugs opened the back and helped Katarina Heinold step gingerly down to the half-frozen mud.

The German patron didn't look as if she had been kidnapped. She didn't look upset at all. "So she came willingly?"

"We were just giving her a ride from Zürich Airport."

"This doesn't look like her hotel."

"Not everyone is unreasonable, Ms. Primakov. Once we explained the situation, she became quite cooperative."

"You told her everything we know."

"A version of everything."

They all went inside, where in the off-season the place was mostly empty. The stable owner, a heavy woman in a smock, shook Oskar's hand and led them to a musty, warm office in the back. It was just large enough for four people—Oskar, Alexandra, Katarina, and one of the thugs, who sat in a corner picking his nails.

"For the sake of our guest," Oskar said to Katarina, "please let us speak English."

Katarina examined Alexandra from her chair, judging. "You are Milo's sister?"

Alexandra nodded.

"I've heard about you. You worked behind the scenes, yes?"

"I got librarians out of trouble," Alexandra said.

"Until you got into trouble yourself."

Alexandra rocked her head, accepting the little jab. "And now, Ms. Heinold, it's you. When did you first become involved with Northwell?"

She frowned and looked at Oskar. "I have already told you this."

"Please," he said. "Again."

Reluctantly, she turned to Alexandra. "I am not involved with North-well. Not directly. I communicate with Investition für Wirtschaft. We have mutual interests."

"What mutual interests?"

"Money," she said, and shrugged. "They approached me in New York and established an open line of communication."

"So they already knew about the Library."

"Oh, yes. It was disappointing to hear, actually. That the thing we be-lieved only a small circle knew about was actually well known."

"Thanks to Kirill Egorov."

Katarina shrugged again. "So I was to tell them if intelligence came up about them, so they could be prepared."

"And what did you get for that?"

"The knowledge that I was helping German business to succeed."

"And money," Oskar said glumly.

"And money," she echoed. No embarrassment, no shame.

"It wasn't just you and IfW." Alexandra said. "That meeting in Septem-ber. Sardi's. Beatriz Almeida was there. Grace Foster and Gilbert Powell, too."

"It was time for me to learn more. The operation was expanding."

"You wanted Portuguese intelligence? From Almeida?"

Katarina shook her head slowly. "Beatriz was not interested. The liquid-ity of German banks is not her concern."

"So she left the lunch without agreeing to anything?"

"I think she was angry. I invited her to dinner, but she didn't even reply. That lunch was a mistake."

Warmth flooded Alexandra's cheeks, and she tried to control her voice when she said, "So you were a mole."

Katarina sat up straighter, defensive. "Germany did not support the Li-brary because we loved the Library. None of us did. We supported it because of what it could give our countries. I have no excuses to make."

Alexandra sighed. "Okay, then. But right now we need to know when and where Northwell's meeting will be."

To Oskar, in German, Katarina snapped, "I'm tired of repeating myself."

At that moment all four of them jumped at a cracking sound from outside. Everyone except Katarina knew what it was, for when they got to their feet she remained in her chair and said, "Was that an automobile?"

The thug was heading out the door to meet his partner, a small pistol in his hand, and Oskar moved to the office window as Alexandra took out her Glock. Katarina's eyes widened, and only now did she rise in shock.

"Scheisse," Oskar muttered, peeking out through the blinds.

Alexandra joined him. The driver's side window of Oskar's SUV was smashed, and though the tinted windshield hid him, she knew his driver was in there, dead. But her eyes were immediately drawn to the foreground, where two tall men in tailored long coats carried pistols toward the stable's front door. She hadn't yet seen the Tourists that had been after them these three months, but by the cut of their suits and the blank, hard looks in their eyes, she knew what they were.

Oskar said, "They're coming for you, Katarina. They're coming to kill you."

As a barrage of gunshots sounded from the direction of the entrance, Oskar pushed open the office door and carefully looked out. He waved for them to follow, then pointed to the left, farther down the corridor. He, though, stepped to the right, toward the entryway. Katarina, stunned, didn't move, so Alexandra grabbed her arm and yanked hard. "No," the woman sputtered.

"Come," Alexandra said, dragging her along.

It was loud in the narrow hallway, and behind them Oskar was reaching the main entrance. When Alexandra looked back, she could see the proprietress huddled down behind the counter, weeping.

Alexandra dragged the patron toward a small door with a Plexiglas window, through which sunlight shone, and she thought she heard a siren wailing behind the rear wall—no. Not a siren, but the terrified whinnying of horses who could sense the bloodbath going on. Katarina was in tears. When they reached the door, the gunshots ceased, and there was only the frantic sound of the horses. She looked back—Oskar, pistol raised, turned the corner, disappearing, and gunshots roared again. Alexandra pushed through the door into the bright cold and told Katarina, *"Run,"* before breaking into a sprint in the direction of her car. Katarina didn't need prodding; she ran in her heels through the wet earth.

Once they cleared the building, Alexandra looked back to see that by the open front door, a man's body lay in the mud. She couldn't tell who it was. Then a flash of gunfire inside the building, followed by a figure in a long coat stepping outside and spotting them. His pistol rose, held steady in two hands. She felt an urge to stop and raise her own gun, but the lot was wide open here. By the time she got into position she would be dead.

"Faster," Alexandra gasped, and was surprised by how well Katarina kept up; she was a bureaucrat fueled by pure adrenaline now.

The gun exploded in the Tourist's hand, just once. But Alexandra felt nothing. She kept running and was almost at her car when she realized she was alone. She looked back and saw the gray coat and heels of Katarina Heinold. Her body twitched in the mud, but her head, pulverized by a direct hit, lay still, half buried by the impact of its fall.

Another explosion sounded, but when she looked the Tourist was no longer standing in his professional position. He was, instead, down on one knee, gripping his side, trying to figure out what had happened. Leaning against the doorway, blood on his face, Oskar aimed his big pistol at the man. When the Tourist raised his gun, Oskar fired once more, and it was done.

14

My guard was a small, dark CIA officer named Samuel who sat by the window and thumbed through phone messages while I watched local coverage of the day's Forum. Samuel and I talked a little, mostly office gossip—he had heard rumors about some romantic relationships in Africa section, and I either debunked the rumors or played them up, depending on what he seemed to want to hear.

I spent a lot of time looking out the window. Our room had a view of mountains and the flat, gravel-covered roof of the Congress Center cluttered with rows of solar panels. On the far end of the roof, two ever-present snipers in heavy white coats chatted and peered down into the park on the other side. All I could see of the park was bare treetops, but right below my window was a triangle of snow-covered courtyard between the Congress Center and the hotel, and sometimes Forum attendees stepped out onto the metal stairs leading down to the snow to have a smoke.

We ate room service meals delivered on draped carts by harried staff, and it was at our early dinner that the petite server, a girl no older than twenty, locked onto my eyes as she uncovered the plates. It was a look that I couldn't quite decipher. Flirtation, or fear? Her eyes self-consciously flicked down to one of the two water glasses covered with cardboard lids to keep out dust. Then she was back to my eyes again, a significant look before taking the signed bill from Samuel.

"Smells good," he said as the server left, and I took the water glass and drank deeply, flipping over the cardboard disk. On it was a simple message: *Come down for a drink*. I pocketed it, wondering, and settled by the window to eat. In the gathering darkness I saw the two snipers still on the Congress Center roof, and to the south of the park, along Talstrasse, I saw another sniper atop a low apartment building. There were many more, I knew, that I couldn't see from my window.

"I need a drink," I said, turning away from the window.

Samuel looked up from his phone. "What?"

"You need to keep me in this hotel, fine. But I'm going to go crazy stuck in this little room. So will you. I saw a bar down near the front desk."

Samuel looked surprised by the idea. "I don't—" he began, then stood up. "Hold on."

He made a call in the bathroom, and from the defensive sound of the murmurs I guessed he was being scolded for even suggesting a trip downstairs. When he came out, though, he was blinking, surprised. "Well, they said it's okay."

"Really?" I asked. "They weren't pissed off?"

"They were pissed off I wasted their time asking."

There was no bar, per se, but four stools in front of a counter and guests lounging at low tables, sipping drinks. We took two of the stools, and I ordered a vodka martini, offering to buy one for Samuel. He hesitated, unsure, and shook his head no, but I ordered another anyway. I didn't want to drink alone, and despite his job I actually liked Samuel.

When he learned I had a six-year-old, he became very interested. He had a girlfriend back in DC who wanted children, but the thought of that kind of responsibility terrified him. So I tried, with as much honesty as possible, to take him through the rigors of parenting, balancing the easily catalogued cons with the less apparent pros. As he began to form a picture of his possible future, he sipped at his martini without shame. Eventually, he looked around. "Know where the bathroom is?"

"I think it's back there," I said, pointing to a corner.

"I'll be right back. Don't run. You're not going to run, are you?"

"All I want to do is go home," I said, and I wasn't lying.

He grinned. "Wouldn't be able to anyway. Frank, at the exit, is built like a linebacker."

When he left, I finished my drink and asked the bartender for another. I hunched over it, trying not to spill my first sip, and that was when I felt a pat on my back and turned to Samuel's stool. But it wasn't Samuel. It was Haroun. And he was grinning wildly.

I was lost. Anger and confusion and a lifelong love clashed in my chest. All I could do was open my arms and hug him tightly. He smelled of some sharp, unfamiliar cologne.

"Brother," he said. "What are you doing here?"

"What am I . . ." I shook my head, trying to clear it. I exhaled loudly. "No, no. You. You're the one who needs to talk."

"Fair enough," he said, then reached casually over to Samuel's glass and took a sip.

"What happened?" I blurted. "How did you become—"

"Become this?" he asked, setting down the glass. "Come on. I'm the same kid who fought your bullies in middle school."

"You're not."

"You're the one who's changed, Abdul. A wife and—how old is Rashid now? Four?"

"Six."

"See?" he said. "You've become part of the machine."

"What machine?"

"Money."

I sighed, remembering how frustrating he could be. "Your people," I said. "*They're* the machine. Capitalism run amok." He seemed to find that amusing, which irritated me even more.

He said, "How is what we're doing any different from Iraq? Half a million Iraqis and four and a half thousand Americans slaughtered to control a dwindling resource. Next to you guys, we're amateurs."

I counted on my fingers: "Schoolgirls kidnapped and enslaved, dozens of sailors drowned, CEOs murdered. And that's only what we've been able to uncover."

He leaned back. "But next to American history . . . ?"

I was stunned by his coarseness. He'd always been that way, but now his cynicism had gone off the charts. "Who the hell *are* you, Haroun?"

He drank the rest of Samuel's martini and glanced around the room. We looked so similar. I was Haroun, if he let himself go, and he was me, if I'd lived an athletic and dangerous life. Around us people were laughing and dealing, and they had no idea what earthshaking events were happening at the bar.

"Right," he said, a decision made, and turned back to me. "In 2009, I was working for Global Partners in Yemen."

"You told me about it when you got back."

"That's right. Yemen's like a lot of the world: great people, shitty situation. I'd seen it before—Congo, Somalia, Sudan . . . but Yemen?" He paused. "Didn't we argue?"

"You told me the world was falling apart in slow motion."

"Sounds like me," he said. "That's because I'd just been someplace that was heading in that direction fast. Then I come back home, turn on the TV, and there they are, all the signs. The empty political rhetoric. The exploitation of the underclass. The gaudy hoarding of wealth. The roads—Jesus! A land with so much money, and it can't even keep its bridges up? Everywhere I looked, the edifices were crumbling."

"You were prime for activism," I noted. "You could've joined the Massive Brigade."

"Activism, or nihilism," he said. "Because who the fuck was I? You were always the smart one. The career path. The focus. The *faith*. Someone like you, if you put your mind to it, might change things for the better. Me? I would only grow angrier, until I exploded. And that, my brother, was when I received a visitor. She invited me to join something bigger than myself. *This is real power,* she told me."

"She would show you how the world really worked," I said, feeling an uncomfortable tingle across my scalp.

"Something like that."

"Was it worth it?" I asked. "Giving up your family? Me?"

He sighed, then glanced around the room again. "I only have one life, Abdul. Give me a second one and I'll try an alternate path."

We were both silent for a short while. I drank, wondering what to say to all of this. There were arguments to be made, but was this really the time for them?

He finally said, "You know, it really is good to see you. Back in Spain, I was terrified you'd end up dead. By us, or by them."

"Them?"

"Your friends. The Library."

"I'm with the Agency."

He furrowed his brow. "Isn't the Agency working with the Library?"

"I don't know," I lied, not wanting to be the sentimental fool who let family milk him for information.

He looked like he didn't believe me. He said, "Working with the Library would be a bad proposition. Word is Milo Weaver and Ingrid Parker are joined at the hip. She's apparently in the neighborhood."

I wanted to tell him about Ingrid Parker's doppelgänger, but I didn't. Because he wasn't my brother anymore. He was one of *them*. A decade-old decision had placed us on opposite sides of a divide that not even blood could bridge.

"Uh-oh," Haroun said, rising from the stool. He looked across the restaurant to where Samuel was stumbling out of a corridor, hand on his head, looking as if he'd just woken. Haroun grabbed my hand and looked into my eyes. "I love you, brother. Please. Go home. You don't belong here."

And then he was gone, hurrying toward the lobby.

Samuel found his balance and sprinted past me, chasing Haroun. They were both gone—I could, I suspected, walk out of there—but I didn't move. I was shook. Again. But not from being face-to-face with Haroun. No. I was shook because of one small thing he had said. Both of our lives had been irrevocably altered by the same promise: You will understand how the world really functions. You will become intimate with secret knowledge scratched onto the stone tablets that run civilization. Haroun and I were the same.

Not just us, I realized, but Sally and Mel. Paul. Milo Weaver, Alexandra Primakov and Leticia Jones—*all* of us, in each of our secret societies, had been promised infinite knowledge. The Massive Brigade, too—Martin Bishop had promised the same thing, and Ingrid Parker continued that tradition. The BND, GRU, Guoanbu. Not just knowledge but *power,* the ability to shape human history. Each group, in its own way, promised the same thing. We had all been seduced completely. And we had all been lied to.

Yet we still fought. In our blind devotion and fear—or was it pride?—of admitting ignorance, we devoted our lives to empty promises and even died for them, along the way abandoning those we loved. Haroun had abandoned his family, Milo's was under a death sentence, and mine . . . were they any less abandoned as I sat in a Swiss bar having spoken to my dead brother?

Samuel returned, gasping, from his vain chase. He dropped onto his stool heavily, wiped sweat off his upper lip, and reached for his glass before realizing it was empty. "Who the fuck was he, Abdul?"

"I don't know," I said, my voice surprisingly cool and measured. "What happened to you?"

"He attacked me in the goddamn bathroom."

Only now did I notice the red mark on his right temple. Tomorrow that would be a nasty bruise.

"I think he might've knocked me out," Samuel said. "How long was he here?"

"Just a minute," I lied. "He was ranting to me about the one percent."

Samuel looked over his shoulder at the exit. "How did that nut even get in the hotel?"

"I don't know," I said, but was thinking, *You don't know anything, I don't know anything, Haroun doesn't know anything.* I picked up my drink, then set it down again when I saw that it, too, was empty.

"Listen," Samuel said, now sounding like he really wanted to be my buddy. "If anyone asks . . ."

"We had a drink, and you never left," I said, and he finally relaxed.

15

The lonely Restaurant Clavadeleralp had been packed up since September, so Milo was taking chairs off tables and arranging them in the large dining area. Kurt, Oskar's surviving agent, a bearded tough with big, morose eyes, worked on other tables while Oskar stood by the wall-sized windows, his arm in a sling. Outside, the snow-covered ground sloped downward along this side of the Clavadeler Alp, lit by the moon and the glow of the restaurant's lights.

Given that he had lost two of his men that morning and taken a bullet in his shoulder, Oskar was remarkably steady. Maybe steadier than Milo, who was starting to feel this was all heading toward disaster. He'd sat for an hour with Alexandra in their little room, trying to talk her through the trauma of witnessing murder. This was something she'd never really had to deal with in the Library, and in the end she'd settled on what Milo considered the most constructive reaction: "We need to ruin these people."

The immediate problem, of course, had been the disaster at the stables. There was the traumatized proprietress, Agota, and a couple of workers who had been around the rear of the building when the firefight occurred. There were five dead bodies—two Tourists of unknown origin, two BND officers, and a deputy ambassador to the United Nations. The only stroke of luck was that all the fighting had faced a wide field of grazing cows and horses, and the few buildings in sight were abandoned for the season. So Oskar and Kurt had brought the bodies inside and sat with Agota until a cleanup team from

Munich arrived a little after two. In the meantime, Milo came to retrieve Alexandra and found Agota and her two workers sitting calmly in a back room with Oskar. "We have made arrangements," he assured Milo. "The Swiss are always amenable to deals."

Now Oskar held up a wireless camera with his good arm. It was no bigger than a matchbook. "Where do you think?"

Milo looked around the open space and up at the exposed rafters. "High enough for a good angle. We need as much coverage as possible."

"Kurt," Oskar said, and when his agent looked up he said in German, "A ladder, please."

They had prepared three long tables in the center of the dining room with space for a couple dozen chairs. When Kurt returned with an old, paint-spattered ladder, Milo climbed it and lodged the camera on a beam, while Oskar used a tablet computer to check the image, calling directions to Milo. They adjusted it until, eventually, the shot took in three quarters of the restaurant, the prepared tables square in the center.

"Should we set out water?" Oskar asked.

From the kitchen, they brought out six glass bottles of San Pellegrino and three towers of glasses. Once everything was arranged, Milo stepped back and had a good look at it all, then checked the image on the tablet again. "That's it."

Outside, they left Oskar's Mercedes parked by the restaurant, then trudged through the darkness, crunching snow as they pressed into the mountain wind, heading up the incline to the nearby Schaukäserei Clavadeleralp. Both were owned by the same family, which had been happy to rent the shuttered restaurant and cheese-making house to Oskar for "a party for foreigners." Foreigners could only mean guests of the Forum, so the owners had asked an exorbitant price, and it had taken a while to haggle them down. At the center of the Schaukäserei was a large vat, long since cleaned out and covered, and a full kitchen that, during the warmer months, was open to tourists and hikers. Now, though, the place stank of rotten milk, and the cold pressed through the walls.

"No lights," Milo said when Kurt eyed an electric panel full of switches. "And no heat."

"How long?" the German asked, sounding disappointed.

Oskar checked his watch. "Half hour until eight."

"The others know not to come, right?" Milo asked.

"Relax," said Oskar.

And so they waited, bundled tight, sometimes pacing in order to keep their blood flowing. Kurt kept checking his SLR camera and its telephoto lens, while Milo checked the tablet to be sure the signal from the matchbook camera made it this far; the picture remained bright and clear. Oskar sat next to him by the window, looking down at the restaurant twinkling in the dark. "This is a long shot," he said.

"Everything we've done is a long shot," Milo said. "It'll give us nothing, or it'll give us a lot."

Oskar grudgingly agreed, and together they watched the restaurant, foggy breaths spilling from their mouths. "I am still unsure about you," Oskar finally said. "Erika—she is a believer in history. She has history with you, and that means something to her. I am a believer in the present. What you were is not necessarily what you are."

"Do you think I'm setting you up?"

Oskar rocked his head. "I would not put it past you. Or," he added with a little flourish, "I would not put it past the person you *were*. I am still trying to understand the person you seem to be."

"How?"

"The old Milo Weaver would walk up to Grace Foster and Anthony Halliwell and put bullets in their heads."

Milo considered that. Was it true? Maybe. But the old Milo would have at least convinced himself that he had no other options. Violence was what was left once he'd run out of other plays. At least, that's what he had always told himself. He said, "Let's say we did murder Foster and Halliwell. What takes their place? Who is Halliwell's second in command? Or maybe MirGaz and Nexus and Salid take over the operation. Maybe IfW. We don't know."

"It's better than doing nothing, don't you think?"

Milo sighed. "Maybe it's worse."

Oskar chewed the inside of his mouth. "It might put fear into them. Right now, Northwell does not fear us at all."

Milo looked at him, and in the moonlit darkness the German's face was gaunt and drawn.

"There," Kurt said from the other side of the room. He raised his camera and pressed the long lens against a window that faced the road crisscrossed with ski tracks. A black sedan was coming slowly, its chains biting into the snow.

Oskar pulled out a pair of binoculars, and they all stood in the darkness watching the car pass and head toward the lights of the restaurant, eventually parking beside Oskar's Mercedes. Three figures got out, and Oskar climbed onto a low table to get a good look over the slope of snow. "It's the Second Bureau," he said.

The three figures spoke among themselves, and one pressed a hand to the hood of Oskar's Mercedes, checking for warmth; then they went inside. Milo woke the tablet and watched as the three Chinese men—among them Chen, who had met with Leticia—entered the restaurant and took off their hats, carefully looking around. Milo tapped a button and began to record.

The men were quiet at first, warily poking around. One opened a bottle of San Pellegrino, filled a glass, and drank. In Mandarin, they began to talk.

"Kurt," Oskar barked, and the agent hurried over to listen.

"They're wondering where we are," Kurt said. "The skinny one doesn't like it. The one with the water is telling him that he's paranoid. I think he's the boss."

"Keep listening," Milo said as he handed the tablet to Kurt. "Let us know if they say anything important." Then he walked to the other end of the room, rubbed his arms, and bounced, looking outside at the blue snowy field. He didn't expect anything incriminating from the Second Bureau on their own. He just needed them to stay in that restaurant long enough for—

"He's making a call," Kurt said.

"Who?"

"The one with the water."

"Who's he calling?"

"It's . . ." Kurt listened. "I don't know. But he's agreed to stay ten more minutes."

"Damn." The only way Milo could stretch out their stay would be to walk over to the restaurant himself, but that was more danger than he wanted to face. He squinted down to the line of black pines, then to the road that came from town. No headlights, no heavy vehicles. It would be a wash, and now his only worry was Leticia.

"Milo," he heard, and when he turned he saw Oskar at the opposite window, looking east, up the hill. Milo saw it, too: seven skiers in black, a loose group gliding slowly down the hill, converging. Strapped to their backs, Milo saw once they were closer, were submachine guns; their heads were covered in black balaclavas. Eventually, they came to a halt behind the restaurant, by the cars. They squatted as one, unclipping the skis from their boots, pulling their guns around into their hands, and then they split up on either side of the restaurant.

"Oh, shit."

Milo glanced over to see Kurt, hands white with cold, recording everything with his SLR. Oskar squatted on the table with the tablet, and Milo joined him. They watched the three Chinese men wandering around, arguing in Mandarin. The fat one finished his water.

Milo looked out the window, and from this vantage he could see four of the Tourists creep around to the front of the restaurant, where the big panoramic windows offered breathtaking views and a strategic weak spot for anyone hiding inside. Then the Tourists disappeared around the edge of the restaurant. The snow in front of the building lit up with the flash of automatic fire, and when they heard the *thump-thump-thump-thump,* three startled Chinese men in the little tablet screen jumped and jerked and fell as the window shattered from the hail of bullets that filled the room.

It was fast—no more than a minute—but the destruction was complete. Chairs, hit by stray bullets, had flipped. Three glass water bottles had shattered. Red bits of human—garish pink spots in the video feed—were scattered across the tables. And then there was silence. Instinctively, Milo and Oskar crouched lower, bringing the bright screen down with them, and in it they watched four hooded figures enter, guns at their sides. In English, they heard:

"Where are the rest?"

"Something's not right."

"You going to call this in?"

One of them took a satellite phone out of his coat and stepped toward the shattered windows. Before he stepped outside to call, he said, "The cunt set us up."

Milo knew who the cunt was, but he had no way to get in touch with her.

So he watched as the man with the phone stepped out through the window frame and made a call they couldn't hear. Five minutes later, the seven Tourists made their way back around the rear of the building, put on their skis again, and slid down the hill toward town.

16

"What time is it, handsome?"

Pretty, blue-eyed Lance, who had stationed himself in the desk chair with a view not only of Leticia lying on the sofa but of the busy lit-up Promenade in front of the Belvédère, framed by the French doors, sighed and checked his expensive wristwatch. "Quarter till eight."

Not long, she thought as she stretched out. "You know," Leticia said, "I used to be you."

Lance had a preternatural ability to sit in silence, and had been demonstrating it for hours. Now he perked up, just a little. "What?"

"You. A Tourist."

He blinked dumbly, and she wondered if they even called themselves Tourists. "Have passport, will travel," she said. "For years, I traveled on the government dime. Making things right. Sometimes making them wrong. It's relentless. How long you been on the payroll?"

He looked out the windows, considering whether or not to answer, then said, "Two years."

"A lot of miles?"

He nodded slowly.

"It gets easier," she said, "before it gets harder."

Lance frowned at her, and she almost said, *You should smile more,* but instead said, "Right now, honey, you're probably pretty high on yourself. You travel the globe and sometimes you hurt people, but the law never catches up to you. You appear and disappear, like magic. And you're right, it *is* a little bit like magic. And you *are* special, just like they tell you. But then, eventually, you start hearing that voice in the back of your head. The one that says there's no point."

He shifted, looking uncomfortable. "You don't know what you're talking about."

She gave a good long smile. "I'll tell you where it happened to me. Cambodia, 2007. Simple thing. Take out a bent politico and disappear. I didn't take the kid into account." She paused, remembering, for at this moment she was giving him something real, and she wanted to get this right. "And my first thought, like anybody's, was *collateral damage*. We're not going to cry about dead flower girls when the drones take out a terrorist's wedding, right? But then the new thing happened. I started thinking back over the years. How much collateral damage had there been? I even used a paper and pen. Math never lies. And it hit me, finally, that the collateral damage I'd done over the years wasn't some side job—it *was* my job.

She watched him think on this, watched him scratch the side of his cheek and look out at the Swiss evening full of fancy dresses and the stink of money. Was he thinking about his own missteps, or the series of decisions that had brought him to this hotel room? She didn't know, and she didn't have time to puzzle through his psyche. So she climbed off the sofa. "I think I'll take a shower. Want to join me?"

He looked briefly shocked, and it gave her pleasure to know that there really was a human under that façade. Then his face relaxed into an appreciative, cocky smile as he measured her body with his eyes. "Another time."

He really was full of himself. She gave him a wink. "Suit yourself."

Leticia headed through the wardrobe room and bedroom to find an expansive bathroom with a whirlpool tub, flat-screen TV, and large, sealed window looking back at an empty, snow-covered hillside. She closed the door and turned on the shower, then watched herself in the mirror, searching for lines. She thought about what had brought *her* to this room, and the choices she had made. In Wakkanai, Hong Kong, Shanghai, Laayoune, and here. What was it about her that kept finding trouble? Was this what penance really looked like?

And yet—and *yet*—she had survived it all. The scar on her arm from Haroun Ghali's Hong Kong bullet was just part of the terrain of her body, so many nicks and scratches, but nothing that had put her down. *That* was black girl magic right there.

Though she expected it, Leticia still jumped at the sudden *wee-wah* of the fire alarm blaring throughout the hotel. She put on her game face and returned to the living room, where Lance was stepping out to the patio, looking for smoke.

"So?" she asked.

He stepped back inside. "Probably false alarm."

"Sure," she said, and returned to the bathroom. As the steam collected, she counted down the seconds. She'd survived so many dangerous places, but what about now? Would Lance's obstinance really lead to her dying in *Switzerland*? Come on.

But she had to play the game, so she took off her blouse and was unbuttoning her slacks when she heard the pretty tone of the doorbell. Through the wall came a muted conversation. Then the door shut, and after a moment Lance knocked on the bathroom door. She opened it fully, and he hesitated, eyes stalled briefly on her bra. Then: "That was the hotel staff. Turns out it is real. There's a room in flames beneath us."

She made a show of irritation. "I really wanted that shower."

"We'd better go."

"Sure you don't want to go up in flames with me?"

His gaze traveled the length of her body again, approvingly, and she cursed herself—the fool was actually considering it. She forced a grin. "Come on, cowboy. Let's get out of here."

A minute later, they were heading toward the stairs. No hurry. On the second floor, though, a very old woman in gemstones looked panicked and lost. Lance ignored her, and was clearly annoyed when Leticia stopped and spoke to the old woman, then invited her to join them. Helping her on the stairs slowed them down considerably, and they were slowed more when Lance's phone rang. He glanced irritably at the screen, then stiffened and answered, one hand on the phone, the other on the old woman's elbow.

"Yes?" he said. Leticia watched his face pinch in a pained expression. "For sure?" he asked, and though the news he received was obviously not good, he didn't miss a step or forget to keep hold of the old woman. "A fire alarm. Yes, ma'am, it's under control." Then he hung up.

"Something wrong?" Leticia asked.

He shook his head, but his cheeks were very red, and a prescient tingle spread across the width of her back.

Hotel staff were in the lobby, so they passed off the woman, but instead of following her outside Lance grabbed Leticia's forearm. "Over here," he said, pulling her back toward the restaurant at the opposite end of the corridor. "We have to get something."

"Sure," she said, preparing herself.

He pulled her through double doors into the spacious restaurant—pale walls, parquet, and large ring-shaped lamps above their heads like halos. Straight ahead, big windows looked north at the low, snow-covered Davos buildings. As the door closed, Lance's right hand reached behind himself, and Leticia immediately jumped at him, punching the rigid knuckles of her left hand into his trachea.

He gasped, clutching his throat, while the other hand emerged holding his Glock. He got off one shot, which went wild as she dropped into a crouch and stomped hard against his knee. He buckled, gun hand rising as he fell back. She launched herself against his chest, helping his fall. They landed hard, Leticia straddling him, and as he raised his gun hand again she planted her elbow, with all her weight, into his face. It hurt, bone smashing into bone, and his nose gushed a torrent of blood. She quickly rolled off him, prying the pistol out of his weak hand, and kept rolling until she was yards away.

Gasping, she climbed to her feet and looked at him struggling on the floor. A sick, wet moan came from deep inside him. But it was barely audible, just a long, painful exhale pushing through crushed windpipe, smashed nose, and cracked teeth. She raised the Glock and pointed it at him. He was already dying, after all.

Afterward, she stripped off her blood-covered blouse and rolled it into a bundle with the Glock hidden inside. Then she pushed back into the lobby, where the staff, overcome by escaping guests, hardly even noticed the black woman in a bra making her way past them.

Outside in the cold, drivers were moving cars out of the way for approaching fire trucks. The crowd of half-dressed, fully suited, and drunk guests placed hands to their mouths and gaped at thick smoke rising from the other side, from where Leticia had come, into the night sky. Curious, she walked around the building, squeezing through spectators until she saw what they saw: A smashed first-floor window gushed smoke and flickering flames. The smoke was thick and black and, Leticia thought, obviously fueled by some serious propellant.

"You need a coat," she heard, and turned to find Dalmatian taking off his old army jacket. He put it over her shoulders, and she smiled.

"Did you really have to do all that?" she asked as they hurried down the street.

"I don't know, Kanni. What do you think?"

"My name's not Kanni."

17

Alexandra was still deeply shaken by the massacre at the stables, and when she closed her eyes she saw the terrified face of the proprietress hiding behind her counter and heard the frightened horses. But when she opened them, the scene on the bright laptop screen was no better. Three figures trembled and danced. Then they went down in a splatter of gore. Milo raised the volume on the laptop so they could hear:

Where are the rest?

Something's not right.

You going to call it in?

The cunt set us up.

"I'm the cunt," Leticia said, leaning against the wall, still wearing Dalmatian's coat.

And now Leticia was making jokes, for Christ's sake.

But still, Leticia had risked her life so that they could make this video and screen it in the Gasthaus Islen, a pretty little restaurant whose owners had agreed at the last minute to let Oskar use it after midnight. This video was Milo's closing argument.

Their guests—Maxim Vetrov with an older, silent Russian who had assumedly come along to make decisions; Xin Zhu's stern agent, Li Fan; and Francis from the Home Office, a paper cup of coffee in front of him—stared aghast at the screen. Sitting with them, but unfazed, was Oskar, his arm in a sling. Alexandra had gained a new respect for him, too.

"Good Lord," Francis said.

"They expected us to be there," Milo said. "They expected to wipe us all out." Then he turned to Alexandra expectantly.

She took a breath and said, "They murdered Katarina Heinold, German deputy ambassador to the United Nations, this morning."

"Why?" Li Fan demanded.

"Because we picked her up," Oskar said, "and they feared she would talk."

"Did she?"

"Yes," said Alexandra. "She told us when and where they're meeting. Wing B of the Congress Center, third floor. The Parsenn-Pischa room. Immediately after the closing performance."

"So we go in and do this to them?" Vetrov asked, motioning at the corpses on the computer screen.

Milo shook his head. "We don't need to."

Dalmatian, who had taken a position by the Islen's front door, turned to eye passing headlights. Poitevin was outside in the snow, ready to call in any sign of approach. After a moment, Dalmatian turned back, looking uncomfortable; Alexandra wondered if there was trouble.

"The question," Milo went on, "is: Does this convince you all? This, on top of everything else. We need a decision now."

The guests looked at one another, and Li Fan was the first to speak. "The Sixth Bureau will help."

Alexandra had expected China to hold out, if only for show. But no, of course not. Beyond African oil pipelines, Xin Zhu was terrified that the files chronicling his decade of assistance to the Library would become known. He was fighting for his life, whether or not Li Fan knew it.

The old Russian muttered something into Vetrov's ear, and Vetrov said, "A question, please. How, exactly, *do* we deal with this? If we do not attack, then what?"

"We need to confront them as one," Milo said. "Northwell and its clients. They need to know that they will be prosecuted, or worse, in their home countries."

"But Northwell," said Francis, tapping the tabletop. "We don't have any sway over Northwell headquarters. That's the Americans, and I don't see them here."

Alexandra sighed. Erika had warned them about this. She watched Milo lean closer to his audience, hands on the dining table. "Northwell, particularly its Tourism section, is funded directly by its clients. That's how it's able to hide its finances—which, I imagine, was documented in the records Joseph Keller originally stumbled on. The Library worked the same way. Without patrons, we were nothing. Take away Northwell's clients, and the Tourism section withers away."

Again, the old Russian leaned over to whisper to Vetrov, then changed his mind and looked directly at Milo. *"Da,"* he said with a sharp nod.

Alexandra looked at Francis, who seemed most troubled by all this. "The Booths," he said finally. "So we arrest Oliver Booth for financial crimes. Maybe his wife, Catherine, as an accessory, though *that* would be a political minefield. You," he said, nodding at Oskar, "put a team of financial regulators onto IfW's funding schemes. The rest of you put some people in jail. But if we don't have the Americans, Northwell will keep Nexus as its client, and next year Halliwell and Foster will be back here gathering more customers. This will cripple them, yes, but not for long."

"Nothing is static," Alexandra said. "This year, we knock out most of their clientele. Then we have a year to get the Americans on board. A year is a very long time."

"That's assuming a lot," Francis said.

Alexandra looked to the others, to Li Fan and Vetrov's old man, and in their faces she saw the same kind of anxiety. Even in Oskar's face.

"This is what we have now," Milo said. "The alternative is to do nothing and let your economies be disrupted by people who don't give a damn."

Francis raised his brows, and finally shrugged. "It's what we have." He rapped his knuckles on the table. "All right, then."

"Good," said Milo. "Alex?"

"Right," she said, surprised that they had actually agreed. "Tomorrow we meet outside the Congress Center, and together we enter and join the meeting. Milo will explain the situation, and each of you, if you like, can explain the threats in more detail."

"I am bringing my men," Vetrov said definitively.

"Yes," Li Fan agreed.

"Only one each, please," Milo said. "We have no reason to expect violence. With the security cordon in place no one will be armed. They can't get any weapons in. Neither can we." He opened his hands. "No one gets hurt. We walk inside, have a chat, and leave."

"What about the Massive Brigade?" Li Fan asked.

"What about them?"

She looked at Oskar. "The Germans think they are here, yes? Does that change our calculations?"

Milo shook his head. "Not unless the Germans have a place and time that they will strike. Oskar?"

The German shook his head sadly.

"Then, no. It changes nothing."

The old Russian rose to his feet, and Vetrov followed suit, saying, "We have what we have. We thank you." Dalmatian opened the door, letting in the night wind, so the two men could leave. Francis took another sip of his coffee, nodded sharply, and followed them out.

Li Fan lingered, slowly packing her phone into her purse, then turned to Milo. "Xin Zhu sends greetings. He says that today we are friends."

"And tomorrow?" Alexandra asked.

Li Fan looked over at her and smiled, then exited as Oskar took the flash drive with the video out of the laptop. "It will be over soon," he said, then raised his sling a little and smiled. "Talk tomorrow." They watched him make his way out.

The whole conversation had left Alexandra unsettled. Not the words necessarily, but the space between the words. Like there was something their co-conspirators were leaving unsaid. Something only they knew. But she had no idea what it was.

Once Dalmatian had locked the door again, she turned to Milo, who was closing the laptop. "Did you see that?"

"*I* did," said Leticia, finally getting off the wall and heading to the table.

Milo seemed confused. "What?"

"They're not telling us something," Alexandra said.

"Exactly," said Leticia.

"No one ever tells us everything," Milo protested.

"It's a group thing," Alexandra said. "There's something that they, *as a group,* are not telling us."

Milo swiveled his gaze between the two women, looking a little dumb, and she wondered why her father had chosen him. There was nothing special about her brother, not really. He furrowed his brow and looked over at Dalmatian. "Did you see it?"

"Wasn't my focus," he said. "But I can't say I trust them."

"Nobody *trusts* them," Milo said, then turned to Alexandra. "Do you think we're walking into a trap?"

Did she? She shook her head. "Not necessarily."

"But they certainly don't like the plan," Leticia said.

"Agreed," said Alexandra.

"Yet they're all on board," Milo said. "Maybe watching a slaughter is more convincing than you think."

"I don't know," Leticia said, stifling a yawn.

"Go to bed," Milo told her, then looked at Dalmatian. "How are the stitches?"

"Holding," he said, then broke into a queer smile for Leticia. "Good enough to take her back to our room."

Leticia's eyes widened in surprise. She looked at Alexandra. "He's learning."

They left together, and Alexandra went to turn off the lights. Milo stood waiting by the door, looking out at Poitevin, who was walking carefully across ice to reach them. "What are you going to do afterward?" he asked her.

She thought of her eternal debate between a man and a dog. And, perhaps for the first time, she thought, *Why not both?* "A vacation," she said. "You?"

Alexandra wasn't surprised at all when her brother said, "Retirement," though she doubted he had any idea what that really meant.

18

Samuel had been relieved by Frank, a stout thick-necked Minnesotan who, as Samuel had told me, was built like a linebacker, albeit a short one. Frank seemed as if he'd only just gotten the job and wanted to impress his bosses with his understanding of regulations. He searched the hotel room when he arrived that final morning of the Forum, claiming that he couldn't be sure Samuel had checked it (he hadn't), and when he didn't come up with any contraband he parked himself at the door rather than by the window, where Samuel had lounged the whole night, nursing his bruise. I don't know how Samuel ended up explaining it.

There was nothing to do but reflect on those traumatic minutes at the bar. Haroun, in the flesh, explaining to me how his life had ended up where it had, and how he justified it all. He was a creature of loss—the loss of belief—and cynicism. More specifically, his was a story of temptation as old as Genesis, but inverted: Instead of learning of good and evil, he had learned that neither existed. There was only profit and loss, and somehow he had decided that those values were worth risking his life for.

Or maybe I was overthinking it. Maybe he only saw his job the way most people did, as a way to earn a living so that he could live life. But he hadn't said a word about paychecks or a splendid lifestyle at coastal resorts. No girlfriends, no children, no mortgages. Haroun had tried to justify his life on purely ideological grounds, and that was why I was still shook.

It was just after noon when Mel showed up. She asked Frank if I'd given him trouble, and when he shook his head she sent him out of the room and pulled a desk chair up to the side of the bed. Elbows on her knees, she looked at me, pressing her fingertips together, and said, "In your report, and in the recordings, there's nothing about Milo Weaver's plan."

"Because he never told me."

She nodded slowly. "Late last night," she said, "he met with intelligence officers from the UK, Russia, Germany, and China."

"That's the meeting he invited you to."

"Yes, of course, but there's more. Yesterday morning a German representative to the UN disappeared after landing in Zürich, heading for Davos. Last night, Swiss police found three dead Chinese intelligence officers up the side of a mountain—they're trying their damnedest to keep it quiet. Then Milo has his meeting. And this morning, his four intelligence officers met on their own, inside the security ring. At a café in the Congress Center. We didn't get audio, but they seemed to be debating something."

"Probably Milo Weaver's plan."

She took her phone from inside her blue business jacket. "Sure. Then one of them went outside the security ring and headed down to the train station, where he met with this person." She pulled up a photo and handed the phone to me.

It was a photo of a small white man with a mustache, his arm in a sling, walking alongside a younger woman whom I recognized even though her hair was longer, cut into a bob around her jawline, and her makeup was different. I said, "That's the woman who looked like Ingrid Parker. Back in Klosters. Who's he?"

"German. BND."

I frowned, remembering a stray character from Milo's story. "Oskar Leintz?"

"Yes," she said, not surprised that I knew.

"Maybe I was wrong," I said, handing the phone back. "Maybe that *is* Ingrid Parker."

"It isn't," Mel said.

I squinted at the image, not entirely sure myself now. "How do you know?"

"Because yesterday the FBI confirmed a sighting in West Palm Beach, near Mar-a-Lago. Secret Service is shitting itself."

"I thought you didn't trust the FBI."

"I trust them. I just don't respect them."

I opened my mouth, shut it, then said, "Why would the Germans falsely report that Parker is in Europe, and then go meet her doppelgänger?"

"That's the question, Abdul. What are they up to?"

I put on my analyst's hat and thought about what I knew. Leintz's fraught but essentially cordial relationship with Weaver. Weaver's desire to put an end to Northwell's private army, and his decision to enlist countries to help his fight. But this—this particular detail—what did it mean?

"We don't have enough information," I admitted.

She didn't like that but didn't say a thing.

"Did he call again?" I asked.

"What?"

"Milo. I thought he might try again."

She shook her head. "I don't think he ever wanted our help in the first place."

I remembered the trouble they had gone through to get me to Madrid Airport. "No, he did want your help. But after that call he doesn't trust you. He thinks you'll undermine him."

"But he trusts the *Russians*?"

I looked past her to where the sun was sitting high in the sky, illuminating a fresh layer of snow that had covered Davos overnight. From my angle, I could make out one of the snipers on top of the Congress Center. I thought about those intelligence chiefs meeting inside that heavily guarded building, a place they knew Milo wouldn't find them. Oskar Leintz making contact with the fake Ingrid Parker . . .

Oh.

As the thought came to me, I said, "They're setting him up."

Mel's face settled into a stiff mask. She said, "Explain."

"I can't. But all the reports about Ingrid Parker are from the Germans. Yes?"

"Yes."

"Nothing from the Swiss, the French . . . no one else?"

She sank deeper into her chair. "Correct."

It still didn't make complete sense, but I could feel a truth pushing up from under the surface. "I don't know why, but the Germans are running a parallel game Milo doesn't know anything about."

"What game?"

"Something that requires us, and other countries, to believe Ingrid Parker is here."

Mel blinked at me, absorbing this.

I said, "My suggestion is to contact Milo Weaver and show him that photo. You don't lose anything by it, and he might be able to stop a disaster."

"What if Milo's plan *is* the disaster?"

I shook my head. "He's not here to make more trouble. He only wants his family to be safe."

She continued to stare hard at me, stiff, and then her features relaxed. "Come with me," she said.

We went out into the corridor, where Frank stood erect and obedient. "We'll be right back," she told him, and he watched us head to the far end of the corridor. Mel knocked on a door, waited, then opened it and brought me inside.

What I saw was a shock, though it shouldn't have been. Standing with Sally in the room was an angry Gilbert Powell, founder of Nexus. Like a lot of other powerful men, he was taller than expected, and he barely noticed us enter—he was in the middle of a rant.

"What do you think? That I couldn't *find* seed money? For fuck's sake, I didn't *need* yours!"

"Yet you took it," Sally told him in a calm, quiet voice, raising a finger to Mel for patience. "Our terms were never hidden. You signed."

"Enough!" he said. "I'll write you a check right now. Give me a number. Just stay out of the system!"

"Gilbert," Sally said, still measured and cool, "have you met Abdul?"

I was surprised to be brought into this, and Powell seemed surprised by this as well. He shook his head no and turned to the window, not interested in knowing me.

"Well," Sally said. "Abdul has brought us the most interesting story about Northwell and its relationship to Nexus."

Slowly, Powell turned back and focused on me. But he didn't speak.

"It used to be called Tourism," she went on. "I don't know what you call it now."

"I don't know—"

"Remember Lou Braxton?" Sally cut in. "Where4 was a hell of a platform. Gave Nexus a run for its money. It was a shame he died so young."

Weak now, Powell sank onto the edge of the perfectly made bed and looked at all of our faces.

Beside me, Mel said, "Principled, too. He refused to even sit down with us."

"I admired that," Sally said, then looked a long moment at Gilbert Powell, who seemed to be closing down. "There is a way out for you, Gilbert, and it's so simple. You do nothing. Everything remains as it is. You do not block our access. If you do, then everything comes crashing down. Everything."

Powell rubbed his forehead, thinking, then looked up. "You would go down, too."

She shook her head. "We don't need customers to buy into our product. There would be a minor storm, a scapegoat would be found, and a year later it's business as usual. Nexus, though—I give it a month of solvency. No one would trust you. Your pariah status would last a lifetime."

He breathed loudly through his nose, trying to figure a way out of the trap. But, for now at least, there was no escape.

"Go on, Gilbert," Sally said. "Think about it. We'll talk later, before the flight home. And if you get a chance, tell Anthony Halliwell we'd like to speak to him, too. We're in Davos, after all. This is a place for acquisitions."

I watched Gilbert Powell shuffle out of that room, defeated, and knew that I would never see him the same way again. I said, "We're inside Nexus?"

Mel ignored my question and brought me deeper into the room. To Sally, she said, "Abdul's assessment is that Weaver's being played. Tell her."

I repeated my argument, which, though thin, was no worse than any arguments they could come up with. "It wouldn't hurt to tell Weaver what's going on," I said.

"It might," Sally said, sounding a lot like Mel a few minutes ago. "Maybe the Germans are setting up a coup. Get rid of Weaver so the adults can take care of Northwell."

"Or maybe, like you, they're thinking of acquiring Northwell," I said.

Witnessing her conversation with Powell had crystallized that thought. "I don't think you want German Tourism."

Sally seemed to take that seriously, but she made no move to admit it. "Put him back on ice," she told Mel. "You and I have some thinking to do."

19

After parking in the garage, Milo found a demonstration outside the Rätia shopping center, about a hundred people in caps and heavy coats, puffs of fog rolling from their mouths as they chanted in German and held signs in English. A banner said SYSTEM CHANGE NOT CLIMATE CHANGE; another: "LET THEM EAT MONEY," with the *A* in "eat" a scrawled anarchy symbol. Some were wordy—IF WAR IS AN INDUSTRY HOW CAN THERE BE PEACE IN A CAPITALIST WORLD?—while others were succinct—NOT WELCOME printed under the faces of Benjamin Netanyahu and Jair Bolsonaro. On the wall of the Rätia, in large characters, someone had spray-painted M3.

But he didn't linger. He pushed through, walking up the Promenade before turning off onto a side street and continuing to fortified Davos Park at the center of town. The soldiers in black eyed him as he approached the press center, where more guards waited with metal detectors and an X-ray conveyor. They checked the press pass Oskar had supplied carefully enough that he grew worried; then they rifled through his bag, where he'd stashed notebooks, a voice recorder, a camera, and a couple of energy bars. It was as boring as he could make it, and they let him in.

The closing performance, a musical program by the Sphinx Virtuosi chamber orchestra with images of Earth from space, was about to wrap up, so the park was scattered with milling journalists catching smokes and waiting to get a final word from attendees. By a snowbank along the ring of trees, he eventually spotted Leticia talking with Poitevin. Poitevin saw him first, but all they did was meet eyes. Conversation would have to wait.

To the left, Alexandra and Dalmatian pretended to work on their phones, standing a good five yards apart. And up ahead, to the right, near the Congress Center's Talstrasse entrance, he saw Vetrov smoking with Francis, while Li Fan and Oskar, still wearing his sling, conferred. Not far away, four bodyguards stood listlessly.

"Milo Weaver," he heard, and turned to see a pale woman with intense, businesslike eyes catching up to him. She was clearly American, and he wasn't sure what to do.

"Do I know you?"

"Sally," she said with a sudden, beautiful smile.

"We spoke on the phone," he said.

"Yes. I wanted to show you something."

She held out her hand, and in it was a photograph printed on paper. He took it. Oskar, walking with a young woman. "What's this?"

"We know who Oskar Leintz is," she said. "The problem is the other one. Abdul saw her in Klosters, made up to look like Ingrid Parker."

Yes—it had been months, but he remembered the woman. It was Lana, Oskar's lavender-lipped associate from Tegel Airport.

Sally flashed another smile. "They're trying very hard to convince everyone that Ingrid Parker is here, when we know she's not. She's in Florida."

Milo examined the photo again. He didn't trust Sally. She was, he had decided, only interested in keeping a tight grip on Nexus and its intelligence riches. "Does this have to be nefarious?" he asked.

"Abdul thinks it is. He's the one who convinced us to share this with you."

That was something. "How is he?"

The question seemed to surprise her. "He's fine. He'll be on a plane home by tonight. He's disappointed he couldn't get us to work together."

"Me, too," he said, which was at least partially true. He nodded toward the Congress Center and his waiting co-conspirators. "You're not planning to interfere?"

She shook her head. "You do what you have to do. Make your deals. We will do what we have to do."

"You understand what you're dealing with, right? If you think you can control Northwell, or use them, then you're playing with fire."

"We'll see," she said and, with another smile, turned and walked away, back toward the press center. When he looked around, all four of his people were staring at him with anxious curiosity, but he didn't bother with that. He continued toward the Congress Center, and behind him the others began to follow.

When he reached the entrance, none of the intelligence officers made an attempt to shake his hand. He said to them, "Five minutes. They know we're unarmed. There shouldn't be trouble."

Vetrov grunted, "If you are wrong, I do think this will not be the first time."

Milo gave him a wry grin, then turned to Oskar. "Can we walk?"

Once they were out of range of the others, Milo handed him the photo. Oskar squinted at it. "Who is this from?"

"CIA."

"*Scheisse,*" Oskar muttered, then began ripping up the picture.

"What is it?"

He shook his head, not speaking.

"Oskar. Ingrid Parker isn't in Europe, is she?"

But the German turned around and began walking slowly back to the others, not even looking at Milo. Finally, he said, "This was a group decision."

"What are you talking about?"

"This is the best way. Even Erika agrees."

Milo stopped short and grabbed Oskar by the lapels, his face very close. From nowhere, Kurt appeared and clutched Milo's shoulders from behind, pulling him off.

"It's okay," Oskar told Kurt, and Milo was released. Oskar brushed at his coat, as if getting Milo's dirt off it. "It's fine, Milo. Everything is going to be fine." Then he left and joined the others. Together, they spoke quietly, occasionally glancing back at him.

Leticia joined Milo, watching Kurt join the other bodyguards. "What's going on?"

"You and Alex were right. They're up to something."

"Then let's call it off."

What was she thinking? This moment, right now, was why he'd waited months in the desert. "This is our only chance," he said.

"Not if we end up dead, it isn't."

He didn't want to get into an argument with her, so he walked away and stood alone, looking down the park at its milling journalists, then over to the intelligence officers talking among themselves. What were they up to? He remembered Erika telling him, very seriously, that Ingrid Parker was a variable he would have to take into consideration—but no, Parker was in America, and she'd been there all along. Erika had only been planting the story so that it would grow in his mind, and the minds of other intelligence agencies. For what purpose? Why drag a story of the Massive Brigade to Davos?

What had been Erika's concern? He thought back to that stuffy house in the Black Forest, and it came to him: *If you cannot convince the Americans to join your crusade, then I do not expect the others to commit.* She'd spent a lot of time explaining why that was crucial, and yet, even without American support, they *had* committed. China, the UK, Russia, and Germany. All had come together. Even in that meeting, with the video of the Second Bureau's slaughter, he'd been surprised that it had worked. Yet he hadn't seen it. The others had. Alexandra, Leticia, and even Dalmatian had known that something was off.

His stomach twisted as he realized that their final meeting in the restaurant had been a charade, because they had already committed themselves—not to Milo's plan, but to Erika and Oskar's. He'd never had to set up the Second Bureau. No one had had to die.

What were they planning? Did Oskar think that he could make a better speech? Fine—if he wanted to make a more convincing threat, then let him. But if that was all he wanted to do, why keep it secret from Milo? No. It was something else, something that Oskar knew Milo would fight against.

What now? Do as Leticia suggested, and call the whole thing off? How would they survive the next twelve months, looking over their shoulders as Northwell's Tourists homed in on them?

He checked the time on his phone and saw that it was too late. He caught

Leticia's eye—she, too, was lost in thought, but she noticed him looking and nodded seriously. He nodded back. Leticia turned to the others and called for them to follow. Milo walked over to the Talstrasse entrance and said to the waiting intelligence officers, "It's time."

20

Leticia didn't like Milo's attitude, but she understood it. There was only one outcome that interested him, and that was the safety of his family and the people who had worked for him this last decade. Milo wasn't an ideologue; he wasn't fighting for some better version of the world, and for someone like him the aims were always primitive and foundational: Take care of me and mine, and try not to kill too many people along the way.

Fair enough.

To a certain extent, Leticia felt the same. The first principle of life is to stay alive, because without that nothing else can be accomplished. However, once survival was assured, there were other things to consider. Nigeria had taught her that. Other places, too, but Nigeria had hammered it home. And unlike Milo, she'd lived a long time without the incessant chatter of family and colleagues that always distracted you from the big picture. The big picture was this: Northwell and its clients were the reason why little girls in Nigeria were being ripped from their homes and raped and brainwashed and forced into labor. She could list a thousand travesties to justify bringing them down, but there was no need. A single girl was enough to convince her that whatever happened to Northwell couldn't be a slap on the wrist; it had to be crushing.

She just wasn't sure they were going to be able to do the job today. The groundwork they'd done in the last three months had been the minimum, a quickly assembled house of cards. If it failed today, she doubted they'd get another chance. And if it succeeded . . . well, she had no illusion that there wouldn't be more work to do.

But she didn't fight him. She hurried ahead to open the door and step into the airy, glass-fronted entryway, where security guards were waiting to check their IDs. She handed over hers and stepped through another metal detector, wondering why she didn't just leave.

She knew why. It was because the other thing she'd learned was that going it alone never really got her what she wanted. Even today's half measures were better than what years on the road had gotten her.

But it was more than that, wasn't it?

Yes. She was tired. Tired of the disposable life, where when the dark moods came there was no one to turn to, only a mirror, and in that mirror the emptiness could no longer be ignored. Then she'd come to Zürich and discovered something in Milo's Library that she didn't even know she'd needed.

At the far end of the corridor, some journalists were huddled with their phones, and when Leticia, then the others, approached they looked up, squinting. But none of her crew were well-known politicians worthy of a byline, so they went back to their phones.

Looking to Alexandra, Leticia said, "Parsenn-Pischa, right?"

Alexandra nodded, and Poitevin joined her as she went through the floor plan in her head, calmly walking past small meeting rooms called Flüela and Sertig. Before reaching the journalists, she turned down a broad staircase under a banner that said ANNUAL MEETING 2019 to the large main hall, where workers were breaking down displays and screens and stacking chairs. Off to the right, nondescript bureaucrats and businesspeople networked in low tones and sudden bright laughter, but Leticia led her people to the left, past the kitchen and VIP entrance, up concrete stairs to automatic glass doors marked with a blue sign with a large orange *B*.

When they stepped through to B-Wing, she and Poitevin paused. It was a small area that wrapped around an elevator, and to their immediate right narrow stairs led up to the third floor. She waited until all of them—the bureaucrats, their guards, and the remnants of the Library, thirteen in all—were through the doors, then turned to Milo. "One floor up," she said. "I'll go first."

She began to ascend, Poitevin right behind her, and paused at the top step, where she could see on a far wall a sign that said B3—the characters overlapped, she noticed, like the M3 of the Massive Brigade. Then she stepped forward and turned right, where, on the far wall, between two sets of double doors, a small TV displayed:

PARSENN-PISCHA

PRIVAT

Between her and that TV, though, seven men and two women stared at her. One of them was Haroun Ghali, while another, wiping his nose with the back of a hand, was the man who had faked incompetence until the moment he murdered Noah and Kristin—the man they only knew as Joseph Keller. And there, in the back: Karim Saleem, from Nigeria.

Haroun was at the front, and he stood stiffly about ten yards away. He put a hand on his jacket, at the hip, but then dropped it. Instinct had made him reach for a gun that wasn't there.

"Leticia," he said, the corner of his mouth twitching in amusement or panic—she couldn't be sure which. "You really did a job on Lance."

"Sorry," she said as the others emerged from the stairwell behind her.

Haroun looked them over, frowning. "So what brings you here?"

Milo appeared at her side and kept walking forward, so she stayed with him until they were both facing Haroun. The other Tourists crept closer. Milo said, "I need to talk with Grace Foster."

"That's not happening."

"We don't want to fight," Milo said, "but we will. Please tell her we're here."

Haroun looked back to his colleagues, who formed a shallow arc of tense figures ready to attack. They didn't need guns to do serious damage. Joseph Keller's expression tensed when he met Milo's gaze, but Milo maintained his self-control—admirably, Leticia thought. His features betrayed none of the fury that she knew was bubbling inside of him.

"This is just a conversation," Milo said. "Like you, we're not armed." He spread out his arms. "Check, if you like."

Haroun looked back and forth between the two of them, then raised his head to peer at the others again. It struck Leticia that Abdul's brother was out of his depth. He was a man who had been trained for action and little else. Conversation was uncomfortable to him. Back in Nigeria, Karim

Saleem's act as a Literacy Across the World humanitarian had been forced and awkward, which was why she'd dug deeper. Northwell might have used the Tourist playbook, but they'd picked up only what they really wanted: the hierarchy, methods, and fighting skills. They'd ignored the most important part: the twisted logical skills of the Tourist that made for the perfect story-teller. The misdirection and the instinctual camouflage. No, what they had here was bargain-basement Tourism.

"Hold on," Haroun finally said, then turned to head inside, telling his colleagues to keep an eye on them. He opened a door and slipped inside the two rooms they'd reserved, the Parsenn and the Pischa.

"What do you think?" Milo asked.

"I think he's confused."

"Me, too." Milo glanced back at the intelligence officers and spoke without moving his lips. "They're going to try something serious in there."

"Like what?"

"I don't know, but if they don't think CIA will take care of Northwell, they'll do it themselves."

Alexandra approached and said, "So?"

"Your brother thinks there's going to be trouble."

"So what do we do?" Alexandra asked.

Milo looked back again, and Leticia did too. Francis checked his watch and chewed the inside of his mouth. Oskar's frowning face was deep with lines as Vetrov glanced distractedly at his phone. Only Li Fan seemed re-laxed, her eyes shifting to look right back at them, as if trying to decide which of them to eat first.

Milo said, "What do they want?"

"The same damned things we want," Leticia said.

The far door opened. Haroun held it open, and out came the bitch. Grace Foster hesitated at first, as if only now believing what Haroun had told her inside, then collected herself and walked over, her high heels clicking rapidly. She eyed Leticia, a disappointed look, then approached Milo. "What the hell are you doing here?"

"We're here to talk to your group."

"No," she said, shaking her head. "Get out of here while you still can."

The half-circle of cut-rate Tourists tightened, and Leticia planted her feet wide, preparing to fight.

Milo sighed, trying to look merely put-out. "You see the people behind me? Do you know who they are?"

She looked past him, recognizing them all.

"They're on board. It's settled. I'm offering you a way out. No one gets killed. No one even gets arrested."

Again she looked past him. "I don't see the Agency."

"That's between you and them. But this, right now, is the only way you get out of Davos with your freedom and your lives intact."

Leticia couldn't tell how Foster was taking all of this. Her white cheeks didn't flush, and she held on to Milo's gaze. God, she was cool. "What," she asked, "do you intend to say?"

"We'll explain that it's over. Everyone's done well, everyone's profited from their investment. But now it ends. They rip up their Northwell contracts, and all is forgotten." He opened his hands. "If not, or if you don't let us inside, each of your clients ends up in prison when they return home."

Finally, a smile reached Foster's face. "You think they'll scare that easily?"

"If they're smart they will."

She raised her chin to look down at him condescendingly. "You don't know these kinds of people, do you? They live on a different planet from you. From me, too. Prisons, laws—they'll tie your friends up in court for years while ripping them to pieces in public. No one scares them."

Leticia's optimism, low as it was, sank even further. The bitch was right. And Milo wasn't getting it. Despite all the things he had done and seen over the years, Milo Weaver was naïve. He still thought shame existed in the world. He still had faith in *process*. Had she really hooked her cart to this man?

After thinking a moment, Grace Foster shrugged. What did she have to lose? "Okay, then. Make your pitch. But *she*," Foster said, pointing at Leticia, "stays out here."

Smart girl, Leticia thought.

It took a moment, Haroun and his colleagues patting down everyone except Li Fan, who slapped Haroun's hand and simply said, "No." Haroun didn't try again, and Foster didn't press the issue. While they bickered, Francis scratched at his forehead, looking embarrassed. Oskar kept checking his phone, and Vetrov pulled on white gloves, which didn't seem very GRU to her. Then the bitch led Milo, Alexandra, and the four intelligence officers inside. This time she got a view of the space, of chairs and backs lined up in front of a podium by a glass wall. Behind the podium, Anthony Halliwell, against a backdrop of the Northwell logo on a projector screen, said, "twenty percent growth," then noticed the visitors and paused. What struck her was the number of people in the audience. She'd expected a dozen. But there were so many more.

As the door shut, she turned to find Haroun staring at her with an expression she couldn't interpret. So she walked slowly over to Poitevin and Dalmatian and the four bodyguards whose names she didn't know. They stood together, facing the others, who, she hoped without hope, would be the last Tourists she would ever have to face.

21

The crowd that had surprised Leticia shocked Alexandra, and that was when she first wondered if they were out of their depth. They had known of four or five companies that used Northwell's services, but here were—she did a quick estimate—over sixty men and women in suits, filling the seats to overflowing, all focused on Anthony Halliwell at his podium, and then turning to look at the unexpected half-dozen visitors. They were multitudes, these Northwell clients—Africans and Asians and Arabs and Europeans. There was a face she recognized as part of Jair Bolsonaro's entourage, and in the front was the unmistakable face of Gilbert Powell, his head swiveling to take them in. In the second row, Sergei Stepanov was sitting with his English banker, Oliver Booth. The lamps in the low ceiling were dark, but plenty of light came in from the floor-to-ceiling windows and glass door that led to the small, snow-covered courtyard between the Congress Center and the Congress Hotel.

"What is this?" Halliwell asked through his mic.

"Sorry, Tony," Foster said, sounding entirely casual. "Something unavoidable came up. But it won't take long."

She led them up to the front, while Halliwell looked like he wanted to shout—he wasn't a man who liked surprises. On the screen beside him a color-coded pie chart chronicled the expansion of operations into each of the continents. How simple a chart could make all this look.

At the mic now, Foster took Halliwell aside and whispered. His flushing face did a poor job hiding his shock and anger. Foster then turned to the mic and said to everyone, "This man over here is Milo Weaver. You'll know the name because of the numerous Interpol Red Notices out for him. He is a known criminal, but one with powerful friends. Which is why we're letting him have five minutes of our time. Once he's had his say, the meeting will continue."

She stepped back and offered the podium to Milo, who suddenly looked unsure of himself. Though she felt a flash of frustration, Alexandra could understand. This wasn't the kind of crowd they thought they would have to win over. A dozen, maybe twenty, but this? The others—Francis, Li Fan, Oskar, and Vetrov—looked equally surprised, and Li Fan leaned in to whisper to Oskar, who nodded.

Milo cleared his throat and said, "The people I've brought with me represent the intelligence communities of the UK, Germany, Russia, and China. All four countries are aware of your relationship to Northwell, and the criminal acts you've hired them to commit. Each of you, in the next week, will have warrants out for your arrest. Unless you hereby sever your relationship with Northwell."

God, he was bad. Alexandra had never seen Milo before a crowd, because he'd never needed to talk to any group larger than the twelve patrons. His stilted speech was like trying to heat a large room with a single match. As she watched, Li Fan whispered to Oskar again, showing him her wristwatch, and Oskar approached Milo from the side. Li Fan also moved, getting closer to wide-eyed, scarlet-faced Anthony Halliwell. Francis and Vetrov, watching all this, fidgeted with what was plainly secret anticipation. Whatever they were planning, it was happening now.

"The fact of the matter," Milo went on, "is that no country can afford this kind of lawlessness, and so you have a choice. If you choose to not act, then in a week you will be imprisoned and your companies will be taken away. Many of them will collapse. A deal is being offered. I suggest you take it."

Oskar whispered to Milo, who nodded and stepped back. Oskar moved to the mic and said, "My friend states the facts plainly. Let me put it more simply: This ends today. Each of you will play along, or you will share the fate of these two leaders of Northwell."

Halliwell shook his head and barked, *"Really?"* He sounded ready to laugh.

That was when a low, staccato series of booms sounded. They came from out in the courtyard. The glass trembled slightly, and all heads turned to see smoke fuming from holes in the snowy ground, rising to obscure the hotel. The noise and smoke surprised everyone, except, she noticed, the four intelligence officers. As if on cue, Li Fan reached into her coat, took out a pair of blue latex gloves, and slipped them on.

22

"Two hours until your car comes," Samuel said from behind me, scrolling through his phone, legs stretched out on the bed.

I was staring down at the white solar-paneled roof of the Congress Center, hardly hearing him.

Samuel said, "This time tomorrow, you'll be ordering Starbucks ventis."

I turned back to him. The bruise on the side of his face had purpled, a reminder of Haroun's strength, and despite the pleasure his words should have evoked, I just couldn't picture myself in America. Not at Starbucks, and not at home with Laura and Rashid. It was a dream I'd held on to over the past ten days, something to keep me going, but now it wouldn't come. Why?

I suspected it was because, unlike Haroun, I'd always only been an analyst. It was what I did. It gave my life meaning. But I'd been unable to analyze this situation to my satisfaction. There were too many loose ends. Too much chaos in the data.

I was sure the Germans were using Milo, but to what end? Weren't they getting what they needed from him? He had revealed a globe-spanning secret army and had brought them to the convergence point of that conspiracy. He had handed them everything. Yet they were lying to him about the Massive Brigade. Why?

The door opened, and Sally and Mel filed in. I hadn't seen Paul in a day, but I also hadn't bothered to ask after him. I supposed his presence was no longer necessary, and so he'd been sent home. Samuel scrambled to his feet, but neither woman seemed to care if he was doing his job or not. Mel just ordered him to step outside, and he did so.

"Did you tell him?" I asked.

Sally nodded and settled on the desk chair. She, too, seemed deep in thought.

"And?"

"And he listened," she said. "I suppose he's adding it to his calculations."

Mel settled on the corner of the bed. "We should be down there."

Sally glared at her. "If there's an international incident brewing, we are *not* taking part."

"There isn't," I said, and they looked at me. "At least, Milo's not planning one. He'll want to get this done entirely under the radar."

"He's not the only player," Sally said.

"Which is why we should—" Mel began, but Sally cut her off with: "Enough, okay?"

The tension between them was distracting, and I didn't want to be distracted. So I returned to the window. Why would the Germans peddle lies about the Massive Brigade right here in Davos? Why sell that to us and, presumably, to other intelligence agencies?

Along Talstrasse, just south of the park, I saw that sniper on his rooftop, keeping an eye on pedestrians. This was perhaps the most secure city in the world at that moment. What could really go wrong?

"Distraction," I said aloud, and though I continued staring out the window I knew they had turned to me. "They're distracting us from something."

"From what?" asked Sally.

I didn't answer, because I didn't have an answer, and that was when I looked down at the Congress Center roof and realized it was empty. The two snipers I'd grown used to seeing down there, pacing with military regularity, were nowhere to be seen.

"What do the Germans want?" Mel asked behind me, but I was absorbed by the empty rooftop—where had they gone? When two figures emerged from the rooftop access door, I relaxed. Just late for their shift. They—

No. Not snipers. They wore red and blue hooded overcoats, and one carried a heavy duffel bag. They hurried around the solar panels to my end of the roof.

"To stick it to us," Sally said, answering Mel. "That's what they want."

"But why?" Mel asked, sounding unsure. "What the fuck have we done to them?"

"You have to ask that?"

The two figures crouched at the edge of the roof, over the courtyard between our buildings, and opened the duffel bag. Together, they removed a dozen or so metal balls and what looked like an aerosol can. What were they—

"Oh, shit," I said as the pieces came to me, the way a problem left to fester in the back of the mind will suddenly present its solution when the final piece is witnessed. And there I was, witnessing it.

"What?" I don't know which of them said that.

"The Germans know you want to absorb Northwell," I said. "And they can't allow that."

The figures were dropping the balls into the courtyard, where they poked holes in the snowbank. One of them—the one in blue—took something out of his pocket, extended an antenna from it, and pressed a button.

Boom-boom-boom-boom.

"What the fuck?" Mel said, standing.

Sally said nothing, but she was suddenly at my shoulder. Together we looked down at the courtyard, where the balls were exploding, spitting out streams of smoke that quickly began to fill the space between the hotel and the Congress Center.

As the blue-clad figure ran off to the access door, the one in red shook his aerosol can and, on one of the solar panels, raggedly scrawled two shapes in red spray paint: M3.

23

Through the windows, the back of the hotel had been replaced by the milky white of smoke as Northwell's clients were on their feet, some gasping, most silently stunned.

Unlike Alexandra, Milo hadn't noticed Li Fan putting on her latex gloves, but he had seen Vetrov's white ones. Now he turned to see that Vetrov had moved to join Li Fan, who reached into her coat and handed the Russian something small and white. And that was when he knew. That was when he remembered Whippet's long-ago report on Chinese technology. He knew what would happen, and how.

Oskar, at the microphone, said, "No need to worry. Please. You are all very safe."

"No!" Milo shouted, but Li Fan was already taking three long steps toward Halliwell, who stood gaping at the window. Li Fan raised her arm and pointed her own white object at the back of Halliwell's head. She pulled the lever, and the 3D-printed plastic gun fired, popping loudly in a bright flash. She tossed the wasted gun aside, but by then it had served its purpose, shooting a single plastic bullet into the back of Halliwell's skull. The front of his forehead exploded, a burst of bone and brain spraying across the window, and he dropped to his knees, then onto his face.

There were screams. There was panic.

"Please," Oskar said in his calmest voice. "Settle down."

That was when Foster, shaken and stunned, realized Vetrov was approaching her, raising his own plastic gun.

Milo began to run.

Foster turned to flee just as Vetrov pulled the lever, shattering the gun and blowing out a piece of her skull. She fell. Vetrov tossed the weapon aside and approached, but Milo got there first and shoved him away. He crouched to take a look at her. Foster was still conscious, gasping. It had been a bad shot, leaving her skull open and the mangled brain visible. She was going to have to live through all of it until she bled out.

Lips trembling, she told Milo, "I don't feel it."

He heard someone clearing his throat over the speakers. It was Oskar, at the podium. Fucking Oskar Leintz. And fucking Erika Schwartz.

Beyond the podium, Francis had walked over to the glass door to the courtyard stairs and pushed it open. Smoke began to creep inside. He was so calm. They were all so calm. Then Haroun and the man they had known as Joseph Keller burst inside from the corridor, followed by Leticia and Poitevin. Then the others. They looked at the bodies and then the open courtyard door, where white smoke billowed inside, almost swallowing Francis. The outside world, it seemed, had vanished.

"Excuse me," said Oskar, now holding the mic. "Please. Everyone please calm down."

They didn't calm down, so he went on, louder this time.

"What you have just seen is a shot across the bow. So that you understand the seriousness of our proposal. Northwell is over. Your contracts with them are void. Understand: If any of this is revived, we will not arrest you. We will murder you."

Someone, somewhere in the crowd, was weeping loudly.

Oskar raised a finger. "One more thing—this is important. You will be questioned. You will all have the same story. It is this," Oskar went on, pointing at the door where Francis stood: "Two members of the Massive Brigade came through there and killed these people. One was a woman named Ingrid Parker. They did not give a speech. They did not say a thing. They opened that door, walked in, committed murder, and left. The savages."

Milo looked down at Foster. Her eyes were still open, flicking around, confused, and though her mouth moved nothing came out.

Oskar turned to Li Fan and Vetrov. "I think that covers it. Yes?"

Li Fan shrugged, and Vetrov nodded, but his eyes were on the third row, where Sergei Stepanov was standing at the edge of the crowd with two other Russians. Stepanov's face seemed to contain worlds: anger and confusion and fear. Slumped in a chair not far away, Oliver Booth looked as if he'd been tranquilized.

"Okay," Oskar said, and laid the mic back on the podium with a *clank*. Francis joined him, and the four intelligence officials left the room together. Haroun Ghali, stunned, only watched them pass.

Leticia, perhaps also in shock, even opened the door so they could leave. Then she came over to Milo, squatted next to him, and said, "She's dead."

He looked down at Grace Foster's corpse. Around them, everyone started making their way out of the room in a hurry. They were quieter than he would have imagined, each only interested in their own escape.

"Alex?" he called, looking around, and quickly saw his sister standing against the wall, arms around herself, vacant. Dalmatian maintained a respectful distance, but his swiveling, careful eyes showed that he was still on the job.

"Come on," he heard. Leticia was offering a hand. He let her help him stand.

"I'm pissed off, too," she said, "but maybe this was the only way."

He exhaled, shaking his head, watching CEOs file past him. The room was emptying quickly. The remaining Tourists, unsure of what to do, were also leaving. Two dead bodies, that was all it had taken. And despite the outrage bubbling up, Milo knew Leticia was probably right.

"So what now?" she asked.

AFTERWORD

THE LAND OF
DISSIDENCE

7 8 9 0

1

I did not get my Starbucks venti the next day, nor the day after that. Instead, after the police converged on the Congress Center and we were allowed to leave the hotel, Mel and Sally hustled me to a black SUV, and Samuel drove us all the way to Zürich, where a private plane was waiting. In the air there was little conversation. Mel and Sally conferred between themselves and talked on satellite phones, Sally eventually turning to me to say, "Did you hear the news?"

"No."

"The government shutdown is over."

That meant nothing to me.

When we landed, they brought me directly to Langley, where I was questioned periodically for hours in a cell located in a part of the building so deep in the basement that I hadn't known it existed. How, they asked, did I know? How had I known what was going to happen? That I figured it out mere seconds before it occurred didn't seem to faze them.

I'm an analyst, I told them. It's what I do.

Only after two days of this did they finally call a taxi and send me home. Rashid was at school, and in answer to Laura's anxious questions I took her hand and walked her into our bedroom. I sat her down, put my head in her lap, and wept.

When she asked about Haroun, I shook my wet face against her thigh and told her I'd been wrong. Haroun was not alive. He had died in 2009 in Mauritania. "I'm never leaving again," I told her.

Though Sally and Mel never returned, Paul periodically took me from my desk to answer more questions from plain-faced white men. Their questions diverged into territory that was unfamiliar to me. For example, they wanted to know what Milo Weaver knew about Nexus's relationship with CIA. I didn't know. What I *did* know—and I repeated this—was that the murders at Davos had nothing to do with Milo Weaver or the Massive Brigade. Though they claimed to agree with me, in government press releases the administration blamed only the Brigade for the chaos. The witnesses, after all, unequivocally backed up that story. Switzerland promised greater security at next year's Forum, and President Trump claimed that his administration had tightened the screws so much that the Brigade had had no choice but to head to Europe. "They're weak on security over there. So weak. We're so much stronger on security than the last administration."

A week later, a Massive Brigade bomb erupted inside a suite in the Mar-a-Lago club in Palm Beach, the fire and smoke destroying half of the residential spaces. Luckily, no one was killed. The president had left just a few hours earlier for Bethesda, Maryland, for his annual physical examination.

Something they never asked me about, oddly, was Haroun. They never asked if he'd contacted me—perhaps they were monitoring me and knew he hadn't—or what I knew about his life. So eventually I started to bring it up myself. "What happened to the Tourists? What happened to my brother?" They frowned and looked at their notes and told me that this was beyond the purview of their expertise. "And the Library?" I pressed, only to watch my interrogators feign ignorance.

One question they did answer was: "What happened to the snipers?" It had bothered me for a long time, the way the people in blue and red were able to take over the Congress Center's roof without resistance. It was one of those small details that an analyst can't let go. They told me that the snipers had been found after the event, drugged and tied up just inside the rooftop access door. Neither had been able to identify their attackers.

Eventually, over the space of weeks, I revealed almost everything to Laura but said nothing about Haroun. I didn't have it in me to tell her what he'd become. She absorbed each fragment of the story like little blows to the body, then threw a series of smart, pointed questions back at me. Each, it seemed, required me to reveal more, and I eventually would have to stop her and say, "Later, okay? I can't give it to you all at once." After years of me telling her nothing, this arrangement was more than she could have hoped for.

By late February, she knew almost all of it. She understood why, that first day back, I furiously deleted Nexus from all our devices. And as she learned more, she began treating me differently. The mistakes that would once anger her, the ones I still committed, no longer evoked her wrath. She was patient, perhaps seeing me differently. Not as a better person, but as one, perhaps, who needed a little more guidance. And knowing that she understood me better, I made an effort to be more open, allowing her to help me along the way. I was often in awe of her wisdom.

"What matters," she told me one night, "is that you know you're doing right. As soon as you feel like what you're doing—for the job, or in your personal life—is actually wrong, it's time to leave." A part of her was echoing her Communist father's suspicion of my employer, but she wasn't her father, just as I wasn't mine. She said, "I'd rather struggle with the mortgage than have your spirit broken."

And then, in late March, behind the headline news of Special Counsel Robert Mueller's report implicating the president in ten instances of obstruction of justice, we learned that Sergei Stepanov, head of MirGaz, had been arrested in his Moscow apartment on charges of tax fraud. In April, the Berlin offices of Investition für Wirtschaft were raided as part of an extensive money laundering investigation, and Germany was demanding the extradition of Oliver Booth from the UK as part of it. London, reports suggested, was leaning toward handing him over, even as catastrophic Brexit negotiations were breaking down.

I had to look hard to find the news about Salid Logistics. The Oman conglomerate was being taken to court under antitrust laws. Economic analysts were surprised by the move but opined that the company would be broken up within the year. Tóuzī's demise didn't even make American papers. Two of its Shanghai managers were arrested, and within days the offices were simply shuttered.

Northwell's woes took longer to surface. After the murder of its founder, a power struggle erupted. This was complicated by German regulators connecting the company to its IfW investigation. Cued by this, American regulators demanded Northwell's account books and discovered a discrepancy between assets listed and assets owned, to the tune of half a billion dollars. Though government contracts remained in effect, all other Northwell operations were frozen until everything could be balanced. No one knew when that would be.

Nexus, on the other hand, blossomed. It continued to take over Facebook market share, so that by the summer analysts predicted half a trillion in revenue by the end of the third quarter. We, though, remained a Nexus-free household.

Yet with all this news coverage there was no mention of Milo Weaver, Alexandra Primakov, or the elusive Leticia Jones. Certainly there was nothing about the Library—had it really disbanded, as Milo claimed? After Davos, all the Red Notices against Weaver were revoked, though the Interpol database never mentioned why. I scanned reports coming to the Africa desk, searching for any sign of the librarians, or even the Tourists I still feared were out there in one guise or another. But there was nothing.

2

In June I was invited to a conference on African security in Paris, in August, cohosted by a private think tank and the UNIDIR—the UN's Institute for Disarmament Research. The organizer, Dr. Edward Berger, had discovered my little essay in *Foreign Affairs* on the Sahrawi and asked if I could expand the piece for a half-hour presentation and take part in a panel discussion on cybersecurity that needed a fourth member. "What do they think you do for a living?" Paul asked when I brought it up with him.

"Freelance consultant. That's what I told them."

"Really?" he asked skeptically, but by the end of the day the trip had been cleared.

Laura, excited, threw herself into planning every moment of our three days in Paris, and I worked on expanding the five-page published sketch to thirty. The subject—Sahrawi resistance to French and Spanish assimilation—was only tangentially connected to contemporary African security, and I had to work to bring the thesis into line with the present, positing that the resolute, immovable identity of these nomadic peoples virtually assured that the Polisario Front's push for independence, despite relative peace, would not go away until the Sahrawi Arab Democratic Republic had been established. I took the paper's title from the precolonial name for the region used by the sultan of Morocco: Bled es-Siba—"the Land of Dissidence."

I spent a long time working on the speech, probably too long for the sparse crowd that showed up in the small conference room of the Hotel du

Collectionneur in the 8th Arrondissement. Still, it went well, and after the presentation, I spoke to a few attendees who preceded their criticisms with compliments so that I would better listen, and when they cleared out I saw that one person was still in her seat. She was a young white woman with long dark hair and light features. She had a phone to her ear, but she was staring directly at me, as if having a conversation about me. When I approached to ask if she had any thoughts, she lowered her phone and lit up with a charming smile. "I'm sorry," she said, sounding like an American who had spent a long time overseas, "but I don't know much about Africa."

"That's all right. Did you learn anything?"

"Yeah." She cocked her head, looking surprised. *"Yeah."*

"I'm glad," I said, and both of us laughed.

"Did you know," she finally said, "that this is the same conference that Kirill Egorov went to?"

A chill went through me, and I instinctively took a step back. "What?"

Her head bobbed. "Yeah. He wasn't a speaker, but he hobnobbed. Then he went and grabbed Joseph Keller and . . ." She shrugged. "You know the rest."

"Who are you?"

"Do you like parks?" she asked.

"Uh, sure," I said.

"Cool. You know, you should go to the Luxembourg Gardens. Have you been?"

"I've never been to Paris before."

Her eyes widened into saucers. "Oh, you *must*. Big, open space. Bring your family. It's *great*. My aunt takes her dog—the French *hate it* when Max craps there."

"Who," I said again, "are you?"

She got up and smiled. "Go see the Luxembourg Gardens. Tomorrow morning would be good. Don't waste your time indoors."

Slipping her phone into the back pocket of her jeans, she walked out of the room, leaving me stunned. Because even though I'd never seen her before, I knew who the girl was. And my guess was proven right the next morning when Laura and Rashid and I took a taxi over to the huge, sculpted park leading up to the Luxembourg Palace and, walking alongside the enormous pool, I saw a tall woman coming toward us in a fashionable scarf, with a dachshund at the end of a long leather leash. *My aunt.*

I thought she would pass me—what, really, did we have to discuss?—but she stopped in her tracks and did her best to act surprised. "Abdul? It *is* you!"

"Alexandra," I said. None of this made any sense. Laura noticed my consternation and frowned at me, then turned and stuck out a hand.

"Hi, I'm Laura."

Alexandra Primakov shook her hand vigorously and said, "Alex."

"Primakov," I said to Laura. "I told you about her."

Laura inhaled loudly, remembering.

"And *this*," Alexandra said, lifting her dog off the gravel, "is Max."

"Oh!" Rashid said, hustling over. "A dog!"

Alexandra squatted next to him and let him pet the dachshund, which licked Rashid's hand. "You must be Rashid. Rashid, would you like to walk Max?"

"Could I?" he asked, glancing up to his mother for assurance. Laura shrugged.

And, like that, it was arranged. Rashid laughed as Max dragged him in a zigzag path, and Laura, grasping the situation with admirable speed, tagged along after him, shouting instructions Rashid largely ignored, while Alexandra walked with me.

"Cute family," she said.

"Don't be patronizing."

"I'm not, Abdul. They are cute. How's the conference?"

I chewed the inside of my mouth, irritated, but played along. "I think my presentation went well. Tomorrow night, I'm part of a panel discussion."

"Oh? What's the topic?"

"Cybersecurity in North Africa."

"I didn't know you were an expert."

"I'm not."

She nodded, smiling with her eyes.

"Where's Milo?" I asked, tired of the pointless niceties. "Why is his daughter contacting me?"

Alexandra shrugged. "Coming to Paris was her idea. Milo didn't like it, but she's determined when she wants to be."

"Wait a minute—did *you* get me invited to the conference?"

She squinted in the Paris light. "Milo talked to a friend in UNIDIR."

I felt a tingle of embarrassment and irritation—once again, I hadn't been drafted into service for my own qualities but for someone else's use. "Why?"

Alexandra hesitated, then: "You should understand, Abdul: Our only real mistake in Davos was not getting your people on board. That's why the others insisted on killing Foster and Halliwell—the risk of the CIA taking over Northwell's operation was too great. They couldn't allow it. Not even Milo blames them for that."

I took that in, remembering Mel asking about "intelligence officers from the UK, Russia, Germany, and China" meeting secretly in the Congress Center. Those were the ones Milo didn't blame for double murder. "But that didn't end it," I said.

She shook her head. "You've seen the news. One by one they're going down—MirGaz, Investition für Wirtschaft, Salid, Tóuzī—but not because each country *wants* to attack its own industries. Davos taught Milo a lesson he should have learned long ago: The only way to get the results you want is to shepherd them all the way to their rightful conclusion. And to do that, you can't be shy about using all the tools at your disposal."

I suddenly realized that the news I'd been following for months had been guided by the hidden hand of Milo Weaver. I suddenly saw him differently. I said, "You mean the Library files."

She shrugged. "They're a rich resource. They can be used to convince or cajole. That was always true, but Milo never wanted to use them aggressively. He knows better now."

I imagined Milo taking choice items from his files to blackmail this attorney general or that law enforcement czar. Meticulously forcing the advancement of justice all over the world. Active measures, yes, but the kind even he could approve of. "Why?" I asked.

She looked confused.

"Northwell was the problem, not those other companies."

"You don't think so?" She shook her head. "They knew damned well what they were paying Northwell for. And they'll do it again as soon as they get the chance."

It was an argument, all right. "Milo really has gone active, hasn't he?"

Alexandra smiled and shrugged.

"So Tourism is finished?"

"The Tourists," she told me, "are scattered to the four corners."

"My brother?"

"South Africa. Do you want his contact information?"

Up ahead, Rashid was on the ground, and Max was licking his face. Laura was laughing. "I don't know," I said honestly.

"We'll get it to you. Use it if you want."

"And the Library?" I asked, sounding sharper than I wanted. "What's its status now?"

She didn't answer immediately, just looked at my family playing with her dog. "It's . . . it's figuring out what it is."

"Are they safe? Milo and his family?"

"No one has tried anything yet, but they're being careful. Only one thing stands in the way of Milo and his family breathing easily."

"Nexus," I said. "They asked me what he knew about them. He knows?"

"Yeah," she said, looking across the park to where Stephanie Weaver was sitting on one of many scattered metal chairs, scrolling through her phone and chewing on a thumbnail. "And as long as the Agency worries about that, he's not safe. None of us are."

"Are you planning on doing something about that?"

"I've got a friend named Vivian," she said with a smile, because now she'd finally reached the *why* of them bringing me to Paris. "Very good journalist. She's got a lot of the story figured out, but she can't find any CIA sources."

It took me a full second to make the connection, and when I did I just stared at her, aghast. Was she *really* asking what I thought she was asking? Right over there, turning back in our direction, my family was working its way back to us. "You're fucking nuts," I said.

3

In the morning, the front desk at our hotel called—a message had been dropped off for me. It was a plain envelope with my name scrawled on it, and inside was a slip of paper with two phone numbers. One, labeled *HG,* began with +27, the South African country code. The other, *VW,* began with +44, for the UK.

When we'd gotten back to the room the previous day, I'd told Laura what Alexandra had asked of me but avoided mention of Haroun. To my surprise, she didn't immediately explode with anger. Thoughtfully, she said, "But she wouldn't use your name, right?"

"That's beside the point!" I yelled. "It's too much of a risk."

Now I brought the phone numbers back to the room, where Laura was already packing for the next day's flight home. I said nothing about the message.

After breakfast, we stood in a hot line for an hour, waiting to take an elevator to the top of the Eiffel Tower. Once we were up there, looking over the grand city, Rashid suicidally trying to climb the railings, Laura kissed me firmly on the lips. We aren't the kind of couple who show affection in public, so it was a special thing. She said, "What matters is that you know you're doing right."

It took a second for me to realize she was finishing yesterday's conversation. Then I wondered—what kind of "right" was she speaking of? The basic right of keeping your family safe, or the grand, historical right of protecting people from the onslaught of Big Brother?

In the afternoon, we went to the Louvre. When faced with paintings, Rashid slumped in boredom and didn't perk up until the museum store, where he found a comic book he begged us to get. It didn't matter that it was in French—the superhero, a teenaged Muslim girl, in a hijab no less, was the coolest thing he'd ever seen. Back at the hotel he and Laura crashed, and I went down to the hotel bar, ordered coffee, and took a quiet seat in the corner to look over notes for the evening's panel. I'd spent weeks boning up on cybersecurity so that I wouldn't look too ignorant onstage, but I still wasn't sure I'd be able to pull that off. Besides, I couldn't focus with those phone numbers in my pocket. I took them out and, after knocking it back and forth in my head too many times, called *HG*.

The transcontinental line crackled as it rang four times; then it connected and he said a hesitant "Yeah?"

"Brother. It's me."

There was a long pause, and when he finally spoke he sounded choked up. "How'd you get . . ." He coughed. "This means they've got it, too. Do you know how long I have?"

"I got your number from Milo Weaver's sister."

"Oh," he said, sounding relieved.

"How are you?"

"Well, I'm glad you can't see the flea trap I'm living in now. But anything to stay off the radar. What about you? Where are you?"

I told him about the conference, and he asked pointed questions about Rashid and Laura that I answered calmly until the emotion built up inside me. "Come back, Haroun. Come back to America."

"An American jail?"

"I don't know. Maybe. But it's better than running."

"I'd never make it to a jail cell."

"You don't know that."

He coughed again, then said, "Your people won't let me."

"What does that mean?"

"They're all gone. The ones I stayed in contact with are gone. A traffic accident in Mumbai. A suicide in Stockholm. A shooting in Brisbane. I don't know, brother. I might be the last one."

"How," I began, then hesitated. "How do you know it's CIA?"

"They're getting rid of people who know about Nexus, and all of us did."

He snorted a cynical laugh. "Turns out the Agency isn't as incompetent as I thought."

"There has to be a way," I said. "Maybe I could—"

"Remember what I said in Switzerland?" he cut in. "If I had another life, I would try another path. But I made my bed, and there's nothing I can do about it. It's fine. Despite the things I've done I never wanted to hurt you. I hope you believe that."

I did, but I didn't tell him. Instead I asked if I could do anything to help him.

"No one can help me, brother. But you know what you *can* do? Live your life well. Take care of that family of yours. I need to know you're happy. I need to know you're good."

Afterward, I ordered another coffee and sank into a quiet depression. Haroun couldn't start again and live another life, just as I couldn't. We'd made decisions early on, and those decisions had changed everything. Neither of us could go back in time and try the other path.

Back upstairs, Rashid was looking at his comic book on the toilet, and I brought Laura out to the terrace. The noise of traffic enveloped us, and I had to lean close for her to hear my words. As she gradually absorbed Haroun's story, she turned to gape at me. "Why didn't you tell me before?"

"I don't know," I said. "I was frightened, maybe."

"Of what?"

"That you would see him in me."

She held my face and kissed me deeply.

Two hours later, I made it out to the same Hotel du Collectionneur stage I'd used before, this time to join the three other guests—an Algerian, a Russian, and a Frenchwoman. I was shocked by the size of the crowd and the presence of television cameras embossed with the logos of France 4 and i24. None of this was for me, of course. I just happened to be sharing the stage with an Algerian intellectual whose controversial book on Islam had made him momentarily famous. He was well prepared for his fifteen minutes of fame, speaking in a thoughtful, measured manner about the contradictions between Islamic rules and the image gratification of social media.

The Russian professor spoke about the use of deep fakes in Moroccan media, and its influence on the country's political stability. The Frenchwoman delved into history, arguing that France's colonial history, and the West's responsibility for these new media, obliged the Macron government to take the lead in securing North Africa's data protections.

After their erudition, I felt there was nothing for me to say. But I was the only American representative; I couldn't go down in flames. Not here, in front of these cameras.

"My concern," I said hesitantly, "is the security of the individuals using these services. In March, Egypt passed sweeping regulations fining purveyors of so-called fake news fourteen thousand dollars. The government has the authority now to decide what news is or isn't fake. This is a dangerous precedent for the free press."

"And that's why Nexus is so popular in North Africa," the Algerian cut in suddenly, throwing me. He was leaning back in his chair, legs crossed at the knee. Not only was he prepared for stardom; he relished it. He said, "Not a single group has been able to crack its encryption, and governments have no way to trace users. *That* will change the face of North African democracy. Don't you think?"

As he waited for a reply, I looked to the audience, and in the glare of the bright lights they momentarily disappeared. I was enveloped in white. But I wasn't alone—beyond the crowd, through the cameras, were thousands, maybe millions. What was right? What was right for Rashid, now and in the long run? For Milo? For Haroun? For Laura? For me?

"Actually, no," I said. "Nexus was cracked a long time ago."

"Is that so?" the Algerian asked doubtfully.

"Yes," I said. Then I told him how.